THE COLD LIGHT OF STARS

THE COLD LIGHT OF STARS

ICARUS CODE BOOK ONE

RYSA WALKER

STARRY NIGHT BOOKS

There is no light in earth or heaven
But the cold light of stars;
And the first watch of night is given
To the red planet Mars.
~ Henry Wadsworth Longfellow, "The Light of Stars" (1843)

————

Two possibilities exist: either we are alone in the universe or we are not. Both are equally terrifying.
~ Arthur C. Clarke

For Pete ~
With love and gratitude for many long and spirited conversations that
*sometimes, **eventually** turn into books. This one wouldn't exist*
without you.

CONTENTS

PART I: AD MARTIS

FROM THE JOURNAL
OF EBERIN DAS

27.17.505

THE GREATEST TESTS of character come when a choice must be made, even though all of your options are bad. One of our philosophers wrote that, although I can't for the life of me remember which one. I think it's true, though. How do you come to a decision in that situation? Do you adhere to the ethical or religious rules of your society? Do you employ a strict, utilitarian calculus? Or, perhaps, the truly moral thing in such a case is to take no action at all, regardless of the consequences?

These questions were intended as a thought experiment, and yet that evening, as I stared across the table at my own personal test of character, I found myself on the verge of decision paralysis.

Regardless of how I justified it later, it had to be done. Arrangements had been made, the die had been cast, and refusing to act was no longer an option. Had *never* been an option, truth be told, unless I was willing to consign my entire civilization to oblivion.

And I was *not* willing to do that. Therefore, my dinner partner, who was well into his second drink and explaining his research to me in minute detail, had to die before that night was over. And unless he choked on his dinner or suffered a convenient heart attack, his death would be at my hand. There was no other choice.

I sat at the table, trying to remember the name of that philosopher. It must have been clear that I'd tuned out the conversation because the man gave me an uncertain smile.

"I'm sorry," he said. "Did I lose you? This is really technical and sometimes I get carried away."

That made me feel worse. The very least I could do was listen attentively, even though I already knew everything he was telling me. There was no excuse for insulting the man during his final hours. The fact that I was going to murder him was awful enough.

And yes, taking his life *was* murder. My counterparts might have been able to convince themselves that their own "tests of character" were akin to taking a life in battle, but we are not soldiers. This man was no soldier, either. To the best of my knowledge, he had never harmed anyone. Never even threatened anyone. And he likely would have continued on that same blameless path had I decided to walk away.

"No, no," I assured him. "My mind just got a bit sidetracked for a moment thinking about all of the potential applications. Relax, okay? The job is yours if you want it. I think you'll be very pleased with our compensation package. So, you were saying something about how the latest iteration could help with organ repair?"

"Oh, yes. Definitely. Here...let me show you the details." He pulled a small tablet from his pocket and began sketching something onto it, talking excitedly as he drew.

After that, I listened carefully, nodding in all the right places. I couldn't change the man's fate, but I could ensure he died happy and at peace. And I did. His end was as quick and as painless as I could make it.

God, what is the *name* of that philosopher? All these years later, and I still can't remember it. It's frustrating as hell when I have no way of looking it up.

I still don't know if killing the man was the morally correct choice.

But whether the act meant I passed or failed my test of character, it is done.

The important thing now is to ensure that the sacrifice of my conscience and the far greater sacrifice of that man's life were not in vain.

(Confidence interval: 89.7%)

ONE

THERE WAS A FAINT METALLIC CLINK, almost like a pin drop, and then the man on the screen mumbled a curse. "That's five today. *Five.* Unbelievable. What the hell is this thing made of?"

Pale orange light filtered into the cave from his upper left, blending with the bluish-white glow of portable lamps that cast odd, elongated shadows on the walls. These shadows, along with the slight echo in the recording made it hard to determine which of the people in the video were speaking, but Claire thought it was the one crouched near the ground, guiding the massive drill. The other two hovered around, craning their necks to see what he was doing. They all wore identical suits and helmets, bulky and shapeless, that obscured their age, gender, and other identifying features.

"Well, did we at least make some progress?" That was a voice that Claire recognized—Dr. Laura Brodnik, the astropaleontologist who had organized the meeting.

"Yeah," the first guy said, looking up from the drill as one of the others handed him a replacement for the broken bit. "Maybe two centimeters, which puts us at around ten altogether. We've eaten through half of our drill bits, though. If this casing is thicker than twenty centimeters, we'll be going home with a major cliffhanger."

Brodnik chuckled humorlessly. "The hell we will. *We* found this. It's ours. We've got thirty-six hours left, and if that last drill bit shatters, I'll shift to using a pick and hammer. If that breaks, I'll use a nail file. No way are we going home until we at least put a camera inside this thing."

The man lowered the drill into the hole and went back to work. About thirty seconds of noise from the drill followed, mixed with random chatter from the others on the screen, and then the drill's monotonous whine abruptly changed pitch.

"You cracked another one?" Brodnik asked. "Already?"

"No. We broke through! Give me the camera."

One of the other spacesuits stepped forward to hand the guy a spool of wire. A tiny cylinder dangled from the end. He lowered this into the hole and gradually fed it in. Then Brodnik, or at least Claire *thought* it was Brodnik, nodded to an assistant. They must have flipped a switch of some sort, because a thin corona of light now surrounded the wire inside the hole.

The image froze at this point, and Brodnik explained that she was shifting to the view from the camera. Not the spacesuit-clad woman on the screen this time, but the actual woman sitting across the conference table in jeans and a pale blue sweater.

Claire glanced around at the other four people at the table, none of whom she'd met. One of them, a beefy dark-haired guy who, aside from her, was the only one in the room wearing a business suit, seemed as out of place as she felt. Of the other three, one was a Black man around Brodnik's age, early- to mid-forties, and exceptionally tall. The other two, a guy with Asian features and a pale woman with white-blond hair and freckles, looked to be in their late-twenties. Closer to Claire's own age than to Brodnik's, so she thought they were probably grad students. All three seemed to know each other pretty well, and they weren't watching the screen as closely as Brodnik was. Or as closely as Mr. Suit was, for that matter. It wasn't like they were bored, exactly, but more that there was no sense of anticipation on their part. Whatever was coming next, they'd already seen it. Probably in person.

For a moment, the monitor behind Brodnik went completely dark, and then a wall came into focus. Not a cave wall, which was what Claire had expected, given that they'd been digging inside a cave. The wall wasn't even made of dirt. It was smooth, metallic, and slightly reflective. As the camera steadied, the picture came into focus revealing walls covered with markings. It looked like writing, although the symbols didn't correspond to any language she'd ever seen.

The room on the screen appeared to be rectangular, but it was hard to get a sense of the size. There was nothing in the picture to provide perspective and the light from the camera wasn't strong enough to illuminate the entire area. But those were definitely symbols of some sort.

Symbols.

Etched into the metal wall of a buried chamber on a planet previously assumed to have supported only microbial life. Claire's first thought was of hieroglyphs inside Egyptian tombs. Or maybe Chinese pictograms, although these weren't nearly as detailed.

Her mind raced as she considered the implications of this find, both on the broader scale and on the very personal level of her career. This was quite literally the story of a lifetime. Brodnik could have given it to any science reporter she chose, most of whom would have cheerfully killed their firstborn just to be in the room.

Claire pulled out her tablet and began typing questions to ask once the main presentation was over. One of the biggest questions, of course, was why Brodnik wasn't holding a major press conference to announce something of this magnitude, but *that* was a question Claire definitely wouldn't be asking. An exclusive on the story of the century was perfectly okay with her, so she simply gave the woman a grateful smile.

What she got back was a confused look, and then Brodnik continued. "The footage you've just seen was recorded two months ago in the Tharsis Colony, near Icarus Camp. We tried to drill a second hole at another location inside the chamber, but only got about halfway through the metal—and yes, it's definitely metal—before our last bit broke. Our transport was leaving the next day, so we plugged the hole and added this to the list of sites with biological life that need to be examined more closely before KTI moves forward with the next stage of their project."

"And you're certain that it contains biological life?" the guy in the suit asked. He had a faint accent. Russian, or maybe Eastern European?

Brodnik raised an eyebrow. "At some point, yes. Obviously. Do you really think a metal box with symbols etched into the walls is a *natural* formation, Mr. Macek?"

He laughed. "No, no. Of course not. But there's a big difference between biological life being present now and biological life having been present in some... well, I was going to say *prehistoric era*, but we don't have a history for Mars, so that's not right. The point I'm making is that nothing KTI is doing in stage six, or really in any of the future steps, poses a threat to what is clearly a find of unbelievable scientific importance. The only reason this would justify a delay is if something was *still* living inside this box that was buried below the surface hundreds of centuries ago."

It was a valid point. The next stage of the Mars project headed by KTI, or Kolya Terraforming Incorporated, would be the introduction of millions of recombinant biobots at carefully selected locations around the planet. Work over the previous five decades, most of it funded by companies setting up bases for asteroid mining, had gotten a magnetic shield in place and there was now enough of an atmosphere that specially engineered bamboo, lichen, and a few other hardy species were surviving in the open in two or three regions of the planet. Mars still wasn't the kind of place you'd want to raise your kids, but there were several massive biodomes that housed a steady influx of scientists, construction specialists, and—for the past five years—student groups and a rapidly growing number of tourists. Anton Kolya's fondest wish was to increase that last, lucrative group over the next decade as the terraforming process continued.

The guy sitting just to the left of Brodnik snorted. "Wait. You think that chamber was buried *hundreds of centuries* ago? More like thousands of millennia."

Macek gave him a tight smile. "Which would make it even *less* likely that something is still alive, wouldn't you agree?"

"The point here is that we do not *know*," Brodnik said. "And that's why I've asked permission for my team to be on the next transport back. I know we're not scheduled to return for another eight months, but…"

Macek waved a dismissive hand. "That's not a problem. Mr. Kolya has already approved transport, at KTI expense, for you and your team. He has also authorized me to provide you with any assistance you might need for the excavation."

Claire stifled a smirk, already envisioning how Anton Kolya would use this discovery to his advantage. No doubt the excavated chamber would be set up outside the biodomes so he could charge tourists a few thousand dollars extra to explore it. As long as this discovery didn't significantly delay the launch of stage six, he'd treat it the same way he did everything else—as a resource to be exploited to the maximum.

"We have a worker transport departing from Tranquility on the sixteenth," Macek said, "which would be…"

"Eight days from now," the blond woman sitting next to Brodnik said excitedly. "Works for me."

Brodnik and the two guys nodded.

"Does that schedule work for you as well, Ms. Echols?" Macek asked.

Claire looked up from her pad, momentarily stunned into silence. "I …assumed I was simply here to write a story about the discovery. How long would I be gone?"

"Roughly nine weeks," he said. "Unless you think you'll need longer than two weeks on the planet, Dr. Brodnik?"

She shook her head and Macek turned his gaze back to Claire.

Her immediate physical reaction was a firm, unqualified no. Nine weeks of recycled air. Nine weeks without a piano to help her unwind. Nine weeks…most of which she would be cooped up in a tiny ship with a bunch of strangers. It was pretty much her personal idea of hell.

The rational side of her brain, however, immediately launched a protest. This story was going to be seismic. She would be insane to pass it up.

"I'll have to juggle a few things around and check with my editor," she told them, "but I can't imagine him saying no. Not for something like this."

What she didn't add was that work responsibilities weren't going to be the biggest hurdle. Nine weeks was an eternity to a four-year-old, and Jemma didn't even remember a time when Claire hadn't been around. Since she worked mostly from home, Claire usually watched the girl when Rowan Martinez, her roommate, had to work outside of Jemma's preschool hours. Science reporters rarely get called out on assignment at the last minute, so they hadn't exactly built a deep bench of people to call upon. Jemma's dad was about as reliable as a wax teapot, and eight days wasn't much time to line up a full-time sitter with a flexible schedule.

"Can you trust your editor not to leak the story?" Brodnik asked.

"That's an excellent point," Macek said. "Mr. Kolya doesn't want this to get out until everything is in place to do it properly. I mean, it's been waiting for eons, right? What's a few more weeks?"

Well, that explained why they hadn't opted for a press conference. Kolya wanted to give this the red-carpet treatment. It still didn't explain why they'd chosen a junior reporter to cover it, but again, Claire was absolutely not complaining.

"He won't leak it," she assured them. "In fact, he wouldn't

dare publish it until I have proof. This...well, it's going to be explosive, to say the least."

"Indeed. The story of the century."

Macek's words were an eerie echo of Claire's own thoughts from a few moments earlier, and something in his slightly amused expression bothered her. This *was* the story of the century for now, but it would soon have some serious competition for that title. Did Macek *know* that? Was Kolya's organization aware that a story lurked on the horizon that would make the discovery that there had once been intelligent life on Mars seem positively mundane to many people?

It seemed unlikely, given the detailed non-disclosure agreements Claire's mother required of every single employee at Jonas Labs, from top-level scientists down. Everyone in the company was a stockholder, too, and leaking company secrets about something that was still not guaranteed wasn't generally in their best interest.

But who was she kidding? Anton Kolya could have paid any one of those employees enough to make it in their best interest. *Of course* he knew...and that explained why they were holding off for a bigger, more spectacular reveal of the discovery on Mars. Kolya was timing the release of this story to steal her mother's thunder.

And Claire was one hundred percent okay with that.

TWO

ON SECOND THOUGHT, Claire decided that she was *ninety-five* percent okay with that. Maybe ninety.

Because stealing her mother's thunder also meant stealing Joe's thunder. And if her brother was the sort who gave a single damn about fame and recognition, she'd have downgraded that percentage a whole lot more. But she knew Joe well enough to be certain that he'd welcome the distraction of a competing story if it allowed him to get away from the cameras and back to his lab. And she knew beyond a shadow of a doubt that he'd tell her to seize this chance.

Claire stayed behind after the others left, in part to sign some initial paperwork, but also to personally thank Brodnik for the opportunity. Brodnik gave her another confused look, however, and then shook her head.

"Don't thank *me*. I really didn't have anything to do with this. Word came down from above that you were to be included on the roster for our return trip to Mars. They want this discovery fully documented."

"Well, sure. I'm not surprised that they want press coverage, but..." Claire trailed off, leaving the rest unspoken. She wasn't even the lead science reporter at the *Atlantic Post*. She had finished her master's only two years ago, and while it was true that she had carved out something of a niche with the *Simple Science* series, it was aimed at non-scientists. Her work history shouldn't even have put her on the short-list to be in the press room for the announcement, let alone have ensured an exclusive.

Her name, though? Even though she went by Claire Echols

professionally, it wouldn't have taken much digging for Brodnik to find that her legal name was Claire Jonas-Echols.

"Your mother is on Columbia's science advisory board, Claire."

On the one hand, Claire wasn't surprised. Her mother sat on dozens of boards, although it was hard to imagine her actually attending meetings as long as there was work to oversee in the lab or a new contract to bid on. Then again, would this science advisory board have expected her to actually show up? Merely having Kai Jonas's name on their roster would be a coup for most universities.

But Kai lifting a single finger to help her daughter get this position was far more improbable than what had just been discovered on Mars.

"Dr. Brodnik, my mother did *not* pull strings to get me this assignment."

Claire didn't elaborate, choosing to leave it at that one, simple statement. If Brodnik was curious, she could find plenty of rumors online and she was free to make of them whatever the hell she wanted. And truthfully, it didn't matter whether Brodnik believed her or not, because Claire knew her mother. Leaving Jonas Labs for any reason would have been seen as a betrayal. When she had briefly considered a career in classical music, Kai had been appalled. But Claire's decision to become a journalist, a profession her mother viewed with complete and utter disdain? That was an unforgivable sin.

For the past six years, they'd seen each other only at Christmas and on her brother's birthday. On those occasions, they made nice for Joe's sake, although Claire was increasingly convinced that he insisted on family gatherings just so he could watch the two of them squirm.

"Perhaps it was another member of the advisory board, then," Brodnik said, looking a bit uncomfortable. "Or...it could even have been the chair of our department. His wife was part of the stage two trials. Multiple myeloma, and...it would almost certainly have been fatal before Arvectin. Let's just say he's a huge fan."

Brodnik's department chair wasn't alone. Most forms of cancer had been cured during the first half of the twenty-first century, with only a few stubborn and hard-to-detect blood cancers remaining. Those were the cancers that Arvectin targeted with amazing results. In one of the rare instances where being last makes you the perceived winner, Arvectin had been, therefore, heralded as the "cure for cancer." That misperception was one that Claire's mother and the rest of her team at Jonas Labs had assiduously corrected in public and secretly propagated behind the scenes.

"But I have to admit that your skills may be a good fit for this assignment," Brodnik continued. "The coverage will be read mostly by non-professionals, and you have a knack for making complex subjects accessible. We added a few of your pieces to the list of supplemental reading for the department's intro classes last semester."

"I'm glad you found them useful." Claire forced a smile, then moved on to asking about any medical tests or vaccines she might need prior to departure because she didn't want Dr. Brodnik to think she'd taken offense at the presumption that she was included due to nepotism, whether direct or indirect. Even though she *had* taken offense. And even though she knew Brodnik was probably right and her name had been added by some misguided soul who assumed that giving her daughter the assignment of a lifetime would be the perfect way to show gratitude or suck up to the great Kai Jonas.

Because in the end, did it matter? She wasn't turning down the opportunity either way.

Brodnik said she'd send Claire the medical info along with several other forms she'd need to fill out. "You should move quickly on that vestibular training since a week is cutting it close. One of my team only got four sessions in before we left last time and he spent his first two days in his cabin, even with the anti-nausea pills. The artificial gravity can be rough your first time in space, especially on the older ships they use for work transport. Bring stuff that you can lie in your bunk and listen to, because that's probably all you'll want to do for a few days."

"Thanks for the tip," Claire said, pushing back the contrary little voice at the back of her head whispering that this entire thing was a spectacularly bad idea.

Brodnik handed her a non-disclosure agreement. "You might as well get this one out of the way," she said with a wry smile. "Obviously, you can tell friends and family members you're going to Mars. We don't expect you to literally disappear from the face of the Earth for a few months without warning or explanation. You just can't tell them *why* you're going."

Claire read through the form, which was almost identical to one her mother had made her sign with Jonas Labs before taking the job at the *Post* a few years back. It was a lengthy bit of legalese that boiled down to a threat that Kolya's company would sue her ass into oblivion if she leaked information.

Which was another reason that Claire knew her mother couldn't be involved in any of this. Kai liked Anton Kolya even less than she liked her daughter. The man had committed the unforgivable sin of winning the Zimmer Award the year that Kai was nominated for the research that led to Arvectin. Unlike the public, the members of the award committee understood that Kolya's early terraforming efforts were truly groundbreaking, while Arvectin was merely an incremental achievement. As with most things that didn't go her way, Claire's mother had taken Kolya's win as a personal insult.

Once the form was signed and dated, Brodnik extended her hand and gave Claire the first full smile she'd seen from the woman. "Welcome to the team, Claire. We're about to make history."

THREE

AS SOON AS Claire entered the elevator, she sent a message to Rowan telling her to start looking for possible sitters and promising that she'd explain everything once she got home. Then she messaged her brother to see if he could meet her for dinner. Joe could be in New York in less than an hour if he took the loop from Boston and a local shuttle into Grand Central. He loved New York, so Claire hoped it wouldn't take much effort to convince him.

His response was quick and definitive.

> No can do. Middle of something big. You come here. Bring dumplings. From that place...you know the one.

She *did* know the place. Joe had polished off several dozen assorted dumplings along with sushi and a giant bowl of edamame the last time they were together in New York. Her brother could go the better part of the day without food if he was involved in a project. But when he finally decided it was time to eat, he usually devoured enough for three people. Three very *hungry* people.

> Surely you can spare a few hours to come visit with your baby sister? Coming up there will put me really late getting back to DC.

> You can stay here if it's too late. Cruella is in Ontario until at least Tuesday, so you won't have to see her.

The Cruella crack was totally for Claire's benefit. Joe got along just fine with their mother, in part because they were both so absorbed in their work that everything else was peripheral. To Claire's knowledge, the only time they'd ever clashed was when Kai tried to give Joe what she viewed as helpful pointers concerning the research areas he might want to pursue in his graduate studies. Joe had very pointedly ignored her. Fast-forward a decade, however, and Kai was now delighted that he'd followed his own path. At the obligatory Christmas dinner a few months prior, she'd told Claire that Arvectin might have made Jonas Labs a rising star, but Joe's research would take it to supernova. Claire had merely smiled, opting for Joe's sake not to point out that supernovae often become black holes.

There was no point trying to negotiate with Joe when his mind was made up. And Claire wanted to see him. She'd miss his birthday while she was off planet. Plus, she wanted to share the Mars news with him, even if she couldn't give him all the details.

Claire also wanted to pick his brain for info on what Kolya's people were planning for the next stage in their ongoing terraforming effort. It wasn't exactly Joe's specialty, but there was some overlap since her brother's current project employed a similar type of biobot. *Too* similar, according to her mother, who was convinced that Kolya had a spy inside Jonas Labs. Claire's primary source of information was Kolya's own self-aggrandizing press releases and vague rumors that probably came from the same source. Joe might not know anything more than she did, but it was worth a try.

So, Claire resigned herself to spending an hour on the loop carrying enough dumplings to feed an army and to adding an extra hour to her trip home. She messaged back to ask Joe whether she should deliver to the house or the lab, even though she was almost certain she knew the answer.

She stepped through the door and merged into the foot traffic on Broadway while waiting for Joe's reply. It was a rather blustery day, colder than it had been when she left DC, and she wished she'd thought to bring a coat. When the phone pinged, she glanced down and read:

Lab.

Which was exactly what she'd thought.

Claire looked up from the screen and realized she was about to run into a woman who was also staring down at her phone. She sidestepped, but then the other woman did, too, in an effort to avoid crashing into someone on her right. Their shoulders collided a split second later and Claire's phone tumbled to the sidewalk.

To Claire's surprise, the woman actually stopped when she knelt down to retrieve the phone.

"I'm *so* sorry. I shouldn't be trying to work and walk at the same time. Is it broken?"

"I don't think so."

A gust of wind came around the corner and the woman laughed as she grabbed for her hat an instant before it would have been airborne. Claire's phone pinged again with another message from Joe.

Bring some for Beck, too. Lots of dumplings.
ALL the dumplings.

"Well, I guess that answers the question definitively." The woman reached a hand down to help her up and then melted back into the bustle of people on the sidewalk as Claire stepped out of the crowd to place an order for *ALL the dumplings*.

Even though she called ahead, she still wound up waiting at the restaurant, not that she could really complain given the size of the order. Unfortunately, that put her smack in the middle of rush hour by the time she made it to Grand Central, so the local shuttle to the hyperloop terminal in New Rochelle was crowded. She managed to get a seat but had to prop her legs on her messenger bag and hold the dumplings in her lap. The man next to her was not impressed.

Holding the bags wasn't feasible on the loop itself. The last thing she needed was for dumplings to go flying when the thing accelerated. So she rented a locker, made sure everything was secure, and then strapped herself in for the thirty-minute ride.

Thankfully, there was no need for a shuttle from the loop station in Boston. When her father had bought the land for the new Jonas-Echols research campus a few decades back, he'd chosen a spot within easy walking distance of the Lynn terminal. From the exterior of the building, you could even hear the roar of the trains coming and going.

Claire retrieved her bags, sending up a fervent prayer that the next person to use the locker didn't mind the smell of chili oil. Then she stepped out into the warmth of the early evening and began the short walk toward the building where she had spent a sizable chunk of her childhood.

That was not a complaint. Her father had designed the place, from the architecture to the landscaping. Claire had vague memories of crawling into his lap and seeing the plans for it on his computer when she was still in preschool. The actual house where she'd grown up, where her mother and Joe still lived, had been built by a firm her paternal grandfather hired around the turn of the previous century. It was a sterile, neocolonial monstrosity, and her dad had dreamed of building something more in line with his personal tastes. But his own mother had loved the house, and all of her memories were tied up in it, so he had waited. In the end, Grandma Echols had died only a few months before her father did, so his design for a new family home never got beyond the blueprint stage. Claire knew that if any of Martin Echols's spirit still existed in this world, it didn't reside in the house where he'd lived. It lived on in the clean, modern lines of the Jonas Lab campus and the lush eight-acre biodome in the center quad. Stepping inside felt like walking into her father's hug.

Well, most of the time.

On this occasion, it was her mother's face that greeted Claire when she stepped inside and that cast a bit of a chill over the usual warm glow. The wall screen on the far side of the atrium, beyond the reception area and security checkpoints, stood several stories high. It played a closed-caption press reel nonstop, updated regularly with sound bites from Kai's latest media event or awards ceremony. Kai's face, far larger than life on the giant screen, was a mix of Polynesian and Germanic features. Claire's own hazel eyes and more pronounced jawline were inherited from her father, but otherwise, the woman on the screen could have been her decades older, slightly taller twin.

"Of course, everything we do at Jonas Labs is a team effort," Kai was saying in response to a question. "I'm just the lucky person who gets to bask in the glory of our successes...and face the heat when we fail. There was a lot more of the latter during our first two decades, if you recall, so it's not all sunshine and roses."

Claire's father had been the one to insist that having a single face out front representing the company was better for public relations and there had never been any question that her mother would be that face. Kai had both the necessary poise and the expertise, given that she'd led the research arm of the company before she married Claire's dad. He was the sole heir of Echols Pharmaceuticals, a company founded by his grandfather, and a few years after their marriage, around the time Joe was born, he'd announced that the company would henceforth be known as Jonas-Echols Labs.

Nine years ago, the company had been rebranded again as Jonas Labs. The name change was necessary, Kai had insisted, to shake off negative public opinion after a rather nasty class action lawsuit. As usual, Kai backed her assertions with a plethora of data, to the point that even Claire had to admit that rebranding was the best course of action on strictly financial terms. But coming only a few years after her dad's death, it felt wrong, as if he and several generations of Echols ancestors before him had been erased from the company they'd founded.

Claire pulled her eyes away from the press reel and placed her hand on the scanner at the security desk. The guard ran a wand over the bags of food and peeked inside. That was a first. Normally, any guard on duty didn't even bother once they saw her face. Given that Claire owned one-sixteenth of the company, it seemed rather unlikely that she would be sneaking explosives in with the dumplings.

The guard frowned, then ran the wand over her messenger bag.

"Is something wrong?"

"No. I thought there was a blip on the screen when you first approached, but it's gone now. You're fine, Miss Echols."

Both Kai's suite of offices and Joe's lab were on the upper level, mostly because Joe liked being close to the roof so that he could pace around up there while thinking. He could use the walking paths that wound through the arboretum in the biodome or the gym on the second floor, but Joe found people distracting when working through a problem. John Beckett, known to everyone simply as Beck, was the one exception to that rule outside the family, possibly because Beck was as quirky as Joe, in his own way. They'd developed their own rhythm over the years, and like Claire, Beck was smart enough to steer clear of Joe and Kai when they got that slightly vacant, faraway look in their eyes. Bothering either of them when they were deep in thought would land you in the doghouse for weeks.

Security was tighter on the upper floors in general. You needed a special clearance to venture into those hallowed halls. Employees referred to the sixth floor of Jonas Labs as Mount Olympus, and it was common knowledge that the gods didn't like unexpected visitors. If they needed something from you, you would either be summoned for an audience, or they would come down from on high.

After the unaccustomed scrutiny from the guard in the atrium, Claire half expected the palm scanner inside the elevator to blink red and deny her entry. It didn't, and she saw why as soon as she stepped out onto the sixth floor. The guard on duty, a middle-aged guy named Wilson, had known her since she was nine.

"Miss Claire! We haven't seen you in ages." Wilson's voice still carried a hint of Georgia, even though he'd lived in the Boston area for at least fifteen years. "Your brother is down on four, but I'll send word that you're here. He said you might have someone with you?"

"No," Claire said, a bit confused. "Just me. What's with the extra security detail downstairs?"

He shook his head in disgust. "They're at it again. Crazy sonsabitches. Three threats from the Flock in the past week."

Claire wrinkled her nose. She had expected him to say they were guarding against corporate espionage, since her mother was still making vague noises about suing Anton Kolya. It had been several years since they'd had trouble from the Flock. The preferred name of the group was the Earth Watch Alliance, but even the major newspapers eventually gave up because no one called them that. The Flock's leader, Tobias Alvin Shepherd, was an anti-science, apocalyptic guru who opposed pretty much any medical or technological advancement. He had clusters of camps near major research universities around the globe where thousands of the faithful lived waiting for the mothership—helmed by some nebulous group he called the Sentinels—to return and carry them away. Which wouldn't be a problem, if not for the havoc they wreaked in the interim.

"No more rats, I hope?"

The local branch of the Flock had managed to sneak a crate of live rats into the building a few years back, apparently to protest animal testing—which Jonas Labs actually *didn't* do and hadn't done since the late 2030s. Some of the news articles that covered the incident pointed that out. Claire had made certain that Bryce Avery, her colleague who wrote about the attack for the *Post*, knew the truth, but he'd conveniently left that bit out, something that her mother brought up every chance she got. Not that it would have mattered, anyway. As with most stories, the public only remembered the sensational aspects. In this case, that meant the videos of people screaming and running for the exits as dozens of live rats scurried through the lobby.

"No rats," Wilson said. "They seem to be stepping up their game. They've moved on to bomb threats."

"Whoa. That's…a pretty radical shift. I thought they were supposed to be pacifists. And against technology."

"What they are is *crazy sonsabitches*." Wilson repeated, then inhaled deeply. "I don't know what you've got in that bag, but it sure smells *good*. And it looks like you brought enough for you and me both."

"Joe's command was to bring him *all* the dumplings. But I'll keep some back for you. Check the kitchen when you go on break."

He laughed. "I will most definitely do that, but we both know there won't be a crumb left if your brother is hungry. How long you in town for?"

"Just tonight, then I've got to get back to DC."

Wilson stared at her for a moment. "You got security at your place down there, right?"

The shift from his usual jocular tone caught her off guard. "Yeah. I mean, not like here at the lab, but we have an alarm system. Why?"

He smiled and shook his head. "Ignore me. Occupational hazard. They just got me antsy. Shame you have to rush home, though. You're gonna miss seeing your mama. She's not back 'til Tuesday." There was a teasing edge to his voice. While there were, no doubt, plenty of employees among the roughly two thousand at Jonas Labs who were unfamiliar with their family soap opera, Wilson was not one of them.

"I'm heartbroken, I tell you. Completely heartbroken." Claire shot him a grin and took a right at the corridor, toward Joe's half of the floor. A left would have taken her into Kai's domain where an entourage of assistants were in a constant buzz. It was nearly seven o'clock and a faint hum of activity still emanated from the other end of the building, even though Kai was out of town and at least a third of her office staff traveled with her at all times.

Joe's side was quiet, as usual. His only assistant was Beck, who had come on board about a year after Joe began work on his doctoral thesis. Beck was handpicked for his work on gerotherapeutics, and while he hadn't been her brother's first choice, you'd never get Joe to admit that now. There was a woman from MIT whose research was more cutting-edge, and Joe had been disappointed when she turned down the offer. He hadn't been surprised, though, since taking the job would have meant putting her own research aside to follow a different vision from a freshly minted Ph.D. who was still too young to buy a drink in some states. Joe had started college at fourteen, finished a four-year degree in less than two, and had his doctorate in hand at age twenty. He'd also had immediate access to the labs of one of the top ten global pharmaceutical firms, a firm that had catapulted into the top three a mere eighteen months later when Arvectin finally hit the market.

The door to the lab was partially open when Claire arrived. It was a cavernous space that housed the computers on which Joe and Beck developed ideas for the company's future projects, which were then sent down to the lower floors for actual testing. A conference table, identical to the one that Claire had just sat at in New York, was on the far side of the lab near a glass wall overlooking the biodome, where lights twinkled in the trees along the walking paths. Unlike the conference table in New York, however, she doubted that this one had ever been used for a traditional meeting. For one thing, that would have required removing the white tape borders and the table tennis net strung across the center. She had walked in on many occasions to find Joe and Beck batting ping-pong balls back and forth while they brainstormed or talked their way through some problem.

Claire tapped before entering, thinking that Beck might be inside, even if Joe was still downstairs. But the only person she saw in the lab was *herself,* slowly spinning in mid-air.

FOUR

THE SIGHT of her virtual doppelgänger was something of a surprise, given that Joe now had hundreds, if not thousands, of guinea pigs. Claire had been one of the first, however, to go through the full body and brain scans, physical stress tests, bloodwork, and about a gazillion lifestyle questions. He'd bribed Claire with the offer to take her and her two besties to see Hell's Gravity, a flash-in-the-pan boy band they'd been crazy about. Joe had bought snacks, and t-shirts, and hadn't even complained (too much) about the music. Claire's friends had been crushing on him even before that, but they were positively in love by the time the night was over. She'd pointed out that, technically, she was the one who paid for the evening through several days of literal blood, sweat, and tears, but that hadn't budged him off their pedestal one bit.

The figure hovering in front of her was no longer thirteen. If she had to guess, she would have placed her doppelgänger in her late thirties or early forties, and she was again struck by how damn much she looked like her mother. This older version of her body carried a few pounds more around the waist than Kai—even the older versions of Kai that she'd seen in the lab had negligible body fat. Was this projection of her future health because the initial lifestyle questions were answered by a thirteen-year-old girl who was still growing and hungry all the time? Maybe, although she thought it could also be because she was fonder of chocolate than her mother and less diligent about her morning date with the treadmill.

This was far from the oldest version of herself that Claire

had encountered. She'd seen herself aged all the way into her mid-eighties. Nothing after that, however, which made her a little suspicious that she was not genetically destined to make it beyond octogenarian.

The simulation had been eerily prescient about her health. Joe predicted Claire's appendix would need to come out in her early twenties, and he was right. He also predicted the onset of migraines at puberty, and a predisposition toward the same blood cancer that had taken their father, although that was no longer a potential death sentence thanks to Arvectin. The only thing he hadn't flagged was the broken wrist that she had acquired on a college ski trip, but Joe had gleefully pointed out that the healing followed the same timeline as her *in silico* version, taking a few weeks longer to mend than the doctor predicted because of the migraine preventative she was on. Claire had given him considerable grief about that, noting that the proper reaction of a loving brother to the news that his sister was going to have to wear her cast for another week or so wasn't a big grin and *I told you so*. The simulation had even been uncannily close at predicting her appearance up to the current day if you ignored the fact that the version of her body hovering at the center of the lab was completely bald and, at least in its default form, sexless.

She closed the door, making a mental note to ask Joe what he was doing that had him working with her virtual self, and then headed across the hall. The area opposite the lab housed office suites that very frequently doubled as sleeping quarters, along with a kitchen and eating area. Claire had known Joe to spend entire weeks living out of these rooms, crashing on the cot in his suite, showering in the tiny, attached bath, and sending someone to fetch fresh clothes when he reached the point where Beck complained.

Just as Claire finished arranging the dumplings on plates to reheat, familiar arms circled her from behind to scoop her into a bear hug. And it actually *was* a bit like being hugged by a bear. Physically, Joe Echols was the complete opposite of what most people envisioned when thinking of a guy who spends the vast majority of his time in a lab. At thirty, Joe was a towering hulk with dark eyes, long, untamed hair, and bronzed skin several shades darker than Claire's own. He had been taller than their dad, who had himself been well above average height, by the time he was twelve. She had never seen her brother lift weights, but he could easily pick her up and carry her around under one arm, something he'd taken great delight in doing when they were younger.

The most remarkable thing about Joe, however, was his energy. That was true at all times, but especially when he was involved in a project. Claire had been around scientists her entire life, and she had seen how research drained many of them, including her mother. Joe, on the other hand, seemed to draw energy from his work. He was never so alive as when he was in the thick of a project.

Joe reached around to snag one of the dumplings from the container.

She gave his hand a swat. "Stop that, you pig. They're still cold."

"They're not *cold*," he said around a mouthful. "More luke-warm. Did you get the extra chili oil like I asked?"

"You *didn't* ask. But I still remembered because I'm just that awesome. Dig around. It's somewhere in the bag."

Joe found the chili oil, then rummaged in the fridge for beers. "Thought maybe you were in New York with Wyatt. Isn't he covering the protests at the UN?"

"That was at least three weeks ago," Claire said with a laugh. "Pretty sure he's on the West Coast this week. I'm not getting regular updates because he's in *love*. Again."

Claire had been best friends with Wyatt Garcia since their sophomore year of college, and frequently more than friends when they were between romantic attachments. Or more accurately when *Wyatt* was between attachments. She'd had exactly one romantic relationship, two years back, which had imploded after about six months. Wyatt, on the other hand, came back from assignment two or three times a year convinced that he'd found *The One* halfway around the world. Most of those relationships lasted a month at most before Wyatt got bored or pissed the other person off. Or, more likely, he got bored and *then* pissed the other person off so that he didn't have to do the leaving.

"I'm telling you, he'd drop every single one of them if you showed the slightest interest," Joe said.

"Oh, sure. Because *you're* the resident expert on relationships."

"She knows you too well." This comment came from Beck, who was now standing in the doorway. Tall, thin, and handsome in a bookish way, he was much closer in appearance to a stereotypical lab denizen than Claire's brother. Beck was a good listener, too, as she'd discovered after her dad died. Joe and Kai had been wrapped up in their own grief and in their shared sense of failure for being too late with the cure. Poor Beck had rounded a corner the day of the funeral and found seventeen-year-old Claire curled up in a side room, knees to chest, in the middle of a complete emotional breakdown. She'd expected him to run and get her mother, which was the very last thing she'd wanted. But instead, he'd put his arms around her and let her cry it out. Scream it out, really, because there had been almost as much fury as grief in the mix. As a result, Beck probably understood more about Claire's anger at her mother than Joe did.

"Okay. That's my cue to change the subject before you two gang up on me," Joe said. "What were you doing in New York, then? Last time we spoke, you said you wouldn't be traveling outside DC until my birthday."

"Major change of plans. If all goes as expected, I'll be sending you birthday greetings from Mars." She gave the two of them a basic overview while they ate, implying that her participation was something Kolya's people were pushing to increase tourism. Which was true, but entirely beside the main point of the trip.

Joe smiled and shook his head in amusement. "Mom is going to freak. She still thinks Kolya swiped my biobotics research. Personally, I really don't care as long as he's putting it to use a few hundred million kilometers away. To the best of my knowledge, Kolya's group hasn't done anything in the medical field in over a decade, so why should it bother me?"

"True," Beck said. "And unless Kai decides to shift gears rather dramatically, Jonas Labs won't be getting into the business of terraforming. Still, I'm surprised that you're dealing with KTI, Claire. I seem to recall that Anton Kolya is one subject —quite possibly, the *only* subject—on which you fully agree with your mother."

Claire had to snort at that. "It's a subject on which about eighty percent of the public agrees with my mother. Kolya's an egotistical ass. And a publicity whore, although maybe that's redundant. I doubt he'll be on the planet when I am, but even if we were going to be on the same ship and I was forced to share quarters with the man, there's no way I'd pass on this opportunity. And…while we're on the subject, do either of you know what exactly he'll be doing in stage six that involves the upgraded biobots? All I know aside from the publicly available info is what I picked up from Mom's rant at Christmas when she called him an effing thief."

"Wow. I had no idea that Kai was in such a mellow mood over the holidays," Beck said, exchanging an amused look with Joe.

"That *may* not have been her exact phrasing," Claire said. "Do you think she's right, though? That he's a thief?"

Joe shrugged. "Maybe. But there's also a fair chance that it's just convergent research agendas. Biobotics is a massive field, and Beck and I are far from the only people working in this particular branch of it. Kolya has probably got a half dozen people on his staff doing that sort of research. She's right that there are some odd areas of overlap, but again...not gonna point fingers when they're using the critters in an entirely different realm."

Claire had followed the progress of Joe's *critters*, as he often called them, since just after her eleventh birthday when he'd pulled her into one of the labs to show her his latest find. His critters weren't anything especially remarkable back then, just a slight variation on what used to be called *xenobots*, so named because the first versions were created from cells of *Xenopus laevis*, or the African clawed frog. Skin and cardiac cells were cobbled together to make small, autonomous organic machines. Or animals, depending on whom you asked, but even the most rigid ethicists had to admit they were animals only in the sense that bacteria or similar very basic life fit that definition.

Joe hadn't, of course, been working on projects for Jonas Labs at age fifteen. Even for prodigies, there were limits. He had, however, been given access to a small lab where he worked with a tutor during his high school years and over the summers after he started college. Thanks to the equipment at his disposal, he was experimenting with biological building blocks when most boys his age were still playing with Designabot kits.

"Get a load of this, Claire Bear," he'd said as he dragged her into the lab one day during Christmas break.

What she had seen on the wall screen was a flurry of moving dots. Red, blue, and purple, although the colors weren't uniform. The dots had uneven edges, with a chunk gone on one side, almost like a pizza with one slice missing. While smaller dots were stationary, the larger ones spun in circles across the screen like old-fashioned tops. A faint pulsing had emanated from the center of the whirling dots, almost like a heartbeat. The red and blue dots zoomed around the screen, caroming off the others, and scooping the stationary dots into small piles.

"What do you see?" Joe had asked.

Claire had given him a scathing look, thinking that he was patronizing her. "Xenobots. We studied them in earth science class. Third grade. They're used to clean up toxic waste sites."

"Of course they're xenobots, although the preferred term is biobots. I meant what do you see them *doing*?"

"Reproducing. Making copies of themselves."

"Close. Look again."

She had stared at the screen for a bit longer before realizing that most of the stationary piles being created were the same color as the biobots creating them. In fact, all of the purple piles were being made by purple dots. But some of the red and blue dots were *also* making purple dots.

"They're combining. Red and blue make purple."

"Exactly. Which is cool because they're not supposed to do that. The big question is whether the hybrids can reproduce."

"But the hybrids *are* reproducing."

"They're trying. But are any of their offspring moving?"

They hadn't been, and it had taken Joe several months to pinpoint why. Once he had it figured out, though, he had his dissertation topic.

The research their mother's team had been working on back then, which would eventually lead to Arvectin, targeted stubborn cancers that still eluded modern medicine by using similar biobots created from the cells of the patient as a delivery mechanism. That had been about a year before Martin Echols's diagnosis turned their lives upside down, both at home and at the lab. Every resource that could be freed up within the company had been immediately diverted into the Arvectin program. If her father had been able to hold on for another six months, he'd have been around for the breakthrough.

Since the launch of Arvectin, countless people had told Claire that it must be such a consolation to know that her father's illness led to research that saved so many lives. In a way, they were right. But she could never shake the sense that those people were leaving the obvious unsaid. If Jonas Labs had the ability to save so many people, why had it taken a personal tragedy to fast-track that research?

FIVE

"SO, who's on the team you're traveling with?" Joe asked, pulling Claire's mind back to the present. "If they've got you on a worker transport, those are built for speed, not comfort. You won't have much privacy. Better pray they're not a bunch of assholes, because you're going to be miserable otherwise."

She took a swig of beer to give herself a moment to make sure she didn't say anything that would violate the NDA she'd just signed. "Not sure. I don't know much about any of them. Just that it's a multidisciplinary team out of Columbia. Dr. Laura Brodnik is the lead. She seems okay."

Joe rubbed his chin. "Wasn't she working with...damn, I can't think of his name. Beck, you're the name wizard. Remember a year or so back? Post-doc who gave a talk at a conference claiming that the non-coding DNA they'd found in some of the Mars samples was too uniform to be naturally occurring. Wasn't he at Columbia?"

"Yeah," Beck said. "I think the name was Kimura? Something like that. Why? Is he on the team?"

"Maybe?" Claire said. "There's an Asian guy. Brodnik introduced herself, and one of Kolya's employees was there, but they didn't bother introducing anyone else on the team."

Beck pulled something up on his phone. "Yeah. Daichi Kimura. Is this him?"

Claire nodded. The video was from fifteen months earlier. It had been taken from a distance, but she could still tell it was the same guy she'd seen at the meeting in New York. She was pretty sure that she'd watched the clip before, or at least part of it. But it was short, so she let it play.

Kimura was speaking at a conference—the microbiology working group of the Ares Consortium, according to the title of the clip. There were maybe twenty people in the audience. Kimura clicked to change the picture on the screen behind him and then said, "Which brings me to the biological samples collected from Terra Sirenum that were submitted to the consortium for analysis. Image number four, which you can see on the screen, is an enlargement of the non-coding DNA—sometimes called 'junk DNA'—from one of the three unicellular organisms found near the Arsia mining camp. Careful inspection of the binding sites on this sample of *Deinococcus aganippe* shows an unusual regularity. Compare that..." He clicked again, and now there were two images side by side behind him. "To image number five on the right, which is an almost identical sample released two years ago, taken from the site at Noctis Labyrinthus."

There was a clear difference between the two images. The one on the left showed binding sites that were smooth and regular, while the ones in the image on the right were more typical...slightly bumpy and misshapen.

A woman in the audience raised her hand. "So...just to be clear, Dr. Kimura. You're claiming someone *tampered* with these samples?"

Kimura shrugged. "That much is obvious. The only question is who. And, I suppose, why. Although, those answers are pretty obvious, too."

"Really?" the woman asked. Her tone made it clear that it was anything but obvious to her.

"Sure," Kimura said. "It's like anything else. Follow the money."

The clip ended and Claire handed the tablet back to Beck. "I remember seeing that when it came out. But wasn't it pretty thoroughly debunked?"

"Less debunked than yanked," Joe said around a mouthful of dumpling. "NASA got *all* up in arms, thinking the guy was saying that they'd purposefully tampered with the samples. Or that they'd given researchers the *wrong* samples. And since Columbia has a shit-ton of contracts with NASA, they made him walk back his research pronto."

"Well, to be fair to the guy, it's not like there wouldn't be an incentive to do some tampering," Beck said. "There's a lot of money tied up in Kolya's venture and something like that would activate a whole new level of scrutiny."

"Why, though?" Claire asked. "They're about to start stage six. Would they really pull the project now?"

Beck shrugged. "They might. Or at least delay it significantly. There are supposed to be safeguards at each stage. Kolya got the green light to move ahead with his terraforming experiment because they were able to make a convincing case that only unicellular life is native to Mars, and none of it is unique. More complex life can survive there, obviously, otherwise Kolya's project would never have gotten off the ground. They've already introduced a pretty wide array of algae, tardigrades, and so forth at key locations. Some plants, too. But if the microbes they discovered a few decades back had actually been multicellular I don't know if that would have happened at all. And if scientists were to stumble upon other, more complex life forms on the planet now…"

"They're not going to pull the plug," Joe said. "Too much money has been invested by too many powerful people. But it would probably push stage six back a couple of years while they greased a few more palms to get things on track again. Can you imagine the happy dance Mom would do if she learned Kolya had that sort of setback?"

Thirty minutes later, the food was gone except for the small plate of dumplings that Claire had managed to hold back for Wilson. They lingered over a second beer, and then Beck said he was heading home.

"Don't give me that look," he told Joe. "I need to feed my cat. And sleep in a bed where my feet don't hang off the edge.

But yes, I *will* be back in the lab by seven. Claire, you're more than welcome to crash in my office if you're staying the night. It's actually not bad if you're under six feet."

"Thanks, but I should really get back. We leave in a week, and I have to help Rowan find a sitter for Jemma."

Beck said he'd deliver Wilson's dumplings to him at the security desk. He took the plate and then gave Claire an awkward one-armed hug. It triggered an instant flashback to the meltdown after her dad's memorial service, both because she'd just been thinking about it and because that was the only other time that Beck had ever hugged her.

"Have fun fraternizing with the enemy," he said. "But be careful, okay? And I don't just mean the obvious kind of careful since you'll be on a planet without breathable air. I've heard that some of the labor disputes in Elysia and several of the other colonies have heated up in the past few months. And yes, I know it's practically on the other side of the planet from where you'll be, but…"

His pale blue eyes were genuinely worried, and Beck wasn't inclined to exaggerate. Claire gave him a cheery smile, in part to ward off her own nerves about the trip, which were creeping back to the surface. "The main complex at Daedalus City probably isn't a five-star hotel, but from everything I've heard, it's pretty posh. And they must be fairly sure that it's safe…they're bringing in groups of high school students, now. The off-world equivalent of a semester abroad, I guess. I'll probably be safer than you guys from what Wilson said about the Flock's bomb threats."

At the mention of the Flock, Beck made a sound very close to a growl. He and her mother, along with many of the other scientists Claire knew, seemed to take the group's attacks as a personal affront.

Joe, on the other hand, just snorted. "Toby's sheep aren't anything to worry about. There will always be Luddites."

Beck opened his mouth to argue the point. Having heard

both sides of that argument in detail, Claire decided to move the conversation back to something they both agreed on so that the man could get home to his cat and his more comfortable bed.

"I promise I'll be extra careful," she told him. "Enjoy the launch, Beck."

They both rolled their eyes, exactly as she'd known they would. Beck and Joe might argue about the Flock, but they were perfectly *simpatico* concerning the upcoming publicity storm.

Joe chuckled softly once Beck was out of earshot. "Can't believe the bastard stole all the big brother lines, but I guess it saves me the trouble. Truthfully, I'm more jealous than worried. I was thinking about booking a trip to a hut in Bora Bora or someplace off-grid to avoid the publicity hellscape surrounding the launch and you one-up me by going off-planet. I'd love to collect some samples on my own and see if Kimura was right. Although Kolya's crew would probably confiscate them on the return flight."

"I'll see if I can sneak something back in my luggage," she teased. "But…you know Kai isn't going to let you duck out on the launch. And you shouldn't. This is *your* work, Joe. You should be the one taking the bow, not her. Even if it means they put you in a suit."

A wave of guilt hit her again. The Mars story, assuming everything went as expected, would mean that Joe's breakthrough had maybe a week or two in the limelight before being shoved aside, at least temporarily. It could mean that this year's Zimmer Award and God only knew how many others would go to Brodnik and her team, rather than to Joe. Probably not, and Joe didn't really care, but still…

"She's not getting me in a suit," Joe said. "I *do* have a lab coat…somewhere…so she can send a crew in to get some shots of me and Beck in our natural habitat. And yes, I know I'll have to make an appearance at the big bash, but the food will be good, and my stay will be brief. Go in, shake a few hands, then straight back to the lab."

Claire looked up from stashing a plate in the dishwasher. "Speaking of the lab, why are you running Virtual-Me in there? Have any ailments popped up that I should be concerned about given that I'm heading off planet?"

"Oh, no...no. You should be fine. It's just that your duplicate is still one of the few taken from an adolescent for which I have full research permissions, so we were running some tests for Rejuvesce."

When Claire met Joe and her mom in New York for Christmas dinner a few months earlier, they'd both been in a celebratory mood that went well beyond the usual holiday cheer. Kai had been reserved at first, not wanting to go into specifics. But Joe hadn't been able to resist telling her that Rejuvesce was expected to be cleared for market by early spring.

The drug had entered the final stage of human trials with a few hundred volunteers four years earlier, after several rounds of *in silico* trials showed much better than expected results. Those results were borne out in human trials, as well. There were no noticeable side effects and they'd seen a dramatic drop in the rate of cellular senescence in more than ninety-five percent of the participants. The patients in the trial were still aging, but at a much slower rate. Joe predicted that the drug would add at least twenty years to the average lifespan, possibly thirty if people started taking it by age fifty.

"But Rejuvesce is about to launch," she said. "What sort of tests could you be doing at this stage?"

Joe grinned. "I guess you could call it a side goal. Mom says it's just an excuse to avoid the fanfare, and she's not *entirely* wrong, but...I definitely think we're onto something."

SIX

JEMMA POINTED one chubby little finger at the display. "What's that big circle called?"

It would have been a lot easier to finish editing without the girl squirming in her lap, but Claire didn't have the heart to shoo her away, especially knowing that she would be leaving the next day. At least Jemma had stopped asking whether there were bug-monsters on Mars like there were in some movie she had watched at her dad's house the previous month…a movie that was clearly not appropriate for a four-year-old because it had given Jemma nightmares for a solid week afterward.

"That one," Claire said, "is Arsia Mons. It's one of the three mountains in the Tharsis range."

"They don't look like mountains." Jemma snickered. "They look like my daddy's nipples."

"Oh, really? Does he have *three*?"

"Noooo." Her tone suggested that was just plain silly. "I *mean* because they have little pointy things in the middle, but the rest is flat and round."

Claire flipped the view on the screen to show the mountains' height. "Are you sure about that?"

Jemma shook her head. "I didn't know they were that tall. Is that the mountain with the giant slide?"

"Yes. But…this isn't a slide like at the park. This is a special kind they only have on Mars. It goes *up*, super-fast, so that our shuttle can take us back to the ship that will bring us home. It's just like riding on the hyperloop, only it goes into the sky."

"I want to go on it, too. Why do they only have it on Mars?"

"The gravity on Earth is too strong. You remember about gravity, right?"

"Gravity is the thing that made me fall off the couch," the girl said in an annoyed tone, no doubt remembering the bump she'd taken to the head while goofing around the previous week.

"Right. So it would have to be a really, really, really long hyperloop tube to get our shuttle high enough up to escape gravity and get past the clouds. Instead, our shuttle will ride piggyback on top of a big jet, and once we get high enough up, they'll give us a boost and that big sail I showed you in the video yesterday will unfold."

"The one that looks like a giant mirror?"

"Yep. Then they'll shine some really big lasers at the mirror sail and the photons that come out of the laser will push us all the way to Tranquility Base on the moon, where we'll catch the bigger ship that goes to Mars. I'm going to call you from Tranquility Base, and you can tell everyone at preschool that you talked to someone who was on the moon."

"Dane said his gramma went to the moon to gabble."

Claire frowned, then chuckled as she realized Jemma meant *gamble*. Going to the moon clearly wasn't as big of a deal as it would have been when she was Jemma's age.

The girl was now tracing the other mountains with her finger. "Are you gonna slide down these ones, too, since they're so close by?"

"Um, no. The hyperloop is only on Arsia Mons. And the other mountains aren't really all that close. Remember when I went to Dallas, and I showed you how far away I'd be on the globe?"

Jemma gave her a solemn nod.

"Believe it or not, that last mountain is farther away from Daedalus City than DC is from Dallas."

"Whoa."

"Whoa is right."

"But maybe those other mountains are where all of the bug-monsters are hiding, Claire." Jemma tucked her chin against her chest the way she always did when she was trying not to giggle.

"There are no...bug-monsters...on...Mars!" Claire tickled the girl's tummy with each word. "Just the teeny-tiny kind of bugs you can only see under a microscope. You could squash a bazillion of them with just your thumb."

That, of course, prompted Jemma to start smashing her thumb on the edge of Claire's desk. It also made Claire realize that she wasn't nearly as certain about those bug-monsters as she'd been a few days before. After all, she'd also have said that there had never been life on Mars capable of leaving behind a written record, and yet here she was, preparing to head off to investigate that very thing.

"You know what I could really, *really* use right now?" Claire asked.

Jemma shook her dark curls.

"One of those peanut butter cookies I brought back from New York. Think you could fetch one for each of us? Don't forget the napkins."

"Can Siggy have one?"

This was Jemma's latest trick—beg a cookie for the cat so she'd end up with two. But Claire was onto her devious little plan.

"What do you *think*?"

"Probably no?" Jemma said, but her voice was still hopeful.

"*Definitely* no."

The girl hopped up and ran for the kitchen, with no further questions. And now Claire was thinking about the extra padding around her virtual twin. Maybe she should give *her* cookie to Sigrid, not that the picky thing would be likely to eat it. And, anyway, that version of her was years away. A far more pressing problem was that she was going to catch hell if Rowan got out of the shower and found her bribing the kiddo with sweets before breakfast. But she really did need to read through the script for the *Simple Science* segment one last time before sending it off.

Once she had Jemma parked in front of the viewscreen with one of her videos, Claire shooed an indignant Sigrid off her chair and did a final read-through. She was contracted for two *Simple Science* pieces per month, along with various other assignments. Normally, she would have taken several more days on the script and wouldn't have ventured into the office to record the video portion until they'd mapped out the entire storyboard. But the recording was something she couldn't easily do on the ship, so they had juggled things around a bit. She'd seen enough KTI tourist promos to know that Kolya's team had a decent recording studio at Daedalus City, so her tentative plan was to record a short bit of video during their stop at the main lunar base and the rest after they arrived on Mars.

As Claire had expected, Reese Bernard, the science editor at the *Atlantic Post*, had expressed zero qualms about the paper covering the story when she met with him the morning after she returned to DC. The man's jaw had dropped so far that it practically unhinged when she told him about the chamber Brodnik's team had unearthed at Icarus Camp and the only question on his mind had been which of his senior reporters to assign. When Claire broke the news that the team had specifically requested *her*, his response had been a groan. She fully understood why, but it still stung.

"It's not that I don't trust you'll do a good job, Claire," he'd added quickly. "That's not it at all. But surely you see why this is going to cause problems? Shaundra and Bryce aren't gonna like this. Bryce in particular. He's been here nine years. Neither of them will see this as something you've earned."

And they'd be right, Claire thought. At the same time, she couldn't shake the feeling that this was *always* going to be a problem. No matter how hard she worked or how good she was at her job, there would always be someone who believed her entire career fell into her lap due to family connections. There was a grain of truth in the mix if she was being honest. She'd spent the early part of her life learning about other people's discoveries, watching the process from conception to market. Had she been born into a different environment, she might have wound up reporting something else entirely—fashion or politics or economics. But science was something that she *knew*, something that she had absorbed by osmosis, simply from being surrounded by it. Like her father, Claire had never had a desire to *be* a scientist, but she couldn't deny that growing up in that environment gave her something of an advantage in covering the field.

"I'll do my best to smooth things over," Bernard had told her before he ended their call. "But...maybe you should avoid the office between now and your departure? Take a few days off to get ready."

She had been planning to do that even without Bernard's urging since working remotely made it easier to handle interviews with potential sitters for Jemma, schedule her required medical check-up, and go to daily sessions with the physical therapist who conducted the vestibular training that Dr. Brodnik recommended. The first three appointments had nearly made Claire lose her breakfast, but she was now at the point where she could adjust fairly quickly to the level of spin that she'd have to endure both en route to Mars and in the sections of the habitats on the planet that had amplified gravity.

Her suitcase was now packed, and she was officially cleared for Mars travel. It was Rowan's day off and since she couldn't delay it any longer, she was heading into DC to record the *Simple Science* segment and also to cover one of Bryce Avery's interviews. Her decidedly *un*collegial colleague had responded to the news about the Mars trip by calling in to say that his wife and daughter had a bad case of the flu and he'd be out for at least a week. Claire didn't believe it. She doubted that Bernard did, either. But if that was Bryce's attitude now, she couldn't even imagine how he'd react when he discovered that the trip was much more than an in-depth profile on KTI's terraforming project, which was the cover Bernard was going with until the actual story was official.

After work, Claire had dinner plans with Wyatt, who had just gotten back into town. He would have a thousand and one questions, most of which she couldn't answer. Which meant that she'd either have to lie to him, something he usually spotted in a heartbeat, or tell him she'd signed an NDA...which would lead to a thousand and one *more* questions that she couldn't answer. Wyatt hounded people for a living, and he wasn't going to cut her a single bit of slack. She would definitely have to wear her hair up. He'd admitted in a weak moment a few years back that she reflexively tucked her hair behind her ears when she had something to hide.

Claire's biggest worry, however, had been resolved the previous afternoon. She and Rowan had spent the better part of the week interviewing sitters. After two candidates who seemed great on paper but hadn't been a good fit when they met Jemma, Rowan said she'd just ask for an unpaid leave of absence. Claire knew that Ro wouldn't have minded the vacation and the extra time with her daughter, but the *unpaid* part would have stretched her friend's pride to the absolute limit because unpaid leave would have left Claire covering all of the bills for nine weeks—actually closer to ten weeks now, since a last minute change in the itinerary had added a few days to the roundtrip.

Covering the bills wouldn't have been a problem from Claire's standpoint. She had broached the subject of paying a larger percentage of their shared expenses a couple of months after Rowan and Jemma moved in, pitching it as a sliding scale thing, although a true sliding scale would have meant that Rowan bought groceries once every five years or so and Claire paid for everything else. The only concession she'd gotten from Ro was a fifty-fifty split on expenses, rather than her paying extra for Jemma's room and board. And Ro had agreed to that arrangement only until she finished her residency.

Luckily, the last person who answered their post hit it off instantly with Jemma. Ro's pride was now safe. And Claire was pretty sure Jemma would have more fun with this guy—who was being paid to entertain her—than she normally would hanging around while Claire worked all day.

By the time Rowan was out of the shower, the script was off to the office, and Jemma and Claire had both finished their cookies. Unfortunately, she'd forgotten to decrumb Jemma, which meant they were busted.

"Well, at least they're peanut butter cookies," Rowan said, shaking her head. "Actually, if you two little piggies left a cookie for me, we'll call it breakfast and I'll fix an early, *extra healthy* lunch. Let's get you out of those crumb-covered pj's so I can put them in the wash." She tipped Jemma onto her back and tugged at the hem of the girl's pajama bottoms.

"Claire is gonna slide up a tube into the sky wivout us." Jemma's tone made it clear that even though her eyes were still glued to the screen, her mind wasn't entirely on the exploits of Marvel's WonderKitties.

"True," Rowan said. "She can't take us, though. Little kids can't go to Mars yet. You would hate it anyway because once she reaches the ship it will be like she's in time-out all day, every day for weeks. And you *like* Ethan. Remember the silly duck voice he made? He's going to take you so many fun places while I'm at work."

"You also have a really important job to do while I'm gone," Claire said. "I need you to take care of Siggy. And somebody has to play my piano, so it won't miss me."

Rowan rolled her eyes. "Thanks bunches, Claire." She was normally a very patient mother, but Jemma's energetic piano compositions got on Ro's last nerve.

"You're welcome," Claire said with a grin, before turning back to Jemma. "And you have to blow a kiss to me each night that I'm on Mars. That way, I won't feel so lonely, and the pilot can follow the trail of kisses right back to earth. Can you do that for me?"

Jemma nodded, but she still seemed a little sulky, so Claire added, "I've heard they have really good peanut butter cookies on Mars. Maybe I can bring some back."

Rowan snorted and sent Jemma upstairs to pick out her clothes for the day. Once the girl was out of earshot, she said, "You do know she's going to remember that, right? God help you if you don't come home with peanut butter cookies."

"I'll add it to my checklist of things to bring back."

"You should also remember to bring back a full explanation for why you're *really* going on this trip. I couldn't even get you on a three-day Disney cruise last Christmas and suddenly you're signing up for nine weeks inside a smelly tin can?"

Claire laughed, even though Rowan's point was dead on. "Hey, at least on this trip, there's a possibility that my roommate won't snore. In your case, sleepless nights are a given."

"Yeah, right. Still not buying it. I'm expecting you to have one hell of a scoop when you get back. Oh…and you're not going to have any excuse for getting out of that cruise this year, so go ahead and pencil it in for Christmas."

SEVEN

CLAIRE'S HAND was already on the knob when she happened to glance through the window of the small conference room. The man waiting for her—technically, waiting for Bryce Avery—was in his late twenties or early thirties, slightly built, with shoulder-length blond hair that was matted and in dire need of a wash. Not typical attire in their department, although a source coming into the office was unusual, in and of itself. Most of the time, interviews were handled remotely, but if a face-to-face was warranted, the reporter almost always went to the source.

What gave Claire considerable pause, however, was the off-white woven hoodie. Or more precisely, the logo on that hoodie —an eye with a brilliantly colored globe in place of the iris, above the letters *EWA*.

She let go of the handle, turned on her heel, and marched right back to her editor's office. "What the hell, Bernard?"

Reese Bernard looked up from his desk. He was a good editor and an okay boss, but he reminded Claire of an old-fashioned yard gnome—full beard, short and round stature, perpetual scowl, and almost always found in the same spot. All he needed was a pointy hat to complete the look.

He spread his hands, clearly clueless. "What did I do?"

"More what you didn't do. You could have at least warned me that the interview I'm fielding for Avery is with one of the Flock."

Bernard laughed, shaking his head. "Couldn't warn you about what I didn't know. Relax. It's probably just Devin again. The guy's harmless. He latched onto Avery at some conference about six months back and has come in two or three times since then. Always has some hot tip that amounts to nada but gives Avery a story to tell at the bar. Just let the guy vent into a recorder for a few minutes."

"And you don't think Avery did this on purpose?"

"Oh, I *know* he did it on purpose. Absolutely no doubt. And I also know you're going to be a good sport about it. Because as pissed as Avery is now, it's nothing compared to the upcoming shitstorm if this story is what you say it is. And I'd rather not have to take sides in this. You know how I hate breaking in new reporters."

Claire sighed, noting the artful way he'd avoided saying *whose* side he'd be taking in the upcoming shitstorm. "Fine. I'll be a good sport. But I can't guarantee that the guy in there will do the same if he knows my family background."

"If I hear an explosion, I'll send in the cavalry." It was a joke, of course, but it didn't sit well with Claire after the warnings she'd gotten a few days before from Wilson and Beck.

"Jonas Labs has had three bomb threats from the Flock in the past month. Pretty sure they're not the only lab that's been targeted, either."

"Really?" Bernard's smile was gone now, and he shot a nervous glance in the direction of the conference room. "You think I should get one of the guards up here?"

"No. If the guy was armed or carrying anything suspicious, he'd never have made it into the building. And he looks like a strong gust of wind could blow him away. I'm not worried about my physical safety. But I really don't think Avery should be leading these guys on."

Claire headed back to the conference room, pasted on a smile, and opened the door.

"You're not Bryce," the guy said as she took the chair opposite him.

"Sorry. His wife and daughter have the flu, apparently, and he asked me to sit in. Claire Echols. You're Devin, right?"

He nodded, narrowing his eyes, and she jotted the name down on her pad. There was no need for her to ask his last name. Anyone wearing that hoodie would have had it legally changed to Shepherd. Many of them tossed their first names away, as well, adopting what they called *Earth names,* like Skylark or Daffodil.

"I was supposed to meet with *Bryce*. Bryce Avery. *We had an appointment.*"

His voice was strained with suppressed anger, and despite the fact that he was barely above Claire's own height and weight, she was beginning to question Bernard's characterization of the guy as harmless. On the plus side, her name and face hadn't seemed to trigger any recognition.

She paused, debating whether to repeat Avery's cover story, and then decided to just punt the ball. "Bryce should be back in the office next week, if you'd prefer to wait and—"

"That's too late! He *said* he'd be here. I came all the way up from Culpeper and we don't have another work detail in the city until next month." He reached across the table and grabbed her arm. "Can you give me his personal number? Please. Things have…escalated, and I really, really need to talk to Bryce."

"No." Claire pulled her arm away and slid her chair back, just out of reach. "Even if I had that information, which I don't, I couldn't give it out. But you're right. He should have called to let you know."

Devin's eyes widened. "What? No…no calls."

As soon as the words were out of her mouth, she realized they were stupid. Avery couldn't have called, even if he'd been so inclined. Members of the Flock handed over their phones along with their last names and all personal possessions. The main office of each compound was connected to the outside world and that was the only way to get a message to one of the members. If this guy was here, he obviously didn't want his main office to know.

"Is there anything I can do to help you? I'd be happy to get a message to Bryce if you'd like to record it. Or I'm sure he's checking work mail, so you could try contacting him when you get…home." Claire sighed. "Sorry. I guess they don't let you do that, either."

"I can *do* anything I want. My life, my choice. *We're not prisoners.*" He punctuated the last three words by pounding his fist against the table.

"Okay, okay. I'm sorry. Do you want to leave him a message or not?" The guy was almost in tears now and all Claire wanted to do was get out of there before she said anything else to set him off. "Write it down or record it. Either way, I promise Bryce will get it today."

That was a promise she fully planned to keep, too. And Bryce Avery would also be getting a few choice words along with the delivery. This had gone well past the point of her being a good sport.

The door opened and Bernard stuck his head in. "Everything okay in here?"

"It's fine," she said.

Devin gave a bitter laugh and stood up. "Yeah. It's fine. I'm leaving. Should have known better."

Bernard stepped aside to let him pass. When the guy was out of earshot, he said, "I take it he recognized you?"

Claire shook her head. "Don't think so. But I'm going to reiterate what I said earlier. Avery shouldn't be yanking their chains."

"Yeah. You're right. I'm heading out for the day. You have a good trip, okay? Check in when you get there." He lowered his voice. "Try to give me a subtle heads up a day or so prior to the big reveal."

"Sure. How about I message you to *hold the presses*?"

Bernard snorted. "I said *subtle*. And…I'll talk to Avery about this mess when he gets back."

Claire nodded, even though she knew Bernard would do no such thing.

EIGHT

CLAIRE ARRIVED at Media Res a full twenty minutes early. It was certainly not a restaurant that she would have picked, both because there were at least a dozen in the neighborhood with better food and because it was right across the street from the office, which made it a frequent watering hole for the *Atlantic Post's* employees. Wyatt liked it, though, probably because what the food lacked in quality it compensated for in quantity and they didn't water the drinks.

After the dramatic end to her interview with Devin Shepherd, Claire really wasn't in the mood to talk to any of her colleagues who might wander in, so she considered going ahead into the restaurant. But Wyatt was notorious for being late. Hogging a table for half an hour or more before ordering was probably tempting fate if she didn't want the waiter to spit in her food. So, she parked herself at the bar, ordered a whisky sour, and began going over her pre-departure checklist to make sure she had covered everything.

That nagging voice inside her head was back by the time her drink arrived. Could any story really be worth nine weeks in a smelly tin can, as Rowan had so succinctly put it? Because that was pretty much what it was going to be. They would have a *bit* more room to move around during the day they were scheduled to be at the moon base, and they'd have *much* more room once they reached Daedalus City, but even there, she would be spending a lot of her time inside domes. Claire *was* excited about getting out and exploring the surface of the planet, but she would no doubt be in a group at all times, and when she did make it out of the dome, she'd be encased in a bulky spacesuit.

Nine weeks without a single breath of fresh air wasn't her idea of a fun time.

And the trip wasn't without risk. It had been more than a decade since the last space transport accident, and that had been an aging European colonial shuttle, not the modern commercial ship they would be taking. According to a KTI publicity spiel published the previous year, twenty thousand tourists had now visited Mars and the company had zero fatalities. If you looked closely, there was an asterisk and a statement in small print that noted one man had died of a heart attack on Mars, but a team of physicians said that he'd likely have died the same way on Earth within the year. The clear implication was that it was unfair to count that one against them.

Or at least, his death was the only one *reported*. KTI was rumored to have coughed up a huge amount of money to get that man's family to drop the case, and the company had quietly beefed up the required health scan after the incident to include a few extra tests for prospective tourists over the age of fifty. KTI had a knack for keeping secrets that Claire's mother envied, although that was no doubt easier to do in Minsk than in many other parts of the world. It was probably easier on Mars, too, now that Claire thought about it. Were there even any press outlets on the planet aside from the publicity departments of the various corporations that ran the colonies? For all she knew, there could have been dozens of deaths…

Encouraged by the morbid turn her train of thought had taken, the voice in her head—which, of course, sounded far too much like her mother—began ticking off all of the other negatives. Claire responded by tossing back the last of her drink and considered ordering another one. But that might loosen her tongue too much once Wyatt started asking questions about the trip.

It might loosen her inhibitions, too. That could be both good and bad. Sex with Wyatt was always great, and they cared enough about each other that the snuggle afterward was never forced. But she had promised Jemma that she'd be back in time to read the girl a bedtime story since it was her last night before the trip. Ro had decided it would be best for Jemma and Claire to say their goodbyes the night before, since they didn't want to risk the possibility of a meltdown before preschool.

Also, Claire had no idea whether Wyatt was still seeing the woman he'd met in Ottawa. And even if he wasn't, did she *really* want to give him more time to ask questions?

Have the drink, the little voice said. *Setting aside the whole sex thing, it's probably the last decent liquor you'll have for the next few months.*

"Oh, would you just shove off?" she muttered.

From just behind her, Wyatt laughed. "What did I do now? I'm even on time for once."

"Nothing. I was talking to myself."

She leaned forward and gave him a leisurely kiss, savoring the prickly feel of his scruff against her palm and the familiar cardamom scent of his cologne.

"Mmm. I missed you, too." He took the stool next to her. "So…what has you sitting at the bar talking to yourself?"

"My internal monologue is just working overtime today."

"Probably because you're about to *leave the damn planet.* What the hell has gotten into you, woman?"

"It's a good opportunity," Claire said, knowing that it sounded lame. "Aren't you the one always saying I need to expand my horizons? And you don't have room to talk. Any one of your assignments is more dangerous than a tourist jaunt to Mars."

It wasn't a point that Wyatt could argue, and they both knew it. He had spent his entire career covering separatist and terrorist movements, foreign and domestic. That had been his plan long before they met in college, and after graduation, he'd pursued the job at the *Post* with a single-minded intent that Claire found somewhat unnerving. Wyatt had taken that same determination into every investigation, and his fixation on finding answers often rubbed nasty people the wrong way, to the point that he'd very nearly gotten himself killed in the Hsinchu City uprising and again during the election riots in Istanbul the following year. His recording of a message from a US senator to a supposedly private Southern Sons rally in Tennessee nine months back had resulted in two bomb threats —one at his apartment building and one at the *Post* headquarters, where a bomb had actually been discovered and, thank God, defused. Claire had stared at the *Post*'s internal site nervously on more occasions than she cared to remember, waiting for Wyatt to update his feed so that she'd know he was safe.

"But we're not talking about me," Wyatt said. "*You're* the one with chronic risk aversion. This is about pissing off your mom, isn't it?"

Claire resisted the urge to contradict his characterization of her relatively cautious nature—at least, compared to his—as *chronic risk aversion*. The man was the undisputed king of hyperbole, something that drove his editors crazy. Instead, she picked up on the thread that was at least partially true.

"I'll admit that not being here for the Rejuvesce launch is icing on the cake. But I'd be covering the story even if it *wasn't* Anton Kolya's baby. Which I'm pretty sure is what you were hinting at."

Wyatt held back until they were seated and had placed their orders. Then he said, "I'm not trying to discourage you, babe. It's too late for that anyway since I learned about this trip… what? Two days ago? I really *do* think this could be good for you…and not just professionally. But if I know you, you've been doing a deep dive into the sciency stuff preparing for your explainers, and not paying much attention to the political and economic currents. And there are a lot of them."

She was again tempted to object, but he wasn't wrong. "I've had a week to get ready, Wyatt. Can't do everything. And the sciency stuff, as you put it, is my bread and butter."

"Understood. And the political and social currents are my own bread and butter, which is one reason I'm here tonight to give you the condensed version, even though I've got *this* godforsaken thing hanging over me."

Wyatt's dark eyes flicked upward to the space above his head. Technically, nothing was there, but the shared joke spanned pretty much their entire relationship, and she could now almost see a giant anvil with the word *DEADLINE* in flashing lights dangling above him.

"Then we'd best get on with it, hadn't we? What's the condensed version?"

He grinned. "And that's why you are the love of my life. You understand. Steph didn't."

"So, it's over? That was quick, even for you. I'm sorry." To be honest, Claire didn't know if she was sorry or not. She had never even met the woman.

"I'm not sorry at all. She's back in Ottawa and I'm here. We're still friends, more or less, and we're *both* much happier." Wyatt tossed back most of his drink and then said, "Okay, here's the basic rundown. Kolya's people are going to be working overtime to squash *any* negative publicity. He's dealing with several massive dumpster fires right now. Labor disputes on two planets, plus the ongoing squabble over the constitution for the proposed colonial government on Mars. Three of those colonies want a federal system, which I personally think would be better since they have very different interests. Most of the workers want a direct democracy but I don't think that's likely. Kolya himself is okay with it, but only if it's a unitary system, which would make it much easier for him to call the shots across the planet with a handful of well-placed bribes than when you have a bunch of oligarchs all controlling their own little fiefdoms. Half the companies doing business on Mars are at least partially in Kolya's pocket, and their businesses will all benefit long-term from the terraforming effort as much as his will. So Kolya may well get what he's hoping for, at the expense of meaningful representation for the people who live and work there."

"Doesn't the proposed constitution have to be approved by the UN? I thought they set up a new committee for exactly that purpose."

"They *resurrected* a committee that was primarily focused on colonialism here on Earth and tasked it to work in conjunction with the Ares Consortium. There was a lot of chatter about avoiding the mistakes of the past, but since there are economic incentives for them to make most of those 'mistakes' again, you can bet your ass that they will. The UN is a toothless dinosaur. Half the ambassadors are idealists who are easy to deceive, and the other half are corrupt assholes who are easy to buy. And I'm probably being too generous on the percentage that are idealists because I'm an optimist." He frowned. "You think I'm joking. But if the Ares Consortium was acting with any integrity, they'd have required a complete review of the science when Kolya upgraded the terraforming plan with the new and improved biobots."

"You mean their version of Joe's critters? The ones my mother is convinced Kolya stole?"

"Yeah. What about Joe? Does *he* think Kolya's people stole them?"

Claire shook her head. "Most likely just convergent research, according to him. And even if they did swipe his idea, Jonas Labs certainly isn't planning to go into the terraforming game, so he's not concerned. You know how Joe is about that sort of thing. He'd just be psyched to see his research put to a different use. Kai, on the other hand, lusts after any excuse to sue Kolya. Maybe she'll have cooled her jets by the time the launch is over.

But…I'm not clear why you think switching to more advanced biobots warrants starting the review process all over. It will definitely increase the speed of the project, but they've run detailed computer models. And the models were spot on for Daedalus, which they pitched as their proof of concept."

The waiter arrived with their food, and Wyatt held off on answering until he had finished a bite of his burger.

"First five stages didn't include *recombinant* biobots, though. And neither did their trial run in Daedalus City, as I understand it, although they have been running tests in a couple of smaller domed craters over near Nepenthes. Maybe it's not as big a deal as it sounds to me. You and Joe might have a better idea on that front. The fact that they've switched to the new and improved version means that stage six will take much less time but it's going to require the Martian workforce to spend about six months inside the domes, so that the various life forms are free to multiply on the surface. One prediction says it might be closer to a year, because Kolya is always ridiculously optimistic. The other corporate leaders agreed to this because they know it's going to save them a shit-ton of money in the long run. Some of the smaller contractors that are less fully automated require more laborers to oversee the mining operations than the big outfits do, and they're generally the same companies that don't have the kind of financial padding that will allow them to pay even partial bonuses for six months. They'll be covering base salary only. Which sucks since the bonuses are what lured most of the guest-workers to take the job and six months is a pretty substantial chunk out of a two-year contract. They're not allowed to extend those contracts unless the workers become lifers, and the smaller companies aren't interested in pushing that option."

Claire had heard some of this, mostly through her research on the health effects of working on Mars. The two newest colonies, at Daedalus City and Elysia, had engineered a partial workaround to handle the effects of lower gravity from the beginning of construction, with all sleeping quarters and most workplaces built on what were essentially large centrifuges with the floor tilted at the proper angle to simulate conditions on Earth. This was a lot like the set-up on the ship she would be boarding in a few days. There had been some talk about retro-fitting the quarters for the older colonies with something similar, but it had been abandoned as too expensive. As transportation costs to and from Earth declined due to advances in photonic propulsion, most of the corporations began incentivizing the cheaper alternative of guest laborers instead.

Currently, workers still had both choices, at least on paper. They could take a two-year, non-renewable contract, with several hours of mandatory daily exercise—on their own time, of course—to keep their bodies reasonably Earth-compliant. Alternatively, they could become permanent residents. The latter option was generally viewed as the safest since there were scattered reports of deaths and permanent health problems among those who took the two-year contracts and returned to Earth. Long-term residence wasn't the preferred option for most of the companies running the colonies, however, since they were now dealing with the first batch of colonists reaching mandatory retirement age. Older people were, from a business standpoint, a deadweight. So companies had begun adding bonuses to incentivize two-year contracts. Short-term laborers were also required to avoid pregnancy, so the colonies didn't have to worry about expanding beyond the current low level of childcare and other infrastructure that would be necessary to support families on the planet.

To his credit, Kolya took the opposite track. He claimed his goal was to make Mars an actual alternative to life on Earth, with permanent residents and a planetary government, and he exerted enough pressure that the corporations running the other four colonies were gradually coming around to his way of thinking. But there was still a lot of dissent on the issue among those living and working on Mars.

"There have been protests at several of the mining sites, especially at Lyot, and…" Wyatt stopped and leaned across the table. "If you're getting the feeling that your hair is about to catch fire, there's an exceptionally smug-looking troll at the bar shooting lasers from his eyes."

NINE

CLAIRE GLANCED behind her and saw Bryce Avery sitting with one of his buddies from the sports desk.

"Sick kid, my ass," she said. "I have half a mind to take a picture and send it to Bernard. Avery's got a lot of nerve sticking me with his damn interview and then strolling in here a few hours later."

"What interview was that?"

"Oh, just one of Toby's sheep. The guy got pissed and left when he realized Avery wasn't going to show. Not a big deal, but it made me uneasy after the bomb threats the Flock has been sending out. Wilson, the guard on the upper floor at Jonas Labs, said they'd gotten three in the past month."

"They're not the only ones. Gotta say it seems a bit out of character for the Flock, though. I take it Avery is riled up about your trip?"

"Yeah. In terms of seniority, it *should* have been his. Or Shaundra's, although she told me in no uncertain terms today that she had no plans to leave DC, let alone Earth, so I was welcome to it. And...I can't entirely blame Avery for being annoyed. I'm pretty sure it was one of my mom's groupies who insisted on me getting the assignment."

"Hey. We all get breaks we didn't earn. No reason for him to be a jerk about it." Wyatt pulled out his phone and pointed it toward the bar. Avery looked up just as he snapped the picture.

Claire laughed and grabbed at the phone. "Do *not* send that. Bernard said he was going to talk to him about the whole thing."

"And you believe him?"

"No, but…"

"Okay, okay. But I'll keep the picture in case you need ammo when you get back. Where was I…oh, yeah. There have been protests at Lyot and Ares City over the past few months. A few at Elysia, too. My source at Elysia says there's some chatter about forming a union. They have a better shot now than they've had in the past, given that they have the ability to hold up stage six if they press the matter. But I still don't think it will go anywhere. Most of the mining contracts have a send-your-ass-back-to-Earth clause that discourages any sort of dissent. I can't remember the name, but one of the mining companies even docks your pay for the return passage—at the *tourist* rate, believe it or not—if they have to send you back early. Which could mean workers have zip to show for however long they were there. They could even end up owing *the company* money."

"Well, that sucks," Claire said, realizing that the sentiment applied to her pasta, as well. She doused her plate liberally with red pepper flakes and salt and took a few bites before continuing. "Do you know if the protests have spread to Daedalus? Or Icarus?"

He arched an eyebrow. "Not to Daedalus, or at least, not yet. And maybe they won't. Say what you will about Kolya, but he actually sees to it that the workers inside Daedalus City earn a decent wage, even the lower level service workers. That's easier for him to do, though. Even leaving aside the tourism, there's a lot more money in offshore banking than there is in extractives."

Claire found it ironic that everyone still called it *offshore banking* when more than half of it was now off-planet. Portions of many main banking centers—Seychelles, Mauritius, and Panama, among others—had literally gone underwater in the past twenty years due to rising sea levels. A bit of the damage was being reversed through some of the same techniques Kolya was using to make Mars more habitable, but many of the world's wealthier citizens had been persuaded to put their money somewhere where rising seas weren't going to cause instability for a very, very, very long time.

"But it's funny you should mention Icarus," Wyatt said. "That area supplies raw materials to Daedalus City. It's run by a Korean company...Pada, or something like that. They do some opal mining, too, I think. Kolya was in talks to buy them up, but he backed out. Why? Are you going to Icarus, too?"

Claire toyed with her food to buy some time, wishing that she had kept it vague, and also thinking that there was a damn good reason she didn't write about business or politics. There were too many players, and too many interests that were simultaneously at odds and overlapping, especially when money and politics were both in the mix. Which was pretty much always the case.

"Possibly?" she said. "I'm pretty sure Icarus was on the list of potential locations, along with a few others in the Tharsis region. But that was for the research team I'll be traveling with, and I don't think we'll have the exact same itineraries. I'm guessing I'll mostly be in Daedalus City. There will be plenty to cover there, and...."

And...she was babbling, which Wyatt knew was a tell-tale sign that she was hiding something. So she quickly tossed in a nugget of truth, which had the added attraction of being a diversion. "Icarus just stuck in my mind because I was thinking how many of the names are tied to Ancient Greek mythology when I was showing Jemma the map this morning and reassuring her that there are no giant bugs hiding inside Olympus Mons."

"No giant bugs *yet*," Wyatt said with a chuckle. "Pretty sure Kolya is saving that for stage ten." He finished the last bite of his burger, then said, "Speaking of Jemma, if you're off-planet for nine whole weeks, what excuse am I going to have for visiting my cat?"

Claire smiled. That was the explanation they gave Jemma on the occasions when Wyatt stayed over. Sigrid was *techni-*

cally Wyatt's cat. He'd gotten her a little over a year back when he was in a blue funk after a breakup, named her after some war correspondent from eons ago, and then remembered a few weeks later that someone who traveled as often as he did had absolutely no business owning a cat. Or at least that was what he'd told Claire and Rowan when he pleaded with them to take the creature in. They both suspected he had colluded with Jemma, who'd been begging for a kitty for several months.

"I'm sure Rowan will let you take Siggy back for a while if you ask her nicely."

Wyatt looked as if he were considering it, which made Claire think maybe he wasn't as nonchalant about the recent break-up with this Steph person as he'd suggested.

"Of course," she added, "you'd need to take Jemma, too, because they're inseparable now. And I'm pretty sure that letting a four-year-old wander around your apartment would count as reckless endangerment."

"Fair point. That might even be true for a cat these days. I'll call Ro and schedule a time to come visit. But it won't be nearly as much fun without you, babe. And on that note, I really *do* have to get back to work. I'm pretty sure it's my turn to cover dinner, so…" He paid the tab with his phone, then gave her a grin. "You could always join Bryce and his friend over there if you don't want to finish eating alone."

She flipped him off. He laughed, then leaned across the table and gave her an extra-long kiss that left her wishing they could ignore his *DEADLINE* sign and her commitments for at least a few hours.

Judging from Wyatt's expression when he pulled away, it was clear that he was having similar thoughts. "Nine weeks, huh?"

"Nine weeks, four days."

"I'm trying to remember if I've ever gone that long without seeing you. Pretty sure five or six weeks is the record." He gave her a considering look. "So…what time do you take off tomorrow?"

"We leave Dulles at one. The car is picking me up at ten-thirty."

"Hmm. I'll *probably* be done with this article in a couple of hours. Eleven or eleven-thirty at the latest if you're up for company. I have a meeting at the ungodly hour of eight tomorrow, so I'd have to head out early. You can always message me if you get tired and need to crash."

"I'll be awake." She smiled, thinking this was actually the best of all possible options. They could say a proper goodbye and then sleep, leaving little time for him to ask any inconvenient questions that she couldn't answer. "Just come on over when you're done. And if by some chance I happen to fall asleep early, I'm sure you can come up with some creative ways to wake me up."

Wyatt gave her the lopsided grin that had gotten him out of —and into—more trouble than she cared to recount. "Challenge accepted."

TEN

AFTER A FEW MORE BITES OF her pasta, Claire decided it really wasn't worth the calories and was about to head out when she caught Bryce Avery staring at her again. He then leaned over and said something to the other guy. They both laughed and went back to watching the game on the screen behind the bar.

Wyatt was right. Avery was being a jerk. And if he'd merely been being a jerk to Claire, her inner professional might have won out. But he was also being a jerk to his source, although he clearly only considered Devin to be a source of amusement.

And she *had* promised to deliver Devin's message. The man hadn't bothered to give her anything concrete to pass along, but she had an obligation to let Avery know what little he *had* told her, right?

Avery and his buddy were once again engrossed in the game when Claire approached, so he didn't realize she was even there until she clapped him on the shoulder.

"Feeling better, Bryce?"

The side of his mouth twitched reflexively, although she couldn't tell if it was from amusement or annoyance. "Hey, you know how viruses go. The kids bring 'em in and they zip through the family like a damn tornado."

"Yeah. I'm sure. I'm about to head out...some last minute packing to do. But I thought I'd give you a quick update on that interview I covered for you a couple of hours ago. Bernard said he'd fill you in, but since you're here and obviously feeling just fine, I figured why wait?"

He spread his hands and shrugged. "Fire away."

"Apparently you missed Devin's one opportunity to meet with you for the next month. He came all the way in from Culpeper. And for some reason I can't begin to fathom, you're the only journalist he trusts. Although *trusted* might be more correct. Anyway, he says things are *escalating*. Maybe you know what that means, since Bernard says he's spoken to you before."

"Yeah. It means he's a freaking nut job, Claire. And a colossal time-suck."

"Duly noted." She didn't bother to point out that he'd foisted that colossal time-suck onto *her* schedule for the day. "One thing you might want to consider, however, is that while you might think of the Flock as a bunch of timid souls singing kumbaya around the campfire, they've graduated to bomb threats. And that time-sucking source of yours is now a very angry time-sucking source. Very angry at *you*. See you in a couple of months."

Stepping outside, Claire discovered that the evening had gone from nippy to downright frigid in the space of an hour. So she zipped her coat, pulled her scarf around her face, and decided to cut through Franklin Park to shave a couple of minutes off the walk to Farragut North.

Halfway through the park, she began to get the sense that she was being followed. She glanced over her shoulder, half expecting to see Avery, which was insane. What did she think the guy was going to do, challenge her to a fist fight? He might make jokes and yuk it up with his buddy at the bar, but he wasn't a psycho.

Could she say the same about Devin, though? Or about members of this new, more volatile Flock faction who might be angry if they found out that he was talking with a reporter?

You're being paranoid, Claire.

It wasn't even eight o'clock. The sidewalks up ahead were still busy. But she picked up her pace, anyway. A cluster of young people were moving along the same path through the park, toward the corner of K and 14th, but they were caught up in their own conversation, and clearly weren't following her.

As she turned back, however, she noticed a tiny blip of green light a few yards to her left. It kept pace with her through the park, flashing every four or five seconds. Not a single flash, but three rapid green flashes, the last one a smidge longer than the first two. A drone, but it was much too small and unobtrusive to be one of the standard monitors used by the Metro police. Official monitor drones were closer to the size of a hummingbird, and legally required to display a steady blue light when on patrol. This thing wasn't much larger than a housefly and it didn't look at all legal to Claire.

The nanodrone zoomed upward when Claire reached the sidewalk, and for a couple of blocks, she thought it was gone. Then she spotted it again in the reflection of a storefront—*dot, dot, dash*, long pause, then *dot, dot, dash* again—following along about eighteen inches above her head. She kept walking at the same pace, pretending not to notice, until she reached the coffee shop on the corner. Without breaking stride, Claire stepped sideways, pushing the door open with her shoulder, and slipped inside. The drone stopped, hovered for a moment, and then zipped straight up and out of sight.

Taking the train had now lost all appeal. Claire called for a car and then took a table near the window to watch for it. She also wanted to know if the drone decided to pop back in for an encore.

But there was no sign of the fly-sized drone. The only thing she noticed, aside from the typical K Street foot traffic of commuters heading to the Metro or city-dwellers taking their dogs across the street to Farragut Square for a walk, was a rat sitting near the grate on the sidewalk. That was hardly unusual in the city, but it brought to mind the bomb threats Wilson had mentioned.

They're at it again. Crazy sonsabitches.

When Claire's car arrived outside the coffee shop, she

double-checked the license and then darted out quickly to claim it. There was no sign of the drone, and no reason at all for her to assume that the Flock had her under surveillance. She contacted her security service anyway and upgraded to add twenty-four-hour monitoring of their external cameras for the next few months. If the Flock was keeping tabs on her, they'd soon be disappointed to learn that she was well outside the range of their illegal drones. Rowan and Jemma, however, would still be right there in the city, and the least she could do was give them an extra layer of protection from the crazy sonsabitches.

Water was running upstairs when Claire got home. In the living room, Jemma was kneeling at the coffee table, building some kind of diorama out of pretzel sticks, craisins, and cheese cubes. That meant that she'd shunned dinner and Ro was hoping she'd idly pop some of her building materials into her mouth while she played. It was usually a successful tactic, although they occasionally ended up with more on the floor than in her mouth.

Ro called down that the bath was ready a few minutes later, so Claire offered Jemma a piggyback ride and they headed upstairs. Once the girl was surrounded by bubbles and her flotilla of bath toys, Claire pulled Ro into the hallway so that she could tell her about the meeting with the Flock member, the odd encounter with the drone, and the decision to increase their security.

"Not trying to scare you," Claire said, "but you might want to keep a slightly closer than usual watch when you're out and about. And maybe mention it to the new sitter, too?"

"You really think that's necessary? I mean, I see why you got spooked with the two things happening back to back like that, but it was probably just a coincidence. The drone was most likely just some kid over in Franklin Park with a new toy who thought it would be fun to frighten you."

"If so, someone needs to arrest their ass, because that's an illegal toy. I'm telling you, it wasn't much bigger than a fly."

Rowan thought about it, and then shrugged. "People break that law all the time. I stitched up the palm of a guy just last month who slapped one of the little buggers out of the air. Said his soon-to-be ex was spying on him. And you know I'm no fan of the Flock, especially after they picketed JHH last year."

Johns Hopkins Hospital had run afoul of the Flock the previous year due to a new vaccination program they were piloting. Ro had come home cursing the protestors to high heaven during the two week period before they directed their ire elsewhere, saying they made it impossible for staff to get in and out of the building.

"Yes, the group is annoying," she added. "I'll even go so far as to say they're a major pain in the ass. But they're not violent, Claire."

"I would have said the same thing a few weeks ago, but that seems to be changing. Apparently, there's been a schism. Jonas Labs has had three bomb threats."

Ro paused a moment to take that in, but Claire had the strong sense that she was being humored. "They haven't actually *bombed* anyone, though...right? And I doubt they really would. Toby's sheep are mostly ewes."

The last part was completely accurate. There *were* men in the Flock, but more than two-thirds of their recruits were women, mostly young and idealistic. Some of them grew disillusioned after a few years and rejoined society, with nothing to show for their labors, but many of them stayed. One of the few media pieces that Shepherd allowed had been an article the *Post* had published the previous summer interviewing five people who were celebrating a quarter of a century with the Earth Watch Alliance.

"Women can be violent, too."

"I know, I know," Ro said. "But I still find it hard to take the Flock seriously. Isn't it possible that the new leadership just decided to ramp up the rhetoric?"

Personally, Claire didn't place bomb threats under the category of rhetoric, amped up or not. She was pretty sure that Ro didn't either, but Ro had always believed that she was a little paranoid on the subject of security. As she'd noted when Claire had the sentry system installed, their neighborhood was incredibly safe, especially compared to the apartment building where they'd both lived when they first met.

"Maybe. I'm not telling you to stay indoors or trying to worry you." Claire cast a pointed glance into the bathroom, where Jemma was singing her ABCs while sticking random foam letters on the tub wall. "It's just that I'd much rather have the extra security in place and not need it than the reverse. Better safe than sorry."

Ro followed Claire's gaze and was quiet for a moment as they watched Jemma playing. "You're right. I just hate for you to go to all that expense when you're not even going to be here."

Ah, Claire thought. It was about the money.

"Ro, if this is the Flock, they're doing it because of *my* job, not yours, unless you went on some sort of vigilante spree after the picketing crisis and didn't tell me. It could also be because of my connection to Jonas Labs. Either way, that makes it *my* responsibility. And you're getting off easy. My first impulse was to hire full-time bodyguards for the next nine weeks."

She snorted. "No need, *mi capitana.* I will guard the perimeter."

"Good. Then you're dismissed, soldier. Go have a glass of wine. I'll take over bedtime duty."

Jemma coerced Claire into four bedtime stories, although she didn't quite make it through the last one. Claire sat the book back on the nightstand and pressed a kiss to the girl's forehead, breathing in the soft lavender scent of her shampoo. Jemma wasn't her kid, but she'd been around for more than half of the girl's life and she was about to miss a sizable chunk of it. Yes, she would miss Wyatt and Ro, too, but they'd be pretty much the same when she returned. Once you hit your late twenties, growth spurts and developmental milestones were generally in your past.

A little before midnight, Claire heard a gentle tap on her bedroom door and Wyatt slipped into the room. Sigrid followed, purring softly, and making insistent figure-eights around his legs as he undressed. That was the usual pattern anytime Wyatt came over, and one of several reasons that they usually opted for his place. Siggy would eventually get bored with their antics and skulk out of the room, but she had to be the first one to touch him. If she didn't get dibs, she'd yowl and scratch at the bedroom door.

Wyatt sighed and sat down on the edge of the bed. "Okay, okay. Come here, you needy little bitch."

"I believe the technical term is a *molly*, now that she's been fixed."

He looked over his shoulder and grinned. "Who says I was talking to the cat?"

Claire laughed and swatted him with a pillow. Then, she scooched closer on her knees and began tracing the muscles of his bare back with her fingertips, pressing soft kisses against his neck.

He hitched in a breath. "Careful. Unless you're really sleepy and want the fireworks over quickly, that could be…counter-productive."

"Pfft. I've got several boring weeks in a tin can ahead of me, mister. What makes you think I'm going to let you sleep?"

They did sleep, eventually, and Claire woke up a little after daybreak to find Wyatt already awake, watching her.

"Busted," he said, with an embarrassed laugh. "I was just taking a mental picture—I think I'll call it *Claire in Repose*—and thinking how rarely I get to see you in the morning light. You seem to have caught me in an uncharacteristically sentimental mood."

They made love again, and then he said he needed to get moving if he was going to make it into DC on time. While he showered, Claire crept down to the kitchen and put on some coffee. When it finished brewing, she poured some for herself, and then put the rest into a travel mug that she knew she'd probably never see again unless she dug it out of the rubble of Wyatt's apartment the next time she was there. And after nine weeks, the odds of finding it seemed pretty slim.

Wyatt gave her one last kiss at the door. "Keep me posted once you get there. Daedalus is supposed to be pretty wild. Have fun. Break a few hearts. But…*please be careful*, okay?"

The smile on Claire's face felt a bit stiff now. His uncharacteristically sentimental mood had apparently been fleeting. *Have fun*, sure. But *break a few hearts*? That kind of stung.

So she just focused on the *please be careful* part and kept her tone light. "I'm *always* careful, Wyatt Garcia."

"That's actually kind of true, babe. Which is why I'm only a *little bit* worried."

Claire closed the door behind him and trudged back upstairs with her coffee. Rowan and Jemma would be waking up soon to begin their mad morning rush and she needed to stay out of sight until they were gone so that they could avoid goodbye drama.

Have fun. Break a few hearts.

She sighed and shook her head. Too bad she didn't have a recording of those words for the next time Joe started in on how Wyatt was only waiting for some sort of signal from her to ditch his rambling ways.

ELEVEN

CLAIRE ENTERED her address and held the viewer up to her eyes. For a second, it was still just the distant blue planet where she had spent the entirety of her twenty-seven years. Then the picture shifted and zoomed, triggering a brief wave of queasiness before her house in Elkridge, dimly lit by the early morning sun, came into view. A light was on downstairs, probably in the kitchen. She could almost smell the horrid, burnt-tasting coffee that Rowan made each morning.

"First time?"

"Mm-hmm." Claire continued staring into the viewer, really hoping the guy would go away. The voice seemed vaguely familiar, but it couldn't be a member of Brodnik's team. She had been officially introduced to all of them prior to take off and they *knew* it was her first time. Chelsea Friesen, the only one of the bunch who was still in grad school, and Ben Pelzer, the team's geologist, had in fact seemed rather amused that Claire's brief period of vestibular training had prepared her for the level of spin needed to maintain gravity on Mars, but not for the faster spin of the lunar environment. She had been perfectly fine inside the docking cubicle, but the second she stepped into the main resort it had become clear that she was in for a rough transition.

The front desk gave Claire some anti-nausea pills when they checked in and she popped two of them before stumbling off to the room she was sharing with Chelsea. She'd already been wiped out from not getting enough sleep the night before, due to wondering what she might have forgotten to pack, her lingering unease about the odd encounter with the drone, and the fact that she'd spent several of the hours that she should have been sleeping saying goodbye to Wyatt.

On the plus side, the pills had kept her from barfing. On the minus side, they had knocked her out so completely that she slept through dinner.

Tranquility Base Hotel and Casino, named after the site of the first moon landing over a century ago, was designed as a waystation not just for travel to Mars but also as a convenient shore leave destination for asteroid mining crews, military transports from various countries, and an array of commercial enterprises operating in Earth's orbit. Some of those workers were definitely female, but they were all apparently smart enough not to venture out alone in the wee hours of the morning.

Claire really hadn't had much choice, though. She'd been jolted awake two hours earlier by Friesen's snores, soon followed by growling noises from her own stomach. It was a little before four a.m. according to her tablet, so she had considered waiting it out. But then she remembered the tablet was displaying her default settings for Earth, since she hadn't manually entered the lunar time zone. Tranquility Base was two hours behind DC. Her stomach wasn't going to wait until morning for breakfast, and Chelsea seemed unlikely to stop snoring, so she slipped on her clothes and ventured out in search of food.

Unfortunately, the only place serving breakfast at two a.m. was the casino buffet, and she was asked the *is-this-your-first-time* question twice before she got to the table with her food. Either it was a standard pickup line on Tranquility Base, or she was a painfully obvious noob. It probably didn't help that she was still a bit shaky on her feet, especially if she glanced to the side too quickly. She almost certainly looked drunk. In fact, the only reason she had stopped to pick up the stupid viewer to see if it could find her house was to take a break before staggering the rest of the way to her room.

"Yeah, that's what I thought," the guy next to her said. "The Show-Me-Home viewer is a nearly foolproof virgin detector."

Claire lowered the binoculars slowly, hoping to convey with a withering stare what her lack of conversation clearly had not. As soon as she saw the man's face, however, she realized why his voice—deep, with faint hints of both Oxford and Eastern Europe—had seemed familiar.

Anton Kolya was standing next to her, a cup of over-roasted coffee in hand, wearing a grin that made it obvious that the double entendre had been very much intentional. "I wouldn't have imagined it, to be honest. Your mother visited Tranquility Base several years ago."

She struggled to keep her surprise from showing, since she'd had no clue that Kai ever made a trip to the moon. Not that her mother couldn't afford it, but she'd never shown any interest before. It was, in fact, something that her father had suggested as a holiday excursion about a year before he got sick, although from what Claire had heard the resort was a lot more rustic back then.

"Kai's visit was *before* I purchased the place, of course," Kolya added. "But I did send her an invite to the grand re-opening along with our other previous VIP guests. For some reason, she never responded."

Kolya's voice was a study in innocence, and Claire had to choke back a laugh. Apparently, she wasn't entirely successful because the man's grin grew wider. Oddly, he was better looking in person, without the ubiquitous media filters that disguised even the slightest perceived flaw. He looked younger, too, despite the flecks of gray in his dark hair and closely trimmed beard, and Claire thought that might be due to his boyish grin. She had always assumed the filters were being used to hide wrinkles or a softening of his jaw. Now she was trying to remember how old he actually *was*, wondering whether he'd had work done, and also wondering *why* those thoughts were running through her head. Yes, he was handsome and charismatic, but the man's ego was massive enough that it alone could have provided gravity for Mars if he was willing to stay in one place.

"If I'd known you were interested in space tourism, Ms. Echols, I'd have sent your mother's invitation to you, instead."

The comment was more than a little baffling. Did Kolya actually think she was here as a tourist? Claire had assumed that he'd signed off on the various members of Brodnik's team, and therefore, that he knew she was handling the publicity for the Martian discovery. But maybe he left that sort of detail to his assistants?

That, of course, begged the question of how he'd recognized her, but it wasn't the first time that had happened. Even before the *Simple Science* segments began airing, she had occasionally been stopped on the street by people who recognized her, who wanted an ussie. Quite a few of them thought she was Kai at first, possibly because her mom also had an affinity for the same diffusing filters that Kolya's publicity team used.

"I'm a recent convert to the allure of off-world travel. I suppose I'm the family homebody. My brother took a brief trip on one of the satellite resorts a few years back and invited me to come along, but I declined. Later, I regretted it, but...not enough to book a trip myself, Mr. Kolya."

"Just Kolya, please."

"Ah. Are you working toward achieving mononymity?"

He laughed. "Well, it's better than anonymity, right? You can also call me Anton, if you prefer, but there are maybe five people inside this solar system who use that name. And... please don't tell the tourists, but I don't actually blame you for not going out of your way to visit Tranquility."

That pulled a laugh from Claire. Kolya was quite possibly the world's most outspoken ambassador for off-planet travel. He had shot countless commercials and travelogs touting the wonders of a vacation on the moon, at his various suborbital dens of iniquity, and most recently, on Mars. The vast majority of his fortune was acquired as a result of that pitch, so it was hard to buy his support for someone preferring to stay home with a good book.

"I'm serious," he said, looking a bit offended. "There's nothing on Tranquility Base that you can't get more cheaply at any of my hotels and casinos on Earth, aside from the view. And let's be honest, the novelty only lasts so long."

Claire had to agree on that front. The view of Earth was interesting, but the moon itself was a study in gray and black, alleviated only by the lights of the launch pads off in the distance and what she assumed was a rival resort beyond that.

"Mars, though..." Kolya continued. "That's an entirely different story. Mars is the next human frontier. But the moon? It will never be a place someone could think of as home."

"Is that why you only authorize the two-year guest worker contracts here, unlike on Daedalus?"

He gave her a small nod of approval. "Someone has done her homework. Lunar life takes more of a toll on the body. The gravity here in the resort is roughly seventy-five percent of Earth's. When you reach Daedalus, you'll find the nausea less of a problem because there's some natural gravity and we don't need to tilt and spin quite as aggressively to reach a level that's not harmful to human health. But I think the moon takes an even greater toll on the psyche. It's so very gray. At least on Mars there's some color. That was true, albeit to a lesser extent, even before our terraforming process began. And you have some semblance of normal day and night there. Here, you're bombarded with sunlight for two weeks. Then, back in the dark for two more. It wreaks havoc on the sleep schedule...something that you've apparently noticed."

"Oh, it wasn't the daylight that woke me up," she said. "Which reminds me that I need to check and see if your convenience store has earplugs before I board the ship. I'm unfortunately a very light sleeper and my roommate...well, I think perhaps she's congested from the flight."

"Ah. How was it? The flight, I mean."

"It was…interesting. A bit more intense than your typical air trip, but actually not as uncomfortable or unnerving as I'd thought it might be."

"I think the return launch is more enjoyable, personally."

"You mean the hyperloop stage? I'm looking forward to that, too. Taking the loop up the mountains from Denver to Aspen as a kid was odd enough. Never imagined I'd be using it to leave the surface of Mars."

"So…you like to ski? You'll have to come back and try the Tharsis Range in a few years."

She laughed. "A *few years*? You're kidding, right? From what I've read, even a few decades seems extremely optimistic."

"We had several centimeters of snow on the mid-level slopes of Arsia this past year. It still sublimates higher up, but that's a huge step forward. And I expect to see major changes after stage six. A few years *might* be overstating things somewhat, but definitely within ten. Probably less."

"Since you brought it up," Claire began, wishing she had a recording device running. "What exactly can we expect in stage six? I mean, I know on paper that it's just an expansion on the efforts with bioengineered life from stage three, but…"

"Stage six will be an expansion on the efforts with bioengineered life from stage three." He repeated her words back, completely deadpan. "When I'm ready to say more than that, I'll let you know."

"But … stage six *does* have something to do with the recombinant biobots, correct?"

"Ah. You mean the *critters* your mother has been threatening to sue me over?" he asked with a hint of amusement in his blue eyes.

Claire had been largely agnostic on whether Kolya's company was engaged in corporate espionage before this comment, but Kolya using Joe's pet name for his variant of biobots was suspicious, to say the least. She supposed it was *possible* that Joe or Beck had used the term in one of their extremely rare interviews. Or her mother might even have let the nickname slip to a journalist at some point, although she viewed it as juvenile and unscientific, so that seemed even less likely. Pushing this point with Kolya, however, was probably a bad idea. Getting off on the wrong foot with him could jeopardize her access to information over the coming weeks and therefore, hamper her ability to do her job. And if Joe didn't seem particularly bothered by the theft, why should she be?

So, she gave Kolya a little shrug. "I suspect you know more about my mother's threats of legal action than I do. I learned long ago that the key to a happy life is staying out of Kai's business and making sure that she stays out of mine."

Now it was his turn to look surprised. "That's…odd. Dr. Brodnik seemed to be under the impression that your mother was the only reason you landed this assignment. Something like this would normally go to a more senior reporter, would it not?"

"It would," Claire admitted. "And it's possible that my mother's *name* played a role in the assignment falling to me. But I can assure you that Kai herself had nothing to do with it."

"That must make your position on Brodnik's team…interesting." He flashed her a grin with the final word.

"Indeed. Although, I don't think they'd have been happy with *any* journalist being pulled in. It kind of takes the limelight off the people who made the discovery."

"Well, of course. It should be entirely about the *science*. Can't have your scholarly undertaking tarnished by commerce or by the desire to educate the unwashed masses."

Claire was a bit taken aback, not just at his snide tone, but also at the venom beneath it. "You don't care much for Dr. Brodnik?"

"Brodnik?" He shook his head dismissively. "I barely know her. She seems perfectly nice. It's the general attitude of these research teams that I find distasteful. And the hypocrisy.

Because if you think about it, what did Brodnik's team actually *do*? They drilled a hole and dropped a camera inside. They'll run some tests once the chamber is opened. But they didn't *find* the damn thing. If not for the miners at Icarus Camp, that giant box would still be under several layers of Martian rock. And the miners would never have been there if I didn't need raw materials, both for Daedalus City and for export to fund the terraforming project. But no. They're hungry to take full credit. They're resentful that it's your lovely face that people will remember when they think about the great discovery on Mars and doubly resentful that I'm doing my best to ensure they'll also link the discovery to my work in Daedalus. Even though I'm footing the bill for the trip. My only personal beef with Brodnik is that she insisted on including someone who disparages my efforts at every turn."

Claire frowned, thinking for a moment that he meant her. She had definitely made disparaging remarks about the man, but she didn't think any of them had been in print. And then it clicked. "Oh…you mean Kimura?"

"Yes. It was one thing when he was just one researcher among the hundreds we have pouring through each year, but now he's going to be front and center and who knows what lies he may start spouting in interviews? I may not have his level of expertise, but I hire the best. And besides, the man is a pompous ass."

Claire wasn't inclined to argue with the part about the guy being an ass. Kimura had dismissed her with a single glance as they boarded the shuttle. That was unfortunate, and something she would need to work on. She was curious about his charges that some of the Martian samples showed signs of tampering, especially since those claims seemed to have gotten under Kolya's skin. But given how quickly Kimura's accusations had been slapped down and the professional price he'd paid for it, the guy probably wouldn't be inclined to chat with her about his theories under the best of circumstances…and that went double now that his research team was being hosted by the very person he'd implicated as responsible for the tampering.

"I didn't veto Kimura's participation—or yours, for that matter—because I'd made a promise that Brodnik would be allowed to select her own team for the mission. But in light of your mother's incessant legal saber rattling, would it be unreasonable for me to wonder whether she might attempt to install a spy in my ranks? You will find, however, that I have absolutely nothing to hide. And, on a very different note, my reputation would certainly suffer if it ever leaked that I objected to the company of such an attractive and intelligent young woman as yourself at Daedalus City. After all, my goal is not merely to colonize Mars, but also to beautify it."

With that, he placed a proprietary hand on Claire's shoulder and gave her a broad smile. "I'm afraid that I need to turn in now. It's been a long day. I'll have Stasia contact you mid-morning to begin the full tour. And I'll ensure that she places you at my table for dinner at Della Luna. Until this evening, Ms. Echols."

And then he was gone, without waiting for her response. She managed to hold back her laugh until he was out of earshot, but it was a close call. Did he practice that smile in front of the mirror? And did those cheesy lines actually *work* on women who had no interest in his money? Although, given how much money the man had, that was probably a rather small group.

Unfortunately, Claire thought, money wasn't the only thing he had to use as leverage. She needed information and access for her story, which meant she would have to deal with his crap...at least up to a point.

TWELVE

SLEEP WAS CLEARLY out of the question when Claire returned to the cabin, in part because Chelsea was still snoring away. She tried playing for a while on the piano app she had loaded onto her tablet, but it wasn't nearly as relaxing with only a partial keyboard, so she cranked up some music on her earphones and spent the next few hours reading. Then, she tried out the hydrosonic shower, which she quickly realized was going to take some getting used to. It seemed to get her clean enough, but it took forever to rinse the shampoo out of her hair, and she could already tell that she was going to miss the feeling of hot water pounding against her skin. This was more of a warm mist, and it seemed far more likely to lull her back to sleep than to wake her up in the mornings.

By the time she was dressed, Claire felt her queasiness beginning to creep back, so she decided to take another of the little pills. She only took one this time. Otherwise, she risked spending the entire day conked out in the bed again.

Around eight a.m. lunar time, a message arrived from Stasia Ljubic, who introduced herself as Kolya's CCO—which Claire supposed was short for chief communications officer—and provided her with the day's itinerary. Apparently, the tour Kolya had mentioned was going to be recorded, because she had Claire down for makeup at ten, with activities mapped out for the five hours after that. Claire had planned to simply venture outside and record a few minutes on the surface later in the day so that she would have some footage for work. Kolya, however, seemed to be under the impression that she was here to plug his damn resort.

"Well, at least we now know why we got stuck with a thirty-four-hour layover," Chelsea said when Claire told her where she was heading. "We were wondering about that. Normally, we're out of here in a matter of hours. Your little PR junket is going to cost us a research day on Mars."

"You'll have to take it up with Kolya's people," Claire said, forcing her expression to remain friendly. "This really wasn't my idea. I was hoping to get a few days to acclimate. I'll be lucky if the antinausea pill doesn't knock me out again. Although I guess that's still better than barfing with the cameras rolling."

Claire was sorely tempted to add that she would probably be in better shape if her sleep hadn't been interrupted by what had sounded like a passel of congested pigs holed up on Chelsea's side of their shared room. But she would be stuck bunking with her at least until they reached Mars. And while she seriously doubted that they were ever going to be friends, Claire had no interest in making an enemy of the woman. So, she held her tongue and simply left, wishing the room had a regular door instead of the pneumatic kind so that she could at least have had the pleasure of slamming it behind her. The pathetic little whoosh that followed pushing the button wasn't nearly as satisfying. And she couldn't even stomp off because she still felt a wave of dizziness each time she moved too quickly.

The team's attitude annoyed her, even though she understood it. Brodnik seemed inclined to keep to herself for the most part. She'd been nice enough, but it felt forced and a bit calculated, like she didn't want to risk pissing off the daughter of the great Kai Jonas. The others had been borderline rude. It was shaping up to be a very long, solitary trip, because Claire wasn't part of the team, hadn't been there when they made the big discovery, and they probably thought her mommy bought her this plum assignment. They considered the Icarus chamber *their* find, and they didn't want to share the glory with an outsider.

And no matter how much she tried to make nice, it wouldn't matter in the end because they'd resent the fact that her face was the one out front for the publicity. Kolya's people would make sure he was front and center, as well, as they had a vested interest in keeping as much of the focus as possible on Daedalus City and their terraforming efforts.

To Claire's surprise, she found herself agreeing with Kolya. It wasn't as if Brodnik's team had made this discovery on their own. At this point, their contribution to the project had been miniscule. All they'd done was confirm that the chamber was of huge scientific importance. They would never even have known that the thing was out there beneath the Martian regolith if not for the team of miners who had reported they'd hit a giant metal box.

The miners were the ones who had put in the real sweat equity here, yet no one seemed to be rushing to give them any credit at all. You could even argue that the chamber was *their* find, and it was Brodnik and her team who were pushing their way into the spotlight.

That didn't seem fair, and Claire decided that she would have to find a way to rectify the situation once they got to Mars. Maybe she could ask Kolya's team if they would set up an interview with a few of the Icarus Camp miners who were on the site that day. It would be a good public interest story to get them on camera describing how it felt when they realized they'd hit something that couldn't possibly be a natural formation.

After all, she thought with a grin, it seemed only fair to shine a light on the people who had *actually* made the discovery.

Claire arrived at the resort's public relations office a full ten minutes after her scheduled appointment because she had to stop twice in the hallway due to dizziness. Both times, she found herself thinking longingly of the little bottle of anti-nausea pills next to her bunk and wishing she had canceled and stayed in her room, even if it meant putting up with Chelsea's sulking. But Claire wouldn't put it past Kolya to delay their departure another day if she called in sick, and Chelsea and the rest of Brodnik's team would probably toss her out the nearest airlock.

A tall, impeccably dressed blonde who looked to be in her late thirties stood up to greet her when she opened the door.

"Claire! I'm Stasia—" The woman was smiling at first, but her expression shifted to concern as Claire drew closer to her desk. "Oh, dear Anton said you were having some trouble adjusting, but you look even shakier than he suggested. Maybe we should get them to delay departure until tomorrow evening so we can give you another day to acclimate?"

"No, no, no," Claire said quickly. "I don't think Brodnik's team would appreciate that at all. I'll be fine. To be honest, I had no idea that we were going to be recording anything here at the resort. My segments are science-based, and they only run ten to fifteen minutes, so…"

Stasia's smile widened. "Which is why I have you scheduled to tour the MIT Lunar Lab at eleven. After lunch, we'll come back to take a closer look at Tranquility Base's greenhouse and our artificial gravity system. Although I'm guessing you're not a particular fan of that technology at the moment." There was a teasing tone to her voice, but her eyes were kind. "And after that, since I know some of your segments are used in schools, we thought you might want to record for a while in the zero-G playground at the center of the resort—which is something the youngest members of your audience might find especially interesting. Plus, it will give you a short break from the spin. Anything we record that you can't use now, you can always save for later segments."

"That sounds good. And…maybe we could keep the cameras mostly on the sights and I'll just narrate?"

Stasia laughed. "I think that can be arranged. I'll also get you one of the ear clips. Those helped me far more than the pills when I first began making these trips. The pills just knock you out."

They do, indeed, Claire thought.

The tour ended up being much more enjoyable and informative than Claire had expected. While she doubted that she'd be able to use the vast majority of it in the next few segments, the footage would keep, as Stasia had pointed out.

Joe would have gotten more out of the MIT lab tour than she did, however, and it was hard not to laugh out loud when the scientist leading the tour made a special point of emphasizing their own recombinant biobot research. Claire was almost certain that bit was included at Kolya's urging — *see, everyone's doing it these days. Now tell your mother's lawyers to back the hell off.* It was a little heavy handed even for Kolya, especially when that information could just as easily be presented as evidence for the prosecution as for his defense. The MIT lab was less than a five-minute buggy ride from the resort and Kolya probably had half a dozen contracts with these guys. Who was to say Kolya hadn't given *them* the critters instead of the other way around, as they claimed?

The strangest thing about the morning, however, was an encounter with another group of Kolya's contractors just outside the lab. As Claire and the others were boarding their buggy, which was parked in the airlock tunnel, she noticed something moving outside the small window. Once the door was open, she realized it was a sign being held up by one of about a dozen picketers. Most of the signs called Kolya out for unfair contracts with the mining companies, although one appeared to be stating the same thing about workers in an energy plant.

The signs weren't odd in and of themselves. Claire had certainly seen plenty like them on Earth, often in pictures that ran with the stories under Wyatt's byline. What made the sight surreal was the fact that the people holding the signs were all wearing spacesuits. Some were the sleek biosuit versions like the one Claire was wearing, with mechanical compression provided by a carbon nanofiber and nitinol shell, while others were the older gas-filled models Stasia and Paul had referred to as Stay-Pufts or puffsuits.

Stranger yet, one of the protest signs bore an unmistakable logo. Claire had seen it outside Jonas Labs on more than one occasion and also on the jacket Devin Shepherd was wearing when she interviewed him.

Why was the Flock protesting on a lunar base?

Claire wanted a photo, if only to send to Wyatt, but by the time she dug her tablet out, the buggy had zipped past, and the protestors were only a faint white blur in the distance against the dark gray rocks. Paul Caruso, the guy handling the recording, kept his camera pointed down as they passed the protest, then leaned toward her and stage whispered, "That was what we call a moon mirage. What did you think you saw?"

"Paul…" Stasia said with a hint of warning.

Claire frowned. "I… I saw protestors. In pressure suits. Carrying signs. One of them was with the Earth Watch Alliance."

"Wow." Paul widened his dark eyes in childlike amazement. "I thought I saw an ice cream truck. Which is much better than last time, when I thought I saw this Klingon demon called Fek'lhr. Macek must see *something*, because he snarls in that direction, but Kolya and Stasia don't seem to see anything at all. It apparently has something to do with the way the brain interprets light reflecting off the lunar soil. Isn't the human mind amazing?"

Stasia sighed. "Ignore this man. I keep telling him that if he wants to be a comedian, I'll book him for a comedy tour on some of the cut-rate satellite resorts so he can share his gift"— she made finger-quotes here—"with the world."

"And leave you to a joyless existence with only Macek and Kolya to boss around? I would never be so cruel."

All in all, it was an enjoyable day, in part because Stasia and Paul both seemed genuinely nice. Claire was pleased to learn that they would be making the trip to Mars as well. It was a relief to know that there would be at least a few friendly faces around. Kolya would be on board, as well, but she was much more ambiguous about that prospect, especially since Stasia mentioned that he had a business proposition he wanted to discuss. Given his legendary status as a womanizer and his smarmy comments the night before, she thought it entirely possible that any proposition Kolya had would be personal rather than professional.

Claire was relieved to find her shared room empty when the tour wrapped up. Chelsea had apparently decided to hit the casinos or the spa. She took advantage of the privacy to make some calls, knowing it was probably the last chance she would get for an actual conversation. The lag was manageable for Earth-to-Moon communication, but once they reached Mars, the delay would be several minutes each way, even on the laser-comm system.

No one was home, though, so she had to leave a message. Claire felt a tiny twinge of worry, even though Rowan had pretty much managed to convince her that she was overreacting on the drone issue. Still, she wasn't convinced enough to cancel the extra security. She debated adding the video clip taken at the playground to her message and decided against it. It was all too easy to imagine Jemma deciding to try out a few of the tricks the next time she was at their neighborhood playground, with very different results on a planet where gravity was fully operational.

She messaged Wyatt, letting him know that she had arrived safely and then asked if he'd heard anything about the Flock conducting illegal drone surveillance or taking their protests off-planet. At the last second, though, she erased the final questions, filing them away to ask once she was back on Earth. Who knew how private outgoing messages were? Plus, Wyatt would be curious to know why she hadn't told him about the drone when he was at her place. She had actually considered it, but by the time he arrived, she'd been half convinced Ro was right about her being paranoid.

A few minutes before six, Claire pulled on her versatile little black dress and added the one necklace she had managed to wedge into her luggage. Either she was finally getting her space legs, or the ear clip Stasia had given her before they began the tour was magic, because she was able to skip the anti-nausea pill and was pleased to find that she no longer stumbled around like a drunken sailor.

Della Luna, as she had learned on the tour earlier in the day, was Italian for *of the moon.* It was the premiere restaurant on Tranquility Base, and like its sister location, Della Marte, at Daedalus City, the cuisine was true to its name. Both restaurants used only locally sourced ingredients, with fruits and vegetables cultivated in the greenhouse, as well as lab-grown meats and seafood.

The waiter took Claire's name when she arrived, then escorted her to what must have been the restaurant's version of the captain's table. It wasn't large–just a four-top–but it was positioned in front of a porthole that offered, at least for the moment, a view of the stark lunar landscape with Earth perched on the horizon.

Kolya hadn't yet arrived, but Dr. Brodnik and Kimura were already seated. They were dressed far less formally than anyone else in the restaurant, but Claire doubted that they'd packed with an occasion like this in mind. Brodnik had made an effort to dress up her jeans, pulling her light brown hair back into a neat chignon and applying a touch of makeup. Kim was in the same thing he'd worn every time she'd seen him—khaki pants and a rumpled short-sleeved blue shirt. Chelsea and Ben weren't there, so apparently, they weren't getting VIP treatment.

Claire thought that was yet another thing she'd probably catch hell about when she got back to the room.

"Claire!" Brodnik said. "I hope the tour and filming went well."

"It went very well. I had no idea they were making such a big deal out of it. I'd planned to just get some ad hoc footage outside the resort, but this will be higher quality. And more interesting for my subscribers."

"Well, of course they made it into a big production," Kimura said. "You work for the second largest media consortium in the country. Kolya didn't get where he is today by passing up opportunities. Since you waved free publicity in his face, he's going to make the most of it."

"Dammit, Kim," Brodnik hissed. "You *said* you'd behave."

"What?" Kimura spread his hands out in a give-me-a-break gesture. "How am I not behaving? King Kolya isn't even here yet. Unless you're worried that Claire is going to snitch that I refuse to worship at his altar."

Brodnik gave him an annoyed look, and then said, "You should look on the bright side. The fact that Kolya wants publicity means we're traveling on the *Ares Prime* instead of the standard transport they usually give us."

"Is it a significant upgrade?" Claire asked.

That earned her another derisive sniff from Kim. "Basically the difference between first class and the cargo hold. But it adds four days to our travel time."

"We still have the same number of days on the ground," Brodnik said. "Personally, I'm going to relax and consider the next few weeks a well-earned vacation. One I could never afford on an academic salary, that's for certain."

"I'm pretty sure that I signed up for a research trip, not a pleasure cruise," Kim said. "But I suppose KTI didn't want to inconvenience the celebrity member of our team."

Claire laughed out loud at that, although it was less at Kim's words than at her memory of what her brother had said back at the lab.

Better pray they're not a bunch of assholes, because you're going to be miserable otherwise.

As usual, Joe had nailed it.

THIRTEEN

MERCIFULLY, the waiter arrived to ask for her drink order, and Claire was spared further commentary from Kimura. By the time the waiter left, Kolya was approaching the table. She was actually happy to see the man, since his presence apparently triggered a good-behavior clause in Kim's agreement with Brodnik.

Kolya greeted Brodnik, introduced himself to Kim, and then turned to Claire. "Did Stasia take good care of you today?"

"Oh, yes. She's incredible."

"Indeed she is. Stasia is my trusted right hand. I'd hoped to join you for the greenhouse tour, but I'm afraid something came up."

Claire couldn't help but wonder if the *something* that had come up was connected to the picketing workers she'd seen outside the lab, but it wouldn't have made for polite dinner conversation, so she didn't ask. She would probably get a more honest answer to questions of that nature one on one, anyway, and there would be plenty of opportunities for that given that he was traveling with them aboard the Ares.

Kolya and Brodnik engaged in small talk for a few minutes after that. Kimura sulked, looking miserable, which suited Claire just fine.

She looked over when the drinks arrived and realized that what was showing through the porthole seemed to be the exact same view of the lunar terrain, with the Earth hanging picturesquely beyond the horizon. It should have moved by now given that the resort was perpetually spinning. She kept an eye on it for a few seconds and saw a buggy drive past, but the resort itself didn't appear to be moving.

Kolya was watching her, a faint smile playing at his lips. "You seem puzzled, Claire."

"I am. The view is wrong. It's static, aside from a tiny flicker, and it shouldn't be. Come to think of it, that's been true for all the windows on the station. Given what I learned about the artificial gravity system on the tour this afternoon, we're spinning at several revolutions per minute. So...these must be viewscreens?"

"Exactly." He nodded toward the porthole. "That is a current video from a camera just outside Tranquility Base. It's the one with the best view for this evening, I might add. Owning the place comes with a few privileges."

Kim muttered something under his breath. Then he jumped slightly, leading Claire to suspect that Brodnik had kicked him under the table.

If Kolya noticed, he didn't give any indication. "A stationary recording is used for all the windows throughout the resort. It's the same at Daedalus because we have to maintain the point-seven G mandated by the Ares Consortium. If we were to show you the actual view in real time here at Tranquility, I'm afraid that the little cuff you're wearing on your ear wouldn't work nearly as well and you might lose your appetite. Which would be a shame because the new chef here at Della Luna is a true artist. Tonight's special is the lobster risotto and it's absolutely delicious. You should definitely try it."

When the waiter returned, Kolya ordered wine for the table and a selection of appetizers. Everything was incredible. When it was time to order entrees, Claire was torn. On the one hand, the man was still annoying, and she really didn't want to take his suggestion.

On the other hand, it was *lobster risotto*...

"What do you think?" Kolya asked after she took the first bite.

The question was totally unnecessary. He could clearly tell what she thought from her expression alone. And despite his smug smile, Claire didn't regret ordering it one bit.

They focused on their food for the next ten minutes or so. Kimura even seemed less sullen now, so the steak must have met with his approval.

When everyone finished, Kolya called for the dessert cart. It was easy to see why they rolled them out for inspection rather than giving the patrons dessert menus. Someone on Della Luna's staff had considerable artistic talent.

Dr. Brodnik—they had been instructed to call her Laura after her second glass of wine— widened her eyes in amazement. "I've seen elaborate desserts before, but these take the cake."

It was a truly awful pun, but she was right. The confection closest to Claire was nearly a foot tall. The waitress explained that the multicolored base, which was shaped like a delicate circular staircase, was edible. It had been constructed in a special low-gravity kitchen, which allowed them a lot more flexibility in the design. Each step on the little stairway to heaven held a bite-sized morsel of various shades of chocolate. Claire quickly called dibs on that one, although she was slightly tempted by Laura's choice—a poached pear inside a pear made of woven strands of chocolate inside a pear made of the same multicolored candy fibers as the staircase of chocolates.

Kolya picked a rather plain-looking slice of pie that he swore was the best thing on the cart. Kimura said that he never ate sweets. Claire had no issue with that, but the fact that he added a little sniff of judgment at the end kind of made her want to smack him.

Claire had just popped the second stair—dark chocolate infused with raspberry—into her mouth when Kolya turned to Brodnik. "You'll be happy to know that I spoke with the head of the excavation crew this morning, Laura. The chamber arrived at Daedalus a few hours ago. My construction team is enclosing one of the smaller craters just outside the city for you to use as a lab. It will be ready by the time we arrive, so you won't have to worry about pressure suits while you work."

Brodnik seemed to have suddenly lost her appetite for dessert. Kimura leaned back in his chair, arms crossed in front of him. His expression simply oozed *I-told-you-so*.

"And, on a related note," Kolya continued, "the excavation team—"

"Excuse me?" Brodnik said. "Could we back up a bit? Our agreement was that *I* would be there to oversee the last stages of the excavation. That's the only way that we can be certain there's been no..." She trailed off, apparently deciding it might not be wise to accuse him of outright tampering. "That there has been no inadvertent contamination of the samples."

Kolya glanced over at Kim and chuckled, leaving absolutely no doubt that he was fully aware of the man's claims about someone tampering with the DNA of previous samples collected from the Martian surface. Despite the laugh, his voice was somewhat clipped when he continued. "The chamber is in the condition that you left it, Dr. Brodnik. And I have no reason to *contaminate* anything if that's what you're implying. The Ares Consortium has greenlit stage six based on an analysis of your video and the sensor we lowered into the chamber using the hole that you drilled. It detected no evidence of currently existing lifeforms aside from those previously found on the surface, so we *will* be moving ahead on schedule. That's another reason that I wanted them to get the chamber under a dome, so that it will be protected from any sort of contamination during the terraforming process."

Brodnik shook her head. "I...can't believe you actually reopened the chamber. We were told that the excavation would be done under *my* supervision so that we could guarantee the chain of custody for any samples."

"Yeah," Kimura said. "This is bullshit. My contacts at the UN assured me that the Ares Consortium would be withholding approval of stage six pending a full scientific analysis of the find."

"We inserted a *sensor* through the same hole you used for the camera that photographed the interior," Kolya told them. "And do you really think your team is the only one capable of conducting a full scientific analysis? The entire procedure was handled by scientists on Mars who are working under the imprimatur of the Ares Consortium. I'll have Macek forward you their report later this evening so you can be satisfied that we operated entirely within their guidelines."

Claire could tell from both Brodnik and Kimura's expressions that it was highly unlikely that they'd find the report satisfying in the least. And given the trillions of dollars that had been invested in this project by businesses and governments around the world, not to mention the billions that could be lost if there was a significant delay, she thought maybe they had cause to be suspicious.

Kolya sighed. "I truly thought I was doing you and your team a favor. You'll have two weeks on Mars. Transporting the chamber from Icaria to Daedalus was to ensure that you would have time to fully inspect it and that you'd have decent accommodations while doing so. It also makes it far easier to ensure your security. I'm not sure if you're aware, but there have been a few...incidents at some of the mining camps. Daedalus City is exceptionally safe, but it's harder to maintain control elsewhere." He took another bite of his pie and then pushed the plate away. "But, as I was about to say before you interrupted me, the head of the excavation team informed me this morning that they've unearthed a second, smaller chamber beneath the one you investigated. It's sealed, so you can take any samples you like without concern that they've been *contaminated*. I was going to have them dig that up as well, but if you really want to venture back down to Icarus Camp, I'll simply tell them to hold off until you arrive."

"Yes," Brodnik said before he even got the last words out.

"Please tell them to leave the chamber in place. *Sealed*. We're not afraid of roughing it for a few days. It's what we're used to."

"Absolutely," Kimura said. "Of course, if Claire would prefer to remain at Daedalus we'd certainly understand."

Claire sighed. Part of her *would* have preferred to remain at Daedalus. She was not a huge fan of camping even in places where there was plenty of oxygen, and she was admittedly a little worried about what counted as *roughing it* on Mars. But she sure as hell wasn't going to give anyone at the table the satisfaction of admitting that. Especially Kimura, with his insufferable smirk.

It might also give her a chance to talk to the miners who'd made the actual discovery. And was she really willing to give up the thrill of being on site when they excavated this second chamber just for the sake of a few creature comforts?

No. She was not.

She gave Kimura a chilly smile. "Why should I let you guys have all the fun? By all means, count me in."

FOURTEEN

BRODNIK THANKED KOLYA FOR DINNER, but her voice was far less cordial than it had been a few minutes earlier. Then, she and Kimura excused themselves. Claire pushed back her chair to leave with them, even though she was nowhere near finished with dessert, but Kolya placed his hand on her arm.

"Could you stay for a moment, Claire? As I believe Stasia may have told you, I have a business matter I'd like to discuss with you."

Kimura didn't even try to disguise his eye roll.

Kolya gave her an apologetic smile once they were gone. "Staying behind to chat with the enemy isn't going to help build personal rapport with your team, I'm afraid."

"And yet you insisted."

He chuckled at that. "I really do have a business proposition to discuss with you. One that I very much hope you'll accept."

She plucked another of the chocolates from her dessert staircase. "I'm willing to listen, of course, but as I told Stasia, I'm afraid my work at the *Post* doesn't leave much time for side projects."

"I'm sure that they keep you busy," Kolya said, although Claire didn't think he sounded sure at all. "But this project would take place during your time on board. Probably only on the trip *to* Daedalus as I will be remaining behind for a few weeks after your team departs for Earth. Are you familiar with the *Ares Prime*?"

She shook her head. "I thought we'd been assigned to a worker transport until I arrived at dinner. But from what Dr.

Brodnik said, I gather that we're traveling on one of your tourist ships."

"Correct, although the *Ares Prime* is a considerable step up from our previous forays in space tourism. We launched her a mere eight months ago. This is... the sixth voyage? Or maybe the seventh. Every flight has been fully booked, which is why we're set to launch a second ship next month. Tomorrow's flight was booked, too, but Stasia was able to persuade a few passengers with flexible schedules to adjust their travel plans. We'll have seventy-two passengers on board, most of them paying very handsomely, and we like to keep them entertained. For the majority of them, that simply means a casino that isn't greedy, free drinks, and a talented masseuse. We also try to include a couple of celebrities, for those who like to gawk and brag about their traveling companions. I arrange for an advance showing of a highly anticipated movie on each voyage, as well...with the provision that it won't be released on Earth until several weeks after their return. I'm afraid the vast majority of our passengers are here simply as a way of..." He shrugged.

"Flouting their wealth?"

"Exactly. The trip is a status symbol. And since it is largely their money that finances my goals, I do my best to ensure that they are satisfied. That they return home and tell everyone that a trip on the KTI *Ares Prime* is actually worth the—if you will pardon the pun—astronomical price tag. But we *do* have some passengers who are properly in awe of what we are planning at KTI—and I can assure you, Mars is just the beginning. Those people are here for the real experience, to be part of this next step into the future. Some of them are also potential investors. Either way, they want to learn more, so we try to have a few educational opportunities in the mix, as well. All of that is handled by Stasia's crew, but if I'm on board I make an appearance toward the end of the trip. We have presentations with question and answer sessions on the terraforming process, investment opportunities on Mars, the future of space exploration, and so forth."

"It sounds interesting," Claire said.

He waved a hand. "Most of it is stuff you already know, of course. We try to keep them accessible, much like your *Simple Science* segments at the *Post*. In fact, it was your episode on the Fermi Paradox that gave me the idea for doing something slightly different this time. I'm going to go out on a limb and assume that you're familiar with a group called the Earth Watch Alliance?"

"Of course. The Flock. Or Toby's Sheep, as my brother calls them. I was surprised to see one of them with the protestors outside the MIT lab this morning."

"Oh, that wasn't one of the Flock. That was the Shepherd himself."

"You're kidding? What could possibly have convinced a technophobe like Shepherd to go to the moon?"

"Not just the moon. He'll be traveling with us on the *Ares Prime*."

She gaped at him, stunned into silence for a moment. "I'm not sure if you're aware, but Jonas Labs has gotten three—"

"Bomb threats, yes. KTI, as well. They're not coming from Dr. Shepherd. There was a schism in the Flock. Apparently, a few wolves were hiding among Toby's sheep. He is as resolutely nonviolent as ever, but my team *will* be running his luggage through the same thorough scan as we do all our passengers, so you needn't worry about security. To get back to your question as to what convinced him to take the trip, though, he took me up on my standing offer to give him a first-hand look at the terraforming project. Because at their core, Shepherd's goals and mine are the same."

"Really? You've suddenly decided that you want to stop all human progress?"

"Obviously not," he said. "But that's not Shepherd's *core* goal either. His core goal is to ensure the survival of humanity.

As is mine. We just have differing views on the best way to achieve it. He would have us abandon science and progress, and focus only on what the Earth can sustain. I say that's not good enough. At best, it's a stopgap measure. In the long run, humanity's only hope for survival is to spread our seed far and wide."

Given that Kolya was well known for spreading his own seed far and wide, this could easily have been another of his *double entendres*. But Claire decided it was best to simply take his words at face value. "So, you're trying to convert a cult leader. That seems rather…ambitious."

"Compared to terraforming Mars? I've never been one to shy away from a challenge, Claire."

The comment was typical Anton Kolya, virtually dripping with ego, and yet it was hard to argue the key point. Kolya had taken over KTI in 2078, actually leading the charge that forced his uncle to step down as CEO and convinced the board to put Anton, instead of his father, in charge of the company. Claire wasn't sure how old he'd been at the time, but she knew he'd been under thirty, because her father had commented on the takeover, telling Joe not to get any bright ideas about assuming the helm of Jonas Labs. A joke, of course, given Joe's utter lack of diplomatic finesse and his allergy to all forms of bureaucracy.

Prior to Kolya's takeover, KTI had been floundering, and more than a year behind schedule on their contract with the Ares Consortium to build Daedalus City and the spaceport a few kilometers outside the dome. That would have been bad enough, but Daedalus was the company's proof of concept for the far larger project of terraforming the planet as a whole. If they didn't meet the deadline for the Daedalus project, the other contract would be reopened for bids, and the company was already bleeding cash.

As soon as he took the reins at KTI, Kolya pulled in new investment by expanding beyond companies that were interested in the extractives market, pitching the proposed colony both as an elite tourist destination and, according to rumor, tax haven. He already had experience in the tourism arena, as head of KTI's two successful suborbital resorts, the only branch of the company that was showing steady profits.

With the new influx of cash, he had doubled the size of the construction team, offering lower salaries to workers in exchange for a small stake in the new colony. He convinced the first wave of tourists to purchase their tickets long before the resort was finished. It was a gamble that would have likely failed in less charismatic hands, but Kolya managed to sell it, at the same time adding two additional suborbital resorts and overhauling Tranquility Base. In the end, Daedalus City opened two months ahead of schedule and the terraforming contract remained with KTI.

"Okay," Claire said. "I'll grant that you're willing to take on an uphill climb. But you're also a businessman. Where's the profit in convincing Tobias Shepherd of anything, aside from no longer having the Flock screaming that you're helping to destroy one perfectly habitable planet in your efforts to tame one that's far less hospitable? Not that the scientific community wouldn't be grateful for your service in quieting the Flock, but these are people who gave up everything they owned to split their time between proselytizing and doing manual labor on his farms. Even if they were to disband and Tobias returned their worldly possessions, I don't think any of them will be in the market for space tourism."

"I'm convinced that Shepherd is sincere in his beliefs. And while I'll deny this with my dying breath if you say a word to my shareholders, not everything is about money. At any rate, he's agreed to a public debate. Stasia says we need a moderator, someone to introduce the topic briefly and keep us more or less on track. I thought it would be nice to pull in someone like yourself, with journalistic credentials, rather than a member of my own team. Less perception of bias and, if you'll permit me one completely sexist comment, a welcome respite for the eyes once the audience inevitably tires of watching two middle-aged men argue."

Claire pointedly ignored the flattery, in part because she didn't believe him. He was almost certainly correct that the audience wouldn't be a fan of his debate opponent, but most of the passengers willing to cough up millions of dollars for this voyage placed Kolya on a pedestal every bit as high as the one on which the Flock placed Shepherd.

"What would the topic be? And are we talking formal debate rules? I was never on a debate team, so..."

He waved a hand. "Informal rules are fine. Also, we'll keep it relatively brief. I'm under no illusions about the attention span of our average passenger. I'll leave it up to Stasia to devise the rest. My goal is to make it as fair to Shepherd as possible. Stasia wasn't fully on board with him joining us, either, by the way. For someone who has far more female followers than male, the man seems to have set the teeth of every woman in my orbit on edge. But she seems excited about the prospect of the debate." He stopped. "I'm sorry. You had another question, didn't you?"

"Yes. I asked about the topic."

"Right, right. Again, it was your segment on the Fermi Paradox that gave me this idea. We'll be debating whether humans are alone in the universe."

"Which side will you be arguing?"

"We are alone." He said this as if it were perfectly obvious. "Why? Which side would *you* take?"

Claire had to think about that for a moment. "A few weeks ago, I would have said I was agnostic on the subject. But that was before learning about the chamber at Icarus Camp. I'm leaning a bit toward the other side now, given that we know there's evidence of extraterrestrial life. *Intelligent* extraterrestrial life."

"We know no such thing. The existence of those symbols is fascinating, of course, but they don't change my view at all.

Based on everything we know at this point, those symbols are millions of years old. And my position doesn't discount the possibility that human life began on Mars and migrated. In fact, I consider that to be incredibly likely in light of this new discovery."

"Maybe," she said. "But the discovery also reinforces how very little we know. Which, in turn, reinforces my agnosticism. I don't know if we're alone in the universe. I'm not even sure that it's possible to know at this point."

Kolya grinned. "Which, I believe, makes you the perfect moderator. Will you do it?"

"Can I give you a tentative yes? If you're planning to record the debate, I'll need to clear it with my editor before making a firm commitment. Contract issues."

"We will most definitely be recording but wouldn't want it to conflict with the main story about the chamber. So...you could schedule for a few weeks later, maybe once you're back on Earth. And tell your editor that I'm fine with making it a *Post* exclusive. I'm sure Dr. Shepherd won't have any objections."

Claire was less certain on that front. The *Post* had been one of the first media outlets to shift from treating the Flock as a source of amusement to commenting on the threat that their hostility toward any scientific and medical advancement posed for the nation, even the planet, as a whole. But that was Kolya's problem to address. Being singled out in this fashion would probably make Brodnik's team even more annoyed with her, but she was beginning to suspect that ship had sailed. The exclusive would be a little bonus to make Bernard happy—a debate between Kolya and Shepherd might not draw as many viewers as her upcoming coverage of the Icarus chamber, but it would draw far more than the *Simple Science* episodes.

Still, she couldn't shake the feeling that Kolya was hiding something. He had some sort of ulterior motive where Tobias Shepherd was concerned. She didn't think there was any chance of getting at that answer directly, however, so she decided to chip away at the edges.

"I'm curious. How did you manage to persuade Shepherd to do something like this?"

"The trip or the debate?"

"Both. He has to know he'll be facing a hostile audience in the debate, though. I doubt there will be a single person on board the *Ares Prime* who would be receptive to his message."

"As with any negotiation, I determined the other side's needs and wants, and then I accommodated everything I could without losing ground I did not wish to cede."

"I like how you answered my question without answering it at all."

He chuckled. "Ah, you want specifics. Okay, I promised Shepherd absolute quiet and solitude once we're on the ship, something he claims has been hard to come by for the past decade or so and something that was extraordinarily easy for me to grant. His meals will be delivered to his suite, and he'll have no need to venture out or see anyone at all unless he decides to come out of his cave. I think that alone might have convinced him, but I also granted him the right to speak privately with anyone he chooses on the trip—employees, protestors, colonists. And as for the debate...are you kidding? He seemed perfectly willing, even eager, when I proposed it. Especially after I told him we'd be sure it was broadcast back home. While I'm sure Dr. Brodnik would not consider me a *real* scientist since I choose to reside *outside* the ivory tower of academia, I *do* hold an advanced degree in planetary science. Shepherd has long stated that he is willing to debate scientists on any topic, but no one will take him up on the offer."

"Can you blame them? He's not exactly arguing from a position that lends itself to rational debate. It's entirely based on faith. The views of his followers aren't all that different from people who believe they'll be whisked off to heaven as part of the Rapture. The only difference is that it's *aliens* the Flock thinks will whisk them away to the heavens instead of God. I'll certainly keep my contribution as…neutral and unbiased as possible. But if we open it up for questions from the audience at the end, Shepherd is very likely to face some ridicule. In fact, I can guarantee that he will if Dr. Kimura graces us with his presence. So what does the man stand to gain from this? It almost seems…cruel."

"Have you ever listened to Shepherd speak, Claire?"

"Not aside from the occasional interview."

"He can be very persuasive. And he's a zealot. Even if the entire room is against him—and maybe *especially* if the entire room is against him—Tobias Shepherd will walk out feeling vindicated, because he's convinced that truth is on his side and equally convinced that the truth always prevails in the end. As I said, he's a true believer. His position on this issue may also prove more popular with our passengers than you'd think. The entertainment industry has provided us with no end of interesting and adorable aliens over the decades, and many will prefer that fantasy to stark reality. And…" He gave her a casual shrug. "Perhaps Shepherd thinks he can expand the size of his Flock if word gets out that he bested the brilliant Anton Kolya."

There was a teasing note to his voice on the last part, a tiny nod toward humility. Claire was fairly sure it was mock humility, though. And while she didn't know exactly what the man was up to, she was quite certain of one thing. Anton Kolya was every bit as convinced of his own brilliance as Tobias Shepherd was convinced that he alone held the keys to saving humanity.

FIFTEEN

"CAN you shift about six inches to the left and tilt your chair slightly toward me?"

Claire followed Paul's instructions. Her chair legs screeched against the stage floor, and she winced as the sound echoed in the empty auditorium.

He turned to Stasia, who was seated in the front row. "What do you think?"

"Maybe a touch brighter?"

Paul pointed the remote, apparently amping up the brightness. She couldn't really tell the difference, but Stasia gave him a thumbs up.

"It's weird how quickly spatial perceptions can shift," Claire said. "This auditorium is smaller than our main conference room at the *Post*, and yet it seems almost cavernous after a few weeks on the *Ares Prime*."

"Just wait," Stasia told her. "When the seats are all full tonight, it will seem tiny again. Tiny and stuffy. You were smart to opt for a sleeveless dress."

It was the only dress she had packed, so it hadn't been a matter of choice. And she still had a hard time believing that there would be more than a dozen people in the audience.

"It's a *debate*, Stasia. Unless you're paying people to leave the casino and you plan to turn off all of the viewscreens on the ship, do you really think we're going to get a full house?"

"Oh, it *will* be a full house," she said. "You saw how many showed up for the Timeslip Party and there was only a carefully manufactured rumor that he *might* show up in person for that."

The Timeslip Party had taken place the previous week when

the ship formally switched over from Earth time to Mars time. This change wasn't merely a matter of shifting time zones but involved adding nearly forty minutes to the day. When the first colonies were set up, they had decided to adopt the custom from Kim Stanley Robinson's Mars trilogy, keeping the Earth clocks, and just tweaking them to stop for thirty-nine minutes and forty seconds at the end of each day. The colonies had apparently been less impressed with Robinson's method for syncing up the year, which had nearly twice as many days on Mars as on Earth, because they were still squabbling over an official Martian calendar.

On Timeslip Eve, Claire had joined most of the other passengers in the casino around eleven for something similar to a New Year's Eve countdown. No phones, tablets, or timekeeping devices were allowed at the party. Every attendee had been given a button to push when they thought the clock would begin ticking again, with prizes going to the three people who guessed the closest. And Stasia was right. There had been plenty of chatter among the guests that Kolya would be there in person, but his appearance had been a recorded piece played prior to the countdown...with a personal plug for the upcoming debate.

"I can assure you," Stasia continued, "that our guests are not going to miss their first—and for all they know, their *only*—chance to see the brilliant Anton Kolya. There's a reason we keep him cloistered away for most of the trip. Several reasons, to be honest, but the most important is that it preserves the mystique. Jonas Labs uses the same strategy with your brother, right? And his research partner, too, I guess."

"Oh, no." Claire laughed, stopped to think about it, and then laughed harder. "That's not strategy. Not at all. That's just...Joe. And Beck, as well."

Paul leaned toward her and said in a mock whisper, "In Kolya's case, it's like a horror movie. You never want to show the monster too soon."

Did they joke like this in front of the boss? Claire was beginning to suspect maybe they did, since Stasia had just used the exact same phrase that Kolya himself used at dinner the night before they left Tranquility Base—*the brilliant Anton Kolya.* Was his legendary ego also part of their manufactured mystique?

Kolya had actually stayed in hiding even longer than Tobias Shepherd. Claire had spotted Toby several times in the past few days wandering around the ship, but the only time she'd seen any sign that their host was even on board had been the very first morning when she found a note waiting in her room—her *private* room—along with a box of chocolates from Della Luna.

A small thank you for agreeing to host. I'll be working for the next two weeks but very much look forward to seeing you at the event. ~ AK

Claire didn't know whether the *small thank you* was in reference to the chocolates or to the upgraded accommodations, but either way, she had no complaints. The room, which was a few doors down from Brodnik's, wasn't large by any means, but it had a private bath and a small table that doubled as a desk. Given that she had fully expected to be sharing something roughly the size of a closet with Chelsea, the accommodations felt absolutely luxurious.

For the most part, it had been a pleasant trip. She'd had dinner with Stasia on two occasions, once as a foursome with Paul and his partner Ayman who was also traveling off-world for the first time. At that dinner, Stasia had asked enough questions about Kai and Jonas Labs that Claire had jokingly asked if she was thinking about switching jobs. Stasia had laughed and said she thought about it at least five times a day.

There had also been one somewhat awkward lunch with Brodnik and the rest of her team. For the most part, however, Claire had been on her own, something that suited her just fine.

After the nausea fully subsided and the strangeness of not being on Earth wore off, it had been a bit like a private retreat. While she would have preferred some place with trees or water—and with news coverage that went deeper than a few scattered, mostly upbeat headlines—it wasn't bad. She spent a day or two working on assignments for the *Post*, but most of her time had been free for trips to the gym, catching up on her reading, and watching some of the shows she had missed over the past few years due to having a small and very inquisitive child in the house.

And then, before she knew it, the debate was on the horizon. This was the second meeting she'd had with Paul and Stasia in the past two days—the first to go over cues for the B-roll footage they'd put together for her intro and then the current tech and lighting rehearsal. What she had envisioned as a handful of people in a room listening to two men argue had somehow morphed into a full theatrical production, with a reception to follow.

"Stasia is right about the crowd, though," Paul said. "I'm not sure if you've noticed, but she may have done a *tiny* bit of advance promotion."

Claire laughed because this was a major understatement. One of the first things that had greeted her while waiting in line for the very thorough pre-boarding security scan was an announcement for the debate on the ship's welcome screen. It cycled in a loop with the promo for the "galactic premiere" of an action film, *Nine Ways to Die,* two live performances by one of the supporting actors from the film who also did stand-up comedy, and a long list of helpful travel tips.

Within a few days, the simple announcement for the debate gave way to a slickly produced commercial that she'd seen several times a day since then on the ship's viewscreens, both in her room and in the common areas. At the beginning and end, her face appeared in a small bubble in the top center, with Kolya below on the left and Tobias Alvin Shepherd off to the right. Either it was an old photo of Shepherd or the Flock's guru hadn't changed much since the group first came into the public eye more than two decades earlier. Shepherd was short and thin, with a receding hairline accentuated by the fact that he wore his long reddish-blond hair slicked back from his forehead. His most distinctive feature was his pale blue eyes, which seemed to be in a constant state of alert. Even in the photo, Claire had the sense that the camera had caught those eyes a split second before they darted off in the direction of some lurking danger. He reminded her of an anxious rabbit.

"Now that you mention it, I *have* seen my headshot on a few viewscreens lately. If I ever decide to hire a publicist, remind me to lure Stasia away from KTI."

"*Very* bad idea," Paul said. "The last person who tried that vanished without a trace. Well…except for her pinky finger. Kolya had Macek mail that back to her family in a tiny white box."

Stasia snorted. "Do not listen to Caruso. I guess you can now see why we don't allow him to speak in public."

"Sure. He'd probably tell everyone where Kolya has the bodies buried."

"Why do you encourage him?" Stasia laughed, as Paul gave Claire a high five.

There was a little over three hours before the seven forty-five curtain call, so Claire decided to go back to her room to relax for a while. She opened the auditorium door and took a left onto the Grand Concourse—a rather pretentious name for the fairly narrow strip of hallway that encircled the ship. Grandiose titles were apparently the norm, however, since the small auditorium she'd just left was officially known as the Ares Palladium.

A few yards around, she spotted Tobias Shepherd at one of the portholes that were placed about ten meters apart on the concourse. The Earth and the moon hovered over his shoulder.

Have fun fraternizing with the enemy.

Beck had clearly been joking and he'd also been referring to

Kolya. But his words still echoed in Claire's head, in part because she didn't think he'd have meant it as a joke if he'd known Shepherd was going to be on board.

Still, she was going to have to meet the man at some point. It was probably best to break the ice in advance.

With that in mind, Claire firmly pushed aside Beck's warning and her own memories of rats running through the atrium of the building that her father poured his entire heart and soul into designing and pasted on her most professional smile.

"Dr. Shepherd?"

The man jumped, pulling his gaze away from the window.

"I'm Claire Echols," she said, extending her hand.

Shepherd shook his head briskly as if clearing the slate. "Apologies, Ms. Echols," he said as he gave her hand a brief squeeze. "You seem to have caught me woolgathering."

The phrase was almost comical, both because she had never heard it used outside of old books and because of its obvious connection to shepherds and sheep. For a moment, Claire wondered if it was an intentional attempt at humor, but his face showed no sign that he'd meant it as a joke.

"I'm sorry to have interrupted you. I just wanted to introduce myself before we meet at the debate tonight. I'll go now and let you get back to your thoughts."

"Oh, no, that's quite all right. I was just out for a walk around the ship and stopped to take in the view. It's stunning, don't you think?"

It *was* a stunning view, and one that Claire had taken in often over the past few weeks. Not through the portholes, but through the live feed on the viewscreen in her room, where she had lain in bed most nights before falling asleep, watching those two familiar orbs grow smaller and smaller as the *Ares Prime* carried her closer to their destination.

"I agree," she said. "It's my first time off-planet, and I still have a hard time convincing myself that Earth could actually be that far away."

He raised his eyebrows. "Your *first* time?"

"Yes. How about you?" Claire returned the question automatically, just as she had with several of the other passengers. Given Shepherd's views, she assumed the answer would be yes. To her surprise, however, he shook his head and returned his gaze to the window. Maybe he'd also taken a trip to the moon to *gabble*, as Jemma put it.

His actions felt like a dismissal, so Claire opened her mouth to say that she'd see him at the debate. But before she could get the words out, he spoke again.

"I was just thinking that this view perfectly captures the fragility of Earth. So tiny, compared to the vastness of space. And yet it also *masks* that very same fragility, because from here, there's no hint of how little time we may have left or how quickly it could all end if we don't find a way to curtail our greed." Shepherd chuckled softly. "But I'm sure that your view on all of this echoes that of our host. And that of your mother, as well. Progress, onward and upward, in the service of the great god Science with no concern for what other slumbering gods we may awaken."

Claire sighed, now wishing that she had simply walked past the man. His last comment took them directly into the territory of the debate, and she had absolutely no desire to get into an argument with him. Admittedly, his key point was largely true. She most certainly cared more about advancing science than she did about appeasing his imaginary alien deities. But she was still pissed at his presumption that she was a parrot for anyone else's views and doubly pissed at his subtle suggestion that she might somehow taint the debate with her bias.

"I barely know Kolya, Dr. Shepherd. I barely *speak* to my mother. I'm here in my capacity as a journalist for the *Post*, and as I told Kolya before I agreed to moderate, I am completely agnostic on your topic. I *do* agree that science can be used for evil means as well as good. But there's a vast gulf between the scientists I've known and the mad scientist caricature that you and your followers promote. Enjoy the rest of your walk."

"I'm sorry, but you misunderstand my point, Ms. Echols. I've spent my life as an observer of human nature, and I am well aware scientists aren't cackling over their computer simulations about how their discoveries will allow them to rule the world. Yes, many of them—maybe even most of them—are tallying up the *money* they'll make, but quite a few of that group still have at least some degree of good intentions. What you're missing is that even the purest of motives may deliver horrible outcomes. My followers and I have never claimed that the world will end at the hand of an evil genius. We think it far more likely to be destroyed by a bunch of well-intentioned fools."

SIXTEEN

CLAIRE GLANCED out from behind the black curtain at the edge of the screen backdrop and discovered that Stasia, who was currently onstage explaining the little voting devices the audience had been given, was dead right in her prediction. Every seat in the auditorium was filled. It now looked as small and cramped as some of the DC clubs that Wyatt dragged her out to on occasion. A few people were even leaning against the outer wall.

Warm hands fell on her shoulders and Kolya leaned in to whisper, so close that she could feel his breath against the side of her face. "Did we draw a decent crowd?"

Claire stepped away to let him check attendance for himself, but he didn't bother. Even in the dim light, she could see his grin.

Kolya knew damned well that the place was packed. He also knew he was going to win the debate because almost everyone in the audience was here only to see *the brilliant Anton Kolya.* They were better dressed and wealthy enough to spend an obscene amount of money on this trip, but aside from that, the vast majority of the passengers on the *Ares Prime* had a lot in common with Toby's sheep.

"Poor Shepherd has no chance," she teased. "It's wall-to-wall Kolya groupies."

Kolya gave her a look of mock indignation. "That's absolutely not true. Brodnik, Kimura, and the rest of your team are out there. I could take the position that one plus one equals two and they'd wholeheartedly back the other side."

He did have a point, especially where Kim was concerned.

"And I believe *that* is your cue," Kolya added as a wave of polite applause began.

Claire entered, thanked Stasia for the introduction, and thanked everyone for attending, adding a lame joke about captive audiences that they laughed at much harder than it merited. Then she began her short opening spiel as a deep space montage played on the background screen.

"Throughout recorded history," she said, "humankind has pondered the question of whether we are alone in the universe. Are the inhabitants of Earth the first species that has developed to the point of interplanetary travel and communication? One twentieth-century expert argued rather convincingly that we might well be. Physicist Enrico Fermi was convinced that while humans might not be the only *lifeforms* in the galaxy, we are at the very least the only technologically advanced life. His conclusion was based on the premise that civilizations generally attempt to spread to other regions as they grow in size and power."

She motioned to the footage of galaxies swirling behind her. "This led Fermi to the question at the heart of the paradox that bears his name. With so very many planets in the universe, if we are not the first to become capable of traveling to other star systems, then why have we yet to find evidence of other technologically advanced civilizations? Our resolution, therefore, is as follows: *Resolved. Humans are the only advanced life in the universe.* We will have three minutes for opening remarks, followed by four-minute rebuttals, and then one minute each for closing statements. Upon entry, you were each asked to give your current opinion on the resolution, along with how strongly you hold to that view on a scale of one to ten. You'll be polled again at the end of the debate to see which of our two speakers moved the needle the most. And now, without further ado…"

There was polite applause when she introduced Shepherd, about the same as they'd given her. He'd worn a suit, something he'd never done in any of the video footage she'd seen.

The Flock's standard uniform for everyone, from Toby down to the newest acolyte, was jeans and, depending on the weather, a T-shirt or hoodie emblazoned with the EWA logo. Claire wouldn't even have believed that the man owned a suit, although now that she thought about it, he hadn't been in the standard uniform the various times that she'd seen him over the past few days. Jeans, yes, but the last time she'd seen the EWA logo was on the sign Shepherd carried while picketing with the others outside the MIT lunar lab.

Kolya's reception was far more enthusiastic. They were very well-behaved groupies, though. He made a little hand gesture for them to stop clapping as he took his seat and they quieted almost immediately.

Claire then turned the proceedings over to Kolya for his opening remarks.

"Thank you for that kind introduction, Ms. Echols," Kolya said with a bow of his head as she took her chair center stage. "And my thanks to you, Dr. Shepherd, for agreeing to explore this topic with me this evening. Before we begin, I should note that any former debate team members in the audience will no doubt be saddened to learn that we're dispensing with formal rules. I am not only a participant in this debate, but also Dr. Shepherd's host. I've always believed, perhaps erroneously, that the affirmative side has a considerable advantage under formal debate rules, given that it both opens and closes the arguments. And so, not wishing to put my esteemed opponent at any disadvantage, I will be allowing him the final word this evening. With that said, let me state most firmly that we are *alone in the universe.*"

He spoke these last words in a deep, ominous tone, allowing them to echo through the room. Several people chuckled softly, and he waited for silence to fall again before continuing.

"Simply put, Fermi was right. Whether for good or for ill, most advanced civilizations in our history have colonized other lands. And the historical record since Fermi's death has added an important new data point, as we are now well on our way to colonizing another planet within our solar system. Fermi predicted this, arguing that any society capable of space travel would most likely tend to colonize entire systems, given a hundred million years or so of development. And while that may sound like a very long time, please bear in mind that the universe is about 13.6 *billion* years old, give or take a few hundred million years.

"One might argue, of course, that the age of the universe is irrelevant if there are no planets capable of supporting advanced life. But this is far from true. There are an estimated three hundred million planets in the Milky Way alone that could feasibly support such lifeforms, and our galaxy is only one out of an estimated one hundred and seventy billion galaxies. If there are other civilizations capable of traveling to star systems outside their own, then where the hell are all the aliens? Why, in all of human history, have we had no concrete proof that other advanced life exists?

"The obvious answer is that it *doesn't* exist. Every bit of objective evidence at our disposal tells us that humanity is the only bright, sentient force in the universe, my friends, and as such, we have an obligation to ensure that our light continues."

SEVENTEEN

KOLYA FINISHED WELL within his three minutes, and Claire gave the floor to Shepherd. He handed out the obligatory words of thanks and then turned to the audience.

"I'm going to start by giving you the standard scientific rebuttals, since I suspect a majority of you in this room will find those arguments the most compelling. And to be very clear, there are many scientists who make convincing arguments that despite the lack of concrete evidence my opponent has just given you, it is a logical fallacy to assume humans are the only advanced beings, or even the *most* advanced beings, in the universe. My first argument is one that should resonate with every passenger on this ship. You now have firsthand experience with the exorbitant cost of interplanetary travel, both in terms of time and treasure. Interstellar travel would, naturally, be even more expensive and time-consuming. Perhaps other advanced species know we are here and simply don't think it's worth the tremendous effort required to make their presence known.

"Fermi's premise is also based on *human* motivations," he continued, "and a technologically advanced lifeform could be very different from humans, both physically and in terms of their motivations. Maybe they're just not that interested in *our* world because there are better vacation spots elsewhere in the galaxy, especially for beings whose lungs—or gills or pores or whatever—require a very different mix of gases to survive. Or maybe there are intelligent beings out there who have no desire and no need to conquer other worlds, who are content to live within the bounds of their *own* world because it offers everything they need. Which, I will note, our own planet could easily do if not for incessant greed."

He paused for a second and took a sip from his glass of water, possibly realizing that even a short sermon on greed wasn't likely to sit well with this particular audience.

"If representatives of that sort of civilization have been watching," he continued, "and if they have observed the way the nations of Earth squabble, maim, and slaughter, not to mention the way we squander the resources of our planet, they may well have deemed us dangerous and placed this little corner of the universe in a quarantine zone. Or perhaps they're watching us, waiting for us to develop to the stage where we'll be welcomed into some grand federation of advanced civilizations so that we may boldly go where no one has gone before."

This drew a laugh from the audience.

"That's the best case scenario, of course. I would argue that it's even more likely that they are watching and tolerating us for now, waiting until we become enough of a nuisance that we're worth the effort of swatting away."

Another laugh, but it sounded a trifle nervous this time.

"All of these are perfectly plausible explanations for why extraterrestrial life might choose to ignore us, but it could also simply be a matter of *timing*. Our first radio transmissions began in 1895, less than two centuries ago. The first concerted efforts to locate extraterrestrial life began in the 1970s, although some ambitious souls, including Nikola Tesla, began listening for off-planet signals not long after the discovery of radio. Given the size of the galaxy and the tiny, infinitesimal length of time that we have met even the most rudimentary definition of technological advancement, insisting that we are alone in the universe is similar to looking out your window and claiming that fish do not exist simply because there are none on your lawn at this moment. It's simply *not* a logical argument."

"I'll take your objections in the order given," Kolya said after

Shepherd gave him a nod to let him know that he had finished his opening remarks. "Cost is irrelevant given enough time and curiosity, both of which I would argue are prerequisites for technological advancement. Without that desire to explore, to expand —and yes, even to conquer—no species will make its way out of a cave, so I concur with Fermi on that point, at least. But as critics of Fermi's work and also the Drake Equation have shown—"

He stopped, stared out at the audience, and laughed. "And half of you are now looking for the exit, aren't you? I promised to avoid getting too deep into the theoretical weeds here in order to keep this accessible to the non-scientists, so I'll just say that those of you who are curious will find excellent background on everything from the Fermi Paradox, the Drake Equation, Goldilocks Zones, the Rare Earth Hypothesis, and the Great Filter in Ms. Echols's *Simple Science* segments at the *Atlantic Post.*"

Claire gave him a nod of thanks, and he continued. "I will, therefore, spare you a discussion of the complex formulas that have been used to come up with this vast number of planets that Dr. Shepherd stated could potentially support advanced life and merely note that any of the formulas predicting the number of habitable planets includes about a dozen variables that are...well, highly *variable*. This introduces a tremendous amount of uncertainty into those equations. When you control for that uncertainty, using statistical models, the Fermi Paradox doesn't seem nearly as paradoxical.

"Let me give you the example with which I'm most familiar, and which I believe may be very familiar to some of you as it pertains to our destination. Prior to our terraforming efforts Mars was already considered to be on the very *outer* edge of our sun's habitable zone. And yet I can assure you that even today, after decades of work costing many, many billions of dollars, should you decide to step outside the domed environment of Daedalus City without a protective suit, you will *not* find it

conducive to human existence. A decade from now, however..."
He shrugged.

Kolya was playing extremely fast and loose with the term *habitable zone*. All it meant was that the planet was at the right distance from a star to allow water to exist on the surface. It didn't guarantee an atmosphere or any of the other ingredients required for life as we know it to thrive. Claire was quite certain he knew this, and she was a little annoyed that she couldn't call him on it.

And Claire wasn't the only one. Her eye fell on Chelsea, seated in the fourth row next to the rest of the team, whispering furiously to Kimura.

"And that is just one of the shaky variables," Kolya said. "Early twentieth century scientists made a lot of assumptions. For complex life to develop, every single thing needs to hit the sweet spot—the galaxy, the star, the configuration of planets, the size of the planet, a stable orbit, the existence of a moon, an atmosphere, and even more. They *all* need to line up perfectly in that Goldilocks Zone. Not too near, not too far. Not too wet, not too dry. Not too big, not too small. Miss even one of those benchmarks and you're out of the zone. So the number of potential cradles of civilization isn't nearly as vast as Dr. Shepherd would have us believe."

Kolya's voice took on a slightly mocking tone at this point, but if Shepherd noticed, he gave no sign.

"And even if you have a situation where all of these things line up perfectly," Kolya continued, "there's still no guarantee that life will take hold or that it will follow an evolutionary path that leads to advanced lifeforms. We could give Mars an atmosphere, give it a few billion years to develop, and without the necessary building blocks, without that initial seed of life, you'd not only have a planet where humans never evolve, but also a planet incapable of supporting humans in the long term.

"I will grant you that one caveat about timing. We are the only technologically advanced life *currently in existence*. Yes,

yes," he said to the audience. "I know that slightly alters the position I'm supposed to support, and if you feel you must vote in favor of my opponent in the interest of fairness, I will take no offense. No one will be pushed out of an airlock. You will still be fed, and sheltered, and ferried home after our time at Daedalus City." He paused for laughs and then went on. "The Milky Way is one of the oldest galaxies, formed a mere four hundred million or so years after the universe itself. There may well be an upstart planet a few galaxies over where a species capable of giving humans a real run for our money in another twenty million years or so is now emerging from the primordial ooze. There may even have been such a civilization millions of years in the past. But right now? If we had any competition out there, we'd know it. We are alone."

Kolya paused again and looked around the auditorium. "And that's pretty sobering when you stop to think about it. We are one extinction level event away not from just the end of humankind, but quite possibly the end of all intelligent life. Improving the environment on Earth, as necessary as that is, doesn't protect us from an extinction level event, such as a massive asteroid strike. Terraforming Mars doesn't even ensure that.

"If we are, as I believe, unique…that's a huge burden for our generation. As my opponent notes, we have treated our home world rather shabbily, to the point where I truly do not believe that we can expect it to be a permanent shelter for coming generations. Can we reverse the damage done? We can certainly try, but we'd be fools to have that as our only option. Indeed, even Dr. Shepherd has a backup plan—the Sentinel mothership —for the true believers willing to follow his rigid guidelines."

There was definitely mockery in his tone now. Shepherd had seemed oblivious to it earlier, but his eyes narrowed when Kolya mentioned the Sentinels.

Kolya checked the time remaining on the clock, then picked up the pace a bit. "I agree with my opponent that we have an obligation to future generations. We must ensure that life continues…even if Earth is destroyed. Even if the solar system is destroyed. The first practical step in this is terraforming Mars, and I am delighted to be part of that process. But the only way to guarantee the long-term survival of the human race is to become not just a multiplanetary species but a multistellar species. Terraforming Mars is merely a first tiny step toward that goal."

Ah ha, Claire thought. There, in a nutshell, was the reason Kolya had organized this debate. It was also his game plan for spinning the discovery of the Icarus chamber. He planned to use Mars as a cautionary tale. Intelligent life once existed on Mars, at a time long before its development on Earth. Life on Mars seeded Earth, whether knowingly or through some accidental contamination before it expired. And so, given that sentient life exists nowhere else that we know of today, seeding other planets is not simply a matter of expansion, of conquering the next frontier. It is an obligation passed along to us from the source of our creation.

Shepherd also seemed to have picked up on at least part of Kolya's intent, because he began his response with a soft chuckle. "And there we have it, my friends—the vast ego of the imperialist. In past centuries, they railed on about the White Man's Burden to bring civilization to the rest of the world as they raped and pillaged the land, slaughtering those who resisted their god and their ideas of morality. You simply worship a different god. Your god is Science, and it destroys everything in its path."

It seemed to Claire that they were getting somewhat off-topic, but she supposed that was in the hands of the audience. And she wasn't sure that she could have stopped him anyway. Toby was on a roll.

"It isn't even entirely due to greed or malice. Science *builds*, and what seems harmless or perhaps even beneficial on its face might end up being the tipping point, the change that results in the end of all life on Earth. And because science builds, one change upon the other, we do not know which one will send us into the abyss. The only responsible course is to draw a firm line in the sand and say we have achieved enough. We are *enough*. Progress, scientific and technological advancements…we do not need more of these. We have ample resources to feed, clothe, and house every human on Earth if we allocate those resources wisely. If we refuse to do that—and barring a radical change in human nature, I believe that to be inevitable—then we must accept disease and famine for some groups as the natural result."

Shepherd was out of his chair now, pacing along the front of the small stage like a tent evangelist. This felt like something that should be against the rules even in an informal debate. Claire glanced over at Kolya to see if he had any objections, but he didn't seem bothered by the man's antics, so she held her tongue. A tiny blip of green light from the audience suggested that at least one observer was interested enough to be recording Shepherd's spiel.

"The scientists will tell you no, we have this wonderful new grain that we've modified, which will allow us to feed more people per acre of land. But those people will want more than just food and the *things* they want increase the strain on the environment. And the scientist says that's okay, too, because we have a new strain of artificial life that will scrub the air and the waterways so that the Earth can support more people. Of course, that biobot or whatever the newest thing is has unexpected side effects of its own. But don't worry, my friends! They have another fabulous invention that will mitigate those side effects. And on it goes. I ask you, where does it end?" He stopped and scanned the faces of the audience. "That's not a rhetorical question. Because you *know* where it ends. It ends with the destruction of our planet. And apparently the next planet. And the next."

That little green pulse of light came into view again, triggering an odd sense of déjà vu in Claire's mind.

Dot, dot, dash, followed by a long pause. *Dot, dot, dash*…

It wasn't a camera. Or at least, not a camera operated by someone in the audience. It was a surveillance drone like the one she'd seen in the park the night before her departure.

"And that, my friends, *that* is why the Earth Watch Alliance chooses to live as we do," Shepherd said. "That is why we advocate, even agitate, for others to join us. That is why we target companies that keep pushing us toward the brink, toward that next—" He stopped in mid-sentence. One hand flew up and slapped at his neck.

Something very small hit the stage floor and skittered under the chair where Shepherd had been sitting.

For a moment, the man stood completely still. Then, he slumped to the floor and his body began to convulse.

EIGHTEEN

"LADIES AND GENTLEMEN," Kolya said, "we have a medical emergency. Please make your way back to your rooms and give Dr. Shepherd some privacy. We'll keep you posted on the ship's information channel."

A woman was now on stage, barking a command into her watch. She crouched down next to Shepherd, whose body continued to shake. "Does anyone know if he has a history of seizure disorders?"

"No," Kolya said. "Stasia...can you see if there's anything in his file?"

Claire knelt down to peer under the chair. The tiny drone was on its side, apparently damaged, but the green light was still flashing like a stuttering firefly.

"Are you all right, Claire?" Kolya asked.

"Yes." She took the hand he offered and got to her feet. Most of the audience was following Kolya's instructions and calmly leaving the auditorium. There were still a few gawkers, however, so she lowered her voice. "You should tell the doctor that a nerve agent is more likely than epilepsy. There's a nanodrone under Shepherd's chair."

After relaying her information to the doctor, Kolya came back and bent down to check beneath the chair for himself.

"You have sharp eyes. I didn't see anything approach the stage."

"I thought it was the light from a camera at first. But then I recognized that flashing pattern. I've seen it before."

"Really?" He frowned. "I'm pretty sure Macek is going to

have some questions for you. He's my chief security officer. You met him in New York."

Claire was tempted to ask why his chief security officer was the one Kolya had tasked with meeting Brodnik and the others at Columbia. But maybe he viewed negotiations with Brodnik as a security matter, too, given that Kimura was on her team. Not to mention Claire herself, with Kai constantly threatening to sue KTI for corporate espionage.

A few minutes later, Paul Caruso led her out the back door and through a series of hallways to a small conference room in the administrative section of the ship, where he left her to wait for Macek. About fifteen minutes later, Paul stuck his head back in and said that things were taking longer than expected.

"Can I bring you anything while you wait? The reception was canceled, so we're drowning in a sea of fruit, cheese, and crackers. Wine, too."

Claire's stomach churned at the thought. "No, thanks. How is he? Shepherd, I mean."

"Lucky to be alive, according to Stasia. Dr. Yadav told her the nerve agent they detected in Shepherd's bloodstream is usually fatal within a minute, sometimes less, and it was closer to five minutes before she was able to administer an antidote."

"I hadn't even realized the ship had a doctor on staff," she said. "Although I guess you'd have to, given the length of the trip."

"Well, she's not on staff, exactly. We reserve a few slots on each voyage for people with medical skills and give them a very steep discount if they agree to be on call while we're out of port. Passengers are strongly encouraged to put off anything that's not an emergency, since we have a full medical staff at Daedalus. They'll give Shepherd a thorough examination when we arrive. But he's tougher than he looks, apparently. Stasia says he's sitting up now and bitching loudly about the ship's lax security. Which is going to be a public relations nightmare if he starts talking to passengers. Right now, the audience still assumes he just had a seizure of some sort."

She nodded, getting the point without Paul having to say anything else. They didn't want Shepherd telling the passengers about the drone, which meant they didn't want *her* talking about it, either.

Macek—if the man had a first name, Claire had yet to hear anyone use it—showed up about twenty minutes after Paul left. He closed the door behind him and placed a small clear tube on the table. The drone, no longer flashing, was inside.

He sat down in the chair opposite Claire, took out a recording device, and flicked it on without asking…which had her wondering what set of laws they were operating under. Was there an interplanetary equivalent of international law that covered interrogations?

"You're positive you've seen this thing before?" Macek asked, nodding toward the drone. "Not the same exact device, but the same model?"

"No. I'm not an expert on surveillance drones, so I can't be certain. For all I know, there could be dozens of similar brands on the market. All I know is that I saw the thing flash in the auditorium, maybe ten seconds before Dr. Shepherd was attacked. At first, I thought the light was a recording device being used by someone in the audience, but then I noticed it had the same flash pattern— two short blips of green light, followed by a longer one—as a nanodrone that I caught following me in DC."

He had been looking down at the drone, but his eyes now shot up to meet hers. "When?"

"The night before we left. It might be a coincidence, but since I suspect the first device belonged to the Flock—"

"Why do you think that?" His eyes were laser-focused on her face now, as if looking for some trace of a lie.

"Because a few hours before the drone started following me, I interviewed a whistleblower…or someone who wanted to be a whistleblower...from one of the Flock's farms in Northern Virginia."

"Was this whistleblower trying to leave?"

"No. Devin was actually very defensive about his membership in the group. He implied that he was there of his own volition, even though he was clearly very worried about them finding out he was talking with a member of the media."

"Do you know this Devin's last name?" Macek asked.

"Sure. It's Shepherd."

"Oh, right. I forgot about that bit of weirdness. Hard enough to believe that people would willingly hand over all of their worldly possessions to a group like that, but then they force you to give up your name, too?" He shook his head in disgust.

"Yeah, I find it odd, as well, but I don't think they're actually forced. Devin seemed like a true believer to me. He refused to speak with anyone other than Bryce Avery, a colleague of mine who wasn't in the office at the time. The only thing I got from the guy was that things had escalated since they last spoke. My assumption was that whatever he was planning to tell Bryce concerned the recent schism in the Flock, although that's merely a guess. The other reason I suspected it was their device was a warning from a security officer at Jonas Labs the previous week. He said to keep an eye out and to maybe consider increasing my home security, given that the Flock had upped their game to bomb threats."

"So...what do you know about this schism?"

"Not much. The Flock has always been nonviolent, and then suddenly they're not. And I doubt it's a coincidence that Shepherd decided right in the middle of all this that it was a good time for a little off-planet vacation. But you don't need my speculation on the matter. You can just ask Shepherd, right?"

Macek frowned, then stashed the recording device and the glass tube with the nanodrone into the pocket of his suit coat. "One more thing before I go," he said. "The non-disclosure agreement you signed prior to travel covers this incident, too.

No chattering with other passengers about the drones or your theories about them belonging to the Flock or that you think one of them was chasing you around DC. And no *investigative reporting*. If anyone does happen to ask you, Shepherd had a seizure. That's all you know. Understand?"

Claire raised an eyebrow. "I understand the *point* that you're trying to make, but I have a housemate with a young daughter. And I was concerned enough to increase our home security when I believed that a drone was simply watching me. Now that I know the devices have been weaponized, I *will* be sending her a message so that she can take any necessary precautions. If that violates your NDA—which I *sincerely* doubt—feel free to take the matter up with my attorneys when we get back."

Macek gave her a long look, pressing his lips into a thin, tight line. "As you just noted, Ms. Echols, this drone could well be one of the most common devices on the market. Dr. Shepherd is recovering nicely, so either this was intended only as a warning, or these would-be assassins aren't especially skilled at their craft. The odds that your housemate or her daughter are at any risk—"

"That part's not negotiable," she said, even though she was fairly certain Macek could block the transmission or censor the content if he wanted. "And while I don't plan to go around fueling speculation about this incident, if I saw what happened, I think there's a decent chance someone else in the audience did, too. What worries me most, though, is that the device got through your security scan. The owner is still at large and could easily have others ready to launch. To be perfectly frank, the passengers of the *Ares Prime* make a very tempting target for any violent offshoot of the Flock, given the organization's general distaste for conspicuous consumption."

There was a long pause during which Macek's steel-gray eyes never left her face, and then he sighed. "We have a little under three days until we reach Ares Station, where we'll board the shuttles to the surface. I assure you that my team—all four of us—will be taking every precaution to ensure the safety of you and everyone else on board the *Ares Prime*. But since you seem to feel that you're in danger, I'll arrange to have your meals delivered to your room for the duration. Wait here. I'll have Caruso escort you back to your quarters momentarily."

"Are you actually putting me under house arrest?" Claire asked, struggling to keep the amusement out of her voice.

"Certainly not, Ms. Echols. If you *wish* to roam the ship, you may of course do so. But I would again caution you to keep that NDA in mind should you happen to strike up any conversations with the other passengers."

Even her admittedly cursory reading of the NDA was enough for her to know that it was specific to the terraforming project and the discovery at Icarus Camp. Claire couldn't imagine a court agreeing that it required her to remain silent if the passengers were at risk...and unlike most people Macek threatened, she could afford legal representation capable of fending off Kolya's legendary battalions of attorneys. The primary leverage that KTI had over her wasn't that piece of paper, but access to the story.

"Thank you for the unsolicited legal advice," she told Macek. "No need to bother Paul. I can find my way back to my quarters.

Paul showed up anyway when Claire was only a few steps down the corridor.

"Let me guess. Macek was a complete asshole, and he mentioned the NDA at least three times."

"I believe he only mentioned the NDA twice. But yes, he has an abrasive personality."

"Exactly what Stasia and I were afraid of. I'm sorry."

"I've dealt with jerks before," Claire told him as they turned onto the main hallway. One of the passengers was headed their way, so she waited until the woman moved out of earshot before continuing. "My concern is that he seems to be ignoring the fact that others could be at risk. I *get* why you don't want a panic, and I'm not planning to go around spreading rumors. But if one of those devices got through the security scans, there could be others on board. And when I pointed that simple fact out to him, he said I should just stay in my room for the next few days if I was worried."

Paul snorted. "Yeah, that sounds like Macek. Any security lapse obviously reflects badly on him, and he doesn't take criticism well. But, that's partly because he doesn't have a lot of experience with it. The man runs a tight ship, both in terms of this *literal* ship and KTI as a whole. Assuming this was a targeted attack by someone else on board, he'll find them."

"*Assuming*? What else would it be? This is pretty much the epitome of a locked-room mystery. Yes, a drone can be piloted and monitored remotely, but I seriously doubt it has a range in the millions of kilometers."

"That doesn't preclude it being programmed in advance, though. We decided the time and place of the debate before leaving Tranquility, so that opens the list of suspects considerably. And…um…there's no way to be *certain* Shepherd was the actual target. It could have been aiming at Kolya and Shepherd just got in the way. Or even you, I guess since one of the things was following you in DC." He grimaced. "Sorry. I'm not making things better, am I? Maybe it *would* be safer if you avoided the public areas until we arrive."

Claire was quiet until they reached her door, debating whether to say anything at all. Paul had a job to do, after all, and did she really want to antagonize him and most likely Stasia, as well? If he hadn't seemed like a nice guy and if she hadn't grown to like him, she would probably have just let it go, but…

"Just curious. Did you and Macek set up the good-cop, bad-cop thing in advance?"

His flush was all the answer she needed. "Claire…"

"It's okay. I get it. To be clear, I don't actually think I was the target in the auditorium. I watched that thing zoom straight at

Shepherd's neck. But on the off chance that I'm wrong, I need to get a message to my housemates—remember the little girl whose picture I showed you? I have to make sure her mom is aware that there might be an increased threat. And even though I'm not planning to go into specifics on the nature of the threat, I still think there's a decent chance Macek will block the transmission. If you can promise me that message will get through, I'll stick to my quarters until we dock at Ares Station...even though we both know that drone could travel through the air circulation vents and into an individual room just as easily as it could target someone in the auditorium."

"I really don't think so. We were talking about that a few minutes ago and that drone is much too big to get through the mesh filter over the air vents. But on the other issue... Maybe I can arrange something. Can you hold off for a half-hour or so, long enough for me to talk to Stasia about it? Macek is pretty defensive about what's his territory and what's hers, but maybe she can convince him. Or maybe she can take it to Kolya, instead. And...um...I'm sorry, okay?"

"No hard feelings. But...do you really think Stasia can convince Kolya to override Macek?"

He grinned. "Oh, yeah. If she *tries*, she definitely can. The boss always says Stasia is his right hand and Macek is his left... but Kolya's right-handed, so it's not nearly as equal as it sounds."

NINETEEN

CLAIRE CHANGED out of her dress into pajama pants and a t-shirt, her usual sleeping attire, and had just settled down to play a few songs on the piano app—which was still annoying, but better than nothing—when someone knocked at the door. Probably Paul, she thought, letting her know he'd talked to Stasia about her sending a message to Rowan.

But it was Kolya, still in his impeccably tailored suit, pushing a room service cart that held several covered platters and a bottle of Bordeaux. "I've just been informed that Macek sent you to your room without supper, and we can't have you starving."

He lifted one of the lids to reveal an assortment of appetizers. Claire started to protest that she'd be fine with a granola bar she'd stashed away, but she had skipped dinner, knowing they would be eating at the reception after the debate. And she had to admit that it smelled wonderful.

"That's a *lot* of food."

"True, but I intend to make you share. And while we're easing our hunger"—Kolya reached into his pocket to pull out a phone—"perhaps I can also do something to ease your mind. Stasia says you're worried about your housemate?"

"Yes." Claire stepped aside to make way for him to enter with the cart. "It's probably an overreaction, but Rowan has a small daughter and that makes me very…risk averse. And while I told Ro about seeing the surveillance drone before I left, she needs to know that someone is weaponizing the damn things."

"Agreed. This is my personal device. It's not instantaneous, of course, but it's considerably faster than the standard ship system. And it has the added feature of bypassing Macek's oversight without me having to confront the man on an evening when he's quite busy and apparently very touchy about his security team having missed a threat. Although I assure you that I *will* be talking to him about…" Kolya waved his hands in a vague fashion. "About this situation. He very much overre-acted. I'd appreciate it if you could avoid specifics in your warning to your housemate and please don't mention Shepherd by name, but I see no problem with you giving her a heads-up. If she responds quickly, we should hear back from her by the time we're finished eating."

He punched something into the phone, opened a messaging interface, and handed it to Claire. "Everything is set for the home office, so you'll need to add in the appropriate prefixes and adjust for the time difference. Minsk is eight hours ahead, so I think it should be around dinnertime in DC?"

She glanced at the time display, did a quick mental calcula-tion, and nodded. "Hopefully, Ro isn't on duty tonight. If so, it could take her a bit longer to check her messages."

Kolya shrugged and uncorked the wine. "I'm in no rush. I'd blocked out my entire schedule this evening for the debate and the reception. Oh…be sure to key in your personal number at the top, or she's going to wonder who in hell is messaging her from the EEU."

Claire did as he instructed, then typed in a quick note:

> Ro – I've just learned that the bug I saw the night before I left is even more dangerous than I thought. Neurotoxic, in fact, and potentially lethal. Please—

A bit of music came over her earbuds and she looked up midway through writing the message to find Kolya tapping at the virtual piano on her tablet.

"Sorry," he said. "I didn't realize you were wearing the earphones. Do you play?"

She nodded. "It's how I unwind. My piano is one thing I'd love to have been able to pack. The app helps, but it's really not the same."

"Then I have good news," he said with a smile. "You'll be able to play when we're at Daedalus. There's a baby grand at the bar in our executive pavilion. Occasionally, we have a professional come in to perform for events, but it's mostly there for appearance. And maybe a touch of nostalgia, on my part. I can't play much beyond chopsticks, but my mother played beautifully. Come down and use it anytime you like."

"I will definitely take you up on that. But how do you know my playing won't scare off all of your guests?"

Kolya thought about it for a moment, and then shook his head. "You don't strike me as the kind of person who would be able to play for relaxation unless you were already quite accomplished."

He was right, more or less. Back when Claire was taking lessons, she'd been driven to get every note, every element, of every song absolutely perfect. She'd nearly quit during her second year of lessons because of the wicked second section of *Für Elise*. There were a few pieces that she still played well from memory, but these days, she mostly just sat down at the keyboard and played her own creations, letting emotions flow through her fingers and into the piano.

"But if you're shy about playing in public," he said, "it's digital. Bring your earphones. The bartender will be able to hook you up."

"That's even better," she told him. "No one has run screaming from the room since I was five or six, but it always feels a bit odd to play in front of strangers. Thanks."

Claire returned to Kolya's phone and finished typing out her message:

Please be careful, okay? Give Jemma a big
hug for me and contact Sigrid's father
immediately for help with pest control.

When she finished, she showed what she'd written to Kolya. "Is that vague enough?"

"Sigrid's father?"

"Rowan will understand that it means our security service."

It was actually a bit of code instructing her to tell Wyatt, and Claire really hoped she'd get that point without any additional detail. They had certainly referred to him as the cat's dad often enough. Claire knew that if Ro told Wyatt, he would also understand the need to pass the information along so that Joe could alert the security team at Jonas Labs. And hopefully, the fact that she was using code would clue Ro in that she needed to be equally vague in her response. Otherwise, Kolya was probably going to be pissed.

She placed the phone on the edge of the bed and then took one of the two chairs at the tiny table. He handed her a glass of wine and she watched as he navigated around the room service cart and awkwardly folded himself into the other chair.

"These rooms were a lot bigger in the blueprints," he said, noticing her amused expression.

"Plenty of room for one person. And since I thought I'd be sharing something much smaller, I have no complaints."

"But aren't you accustomed to sharing a room?" He glanced pointedly at the phone.

Claire fought back a laugh. Why didn't the man just come out and ask if she and Rowan were a couple? For a second, she was tempted to tell him they were. That would put an end to the flirtation and innuendo.

Or would it? She could also see him taking it as a challenge.

And did she really *want* to put an end to it? What about Wyatt's parting command to go forth and break a few hearts? He'd probably already found the next replacement for this

Steph person. And there was absolutely no risk of anything serious with Anton Kolya. He was quite a bit older, but there was an undeniable attraction. Why not have a little fun?

"Rowan and I share a *house*," she told him. "Not a bedroom."

"Ah. Did Kai cut you off so thoroughly that you need someone to share household expenses?"

She laughed. "If she could have, she would have. But I inherited one-quarter of my father's shares in Jonas Labs, along with some other assets. I met Rowan a few years back when she lived in the townhouse next to me. Jemma was almost two and Ro was about to start her residency at Johns Hopkins when her husband suddenly decided family life wasn't his jam. I'd been thinking about getting a house anyway. I just opted for a slightly larger one with a nice fenced-in yard."

"And you enjoy sharing your house with an infant?"

"Whoa. The *infant* is four and a half, and she would be highly offended by your word choice. But, yes. I like kids… okay, I like *most* kids. How about you?"

He considered the question for a moment. "I haven't really been around many of them in the past few years. But they seem…time-consuming."

"They are if you do it right. Did your parents do it right?"

"My mother did. Father was rarely home. Too occupied with work. And maybe that was just as well."

"Sounds like the exact reverse of my childhood. But…won't you need at least a few little Kolyas to inherit your empire and carry on your work?"

"Eventually, I suppose. I'd ask if you were proposing a collaboration in that regard, but if the rumors about your brother's research are true, I think I can safely put reproduction off for at least a *few* more years." Laughter flashed in his eyes at her expression. "And just like that, Claire Echols has nothing more to say."

TWENTY

THE FACT that Kolya had referred to rumors about Rejuvesce was troubling. Claire had combed through the ship's pathetic news digest for nearly a week, looking for information about the launch, which should have taken place five days earlier unless they'd run into some last minute issue. Given how certain Joe and Beck had both been, and the fact that Joe was talking about side goals, she really couldn't imagine that happening. But if they hadn't moved forward, she needed to be careful not to say too much. She couldn't ask Rowan or Wyatt, either, since neither of them knew about the launch. Her message to Joe the previous day (*Is everything OKAY?*) still hadn't been answered.

"I have plenty more to say," she told Kolya. "My silence is only on that issue. You should ask Macek about this little thing called an NDA. My mother would have me drawn and quartered if she learned that I was sharing information about Jonas Labs with *The Enemy*."

He chuckled, but there was a trace of discomfort in his expression, too. "The enemy? Ouch. Your mother has a remarkable ability to carry a grudge. Fine. I won't push you for information, even though my interest is primarily as a prospective customer. And if Kai were to approach this logically, she'd realize that our work is more complementary than competitive."

"How so?"

"Global population growth is reasonably stable right now. Even if the Jonas Lab breakthrough yields only a five-year increase in longevity, which is where I've heard the smart money lies, and even if this new drug is prohibitively expensive for the vast majority of the world's population...that's still going to ramp up the pressure for off-world colonization."

"True," she said, not adding that the smart money was probably going to feel pretty dumb when Rejuvesce was officially launched. If Kolya was happy with the thought of what a five-year increase in life expectancy would yield, he was going to be absolutely thrilled with the twenty or thirty years that Joe was predicting.

And sure, the drug wouldn't be available to everyone immediately. But Kai had spent the last four years, from the very first hint of Joe's breakthrough, quietly negotiating partnership agreements with labs around the world, expanding the network the company had built in the early days of marketing Arvectin. They'd even held off on the launch for a few months to make sure that they would have enough supply to deal with the initial demand. Joe had insisted on an accelerated distribution plan, in which Jonas Labs would relax the patent on everything other than his specific variant of recombinant biobots after only two years, allowing other firms to begin marketing biosimilar versions of the once-a-month pill.

"Okay then," Kolya said. "No shoptalk. What did you think of *Nine Ways to Die*? Is it worth two hours of my time?"

It took Claire a second to realize he meant the movie premiere. "Not bad. More special effects than plot, but it's a good popcorn movie, I suppose. The audience liked it more than I did, but it's not really my favorite genre."

"And what *is* your favorite genre?"

"Mysteries, for the most part."

"Which makes sense, I suppose, given your line of work."

The conversation continued in that vein for the next fifteen minutes. Books, movies, music...and it did not escape Claire's attention that this was pretty much the standard first date lineup. They had just moved on to where they went to university when Kolya's phone flashed with an incoming message from Ro.

> Understood. I'll contact Sigrid's father tonight and will caution Ethan to be careful when out with Jemma. Are you okay?

Claire messaged back that she was fine. That she had just wanted to give Ro a heads-up and would write more after they arrived at Daedalus.

"Feel better now?" Kolya asked, after she handed him the phone.

"Yes. Thank you very much."

"Happy to help. To be honest, I think you have some cause to be worried. I'm concerned, too, especially given that we've learned over the past several days about some recent and rather troubling…developments…surrounding this schism in the Flock."

"Odd." Claire cast a pointed look toward the cabin's viewscreen. "There was nothing about it in the ship's daily news digest."

"Well, it's called a news *digest* for a reason. Our communications stream is somewhat limited during transit, so we decided that was the best route. Otherwise, the passengers would all be clamoring for their own favorite news and entertainment outlets, and we'd have a lot more griping about not being able to make instant stock trades. They'll have more options once we reach Daedalus, but tourists are told before they book passage that a vacation in space is also a vacation from the daily barrage of information. I even take a partial break myself, aside from things directly relevant to KTI. It may surprise you, but some people consider tuning out the news to be a feature of this trip, rather than a bug."

"It doesn't surprise me. Given my occupation, however, I'm probably suffering from information withdrawal more than the others."

"True. As for the turmoil inside the Flock, I believe the *Post* has a couple of stories on it. I can send you a copy of those articles if you're interested."

"Yes. Thank you. Do you know if there have been any other assassination attempts?"

"Not that I'm aware of. But disaffected members of the Earth Watch Alliance do seem to have finally coalesced around another, more aggressive leader. Shepherd still has a significant group of loyalists, but concerns have been growing over the past few weeks that the organization might move to genuine acts of terrorism against companies or even individuals on their list of enemies. And obviously, Shepherd would be at the top of that list. I suspect that Dr. Shepherd knew something like this was on the horizon, which might well explain his decision to join us."

"It might also explain his self-imposed isolation for most of the trip."

"Yes. And had Shepherd been fully honest on that account, I wouldn't have suggested a public debate. To be honest, I'm not sure I would even have let him on board. But…we can't roll back time, can we? Macek is keeping him sequestered away from the rest of the passengers until we reach Ares Station, and they'll be going through every bit of luggage with a fine-toothed comb before we leave the ship." He tipped back the last of his wine. "And on that note, I should probably dive back into the chaos and let you get on with your reading."

"So soon? I thought you were going to tell me all about stage six of the terraforming."

He grinned. "Nice try, Claire."

"Seriously, though, who am I going to tell? While I doubt Macek's claim that the NDA could be stretched to cover the situation with that drone, it clearly states that anything I write about the terraforming project prior to the launch of stage six, whether for the *Post* or any other outlet, has to be cleared by KTI before publication."

"I'm sure it does, but..." He stopped and gave her a measured look. "Okay. How about this? I was planning to make a trip to Ehden next week. That's just outside of the Elysian border, in an unincorporated area of Nepenthes Mensae. It's just over a three-hour flight from Daedalus. I could ask Stasia to sync up our schedules so that you can come along. I'm sure there will be at least one day when Brodnik's team is doing tedious stuff that you can miss. We'll stop at some of the demo sites on the way and I can give you a small preview of what we're planning for the next few stages. You won't be able to publish anything about it until after my press conference the day we launch stage six, but you can have it all ready to go. Which should give you a nice head-start on the competition. Sound good?"

"It does. Again, as long as we ensure that it doesn't get in the way of the primary story I'm here to cover, it sounds very good."

"Wonderful. I'm extraordinarily proud of the work we've accomplished, and I'm eager to see it through a fresh set of eyes. You can even collect a few samples to take back if you like, as long as you're willing to go through the hassle of clearing them once we reach Earth. Maybe that will convince Kai to curb her lawyers."

She laughed. "Maybe. The one who would really be interested, however, is my brother. I don't think Joe has a litigious bone in his body, but his curiosity is boundless."

"As I believe I said when we met, I am an open book. In an ideal world, science would be cooperative, not split off into little fiefdoms. My firm ceased doing any sort of medical research long ago, and I seriously doubt Jonas Labs is planning to become a competitor for KTI."

"You sound like Joe." In fact, it was so close to what Joe had said that she wondered for a moment if Kolya *didn't* have a bug in Joe's breakroom.

"Given what I know of your brother, I'll take that as a high compliment. But if I am to remain an open book, I should probably admit that I have an ulterior motive for including you on the Ehden trip."

"And what might that ulterior motive be?"

"I have an exceptionally busy schedule over the next two weeks, and it might be my only chance to spend more time with you."

With those last words, he leaned in to kiss her. It was a well-practiced move, with a pause just long enough to allow her to move away if she wasn't interested…although, given the tight confines of the room, if she had moved more than a couple of inches, her head would have smacked into the storage area over the bed.

It was a well-practiced *kiss*, too… but that didn't make it any less pleasurable. His hand was firm, but gentle against her neck, his tongue lightly tracing her lower lip before he pulled away.

"Another confession. I have been wanting to do that since the night we were at Della Luna. But I thought you might feel a little odd about it, given Kai's…" He shrugged, searching for words. Judging from his expression, Claire's mother hadn't held back when she told him off.

"Kai's vitriol?" She laughed. "The legendary wrath of Kai? Believe me, I am *not* worried about my mother. My path and hers parted irrevocably when I had the audacity to switch majors in college. She already had an executive office picked out for me at Jonas Labs. Probably even had the furniture ordered. I really don't care if I piss her off. It won't be the first time—she's hated every guy I ever dated. Also, a…friend of mine told me I should have a little fun on this trip. Lighten up a bit." She didn't add *break a few hearts*, even though she was definitely hearing Wyatt's parting words in her head. "And, to be honest, you're not quite what I expected."

"Should I translate *not quite what you expected* to mean *not a total asshole*?"

She laughed. "Those are *your* words, not mine."

"But you're not denying it."

"No. All I'm saying is as long as this"— Claire motioned between the two of them—"doesn't interfere with the work I'm here to do, I don't think it's a problem. How about we just see where things go?"

"That sounds like an excellent plan." When he reached the door, he hesitated and looked back. "Listen, you're obviously worried that these people have connected you to this defector you interviewed. And now I'm worried, too. Would you be willing to call reception about ten minutes before you plan to go out to dinner, to the gym, or wherever? I'll have Macek assign someone from his team—plainclothes, so no one will know. It will be like you're out with a friend, only…if you *should* run into trouble, that friend will be armed with a stun weapon and a drone jamming device."

Claire sighed. "Or…I could just stay here in my room. It's only for what? Forty-eight hours, maybe a little more? Macek said it's a three-person team and all of them are probably needed to search for whoever brought that device on board."

"Are you sure?"

"I'm *sure*. I was supposed to have lunch with Brodnik and the team tomorrow, but I'm quite certain I was only included as a formality. I'll tell her I'm feeling off and ask for a rain check once we're at Daedalus."

After Kolya left, she pushed the service cart into the corner and poured the last bit of the wine into her glass. It was hard not to laugh, because Macek had, in the end, gotten exactly what he wanted. Claire would be in her quarters, away from the other passengers.

If bad cop and good cop don't yield the desired result, send in sexy cop.

On the other hand, she had gotten what she wanted, too. Her message was delivered to Rowan, who would contact Wyatt, who would contact Joe. There was an unexpected bonus, too. Bernard would be delighted that, in addition to the exclusive on the hidden chamber, the *Post* would also have detailed, in-depth information about stage six when their competitors were all still parroting what Kolya gave them at the KTI press conference.

And if she had a harmless fling along the way, that was simply icing on the cake.

No hearts would be broken on either side. But Claire would be able to report back to Wyatt that she'd had *fun*...and let him make of that whatever the hell he liked.

TWENTY-ONE

THE PORTER GLANCED at Claire's daypack and shook her head.

"Sorry, miss. Safety protocols require that everything be stored *inside* your luggage. No handbags, backpacks, or personal items of any sort for this stage of the trip. Everything will be delivered to…" She glanced down at the list. "To your suite at the Red Dahlia. You can use the viewscreen here in your room while you wait, and your thumb scan will work if you need to purchase anything once you're inside Ares Station."

Claire sighed and opened the suitcase to begin rearranging her things.

"That's a *really* nice hotel," the porter said. "I'm saving up credits to stay there for my twenty-first birthday. I don't know if you've looked at it in the tourist information, but the Red Dahlia is shaped like a giant flower and each of the petals is a balcony that looks out over Lake Marta."

"It sounds very nice." Claire had definitely seen pictures—it was hard to miss the giant red dahlia inside the dome—but the balcony bit was news to her.

She managed to squeeze everything into the single case. It was a close call, though, thanks in part to the unopened bottle of wine she'd packed. Kolya had apparently decided to send treats as compensation for her solitary confinement, although he hadn't seen fit to stop by and break up the monotony. Each morning, there had been a rose on her breakfast tray. At lunch, the tray held a tiny box of Della Luna chocolates. A full bottle of wine arrived each night with dinner, and it had ended up being one bottle more than she was able to consume in such a short time span.

"You're on shuttle eight, seat 1C," the porter said when she handed over the bag. "That group will board in a little over an hour. Please proceed to the security checkpoint no more than thirty minutes prior to your scheduled departure. They'll send notices over the comm, though, so you don't need to worry about keeping an eye on the clock. If you're wearing enhanced lenses or have any bionic prosthetics or other upgrades, be sure to let them know when you get to security."

Claire thanked her and sat back down on the bed. After a couple of minutes, she turned on the viewscreen. She had already spent far too much time staring at the thing during her solitary confinement, much as she had during her first week on board the *Ares Prime*. That first time around, she'd watched the Earth gradually morph into a tiny blue marble in the ship's equivalent of the rearview mirror. This time, she kept peeking ahead to see if she could make out any new features on the *red* marble that grew larger every minute as the countdown clock on the ship's information channel moved toward zero.

That clock, synched to their expected docking at Ares Station, currently stood at just under seven minutes. The station, which was positioned about six thousand kilometers from Mars, had almost the same orbit as Phobos, the planet's now-defunct primary moon. Phobos had been intentionally demolished in the first stage of terraforming, leaving only tiny, distant Deimos. Well, not *that* distant, she thought. The moon was about fifteen times farther away from Earth, but it was also about three hundred times the size, so it was all a matter of perspective.

Some early plans for Mars had suggested using Phobos as a moon base, along the same lines as Earth's own lunar station. There were even proposals for a space elevator since the same area of Phobos faces Mars at all times. But closer inspection had revealed that the surface was much too unstable to use for that purpose. Phobos was essentially a dark, potato-shaped pile of rubble. It also had an unstable orbit that moved it a few centimeters closer to Mars each year. The Ares Consortium, in the pre-KTI days, had justified the moon's demolition by noting that the Martian gravity would eventually turn Phobos into a debris field anyway. They were just speeding up what would happen in the long run. And while that was true, with thirty million years being the average prediction for how long Phobos had left, Claire thought the words *in the long run* were doing some very heavy lifting in that assessment.

At the moment, most of her viewscreen was taken up by the docking bays. Two ships were currently in port, and the *Ares Prime* was now moving toward one of the four open slots that were visible. Even though the station's lasers had slowed the ship down to little more than a crawl, it still looked like they were about to crash into the side. The view made Claire a trifle nervous, much like the antsy, helpless feeling she always got inside a car that was negotiating itself into a tight parking spot. Not that she was one of those who would prefer to park herself —that would be an utter disaster—but she still didn't like to watch.

She picked up the headset on the nightstand and navigated to the news digest on the ship's information channel, hoping there might be something of interest. It was mostly fluff pieces, along with sports scores from the previous day. Nothing new about the situation with the Flock. She'd strongly suspected that would be the case, but still felt compelled to check. Was Shepherd in his quarters doing the same thing? It wouldn't have surprised her.

There was also nothing about Rejuvesce, but she was much less concerned on that front now. Kolya had been true to his word. Both of the articles about the Flock that he'd promised had been delivered to her tablet the next morning, along with a third article from six days earlier (*Medical Breakthrough Predicted to Add Decades to Human Lifespan*) and a personal note:

No wonder you were combing through the news. Extend my congratulations to Kai and your brother and ask them to put me on the waiting list. ~ AK

That had given Claire a nice laugh. If Kolya planned to take Rejuvesce, he'd better order it under an alias. Otherwise, her mother would see to it that they shipped him placebos. Or worse.

The article itself was essentially a Jonas Labs press release with a photograph of Kai at the launch party and extended quotes from her speech announcing the release. Miracle of miracles, there was also a quote from Joe. "So happy to finally share this one with the world." Ten entire words. Claire thought that might be a record.

She had been surprised to see Wyatt's name in both bylines of the articles about the Flock, along with two other *Post* reporters—a woman who usually covered national security and...ugh...Bryce Avery. The general gist of the first piece was that the Earth Watch Alliance hadn't merely split into two camps but had fractured into four separate factions. A "source close to the matter" claimed that Tobias Shepherd had gone underground—figuratively true, she supposed, even though it was in reality the exact opposite of what the man had done. In Shepherd's absence, two people who had served in the loose hierarchy of the organization for the past decade had begun squabbling for control. Now, however, they were losing ground to a third individual, Corbin Drexel, who had appeared on the scene earlier in the year. The anonymous source—Claire thought it was most likely Bryce's buddy, Devin—claimed that Drexel was the person pushing the Flock toward more drastic forms of protest, telling the followers that Shepherd's half measures were worse than doing nothing at all. At least a third of the members were still loyal to Shepherd, but a lot of them were beginning to think that their erstwhile leader had perhaps been killed as part of the power struggle...or that he'd taken off on the mothership and left the rest of them behind.

The second article focused primarily on scattered reports that droves of Flock members were leaving the group. Several hundred had disappeared, some of them rumored to be starting their own commune and others attempting to return to their previous lives. One of the latter group had filed a lawsuit in hopes of getting back the property that she'd signed over to the EWA five years earlier. Whoever was in charge of the finances now, probably this Drexel guy, must not have been happy about that because the woman claimed that she was now receiving death threats.

Claire had no clue what Wyatt had made of the information about the drone, since she hadn't heard anything from him and hadn't contacted him. She'd known from the beginning that if she sent him coded messages through Rowan, he'd be smart enough not to try and contact her directly. Ro had sent another brief message the next day saying that she'd informed Siggy's dad of the bug problem, and that he was looking into it, after which she moved on to chatting about Jemma and other issues.

The only thing Claire wasn't certain about was whether Ro had passed along her concern that the drone belonged to the Flock. That had been the main theme of her conversation with Ro the night before she left, but given Ro's position at the time, she might simply have assumed that Claire had read something while on board that led her to think the drones *might* be weaponized. It was even possible that Ro would dismiss it once again as an overreaction, but Claire was still fairly sure she would mention the Flock connection to Wyatt, if only so she could grouse about Claire being an overprotective mother hen.

Neither of them would have any reason to suspect that Shepherd was on board the *Ares Prime*, but there were records for off-world travel and Wyatt knew the channels to tap to get that information. It might take a few days, but unless Tobias Shepherd was traveling under a false name, Wyatt could easily put the pieces together. Which meant there was a decent chance that Kolya would figure out Claire was the one who'd tipped him off, even though she and Wyatt were basically on radio silence for the duration of the trip.

Although, she really wasn't sure what difference it would make if word got out. It certainly wouldn't put Shepherd in any additional danger. The folks with the nasty drones who wanted the man dead obviously already *knew* where he was. Plus, Wyatt could easily have known already. It had been obvious from their discussion at Media Res that he had sources who kept him informed about the labor disputes on Mars, so it seemed likely that he tracked lunar groups, as well. As Paul had noted, the debate was on the schedule before the ship left Tranquility Base and Shepherd had been out and about during the time he was there. The man's appearance was nondescript enough that it was entirely possible that he'd gone unremarked by his fellow protestors, especially if they'd only seen him in that bulky spacesuit. It was also possible that Shepherd had gone out with that EWA sign in order to signal to his followers that he was alive and well.

Claire navigated to games and played sudoku for a while as a distraction while the arrival clock in the upper right of the display continued to tick away the final minutes. The bed shuddered very faintly about a second after the clock reached zero—so faintly that she might not even have noticed if she wasn't braced for impact—and then a chirpy feminine voice came through the comm system.

"Welcome to Ares Station. We will begin boarding passengers of shuttle one in fifteen minutes. If you are traveling on shuttle one, please make your way to the security checkpoint now. We hope you have enjoyed your voyage on the *Ares Prime* and look forward to serving you again on your return trip to Earth."

About a dozen puzzles later, the initial boarding call for shuttle eight was announced. Claire made her way to the security gate as instructed, realizing halfway there that one of the guards was following her, no doubt at Kolya's behest. The guard stayed about ten paces back, reversing course only after she reached the young woman at the gate.

"Do you wear any prosthetics?" the woman asked.

"No."

"What about bionic enhancements, including lenses?"

"No."

The guard ticked off a number of other questions, several of which Claire was pretty sure had been added to the roster since they left Tranquility Base. Once all of these were answered to the woman's satisfaction, Claire was ushered into the scanning booth. After about thirty seconds of standing perfectly still, the opposite door opened, and she was told to proceed down the hallway to the station's main concourse.

When Claire emerged from the hallway, the first thing she noticed was the number of people. It was much busier than she had expected, given that they were admitting the *Ares Prime* passengers in small groups. Apparently there had been no such precaution with the other ships. There were probably five hundred people in total, maybe more, with some gathered at the food vendors and others lounging in chairs in front of a gigantic, curved window that looked out on Mars. Most seemed to be workers, but there were a few family groups and one cluster that appeared to be high school students.

The second thing she noticed was the view. And that was the moment that everything became *real*.

You'd think that three weeks on the ship, watching Earth recede and Mars loom ever larger would have prepared her, but staring out through that window at the Valles Marineris, a vast labyrinth of crevasses that made the Grand Canyon look like a roadside ditch, was when it fully hit home.

In just over an hour, she would be *down there*, on the surface.

TWENTY-TWO

CLAIRE WASN'T sure how long she stood awestruck, gaping like a fish out of water at the view outside the station. What finally shook her out of it was hearing someone calling her name.

She turned to see Brodnik standing on the other side of the concourse next to Ben Pelzer, the fourth member of the research team, who towered over his colleague by about a foot. Brodnik waved Claire over. She had planned to go straight to Gate B to prepare for boarding—another thing that would have marked her as a complete neophyte since they had at least twenty minutes left—but she headed over to join them instead.

"Are you feeling better?" Brodnik asked.

"Much. I don't know if it was due to stress or from staring into the lights during the debate, but something gave me a nasty migraine. Are Kim and Chelsea on a different shuttle?"

"No," Ben said, nodding toward the food stalls located at the back of the station. "They're just loading up on snacks before we take off. Everything's way more expensive inside Daedalus and our daily meal allowance from the university won't cover much more than breakfast, lunch, and dinner."

"Why aren't you stocking up, too?"

Amusement twinkled in his dark eyes. "Because I am older and wiser. I planned ahead and filled my luggage with a bunch of the freebies from the *Ares Prime*. Something to remember for your next trip…although I guess you don't need to worry about things like that, do you?"

Claire had actually done something quite similar with the wine that Kolya sent but decided to keep it to herself. If Pelzer wanted to think of her as the idle, wasteful rich, that was fine with her.

"Before they get back, though, let me say I'm in full agreement with Laura."

"In agreement about what?" Claire asked, even as Brodnik shot him a look that very clearly said he shouldn't go there.

"About the accommodations. Kim and Chelsea can snark all they want about you being too friendly with Kolya, but this is my *fourth* Mars trip. The first three times were on worker transports. Those bunks are not designed for someone my height, or my age, for that matter. There are usually four people to a room, and I always arrive exhausted. The *Prime* is one incredibly sweet ride in comparison. Plus, we were told yesterday that our hotel voucher from the university would be honored at the Red Dahlia this time instead of the lower tier accommodations researchers are usually given. So, personally, I say thank you very much for arranging the upgrades. You can travel with us *anytime*."

"I didn't arrange any of it," Claire said. "Couldn't have since I wouldn't even have known what to ask for. It's probably a perk connected to finding the chamber, so save your thanks for Kolya or..."

She had been about to say *Stasia*, but suddenly had a weird sense of reality folding in on itself as she heard the woman speaking behind her. When she turned to look, however, the only thing Claire saw was the student group she'd noticed earlier standing around a holographic information portal welcoming them to Ares Station.

Once she was a few steps closer the hologram came into focus. And while it didn't look *exactly* like Stasia, it could easily have been her slightly younger and more enthusiastic sister. The voice was definitely hers.

"Fifty-seven years ago this May," the avatar said, "Commander Eva Daniels and the crew of the Ares Six became the first people to walk upon another planet. To paraphrase the words of twentieth-century space pioneer Neil Armstrong, it was one small step for a human and a giant leap for humankind. It took many years of training and more than eight months of travel in a tiny module for the crew of seven to reach the Red Planet. For the next three months, they made their home in that module, venturing out in spacesuits to conduct a wide array of experiments and construct a small habitat to shield the next group of explorers from the hostile Martian environment."

The scenes of Daniels and her crew that had been playing on the screen behind Virtual Stasia now morphed into images of the various ships that had been used in the years since.

"When travel to Mars first began in 2035, missions could only be scheduled once every twenty-six months when Mars and Earth are aligned. Today, thanks to advances in photonic propulsion, the journey can take anywhere from a mere twenty days to four weeks, and there is just a single, four-month window every two years when travel between the two planets is impractical. Accommodations now range from basic transportation to the very pinnacle of luxury. Nearly a hundred and fifty thousand people—researchers, entrepreneurs, guestworkers, colonists, and a growing number of tourists—have now made the trip."

A whiff of roasted meat and spice hit Claire's nose. She glanced behind her and saw that Kimura and Chelsea were back, holding bags of packaged food. Kim was also munching a chicken kabob, or maybe it was satay, and watching the orientation spiel with his usual smirk.

"In 2039, the Ares Consortium was established in conjunction with the United Nations to set ground rules for international cooperation and colonization. A colony was set up in the Tarsus sector to oversee mining for the raw materials needed to begin the initial steps toward making the planet habitable. In 2046, workers laid the last meter of superconducting wire along the equator–over twenty-one thousand kilometers in all–to create an artificial magnetosphere that would help shield the surface from radiation. By the mid-2060s, three experimental colonies had been built near geothermal hotspots that were harnessed for most energy needs. The two largest colonies were mostly underground, constructed inside existing craters, each spanning less than fifteen square kilometers."

One of the students raised a hand. The hologram turned toward the girl and said to please hold all questions until the end, promising that she would be first.

"A third experimental above-ground colony was built of ice and bamboo, which grows quickly and is well suited to the Martian soil. It was still a fairly spartan existence, but these colonies were largely self-sustaining within a decade, growing their own food and producing necessities like water, oxygen, and fuel. Currently, nearly thirty thousand people from all over the world make their home in one of the five Martian colonies, either as permanent residents or as guest workers."

"And now… a word from our sponsor," Kim said in a low voice, around a bite of his meat stick.

"In 2071," the avatar continued, "the Ares Consortium contracted with Kolya Terraforming to begin creation of a much larger crater habitat as a proof of concept for their proposal to terraform the planet as a whole. Daedalus City—over seven hundred square kilometers—opened to colonists and researchers in the early 2080s. Venturing onto the surface of the planet outside the dome is still possible only while wearing a spacesuit. According to CEO Anton Kolya, however, that could change within a decade as the organization moves ahead with the next phases of terraforming. Five short years ago, we welcomed our first group of tourists. Just over twenty thousand people have now visited Daedalus City, which is quickly becoming *the* destination for discerning travelers looking for the vacation of a lifetime."

The presentation wrapped up with a cheery invitation to learn more about the terraforming effort while visiting

Daedalus and then Virtual Stasia turned to the girl who had raised her hand.

"How far are we from Earth right now?" the girl asked.

"Two hundred and forty-four million kilometers. Sometimes, the distance between Ares Station and Earth is shorter and sometimes it's longer, depending on where Earth is in its orbit compared to Mars."

Another hand shot up, this time from a little boy of about nine or ten, who was standing with his family. "Are there any animals living outside the domes?"

The hologram gave the boy a warm smile and said, "Well, that depends on how you define the word *animal*. If you include microscopic life, then the answer is yes. A number of extremophiles—that is, lifeforms that thrive in extreme environments—were introduced in stage three and are currently doing quite nicely outside the domes. You can see a few examples of these lifeforms on the screen behind me. Some of these microbes even have jobs of a sort since they were genetically engineered to help with the terraforming effort. One of them, for example, was modified to emit perfluorocarbons that are helping to increase the surface temperature of the planet. The Martian surface is not yet capable of supporting more complex life outside of the domes but some of these deficiencies will be addressed in the next two stages of KTI's terraforming process. Are there other questions?"

There was silence for a moment and then one of the older boys with the school group said, "Yeah, I was wondering if maybe I could terraform *you*?"

The suggestive tone left no doubt what he meant, even if his words didn't make sense literally. An adult with the group whacked the kid on the back of the head with the papers she was holding, as his classmates dissolved into laughter.

The avatar gave the boy a look of amused sympathy. "I'm sorry, but I can't help you there. Perhaps you should check out our extensive digital library in Daedalus City. There are several

guides to human sexuality, including one for complete begin-
ners that you may find very useful."

That provoked even more laughter. After it died off, a man
Claire was pretty sure she'd seen on board the *Ares Prime* raised
his hand.

"Yeah," the man said. "Many experts argue that KTI's
projections for stages six and beyond are wildly optimistic. This
has some investors concerned. Why should we believe KTI can
actually meet these benchmarks?"

"Our history," was the avatar's quick response. "The first
five stages of the terraforming project have exceeded all expec-
tations. For example, while the atmosphere still hasn't reached
the point where we'd be willing to risk people going beyond the
domes without a suit, the atmospheric pressure on most of the
planet is now well above the Armstrong limit—the point at
which exposed bodily fluids boil away. That milestone wasn't
predicted to be achieved until at least 2110. The Global
Magnetic Shield constructed during stage four is also doing a
much better than expected job of preserving the fledgling
atmosphere created in stages one through three, effectively
shielding the planet from deadly levels of cosmic radiation."

"But at what cost?" This was from Kimura.

Brodnik groaned, giving Claire the impression that this
wasn't the first time Kim had joined in the question-and-answer
session. He hadn't bothered to raise his hand, and the hologram
was scanning the audience trying to locate the point from which
the voice had originated.

"Wouldn't the money be better spent on the only planet that
actually supports human life at present?" Kim continued. "Earth
definitely needs the help. The cost of the orbital mirrors in stage
one alone exceeded the annual GDP of most countries."

"Your question is based on the false assumption that these
goals are separate," the avatar answered. "Efforts to terraform
Mars help protect the Earth, as well. For example, the
extremophiles deployed during stage three were genetically

designed specifically for the terraforming effort, but they have been used in wastewater treatment on Earth for the past thirty years, dramatically lowering the rate of CO_2 increase."

"Come on, man," Ben said, tugging at Kim's arm. "Stop trolling the virtual help. You're as bad as the horny kid over there. Finish your food so we can head to the gate."

Kim gave him a humorless grin as he pulled the last chunk of meat off the wooden skewer with his teeth. "Just doing my small part to keep them honest. But you're right. It's a bit like spitting into the ocean."

TWENTY-THREE

THEY BOARDED the shuttle a few minutes later. It was small, with just sixteen seats, four rows of four, and a narrow aisle down the center. Kim and Brodnik strapped themselves into chairs in the first row, across the aisle on Claire's left. Chelsea and Ben were in the row behind them, and various faces she'd seen on the *Ares Prime* gradually filed in to take the other seats, except for the one next to her and a few near the back.

Claire was seated directly behind what appeared to be a windshield, although she thought it was more likely a viewscreen. There was no sign of a pilot, so maybe the shuttles were fully automated. She wasn't sure *why* that bothered her, but it kind of did, much as the sight of the ship docking had unnerved her earlier. It was silly. There was far less out here to navigate around than there was on a street in DC, and she wouldn't think of hiring a car with a human driver.

"Still can't believe they took our devices," Brodnik said over her shoulder to Chelsea. "I'm beginning to think you were right."

"I *was* right." Chelsea flicked an annoyed look in Kim's direction, leaving no doubt about who had been asserting that she was wrong. "I know what I saw."

"So … this isn't the usual procedure?" Claire asked.

"Well, I can't say for sure about the luxury ships," Brodnik said. "Maybe it's standard security protocol. On the other transports, though, they didn't make you turn over your personal communication devices. We even hauled our own bags onto the shuttle."

Ben agreed. "Bags and equipment heavy enough to require a maglev cart on my first trip. Like I said, this has been a sweet ride."

Claire was about to press further and ask precisely what Chelsea thought she'd seen when the rear door chimed, closing behind the last passenger. Looking over her shoulder, she saw Tobias Shepherd slip into one of the two remaining seats.

Kim was watching, too, and he started laughing. "Oh no, Chels. Sure you don't want to demand passage on a different shuttle? You never know...." He pressed the pads of his fingers together and mimed an explosion.

Chelsea flipped him off, and Brodnik jabbed him with her elbow.

It was an interesting exchange, one Claire definitely wanted to follow up on later when other passengers weren't within earshot. For now, though, she followed the instructions of the voice that had come over the comm system and turned her attention to the front of the ship.

A few seconds later, the docking bay belched the shuttle out of its slot. As it coasted away from the station, a video version of the holographic not-quite-Stasia Claire had seen inside proceeded to acquaint the passengers with the shuttle's safety features.

"Our estimated flight time to Daedalus is forty-six minutes," she said at the end. "Feel free to utilize the shuttle's extensive media collection during your trip."

Chelsea leaned forward and hissed, "Did you hear *that*, Kim?"

It was a fair point. Without personal devices, the last part of the orientation made no sense. There were no individual screens at their seats, just the massive one that spanned the front of the ship, showing their destination.

"Proves absolutely nothing," Kim said.

Chelsea slunk back into her seat. "Proves you're absolutely full of shit."

He smiled, then reclined his seat slightly and closed his eyes. Claire thought a nap fit right in with the man's jaded act. This was all *so very* routine for him. No biggie. Just about to land on another planet. Again.

Her own excitement, however, grew steadily over the next half hour. She kept her eyes glued to the viewscreen, wishing she had her camera to document this part of the journey for her viewers. Wishing she could share the moment with Joe or Wyatt or Jemma or anyone else who might understand her enthusiasm. She *did* hear a couple of *oohs* and *aahs* from the people a few rows back when they first spotted the Tharsis range. But she'd never spoken with any of those people and couldn't see their faces, so it hardly counted as sharing the moment.

Aside from Brodnik's team, the only familiar face on the ship was Tobias Shepherd and as the shuttle cruised across Daedalia Planum, Claire's curiosity finally got the better of her. She turned in her seat so that she could see the man and was surprised to find him wearing a look of wonder that mirrored her own feelings. He caught her eye, and a wide, genuine smile transformed his face. Only for a moment, though, before his nervous eyes once again darted away.

By the time Claire looked back at the viewscreen, the dome was on the horizon, and she was hit with a childhood memory of flying into Las Vegas on a family vacation. One minute they were over the mostly barren terrain of the desert, the seemingly unending stretches of sand and rock broken only by the occasional highway or solar farm. Then, in the blink of an eye, the plane was flying over massive buildings of every imaginable sort and lush pockets of greenery.

On Mars, the transition was even starker than it had been in Vegas. Aside from the thin scaffolding holding together the transparent sheets of organosilica aerogel that sheltered Daedalus from the harsher environment outside, the dome itself was barely visible. An unbroken stretch of red sand and rock led up to the dome. Inside the border, however, everything was a riot of color and light. A wide strip of grass, shrubs, and flowers pushed up against the inner edge as if straining to break free of the boundary. The central avenue—lined with dozens of hotels, shops, restaurants, and attractions—ended about a quarter of the way in at the shore of a large, oval lake. Other roads radiated out from the lake like spokes of a partially flattened wheel, ending at a street circumnavigating the dome. Beyond the lake, taking up about four-fifths of the enclosed area, were dozens of small farms, orchards, and communities.

The Red Dahlia was a spinning, tilted flower perched on a stationary platform near the lake's center. Each crimson petal—each balcony, according to Claire's porter back on the *Ares Prime*—was outlined with a narrow strip of iridescent red light that reflected in the water below.

She had seen pictures of Daedalus City, of course, but looking at it now, Claire realized that aside from the stark contrast in terrain, it reminded her less of Vegas than of pictures she'd seen of the Disney theme parks. That was due, in part, to the various hotels and other buildings that were in a constant state of spin to emulate something closer to Earth's gravity. It was dizzying to watch, almost like amusement park rides that were synced up to move in unison. And the coordination didn't end there. Unlike Vegas, which had been created helter-skelter over many decades by many different people, every inch of Daedalus City had been planned for maximum visual effect.

Kolya had created his own version of the Magic Kingdom. Claire could almost imagine Mickey Mouse marching down the central boulevard, followed by a big brass band.

From across the aisle, Brodnik whispered, "Look, guys! There it is."

"You're right," Ben said. "Oh. My. God."

The excitement in their voices took Claire by surprise. This was far from their first expedition to Mars, and Daedalus City would have been open for business for at least the past two trips. And how could they just now be noticing what she had seen for several minutes? Maybe they'd been napping, too?

Then she realized they weren't talking about Daedalus City at all. They were looking out the other side of the shuttle at another, much smaller dome a few kilometers beyond the landing pads.

This one contained no buildings, no greenery, no lights, or other signs of life. It was just a dome with a single object in the center—the plain black box they'd just traveled two hundred and forty-four million kilometers to see.

The sight of the Icarus chamber had a sudden, chilling effect on Claire's mood. Her annoying little internal voice that had delighted in pointing out all of the reasons the trip was a bad idea had fallen silent for the past few weeks, aside from piping up briefly after the drone attacked Shepherd. But it came roaring back now at full volume as a sense of foreboding settled into her stomach like a lead weight.

———

WEEKS LATER, when Claire was back on Earth, she would stumble upon a new KTI ad for Martian tourism and have a vivid flashback to that feeling of dread. Had it been a premonition? Or was her mind creating patterns after the fact in order to form a cohesive story?

Claire didn't know.

All she knew was that KTI was now touting an even more impressive safety record than ever. They'd updated the total number of tourists from twenty to twenty-*two* thousand and, according to the information following the asterisk at the bottom, there was still just that one pesky tourist death from a heart attack marring their otherwise unblemished record.

The new ad made no mention of the ten people who would die during her time on Mars, including two who were with

Claire on shuttle eight as it touched down that afternoon outside Daedalus City.

But technically, the statement was still accurate. KTI hadn't even needed to add another asterisk because none of the dead were *tourists*.

PART II: MARTIS FIRMA

FROM THE JOURNAL
OF EBERIN DAS

21.03.507

EIGHT CHILDREN, none of them more than six years of age, are taking turns spinning themselves around in circles in the play area near the community garden. They hold out their arms as they twirl around. There appear to be rules to guide their actions, because they evicted one little girl from the game after only three or four spins. She now sits on the hill opposite my own, a fellow observer of the game.

I couldn't tell what her infraction was, and her banishment seemed very unfair to me. The girl must have known what she did that was against the rules, though, because she accepted her fate with good grace.

Rules are important. Rules help bind a society together. Even small children can learn this.

But I do wonder whether she would have left the game so willingly had she not been familiar with those rules. Would she have trudged up the hill nevertheless, resigned to her role as a spectator? Or would she have argued with the girl who pointed and said she had to leave?

I, of course, will never have children of my own. Perhaps I would know the rules of their games if I did, and I would have a better idea what the girl had done to warrant her eviction.

Any memories I have of being a child myself have faded to the point that they are almost non-existent, like faint echoes of a dream. But I have spent many hours watching the children play here in the town commons where I often come to write these entries. And I believe that without an understanding of the rules, the girl would have at least questioned why her turn ended so soon.

People *need* to know the rules. Ideally, they should have a say in making them. Power differentials being what they are, that's probably too much to hope for at this time. But at a bare minimum, they deserve to understand what the rules are and what they risk if they decide to break them, or in this case, if they decide to *continue* breaking them.

Otherwise, the whole damned thing is rigged. It's not a fair game, not even a game at all. It's nothing more than a convenient fiction that preserves the status quo and protects those who made the rules, who willfully kept the others in ignorance of those rules, and who have the overwhelming power to punish.

(Confidence interval: 92.1%)

ONE

CLAIRE NEVER SLEPT well the first night in a new place. No matter how comfortable the bed, or how safe and luxurious the accommodations, she was lucky to catch more than a few hours. She had, therefore, been wide awake for her first timeslip on the planet itself, finally nodding off around two. Her time awake had been put to good use, going over some revisions to the intro script for unveiling the chamber and sending a message back home to Ro and Jemma. She also sent a short note to Bernard. *Finally here. Tomorrow will be a very big day for all of us.* Hopefully, he would read between the lines and interpret that as *hold the presses*.

Given the lack of sleep, in a perfect world of her own design Claire would have spent that first morning on Mars sitting on her little red petal balcony, feet up, coffee in hand, taking in the odd mix of scenery under the sepia sky. It wasn't *really* a balcony, of course, but more of a sunroom enclosed behind a curved viewscreen like the ones on Tranquility Base and the *Ares Prime* that disguised the fact that you were inside a spinning top.

Here, though, you could change the view on the screen, with options ranging from various static scenes outside the hotel to a leisurely panoramic tour from a vantage point about three stories off the ground. If you found a view you liked, you could freeze at that spot, and watch people outside stroll by. There was even a daredevil option where you could see the *actual* scenery outside your room. The porter who had helped with Claire's bags the night before had cautioned her to take a seat before trying that, and it turned out to be very good advice. While the view as the room tilted upward was kind of cool, coming down was disconcertingly like being the pilot of a plane headed nose-first toward the ground. One round of that, and she had quickly switched back to the level, leisurely panorama.

Atmospheric controls delivered a gentle, faintly fragrant breeze to the little pod. It wasn't nearly as relaxing as the lanai at the condo she had rented in Hawaii a few years back, mostly because she knew it wasn't real. But it was convincing enough that it would have been a nice place to spend the morning getting her bearings after weeks on a spaceship... if not for the fact that Brodnik and the others were chomping at the bit, raring to get out to the dome where the chamber was housed.

So Claire drank the last of her coffee and headed down to the executive pavilion where they were supposed to meet at nine. It was still a bit early, but she thought it would give her a few minutes to check out the piano that Kolya had mentioned. As it turned out, however, she was the last to arrive. That meant the others were extra early, but it still made her feel like she was late.

Red Dahlia's executive pavilion was a much larger area than Claire had expected—two or three times the size of your average upscale hotel lobby. The far side of the room was clearly devoted to business, with a row of desks and viewscreens, one of which was on and spooling a constant stream of data. Probably stock market figures, although she couldn't tell from a distance. A sleek red granite conference table with at least thirty chairs sat at the back, next to a second bank of elevators and a private patio that stretched out all the way to the water.

The side on which she entered was more like a grand hotel lobby, with a red, dahlia-shaped conversation pit facing the massive stone fireplace. Dozens of small sofas and chairs were scattered about behind it. Above, on the mezzanine level, was a well-stocked bar (which was possibly also a juice bar, given that there were customers at nine a.m.), along with bar tables, and as Kolya had promised, a gorgeous red baby grand. Her fingers itched to hit the keys, but it would have to wait.

Two maglev trams, identical to the one that had carried her to the hotel the night before, were parked in the private driveway outside. A third vehicle was just behind the trams. It was similar to a flatbed truck, with some sort of heavy equipment on the back under a thick green tarp. The tarp seemed rather pointless to Claire. It wasn't as if there was any chance of being hit by a sudden rainstorm, and even a dust storm wasn't possible inside the domes.

All four members of Brodnik's team were dressed in matching jumpsuits and holding helmets, so she was beginning to suspect that she'd missed a memo and wondering if she should have taken Stasia up on her offer to ride over with the KTI crew. They were planning to arrive a little later, after they got the signal that the chamber was almost open. But Claire wanted at least a few minutes to get a sense of the thing and decide if she needed to add any details to her prepared script.

Claire was also getting weird vibes from Stasia. At first, she thought the woman was annoyed about her comment to Paul concerning the whole good-cop/bad-cop situation the night of the debate. But she was now thinking it was more a matter of the uneasy balance between reporting the facts about this discovery and spinning them for maximum corporate gain. Her journalistic training insisted on the former and Stasia's job required the latter, so maybe it was inevitable that they would clash over how to present this find to the public.

Per their agreement, Claire had sent Stasia a copy of the intro they would be recording just before the Icarus chamber was opened. She had also included rough drafts of the questions she planned to ask Brodnik, the other team members, and Kolya, in interviews that she'd be conducting over the next few days. After several years at the *Atlantic Post*, Claire was used to having an editor and being told to make changes. She definitely didn't think her words were sacrosanct. But the changes Bernard wanted were almost always intended to clarify, not to muddy the waters, and even in his case, she occasionally pushed back. But when she'd pushed back on several of what Stasia called *suggestions*, Claire had discovered that they were a lot more like demands. For example, Stasia was adamant that under no circumstances was Claire to mention Icarus Camp or Icaria. All she could say about the location where the chamber was found was that it was within twenty-five hundred kilometers of Daedalus, which covered a huge chunk of the planet. Maybe it was a security issue, but Claire could already hear the howls of protest that she was going to get from Bernard.

Stasia was currently standing off to one side with Brodnik, Ben, and three men Claire didn't recognize. The men were all wearing hardhats. Rather than intrude, she reluctantly headed over to a cluster of chairs where Kimura and Chelsea were waiting.

"That's yours." Kim nodded down at a yellow duffel on the floor near his feet. "This Stasia person wants us in pressure suits."

"But … we're going to be inside a dome, right?"

"They're also for hazmat," Chelsea said. "Apparently, this is a precaution until the chamber is open and the KTI scientists have a chance to let the KTI lawyers know that there's nothing hazardous inside. Then we'll be given the okay to work without them." Her expression made it abundantly clear that she thought this explanation was rubbish. "The good news is that they upgraded us to these spiffy biosuits. But from everything I've heard they're still going to be wicked hot."

Kim, who was tapping his fingers against the helmet he was holding, shook his head not in disagreement, but in shared annoyance. "I don't really care about the stupid suits. But as I was just telling Chelsea, I distinctly recall Kolya saying his team of scientists sent their little sensor in through the hole we drilled on our last trip, in order to make sure there were no lifeforms in the Icarus chamber other than the ones previously identified as native to the planet."

"Yeah," Claire said. "I remember that, too. It's why the Ares Consortium agreed that stage six could go forward on schedule."

Kim seemed mildly surprised that she was backing up his story. "Exactly. But if this sensor of theirs checked the chamber out so thoroughly—as it must have, in order to make that very broad and definitive claim—then shouldn't it have identified any potential hazards?"

"You would think so," Claire admitted.

"I *do* think so. And that leaves us with two options, at least as far as I can see. Option one: this protective gear is a bit of security theater designed to make Kolya's legal hounds happy. That's possible, I suppose, especially since you guys will have the cameras rolling the second the thing is opened so you can do the big reveal that there are symbols inside. Also, even with the stack of legal papers we signed, if one of us got sick, we could make a reasonable case for negligence against KTI if we go in without a full biohazard check. The thing is even on *their* property now, rather than that of a contractor. Kolya has a lease on this section of Daedalia Planum for ninety-nine years or something ridiculous like that. Personally, though? I think it's option two. Kolya lied. They never actually checked for lifeforms."

"There's a third possibility," Chelsea said. "They *did* check, and they found something not previously discovered on Mars. At which point they promptly wiped it out in order to stay on schedule for stage six...and Kolya lied about *that*."

Kim nodded consideringly. "Either way, my money is on *Kolya lied*."

"Or," Claire said, "maybe there's a fourth possibility? It could just be *regular* theater. Or theatrical marketing if you prefer. I've gotten some strong signals that his publicity crew wants to play up the drama of cracking this thing open. Who knows what dangers lurk inside the mysterious Martian chamber?" She delivered this in a spooky, tremulous voice, remembering Jemma giggling as she said *maybe that's where the bug-monsters are hiding*. "I mean, Stasia is the one setting up the shots today. If this was one of my *Simple Science* segments, I'd stick to the facts, but if I were staging the opening for *dramatic* effect? I'd probably put us in the suits. It's a lot more suspenseful and official looking than everyone just standing around in jeans."

"Yeah, well I don't give a damn about building suspense or looking official," Chelsea said. "And I hate to be the one to tell you this, but your hair is going to be completely flat and that makeup you're wearing will be on your knees long before the cameras start rolling."

Claire gave her a pleasant smile, even though she didn't get the sense that Chelsea hated telling her that at all. In fact, she was pretty sure that Chelsea was hoping to get a good laugh out of the sight.

"Well, I guess it's a good thing I'll be wearing a helmet, right? The cameras are barely going to be on me and the folks watching something this momentous won't care one bit what I look like." Claire was tempted to add that they would probably have been doing this step in the puffsuits she'd seen them wearing when they first drilled into the chamber if Kolya had left it at Icarus Camp as Brodnik wanted. And they would be in suits soon anyway, for hours on end, once they arrived at Icarus to inspect the second chamber that the excavation team located when digging the first one out of the rock.

It didn't matter, either way. Claire had never known a reporter—male or female—who would travel to a shoot without makeup in their bag.

A few minutes later, after Stasia headed back upstairs and Claire pulled on her biosuit and boots, the five of them boarded one of the two trams and Brodnik instructed it to take them to

Dome Three. The workers Brodnik had been speaking to earlier piled into the truck and followed along behind them.

Instead of driving down the main strip that they had taken on the way to the hotel the night before, the tram shot out over the lake toward one of the narrower spoke roads that led to the perimeter loop Claire had spotted from the shuttle. She pulled the visor cam out of her daypack, adjusted it to fit over her helmet, and began recording. The others were chatting, but she could always edit it out later. The scenery on the ride to Dome Three wasn't as carefully orchestrated as what she had seen on the ride to the Red Dahlia the previous night, but she found it far more fascinating. Claire wasn't a botanist, or even a casual gardener. She would have a difficult time identifying most plants by name, and she did know there were some truly bizarre varieties on Earth—monkey-faced orchids, Venus flytraps, and corpse flowers, to name just a few. But the flowers and trees lining the perimeter road looked...well, they looked *alien* to her.

Most of the trees were similar to bamboo, which was one of the first crops grown on Mars. But the leaves were oversized, and they were a deeper green, bordering on black. Another tree had similarly dark but very shiny leaves that pointed upward from tightly furled branches toward a tall, rather phallic central spike covered with hundreds of small bulbous protrusions that looked a bit like eyes.

The plants that she had seen on the way into the city the previous night, on the other hand, had seemed like the ordinary sort you'd find in a landscaped municipal park or in an estate garden on Earth. The majority of the trees were conifers, but she'd also noticed a few oaks and other hardwoods. They were fairly small compared to their Earth counterparts, although it could simply be that Daedalus City hadn't been around long enough for much of the vegetation to reach its full height. She'd spotted some flowering trees, too—cherry, maybe?—and the grass surrounding the lake looked pretty much like the stuff her landscape service plopped down in front of her house just after she bought it.

It seemed like KTI's goal for a visitor's first impression to Daedalus City was to convince them that Mars could become New Earth, a second home where humanity could not only survive, but do so with very few changes in their lives. Every building, every tree, every blade of grass was designed to drive home that point, as were the accommodations at the Red Dahlia.

The name itself was a play on words that drew a mental connection between Daedalia Planum and the dahlia, which was native to Earth. During their dumpling feast at Jonas Labs, Claire had told Beck that it probably wasn't a five-star hotel, but if so, she now suspected that was only because no critic had yet made the trip to Mars to assess it. The hotel offered every imaginable Earth amenity, including things that were almost certainly luxuries on most areas of Mars. She doubted that you could find bathtubs in the other colonies, or even in workers' homes within Daedalus City. Most were probably still equipped with some variant of the hydrosonic shower she had used at Tranquility Base.

And then there were the crystal-clear waters of Lake Marta over which the hotel was built, where guests could enjoy a variety of watersports. The lake glowed pale blue at night and remained a vivid shade of aqua during the day despite the reddish gray skies overhead, thanks to a potpourri of phytoplankton that had been genetically tweaked to absorb more of the red light reflected from the Martian sky and the surrounding terrain.

As Kolya had said back at Tranquility Base, the moon would never be a place someone could think of as home. But he needed future colonists (and especially, future investors) to look at Mars as the next frontier for humanity. Sure, the planet was wild and even dangerous, but with a generous application of time and money, Kolya seemed to be saying, Mars as a whole could be as earthlike as the main strip in Daedalus City. Claire thought there was a very good reason that it was the first sight that greeted visitors upon entry, and also the last thing they saw as they began their journey home.

Once you were off the beaten path, though, you got a better sense of the effort that had gone into terraforming. These plants, as odd as they looked to Claire, were thriving in a way that their carefully landscaped cousins in the resort area were not. The bamboo trees—although, technically, she supposed they were grass, not trees—towered over the road like wispy redwoods, stretching so high that she had to crane her neck upward to see the tops. The flora on the outskirts of Daedalus had been engineered every bit as much as plants around the resort, but the goal hadn't been to mimic what grew on Earth. Instead, they seemed to have been created with an eye toward what might do well in an environment that was terraformed enough to support human life, but still uniquely Martian.

They drove through the bamboo forest for several minutes and then the tram turned onto a path next to a new looking sign marked *Dome Three. Security Vehicles Only.* A few meters ahead was a gate, which lifted automatically as they approached. Just beyond that, the path dipped sharply downward into a dimly lit tunnel much narrower than the one they'd passed through the night before when entering Daedalus City. Behind them, the lights of the equipment truck flashed on. Their own tram was apparently made of sterner stuff and not afraid of the dark, because it zipped along with just the benefit of the ambient light from the truck.

The temperature dropped almost as sharply upon entering the tunnel as the road had. Claire shivered despite the extra layer provided by the biosuit.

"I guess lights and heat are only for the main tunnel," Ben said with a chuckle.

At least the cold would be short lived, Claire thought. Up ahead, she could already see the faint glow of the exit.

Chelsea snorted and slumped down in the seat. "Since no tourists will be joining us in Dome Three, we're probably lucky Kolya is sparing us some oxygen. And as I was saying earlier, just wait until the whole menagerie piles into the dome and they start lasering that thing. We'll be plenty warm then."

TWO

LESS THAN A MINUTE LATER, the tram veered uphill and emerged inside Dome Three, which was about one-quarter the size of a football field, with a maximum height of maybe sixty meters at the center. Unlike the larger dome, you could clearly see the joints in the bottom layers of aerogel sheets from this distance.

The tram turned right a few yards inside and stopped on a small charging pad. Claire pulled her helmet into place, hoping to get a closer look at the chamber before the guys with the lasers and heavy equipment started setting up and had to shoo them out of the way. Unfortunately, she wasn't familiar with the helmet or the gloves and couldn't work the seals.

"Hold on," Brodnik said and helped her lock everything into place. "It can be a little tricky at first."

"Thanks. I should have paid closer attention when Stasia was helping me into the suit back at Tranquility Base."

Brodnik said it was no problem, and started to walk over to the construction team, but Claire grabbed her arm.

"Listen," she said in a lower voice. "I just wanted to let you know that you were in the original script. In fact, I had *you* going in first. I wanted you there to give your professional opinion on what we'll be seeing. But Stasia says there isn't enough room for both of us."

This had been the largest of several disagreements she and Stasia had over the script. While Brodnik's team hadn't been able to get a good idea of the internal dimensions of the chamber from the little camera they'd inserted at Icarus Camp, the external dimensions gave them a pretty good idea of its overall size. It wasn't exactly spacious, and they already knew that the metal walls were extremely thick. The entire team couldn't go in all at once, but Claire had written the script with the expectation that she would enter behind Brodnik and let the professor give the viewers her impression of the find. She had the two of them positioned off to one side, clearing the way for the lights and allowing the camera to zoom in and get the first images of the symbols. As she'd told Stasia, they could always take closer, clearer images of the symbols later and piece them into the footage.

When Stasia argued the point, Claire told her that Brodnik really needed to be there to give context, and that was sort of true, but it was also a matter of principle. Even though Brodnik hadn't personally dug the thing out of the side of that crater, and even though Claire fully intended to interview the miners who *had* done that once they arrived at Icarus Camp, Brodnik was still the team leader and Claire thought she should be the first person to enter the chamber.

Brodnik smiled, shaking her head. "It's not a big deal."

"Stasia's just worried that having another person inside would cast weird shadows, and—"

"It doesn't matter, Claire. Really. It's in our contract that *the neutral third party*—that's you—must be the first to enter both chambers to ensure there is no tampering. That's rich, given that they've moved this one a few thousand kilometers and apparently fished around on the inside with a sensor. KTI makes it sound like we're in a legal dispute already."

"Given Kimura's previous public statements, that may well be how Kolya views it. Not saying I agree, but…"

"Fair enough. I should probably have left him off the team, but…" She glanced around. "This is off the record. Kim wasn't wrong about those samples. While it may not have been Kolya, *someone* tampered with them. But getting back to the filming today—I'm far less concerned about being the first one inside the chamber than I am about having plenty of time to examine it once everyone else clears out. And I'm even more concerned about having ample time to examine the one that's still at Icarus Camp. What I want more than anything else is to get this dog and pony show over so we can get to work."

A few days earlier, Claire might have taken offense at the *dog and pony show* crack, since she was the pony being paraded out front. But she was beginning to get a better feel for why the team wasn't entirely pleased about having KTI running the show. It wasn't just a matter of them wanting to claim all of the credit for the find, as Kolya had suggested. They were also worried that they weren't going to be able to do their jobs.

Brodnik patted her on the arm consolingly. "You'll be interviewing all of us later, anyway."

"I know," Claire said, still not liking the situation. "Would you mind if I ran something past you? This really isn't my field, and I don't want to look like an idiot if it's completely off base."

"Sure," she said. "As long as it's quick. I need to chat with the ground crew."

Claire nodded. "My first impression is that this thing could be a tomb. I mean, not just because it's coffin shaped. I thought the same thing when I watched your earlier video where it looked more like a cube. Those symbols gave me a similar vibe as the hieroglyphs inside Egyptian tombs."

"That doesn't sound off base to me at all. In fact, it's my working hypothesis. I wouldn't stake my professional reputation on it at this point, but it's a good place to start."

Brodnik then went over to the leader of the ground crew, who seemed to be waiting for her go-ahead. Claire continued on to the chamber, enjoying the unusual bounce in her step from the low level of gravity. It wasn't nearly as dramatic as it had been during her brief stroll outside at Tranquility Base, but it still felt a bit like walking around inside this inflatable castle she'd had as a little kid.

Viewed from the shuttle, the Icarus chamber had appeared a uniform dark gray, but Claire could now see fragments of rock still attached to the surface. Most of the rocks were a slightly deeper shade of butterscotch than the drifts of desert sand surrounding the dome. But there were also darker fragments, as well as a few with green and purple striations. A pile with similar chunks of rock lay off to the side, suggesting that workers had already chipped away much of the material that had attached to the cube during its eons underground.

The chamber itself was a dull metal cuboid, about three meters high and wide, and a little over twice that in length. Aside from the debris still attached to the sides, it was smooth and unmarked. The first twenty-five centimeters or so of the front face hung over the edge of a narrow trench maybe a meter and a half deep. Claire wasn't sure why it was there at first, but then realized it was the only way, short of flipping the thing over on its side, that the workers would be able to apply the laser to the bottom.

She ran her gloved hand over one section of the unblemished surface. This thing was going to send conspiracy theorists into an absolute frenzy. And while she preferred to avoid that sort of thinking, a little healthy skepticism was probably in order, especially given how much she and everyone else wanted this to be the real deal.

First, were there any known metals that could have survived beneath the Martian regolith for millions of years? She didn't think so. Even adamantium, an alloy that some wit had named after a super-strong metal from comic books, would probably degrade after so much time. But aside from the bits of rock that were still clinging to the surface, this thing looked like it could have been built yesterday.

A second question: was there anyone who had a reason to *fake* a find of this magnitude? Some group opposed to the terraforming project, perhaps? There almost certainly were people who wanted to derail the project, but this seemed like a lot of effort when there were easier methods to gum up the works, especially when the easier methods seemed much more likely to succeed. As Macek had said in that first meeting, the existence of the Icarus chamber simply proved that there *had* been life on Mars at one time, not that there was anything currently here that needed to be protected.

Any group seeking to delay or even end the terraforming would have been better off planting something alive. A manufactured lifeform that they could try to pawn off as the real deal would have had a better chance of at least slowing down the project. Although, as Wyatt would no doubt have noted if he were here, given the amount of money already invested, the Ares Consortium would find a way to move forward even if Jesus Christ and a host of angels came tap-dancing out when they opened the chamber.

That reminded Claire of Kimura's comments back in the lobby. *Had* there been something inside, some native Martian microbe—whether legitimate or fabricated—that KTI's scientists wiped out when they relocated the chamber? And could anyone say for certain that they hadn't done the same thing to the second, smaller chamber still buried at Icarus Camp?

No, Claire thought. She was not going to start going down rabbit holes.

At least not yet. Not when there were actual experts nearby whose brains she could pick. Kim and Chelsea were clearly inclined to lean into the conspiracies, but Ben Pelzer, the team geologist, seemed pretty levelheaded.

She looked around and found Ben on the far side of the chamber. He was running his gloved hand across the surface, examining the metal exactly as she had been doing, except for the fact that his other hand held something that looked like a laser gun.

"Can that handy little gadget tell you what kind of metal this is?" Claire asked after watching him run it over various sections of the wall.

"It *should* be able to. Hell, the cheaper spectrometer I had with me on the last trip *should* have been able to identify it. But this thing usually takes only a few seconds to get a reading. And, as you can see, its metaphorical wheels are still spinning."

"How about an educated guess, then?"

He shook his head. "Nope. I've got nothing. Maybe I'll know something more when I get a sample back to the lab, rather than relying on portable devices to analyze it. KTI denied my request to take a sample of the stuff back with us last time. I think we could have convinced them if we'd had a day or two to make our case, but we barely made it back to Daedalus in time to catch our ride home."

"You couldn't have just delayed your return rather than dealing with an extra off-planet trip? I mean, I'm obviously glad you didn't because I might not be here otherwise, but…"

Ben laughed humorlessly. "You clearly don't have much experience with academic bureaucracies. Icarus wasn't even one of the stops covered by our last grant, which was funded by NASA. It was just me, Laura, and Chelsea on that trip. Kim … well, let's just say we didn't get enough funding to include him. Anyway, we were over near Hyblaeus—" He stopped and narrowed his eyes. "This is *off* the record. Understand?"

Claire nodded. "Absolutely."

"Okay. We're over near Hyblaeus Dorsa when Laura gets a message from KTI asking if we'd be willing to stop by and examine something one of their mining teams had unearthed on our way back to Daedalus, dangling the possibility of future grant money as an incentive. So we compressed our schedule as much as we could to carve out a couple of days at the end. We were thinking it was some unusual rock or *maybe* a fossil formation. And then we find this massive cube—or at least, we *thought* it was a cube—made out of something I've never seen before and that I could barely get a freakin' drill through."

"So…" She lowered her voice. "Can you be certain this isn't some new alloy produced in a lab?"

"Ah." His eyebrows went up slightly. "You're not the first person to consider that possibility. I think that might even have been the key reason KTI wanted us to check it out in the first place. There's a lot riding on the terraforming project and also a lot of people who stand to *lose* money in the short run because of the restrictions during stage six, so yeah…it's not unreasonable to wonder whether some of that last group might have decided to throw a wrench in the machinery. Maybe plant a mystery box in a crater down in Icaria and see if that derailed KTI's plans."

"And…?"

"And, even though I can't tell you what this thing is made of, I can answer *that* question definitively. No way was this part of a hoax. No way. It was found in a section of Clark Crater where they're mining for opal. The crater's western wall looks a bit like Swiss cheese, because they drill holes into the side, excavate the debris, and if they see any evidence of an opal level, sort of like what they call a seam in a coal mine, then they widen the shaft so that they can send the bots in, and eventually, the workers. A few days later, one of the workers gets a chip out of the chisel she's using…and that never happens. Those things are sturdy. They might dull a bit over time, but they don't break. When they brought up the manager to analyze it, he got some weird readings. The workers chipped away at it a little more before they called KTI, but…this chamber was still thoroughly embedded in that rock when we arrived. I've dug enough shit out of rock faces, here and on Earth, to state that with absolute certainty. And see that?" He pointed to a greenish-yellow piece of rock molded around the rear corner of the chamber near her feet. "That is olivine. It's igneous—basically, molten rock that shoots up through other layers. And my handy little gadget *can* date olivine. Step back a few inches."

Once Claire was out of the way, Ben crouched down and held the device against the olivine. A few seconds later, he stood back up and showed her the screen. The number was 3.8 ± 0.3.

"That's in *millions*," he said. "So…3.8 million years ago, plus or minus a few hundred thousand, that bit of olivine shot up through the other layers of rock and shaped itself around the corner of this chamber. Which means if somebody planted this thing, they either traveled back in time to do it or they started working on it when the closest thing on Earth to a human was still spending most of its time in trees."

THREE

THEY RETREATED BACK to the tram once the construction team—or perhaps it would be called a *deconstruction* team, in this case—rolled their scaffold into place next to the chamber. Preliminary tests on the metal had shown no evidence that it released toxic fumes when they applied the laser, but the men needed room to work.

And Chelsea had been right. Dome Three was already getting a bit toasty, especially around the area where the lasers were now heating up the big metal box.

The second tram showed up about twenty minutes later, with Kolya, Stasia, Macek, a three-person camera crew and two people who seemed to be trainees. None of them were wearing protective gear. Of course, if they followed the script, none of those people would be entering the chamber, at least not while the cameras were rolling. Still, given how tiny the dome was, Claire felt quite certain that Kolya, Stasia, and Macek at the very least would be wearing hazard gear if they weren't completely convinced that there was nothing to fear when the thing was cracked open. Her earlier guess that the suits were merely for dramatic effect seemed to be confirmed.

There was no sign of Paul. Claire had thought there might be, since he was the one who had handled the recording during her tour of the lunar base. He'd said it wasn't his usual job, but he seemed to enjoy it. Hopefully, his absence was simply because it was his day off or maybe because this camera crew was KTI's A-team, and not because he was still feeling awkward about her good cop/bad cop comment.

On the other hand, maybe it was just as well. Claire thought there was a decent chance that Kolya's presence alone might provide enough awkwardness for the increasingly crowded dome. It was the first time that she had seen him since the night of the debate, and she was beginning to wonder if perhaps he'd had second thoughts. Not just about the kiss, but about including her on the trip to Ehden. She would survive him regretting the former, although her ego might take a blow, but she was genuinely interested in seeing the demo sites he'd mentioned and also wanted the opportunity to collect some samples for Joe.

And who knew? Maybe it *would* give her mother one less thing to bitch about. Claire certainly wasn't averse to that.

Her concerns were quickly put to rest. As soon as Stasia was out of the tram, she waylaid Dr. Brodnik to discuss scheduling for the next two weeks. "I need to arrange for a full camera crew at Icarus, an excavation team to assist you, and a security detail, so as soon as you can, give me an idea of when you'd like to depart and a rough estimate of how long you'll be there. And do you think I might be able to borrow Claire for a day between now and then? We thought her subscribers would be interested in a closer look at the preparations for stage six, so we'd like to take her on a tour of a few sites within a day's travel. Maybe we could set that up for Friday or—" She stopped, tapped her earpiece, listened for a moment, and then continued speaking to Brodnik. "I'll get up with you later on scheduling. They're saying fifteen minutes, tops, until the chamber is open. Claire, if you'll follow me, we should go ahead and record your intro."

The camera crew was already in place, having picked a spot where the Icarus chamber would be visible over Claire's shoulder. Kolya and Macek were waiting next to them, watching the men with lasers as they worked on the final sections of the two vertical panels. The scaffold the workers had used while cutting along the top edge had now been moved off to the side. In its place were two utility bots with extendible arms that were pivoted around to clamp the top and bottom edges.

As Claire headed over to join the camera crew, she noticed a small contingent of trams—maybe twenty in all—outside Dome Three. The trams were moving toward the dome at a rapid clip, filled with people in full pressure gear, a mixture of the old puff variety and the newer biosuits.

"I thought it might be useful to have some witnesses," Kolya said when he saw her looking beyond the dome at the tram brigade. "It's being shown live on screens in the resort and at a few other locations on the planet, of course. But, given the magnitude of the discovery, it seemed unfair not to allow our paying guests to experience it in person."

Claire was tempted to ask how much extra he'd charged the *paying guests* for that little field trip, but she focused on the more pertinent question—at least to her editor—instead. "I'm guessing all of these witnesses, both virtual and the ones in the trams, have recording devices. How long do you think it will be before they start sending messages back to Earth?"

"Oh." Kolya made an apologetic face. "Didn't think about that being a problem. Are you sure it's not a good thing? Maybe your editor will be happy that we're building up a little buzz for the story?"

"No, he's definitely going to view it more as you *leaking* the story, which isn't really in keeping with something billed as an exclusive."

"You're probably right."

Oh, I'm definitely right, she thought, but kept her expression fixed and her mouth shut.

After a moment, Kolya nodded. "Fortunately, this is very easily fixed." He shot a glance at Macek, who walked away and began talking to someone on his earpiece. "Macek will have security hold all guest communications back to Earth and delay the transmission to the other colonies here on Mars until you can get the piece to your editor."

"Thank you."

"Okay," Stasia said to the camera operators. "After the intro, cut the video and the audio feed to the guests outside the dome. Then we'll wait until they signal me that the wall is about to come down. As soon as that happens, both cameras stay on without a break. One unbroken shot gives the conspiracy types less to chew on." She gave Claire an appraising look, and then turned to Kolya. "Helmet or no helmet? She'll need to have it on once she moves inside, but…"

"No helmet," he said.

Claire thought that was a question that should have been directed to her rather than to Kolya, but she chalked it up to Stasia needing to please the boss.

"Yikes," Macek said with a chuckle after she removed the helmet. "Maybe not. If I'd realized how quickly the heat would build with this many people hanging about, I would have had them put the thing inside a larger dome."

"You *are* looking a little…wilted." Kolya grinned and leaned forward to dab at her forehead with his sleeve.

"Not a problem. We can fix all of…this"—Stasia motioned vaguely toward Claire's face—"in post-production."

"No," Claire said. "No filters. You just told them that you're worried about triggering the conspiracy nuts. I have makeup back in the tram. Give me two minutes."

Stasia gave her a smile that suggested she'd need more than two minutes. And as soon as Claire looked in the mirror, she could tell the woman wasn't *entirely* wrong. She couldn't help but worry, though, about Stasia's radical shift in attitude. Maybe what she'd said had offended Paul more than she knew. At some point, she was going to have to pull Stasia aside—and Paul, too, assuming she could find him—to clear the air.

Claire pulled her damp hair back into a quick knot, dabbed on some powder and a touch of color and called it done. Once she was back in place, the woman operating the first camera counted down *three, two, one.* Claire tucked the helmet under her arm and began the script that she and Stasia had hashed out via messages over the past few days.

"This is Claire Echols of the *Atlantic Post* coming to you from a small, domed crater just outside Daedalus City on Mars, where a team of researchers from Columbia University are about to take us inside what may well be the most amazing archeological find of all time. Three months ago, Dr. Laura Brodnik and her team traveled to a crater about twenty-five hundred kilometers from here to inspect a strange object that had been un—well, I was going to say unearthed, but this isn't Earth, so let's just say *uncovered*—by a group of miners under contract to Kolya Terraforming. The object they found is the one you see behind me."

She gestured toward the chamber.

"Even a quick visual inspection tells us that this is *not* a natural formation. Earlier, I spoke with Dr. Benjamin Pelzer, the geologist on Brodnik's team and while he is confident that the chamber is made from a metal alloy, it's not one that he's been able to identify, despite using the latest in portable spectro-metric equipment. The team was unable to open the vault when it was first discovered, but they did eventually manage to drill a hole into the top that was large enough for them to lower a sensor into the inner chamber."

Claire and Stasia had debated that last section at length. What Brodnik's crew had actually lowered into the Icarus chamber wasn't a sensor. It was a *camera*, and that's what Claire had written in her initial draft, along with the fact that they'd discovered symbols etched into the walls. But Stasia thought that ruined the surprise. She wanted to save the symbols for a visual reveal. And, as she noted, a camera is a sensor of sorts, so it wasn't really a lie, just a minor omission.

Unfortunately, it was a minor omission that meant Claire would have to feign at least some degree of amazement for the cameras. She'd definitely been amazed when she first saw the video in New York, but that was weeks and a few hundred million kilometers in the past. Maybe it was a good thing that she'd be wearing a helmet that partially shielded her face.

"Further inspection by a team of scientists with the Ares Consortium," she continued, "showed no signs of unique biological life inside the chamber, so it was moved to this location, just outside of Daedalus City, where it could be placed under a protective dome for further study. The three men you see behind me now with lasers are just moments away from removing that front wall, at which point we will get our first clear look inside the compartment."

This had been another point of contention. Stasia wanted to omit the word *clear*. Claire insisted that time. The original footage recorded by Brodnik's team would eventually be released. And while you could truthfully say that this would be their first *clear* look, given the poor lighting from the camera they'd used, it definitely wasn't their *first look*. Stasia had backed down, but Claire could tell she was getting annoyed at having the desire for at least some degree of journalistic precision chip away at what Stasia clearly viewed as a dramatic presentation.

When they reached the end, Claire asked if she should redo the bit at the beginning to get rid of the *unearthed* blooper. It was written as *discovered* in the script, but she'd pulled an unintentional ad lib.

Stasia shook her head. "Oh, no. It works fine as is. I'm actually more concerned about you adding the quote from Dr. Pelzer."

"Why? Is there a problem with it? I spoke to him about the chamber's composition after we arrived."

Stasia gave Claire a patient smile. "The *problem* is that you agreed to clear the script with me ahead of time."

"Fine. Do you want to rerecord or simply cut it in post-production?" Claire was annoyed, though, and didn't bother to hide it. She had purposefully kept what Pelzer said vague with Stasia in mind, thinking she'd probably feel that the part about an approximate date for the olivine molded to the corner was spoilerish.

"Just *leave* it, Stasia," Kolya said. "You're not dealing with an actor for one of our commercials. Claire can improvise a bit. She knows what she's doing."

"And the entire point was to have a *neutral third party*," Macek added, echoing the term that Brodnik had used earlier. There was a slight teasing note to his voice, which made her wonder whether that was his wording or Stasia's. Either way, Claire thought it seemed rather hypocritical when the so-called *neutral party* was under a rigid NDA, and everything she recorded would be going through KTI's censors.

Stasia gave Kolya a brisk nod, ignoring Macek entirely. "You're right, Anton. Force of habit." Then, she turned to the woman operating camera one. "Shruti, keep your focus on the chamber so we don't miss the visual of the wall coming down. Pax will be with you. Meadow, you tag along with this guy as he gets into position with the lights. Camera two, wait for my signal and then follow Claire."

Claire put her helmet on again and sealed it as Brodnik had shown her. About ninety seconds later, they heard a loud groan. The wall of the chamber tilted slightly, and the guys with the lasers stepped away. One of them pressed a button and the utility bots began inching backward with the wall in their clamps. Claire could now see that there were symbols etched on it similar to the ones they'd seen in the Icarus video, only these seemed considerably larger in size. The symbols were arranged into two clusters—one group of four, followed by a pair. The first reminded Claire of a backward number two and the second one looked like a trio of steps.

Once the bots had the wall in position, they slowly lowered it onto the tarp Claire had noticed back at the hotel—there was apparently a purpose for it after all. Next, the workers moved forward and placed a wide board across the trench in the sand. Stasia then signaled to camera two and they were moving.

Claire kept up an awkward patter on the walk over, mentioning Daedalus City, which could be seen off to the left of them and the desert surrounding the dome. She felt like she was doing commentary at a sporting event.

As they drew closer to the chamber, Claire saw that Stasia was right about there not being much room inside. One thing the earlier video hadn't revealed was the rectangular platform in the center, which took up about half of the floor space. It stood about a meter high and was made of the same material as the outside walls. The dais made the thing look even more like a tomb. She could almost picture a mummified corpse stretched out on top of it.

To Claire's surprise, she didn't have to fake amazement once she was inside. Seeing the symbols through the narrow frame and limited light of Brodnik's tiny camera was a far cry from stepping into an ancient crypt with etchings clearly illuminated on the walls around her. She was actually so stunned by the sight that it took her a second to remember that the camera was on her, and that she had a script to follow.

"This is nothing short of astonishing," Claire said. "For those who don't closely follow the exploration of Mars, I should note that extensive scientific investigation over the course of decades has confirmed—repeatedly—that nothing more complex than microbial lifeforms currently exists on the planet. That was a prerequisite for terraforming to even be considered. And until the discovery of this chamber, there was no evidence that anything more complex had *ever* existed on Mars. This would seem to blow that assumption out of the water. What we see on these walls are clearly symbols—pictograms or hieroglyphs of some sort—and while I'm not an expert in the field, this looks like a burial chamber to me. It appears to be evidence that an *advanced civilization* existed on Mars millions of years ago."

She stopped for a moment to let that sink in, and then continued. "This is obviously a developing story. In the coming days, I will be talking with Anton Kolya, CEO of Kolya Terraforming, who can tell us more about how and where this remarkable discovery was made. I will also be bringing you exclusive interviews with Dr. Laura Brodnik and the members of her team, who are far more qualified than I am to analyze the chamber and explain how this changes our understanding of Martian history."

FOUR

CLAIRE'S TABLET pinged with an incoming file, and she gave it a look of loathing. The horrid thing had beeped at her pretty much nonstop for the past few days. Most of the messages had been from her editor, and she braced as she grabbed it to check, fearing another demand for information that she did not yet have. The last one had ended with the words *get me some fucking answers*, from a man who rarely cursed. And while Bernard hadn't explicitly added the words *or else*, Claire was smart enough to read between the lines.

The four days after the chamber was opened had flown by in an insane flurry of activity. That first evening had been deceptively calm, as she answered the messages from friends and colleagues that began coming in a few hours after the *Post* published her story on Monday. Rowan's text was short and to the point:

> I knew you were hiding something, but DAMN girl. Hugs and kisses from R, J & W.

Seeing Wyatt's initial at the end had given Claire a little pang. She wanted so badly to discuss all of this with him and hated that she still had nearly a month before she could do that.

The message that had given her the biggest smile and even brought a tear to her eyes was from Joe:

> Congrats, Claire-Bear! Beck and I send a big THANK YOU for deflecting the media storm. So very proud and looking forward to hearing all about it when you're back on terra firma.

Claire had spent a good chunk of the past few days out at Dome Three recording the interviews with Brodnik's team, aided by Meadow and Pax, the two trainees Stasia had assigned to assist her. Stasia had brought the KTI A-team with her when they opened the Icarus chamber but must have realized that the audience would be a lot smaller for the interviews and, therefore, handed Claire over to the newbies.

And they were definitely newbies. Meadow had nodded when Claire said they could use a few seconds of the chamber opening as B-roll footage. The expression on the girl's face and the way she'd kept twisting the end of her braid—long and green, *meadow* green, in fact—had made Claire quite certain that she had no idea what the term meant. Pax also seemed lost when Claire asked him to hook Pelzer up with a lavalier. He'd flushed and apologized when she pointed to the little microphone, explaining that he and Meadow had met while getting a videography certificate back on Earth. They'd been working in food services since they came to Daedalus City two years earlier, but had finally landed these jobs as apprentices, a system that he said was really common on Mars. Claire supposed it made sense. After all, it wasn't like you could place an employment ad and expect a flood of qualified applicants in a matter of days.

Claire's tentative plan had been to take Wednesday afternoon off to wander around Daedalus City, make a few casual recordings about the colony for a future *Simple Science* segment, and maybe spend an hour or so on the gorgeous piano down in the lounge. If recording the interviews and answering personal messages had been the only tasks on her plate, she'd have managed it, but unfortunately, she'd seriously underestimated the number of questions she'd be fielding about the story and the number of requests for interviews she'd get from other news outlets.

Some of those requests were for Brodnik's team, and she passed those along. But a number of the reporters were asking to interview Claire personally. She was *covering* the story and had no intention of allowing them to make her part of it. But she declined very politely, realizing it probably wasn't a good idea to burn bridges when she might well find herself hunting for a new job once she got back home.

The problem was that Bernard was the first stop for most of the requests for information, and despite his initial excitement, he was well on his way to developing a real hatred for this story. Even before Claire transmitted the video of the chamber being opened, she'd sent a message warning him that when it arrived, he wouldn't have long before the discovery began to be at least rumored in other outlets. That meant he had to fast-track it with the editorial board. Bernard had obviously given them a heads-up that *something* big was coming down the Martian pike, but he'd had to keep it vague as a result of the NDA Claire signed. The board jumped to the very reasonable conclusion that the something big was related to the upcoming launch of stage six, not that they were about to reveal that an ancient civilization once existed on Mars. Then, when Bernard was finally able to give them specifics, those details came hand in hand with the news that they'd only have a few hours to examine the video before it hit social media channels, courtesy of several hundred tourists who'd watched the thing in person and even more people who'd watched it live inside Daedalus.

At least a few members of the *Post's* editorial board were worried that the chamber was fake. Claire couldn't blame them, but the way they handled the situation still made her angry. As soon as the story hit social media, they went ahead and published the piece, but they added a disclaimer—which was still at the top of the story four days later—noting that the chamber was being analyzed, and that the *Post* could not yet substantiate the claims made in the video or determine whether the video itself was a fabrication. In other words, they were still trying to figure out whether their own reporter had forwarded them a hoax. Bernard had tried to soft-pedal it, and Claire knew they were all just covering their asses, but it still felt like she'd been hung out to dry.

To make matters worse, she had also had to tell Bernard that she wouldn't be able to deliver the promised video of the debate between Kolya and Shepherd. He actually had the temerity to ask if she could get just the footage of the part where Shepherd had the seizure. When she said KTI had no plans to release *any* of the video at this time and pointed out that it would be kind of ghoulish to publish Shepherd's attack, he countered that just because something was a little ghoulish didn't mean it wasn't newsworthy.

That attitude was extremely out of character for Bernard, which suggested to Claire that he'd been catching hell. The thing that had surprised Claire the most about all of the questions bombarding them, and she thought it might even have surprised Bernard, was that the majority of them were not about the chamber itself or even whether it was a hoax, but rather about the unorthodox manner in which it had been announced to the world. As Wyatt had correctly noted at their dinner the night before Claire left, she wasn't all that savvy when it came to international, let alone *interplanetary* political and economic currents. If Wyatt had known the actual reason that she was making the trip, Claire felt sure he could have predicted that multiple governmental agencies (US and abroad, along with two different subgroups at the UN) would be outraged, claiming that the information had serious security implications and should, therefore, have been reported to them first.

Put it all together, and Bernard was in a bitchy, whiny, garden gnome kind of mood that made Claire very glad that she was currently several hundred million kilometers away from the office. Each time a new complaint landed on the man's desk, he fired off a dozen or so questions at Claire …questions for which he wanted immediate answers, the vast majority of which would have to come from Anton Kolya. Unfortunately,

Claire hadn't seen or heard anything from Kolya since his tram headed back to Daedalus City after the chamber was opened. She was supposed to have recorded an interview with him the next day. It had now been canceled not once, not twice, but three times. The most recent cancellation hadn't even given her a new time and date, but simply said TBD.

With the first two cancellations, she'd assumed that Kolya was busy, most likely fielding the same firestorm of questions and complaints that she and Bernard were. But that morning, as she'd stared at the most recent automated message, it had occurred to Claire that Kolya was more likely *ignoring* those requests. Every single one of the people and entities bugging Bernard (and by extension, her) had ways to contact Kolya directly through KTI. Those people probably even had a specific point person within the company to handle their requests for information. The fact that they were hounding Claire and Bernard so relentlessly probably meant that they weren't getting a response from Kolya.

In his last fun little missive, Bernard had said it almost felt like they were set up. Pick a junior reporter, then stick her with an NDA that prevents advance scrutiny and ensures that she tells the story exactly the way you want it told. And since it's an exclusive, you can be sure she'll be so eager that she won't ask too many pesky questions in advance.

Bernard conveniently omitted the fact that he had been fully aware of the terms, and he'd been just as eager as she was to get this story. Yes, she only had a few years of experience. He, however, was her editor and had more than two decades under his belt. If anyone had failed in the due diligence department, it was him.

Claire was increasingly tempted to ignore his messages and blame it on faulty interplanetary communication. No way was she even going to *mention* the possibility of the trip to Ehden and additional coverage on stage six until the footage was recorded, cleared by KTI, and ready to submit.

As annoyed as she was, though, his comment about being set up had started Claire thinking, and she had spent a good half hour that morning digging around for some background information. It was the kind of thing she might actually have done back on Earth if she'd had more than a few days to get ready. What she found had her about ninety percent convinced that Bernard was right about this being a setup, but she couldn't be sure until she spoke with Kolya.

While there was no way to respond to the automated scheduling email, Claire did have Stasia's direct contact information, so she fired off a message asking her to arrange a brief meeting with Kolya before the day was up. If that wasn't possible, she needed to speak either with Stasia or with Paul. It was high time someone gave her some answers, and if pushing the matter jeopardized the trip to Ehden, currently scheduled for Saturday, then so be it.

Because *they* should have been the ones responding to those questions. Every single decision about how this news was released to the world had stemmed from KTI, either directly or as a result of the NDA that Claire had signed. Kolya's decision to relocate the chamber, for example, had amplified suspicions, leading multiple reporters and politicians to declare that the entire thing was a hoax.

Still, only one critic had, in Claire's opinion, given a plausible reason for *why* Kolya would do something that might jeopardize the terraforming project. A lot was riding on stage six. What if Kolya had gotten results that suggested it was going to fail? If the problems were due to any malfeasance on KTI's part, a delayed launch would come with a fairly steep financial penalty.

And even if it was merely a miscalculation or a classic case of overpromising (something Kolya was well known for doing), it had taken him several years to get the other four colonies to agree to keep their workforces inside the domes for six months. The odds that he'd get them all on board a second time seemed slim. Maybe Kolya just needed a distraction for a few months, a reason to push stage six back until this wrinkle, whatever it might be, could be ironed out.

Again, though…no matter how plausible the reasoning, Claire found it far too convoluted and complex. Why not have Brodnik's team discover something living and tiny to slow down the project? Why go to the trouble of coming up with some previously unknown alloy, building a chamber out of it— two chambers, in fact—and somehow embedding them in the walls of a crater?

And Kolya had seemed sincerely enthusiastic about taking her along to see the progress they'd made in preparation for stage six. That's not the kind of thing someone would do if there was a problem with the preliminary steps. So, no…she didn't buy it.

When Claire picked up the tablet, she was relieved to see that the message wasn't from Bernard after all. Meadow had finally sent the edited footage from the interviews with Brodnik and her crew. She'd also added a note at the top.

> THANKS SO MUCH FOR BEING PATIENT WITH US
> AND NOT COMPLAINING ABOUT OUR MISTAKES
> THIS WEEK. WE'LL BE IN TOP FORM SOON—
> PROMISE!—AND WE'RE LEARNING SO MUCH
> FROM YOU.

Claire felt the last bit was very much a case of Meadow blowing smoke up her nether regions, but since she hadn't planned on complaining about their ineptitude anyway, she just sent a quick thank you. Then she grabbed a bottle of water from the suite's cooler and carried it out to the balcony, where she changed the view from a static image to a leisurely spin around the outside of the resort. She'd make a quick final check and then, assuming there were no major issues, transmit the files to the *Post*, even though she seriously doubted that would do much to appease the skeptics. Yes, all four team members were experts in their fields, but Claire could already hear the board saying that it wouldn't be the first time that scientists had been duped by a clever fraud.

The one bright spot of the past few days was that Claire had found the conversations with Brodnik's team to be very interesting, even if she wasn't entirely satisfied with the camera angles and other technical aspects. Dr. Brodnik (who was again saying that Claire should call her Laura, this time without the benefit of wine, so perhaps they'd made some degree of progress) had pointed out the similarities between the Martian chamber and various historical burial chambers on Earth. Brodnik hypothesized that the writing etched into the walls was a eulogy and said the fact that there had been no evidence prior to this of such burial chambers on the planet might suggest that the person who was entombed had been a leader, or possibly a wealthy eccentric who could afford to go out in style. Her hope was that they'd learn more from the second chamber, still at Icarus. It was even possible that the lower chamber was the one that had held the body, in which case some biological information might remain, although she said she didn't hold out much hope of that after such a long time.

Claire took a short break between clips and leaned back into the chair, watching the world outside spin slowly past on the viewscreen. The area immediately around the lake was landscaped to increase the sense of being on a sparsely populated island, blocking out all but a few especially tall buildings along the main strip of Daedalus City.

People wandered in and out of view as the camera panned around the beach area. Claire had seen a few children at Ares Station, but none since. Maybe the Red Dahlia was an adults-only resort. She doubted it was the price tag that was keeping the kids away. Anyone who could afford to bring the entire family to Mars probably wasn't going to be worried about a few hundred additional credits per night for upscale accommodations.

As Claire watched, one daring soul on a jetboard zoomed

into view. She kept pace with the camera for about a minute, caroming from side to side and churning up white spray in her wake. The woman wasn't bad, and when she stopped on the far side of the building where the lake was wider to work on figure eights, Claire grabbed the controls and froze the view so that she could keep watching.

If not for that, she would have missed what came next. The foreground of the view was the wide patio that Claire had glimpsed a few days earlier on the other side of the executive pavilion. It stretched out all the way to the lake, with several dozen tables and lounge chairs scattered about. The patio was empty when she first paused to watch the jetboarder, but then two men came into view.

One of the men was Macek.

And both of them looked mad enough to kill.

FIVE

CLAIRE HAD FOUND Macek intimidating when he questioned her about the attack on Shepherd, but his expression now was nothing short of terrifying...or at least it would have been if she'd encountered it from across a table rather than through a remote camera. The face of the guy with him, who was at least twenty years older and nearly two heads shorter than Macek, was equally animated, bordering on apoplectic.

She zoomed in as close as possible. While she obviously couldn't hear anything, Claire suspected the short guy was getting a bit loud because Macek kept looking around nervously. He shot several anxious glances in the direction of the patio door, and once, when he stopped and squinted back toward the building, she could have sworn he was looking directly at her.

Short Guy was now jabbing a finger toward Macek's chest. The fact that he had to jab upward to do it gave the scene an almost comical air until Macek reached out, grabbed the man's wrist, and twisted. The smaller man winced, appeared to cry out, and then began nodding rapidly. When Macek finally released him, the guy quickly backed away and stuck the hand in his pocket as if to ensure that it didn't escape and do anything stupid like that again.

He hadn't given up the argument, though. It went on for at least a minute longer, and then he said something that seemed to get under Macek's skin. The bigger man clenched one fist and stalked forward, backing Short Guy against a table, nearly moving the two of them out of the range of the camera.

Claire grabbed for the controls and was about to zoom out so that she could see the entire scene, but then Macek backed off. The other man held his hands out in a placating gesture. Macek listened for a minute and then said something. Claire was no lip-reader, but it looked like he said *okay*. The other guy pulled his phone out of his jacket and tapped away for a few seconds. When he finished, he smashed his thumb against the screen, held it out for Macek's thumbprint, and then they both went back inside.

What the hell had she just witnessed? There was no way to know for sure without the audio, but the last few seconds had almost certainly been a financial transaction. It was hard to say, however, who was paying whom.

The jetboarder was long gone, and with both shows now over, Claire tried to pull her mind back to the video clips. They wouldn't answer any of the questions Bernard had identified as most pressing, but maybe sending them to the man would buy her a few hours of peace.

She had interviewed Kimura and Chelsea together, at their request. It made sense, given that they were in the same field. The official story on why Kim hadn't been included on the previous trip was that he had a personal conflict and couldn't make it. Chelsea, who was currently doing her doctoral research, had been able to step in at the last minute. That might have been true but given what Ben Pelzer had told Claire about their last grant being funded by NASA, she suspected Kim had still been in the doghouse over the comments he made at the Ares Consortium conference and Columbia didn't want to risk pissing their funding source off even more. From what she'd gathered, NASA wasn't involved in the current trip at all. Transportation was at KTI expense, with the rest being funded directly by the university, or in her own case, by the *Post*.

Both Kim and Chelsea were extremely cautious when the cameras were on. There was no sign of their usual snark or combativeness. Chelsea barely spoke at all, letting Kim take the lead. He did note that they'd found it odd that there was no biological residue of any sort in the outer chamber, but quickly added that it was possible that they'd find something from the samples they were taking back to the university lab.

"We're talking about millions, or possibly even several billions of years and what are, most likely, infinitesimally tiny samples," Kim said. "Field instruments are convenient, but they tend to miss a lot. They're nowhere near as precise as what we have in the lab back on Earth. And, of course, we still have high hopes for that second chamber. Assuming it's fully sealed, we may find something interesting."

Kim wore a friendly, open smile throughout the interview. Once the cameras were off, it vanished like mist in the morning and his usual sneer slid back into place. If his microbiology gig didn't work out, Claire thought the guy had a decent future in acting.

The segment with Ben Pelzer was by far the best of the bunch. Claire had him repeat the measurement on the chunk of olivine and explain how it might have ended up wrapped around the edge of the chamber. He was a natural teacher, and it was the only one of the interviews where they could actually demonstrate something, instead of just hypothesizing. She didn't really think it would move the needle with the skeptics— they'd just say sure, that rock might actually be millions of years old, but someone had probably glued it to the chamber when it was being transported to Daedalus City. Still, it was something beyond pure speculation.

As Pelzer's clip was wrapping up, Claire's tablet buzzed with an incoming message. It was Stasia, apologizing for the repeated rescheduling and promising that they'd get Claire on the calendar the next day if at all possible.

> Anything sooner is simply out of the question. Paul isn't in Daedalus, and Anton and I are in a conference with regional mining leaders.

No mention of Macek, but she already knew where he was, or at least where he'd been twenty minutes earlier.

Claire understood why Stasia was gatekeeping. She had a job to do. Managing the boss's schedule was a big part of it. But Claire also had a job to do. And right now, Claire's job required her to get in Anton Kolya's face.

It was a little after two thirty in the afternoon, Daedalus time. That translated to around ten thirty a.m. in DC. Which meant she could easily have six more hours of questions from Bernard. Maybe even more.

Screw that.

As soon as Claire pressed send on the interview files, she stashed the tablet in her daypack and headed for the elevator before she could talk herself out of it. The piano was in the executive pavilion, and Kolya had told her to come down and play whenever she wanted. Given that Macek and the mystery guy had headed back inside, she might even get some clues about the scuffle she'd witnessed. It was absolutely none of her business, but Claire had to admit that she was curious. And if it turned out that they were meeting with these mining leaders somewhere else, she would play a few songs on the baby grand, then grab a drink from the bar and head back up to her balcony to enjoy the oddly Earth-like denim blue of the Martian sunset.

While Claire might only manage to get Kolya's attention for a couple of minutes, that would be long enough to ask him a few questions.

Unfortunately, it was quite likely that one of those questions would ensure that this was their last civil conversation. Because, thanks to her little background search earlier, she was now all but certain that Kolya had told her a big whopping lie when they were at Tranquility Base, and she fully intended to find out why.

SIX

THE ELEVATOR DID a weird little series of hitches before it stopped on the lower level, something that Claire had learned was due to the car shifting laterally onto four separate platforms, each moving a tiny bit slower than the last. That way, passengers had a smoother transition from the gravity-mimicking spin of the residence floors to the stationary levels below.

Looking out through the glass doors of the elevator, the place seemed fairly empty, aside from the young woman behind the bar on the mezzanine level and a couple playing a board game in the conversation pit near the fireplace. The fire looked like the real deal to Claire, but that seemed unlikely. Even if there was enough wood on Mars to use it for creating ambiance, she doubted that they'd want to release smoke and ash inside a domed city.

As soon as the elevator door opened, the illusion of quiet vanished. A steady hum of noise emanated from the rear section of the room where she had noticed the red granite conference table a few mornings back. Once Claire rounded the corner, she discovered that section was now closed off inside a rectangle of dark panels that extended from the floor to the mezzanine level above her. Apart from the racket, it reminded her of the chamber over in Dome Three—another black mystery box full of trouble. The panels were nearly opaque and the only thing you could see were vague shadows of the people inside, dozens of them clustered in small groups around the long table. There was no sign of Macek or the guy with whom he'd been arguing, but four burly men who almost looked like they could be Macek's clones were positioned outside. They wore plainclothes and were trying to look unobtrusive, but it couldn't have been any more obvious that they were security guards if they'd been in full uniform.

While Claire couldn't say for certain that Kolya himself was inside the black box, she thought it was a pretty safe bet. And whoever was in there would have to come out eventually. The good news was that the mezzanine offered an unobstructed view of the conference room and surrounding area, and the piano would give her something to do while she watched and waited.

She went up the curved stairway and approached the young woman behind the bar.

"What can I get you?"

"I'm thinking something local. What would you recommend?"

"Depends on what you're in the mood for, really. We have an excellent selection of Martian beer and wine. If you're feeling kitschy there's a lager called *Little Green Men* that's actually green, but it's kind of bitter, in my opinion. Or if you'd prefer a mixed drink, our house cocktail is the Red Dahlia, made entirely from ingredients produced here in Daedalus City. I'd say it's similar to a cosmopolitan, with locally sourced vodka and house-brewed cranberry and raspberry liqueurs."

She told her that sounded good, and the woman proceeded to grab bottles from the shelves. While she was mixing the drink, the tablet pinged but Claire ignored it. She'd had enough of Bernard for a few hours.

"What's with the noise down there?" Claire asked.

"Mining conference. They were on break until about twenty minutes ago, so you're lucky that you waited to come down. Most meetings you can barely hear at all, but these guys get used to yelling at each other even when they're not arguing. The atmosphere is still a lot less dense outside the domes, so sound doesn't carry well. After a few years out there, some of them seem to forget they have indoor voices."

"Don't they have speakers inside their helmets?" she asked, thinking of the recording of Brodnik and the others at the mining site in Icaria. "I mean, I know the newer ones have a comm system, but I'd have thought they had something in the puffsuits, as well."

"They do, but it gets cumbersome if you're talking to a group. My ex did a six-month rotation over at a thorium mine in Mare Acidalium—good money, but they work the hell out of you. He said the comm system inside the helmets is fine if you're talking to one or two people, but after that, it's usually easier to just yell."

Claire nodded and took a sip of the drink. It was good, if a bit too sweet for her taste.

"When we were on the *Ares Prime*, Kolya offered to let me use your piano and said you could help me connect my earbuds? We really don't need me adding to the noise level."

The woman laughed. "I'm sure it would be an improvement. Hold on a sec, though. I'll have to look up the code."

Apparently, Kolya had been right that the piano didn't get much use because it took a couple of minutes for the bartender to find the code and figure out how to sync Claire's earbuds. By the time she finished her drink, though, she was all set.

As soon as Claire's fingers hit the keys of the baby grand, all thoughts of work slipped to the back of her mind and the noise of the room faded away. She began with the third movement of *Moonlight Sonata* (which Ro called her *pissed-off piece*) and then switched over to "Bohemian Rhapsody." After that, she just freestyled, drifting into mellower tunes as the notes and the movement drew out some of the tension that had been building for the past several weeks.

Sometime later, maybe a dozen people came out, closing the conference door behind them. All but two were men, none of them Kolya. Maybe it was the loud voices or just a stereotype from the various images and videos that Claire had seen from Martian mining camps, but she was expecting them to be in work gear and hard hats, much like the excavation crew at Dome Three. That was stupid, of course. From what Stasia had said, these were almost certainly mining *executives*. They were all dressed in business attire and looked like they could have walked out of any corporate boardroom back on Earth. The oldest of the two women, in fact, was wearing a dark green suit that looked almost identical to the one Claire's mother had worn in the photos she'd seen from the Rejuvesce launch.

About half of the group came upstairs to the bar. Others headed for the sofas on the lower level. A glance at the clock showed that Claire had been playing much longer than she thought—it was already a quarter to five. But she went back to it, mostly as a ruse now, so that she could keep an eye on the conference room door without being too obvious.

In the silence between songs, Claire heard voices directly below her. One of them mentioned Kolya's name, which caught her attention. She kept playing but turned the volume down to a faint whisper, hoping she might pick up something useful. If nothing else, maybe she could get an idea how long the conference was supposed to last and whether it made sense to get dinner and come back later.

"Yeah, well that's bullshit. You know it as well as I do." The voice was husky, but something about the tone made Claire fairly certain that the speaker was a woman. "They keep acting like there's some kind of law to enforce these mandates. But there's not. There's not a single damn one of us who can be certain that our subcontractors will follow these rules if they think it's going to put them out of business. Hell, half of them will break the rules if they think it will give them even a tiny advantage over competitors when we open back up. And I can't blame them. You and I can afford to take that hit—well, we can afford to if he manages to reason with these jerks and they don't hold out for *full* bonuses during the downtime. But some of the smaller companies…this could break them."

"You say that as if it's a bad thing," the man with her

replied. He had a slight lilt to his voice, but Claire couldn't place the accent. "I'm thinking it might be a very good time for those of us with the resources to step in and consolidate some of the subcontractors. Take out a few of the small fry. Maybe after that, we'll have enough power to come together and rein Kolya in if he gets another one of these hornets up his ass and decides to dictate policy for an entire planet."

The woman barked out a bitter laugh. "Are you kidding? If stage six works, nothing short of death itself will be able to rein him in. I suspect it's already too late. You'd think finding that stupid crypt would have put the brakes on at least a little, but the Ares Consortium didn't blink an eye. Didn't even move his target date."

"Kind of a shame that someone went to all that trouble, and it didn't work."

"What?" The woman's voice took on an incredulous tone. "You think the chamber was *planted*?"

"Me? Well, I don't know for certain one way or the other. But I traveled with Westmoreland on the flight over, and he said—"

"Oh, come on. Westmoreland? Are you serious? He's a complete idiot. Anything he says, you should believe the exact opposite. Personally, if I have to do business in Lyot, I pick one of the smaller companies. Wes would cheat his own mother."

"I really don't know him that well. I was just at our Mamers location this week and he asked if I wanted a lift to the conference. Why are you so sure he's wrong about the chamber?"

"Because I talked to Beyon—he's the new head of Pada—a few days after one of his mining teams hit the chamber. It's real."

Claire couldn't be sure of the man's name. The woman might have said Vedon, or Bijon, or pretty much anything. But the company name—pronounced pah-dah—rang a bell, even though she wasn't sure why. Had she seen or heard it in some of her research before she left Earth?

"He said that thing was half a klick *inside* the face of a crater," the woman continued. "So unless you know of someone who has developed a teleporter and found a way to beam a massive hunk of metal into *solid rock*, this thing is exactly what it appears to be. A civilization was here long, long before us and apparently, they screwed the place up big time."

"Maybe," the guy said, sounding a bit peeved. "Or maybe Pada is the one that planted it there. Or pretended to plant it. Wasn't Kolya in talks to buy out their interest? That's what I—"

Whatever he was about to say was drowned out by a loud roar from within the conference room, followed by the screech of chairs. One of the shadows approached the door. It banged open, and a thin man in glasses stormed out, his face a red mask of anger. Four others hurried along behind him toward the elevator. A few seconds later, Macek emerged. He exchanged a look with one of the men Claire had tagged as security, and the guard peeled off from the other three to go with Macek. Stasia joined them, too, and all three took off after the other group, not exactly running, but close.

The two people she had been eavesdropping on had now stepped out from under the mezzanine. Claire moved away from the piano to stand at the railing so that she could get a better look. The owner of the husky voice was indeed female—it was, in fact, the older woman in the impeccably tailored green suit. "Well, damn," she said idly to her companion, a comfortably upholstered gentleman in a Jodhpuri jacket. "That really doesn't look like a successful negotiation to me. Quite the opposite, in fact."

When the door opened again a few seconds later, several other people filed out, followed by Kolya. His face was haggard, and for once, he looked every second of his forty-seven years. He tapped his earpiece, and then his voice filled the larger room. "The MFL spokesman just received word that there was an explosion at the Millex facility in Cerberus about ten minutes ago. There are casualties, and since Cerberus is home base for one member of their delegation, we will be in recess for at least the next few hours and possibly until morning. Have dinner. Keep an eye on your messages. But on the off chance that we *are* able to reconvene this evening, please try to stay reasonably sober."

With those last words, his eyes flicked up toward the bar, moving past Claire at first and then snapping back to where she stood next to the piano. He hooked one imperious finger in her direction and stalked off toward the elevators at the back of the room.

It wasn't a request, but a command, and Claire's first instinct was to flip one of her own fingers in *his* direction. Not that he'd have seen it now that his back was turned. It was also an irrational response, since the entire reason she was hanging out in the executive pavilion—aside from a much needed session with the piano—was to speak to the man. The odds that she would get any answers out of him right now seemed remote, at best, but she had to at least try.

SEVEN

CLAIRE CAUGHT up to Kolya at the elevator. Five other people were already inside—the woman in the green suit, the Indian man in the Jodhpuri jacket, two other middle-aged men, and the short guy she'd seen arguing with Macek. One of them had apparently just asked Kolya if there was any indication whether the explosion was an accident or something more nefarious, because as Claire stepped inside, Kolya was telling them that he had no clue.

"It's entirely possible that it was an accident. They do happen from time to time, as you're all too well aware. Either way, I just hope that the casualties were limited."

"Well, of course. As do we all." The short guy stumbled and grabbed the rail behind him when the elevator did that weird side-shimmy to move the car back onto the spinning upper levels. His wrist was red and swollen. "But accident or not, their representative needs to get back to the negotiation table. I, for one, have a business to run."

The woman gave him a scornful look.

"As do we all," Kolya repeated back to him in a dry voice. "I'll pass along information as soon as it's available, Wes. Although, I'm sure you'll all have your own sources giving you the details by then."

"Do you have any indication as to how many are dead?" the woman asked.

"One of the team said at least three," Kolya told her. "But there may be more."

The elevator stopped at floor seven to drop off all but one of the men, including the Indian guy and the one Kolya had called

Wes. Was that short for Westmoreland, the man who had apparently been spreading rumors about the chamber being planted?
Claire thought it might be, since the woman had called Westmoreland an idiot earlier and her expression had made it clear
that she held this Wes guy in equally low regard.

As if reading her mind, the woman looked over and gave
Claire a quick assessment. She was not impressed with the
jeans. Her eyebrows shot up, however, when she reached
Claire's face. Given that it had been splashed onto viewscreens
across two planets over the past few days, Claire thought it
probably looked familiar.

Once the woman and the other remaining passenger were
gone, leaving Kolya and Claire alone, he leaned back against the
mirrored wall of the elevators and rubbed his temples.
"Remember the other day, when I did you a favor and had
Macek hold all guest communications for a few hours, so that
your editor wouldn't lose his shit?"

What Claire remembered was that it was less a favor than a
required action to uphold KTI's promise of an exclusive. They
also hadn't held the guests' communications nearly long
enough to keep Bernard happy. But the last part was due at
least as much to the *Post's* editorial board and, she suspected,
her own lack of experience. She should have realized that there
would be a lot of legal hoops to jump through before they
okayed the story and that many on the board would assume the
information was a hoax. So, instead of arguing the point, she
simply gave Kolya a curt nod and waited for him to continue.

"Okay, I need to ask you to repay that courtesy and hold off
on reporting the current situation to your paper until I give you
the go-ahead."

She was tempted to note the major imbalance between the
two requests. While he'd held off for a few hours, he seemed to
be asking her to hold off indefinitely. He was also forgetting
something rather important.

"Why would it even matter if I sent this in to the paper?"

she asked. "You just told an entire room. Several of them were already on their phones."

"What? I'm not talking about the explosion. I meant the proposed strike." For a moment, they just looked at each other, both confused. Then, he spotted her earbuds and his expression shifted to a smile. "Ah. You came down to play the piano, not because you were chasing a hot tip."

"Yes. But, in the interest of full disclosure, I was also planning to waylay you once you were done and ask some questions about the whole situation with the Icarus chamber. Stasia made it clear that you're too busy for an appointment, but I really only need a few minutes. And my editor is…"

Claire trailed off, momentarily at a loss for words. The door had opened on the penthouse level, although at first, she thought they were on the roof. She stepped out into a circular area surrounded by eight red petal balconies. There were no exterior walls and no ceiling, just a curved, transparent dome that offered a panoramic view of the colony—Daedalus City in one direction and small clusters of communities and farms in the other. She could also see several smaller enclosures, two of which housed heavy equipment and one that held only the tiny black speck of the Icarus chamber.

The outer ring of the penthouse was designed for entertaining, with furniture arranged to make the most of the view. A bar nearly as large as the one in the executive pavilion sat on one side next to a dining area with seating for twelve. Overlapping crimson panels at the center of the room continued the dahlia motif, separating what she assumed were Kolya's private quarters from the rest of the apartment.

He smiled. "The view kind of takes your breath at first, doesn't it?"

"Yes," Claire said. "It's incredible."

That was true of the room, too. It could very easily have been gauche and overdone, but the designer had been smart enough to keep the furnishings simple so that the view remained center stage.

"It seems to spin more slowly up here than on my level. Or am I just getting used to seeing the scenery zip past?"

"No," he said. "It's slower. This level is on a separate track. I increase the spin when I'm sleeping and when I exercise, but it's nice to view the world out there at a more leisurely pace. At some point, I'll probably dispense with it entirely. But for the next few decades, at least, I'll need to spend a few months out of the year on Earth, which means that I need to keep my body used to the higher level of gravity."

Kolya lifted his face up to the clear ceiling, taking in the last of the late afternoon sun. "The one area where Mars will never be able to compete with Earth is the amount of natural light. We're simply too far away from the source. So I have our architects maximize what little we do have, allowing design to compensate for what nature cannot provide in abundance. Not just here, but throughout the colony." He nodded toward a gray sofa. "Now…what were you saying about your editor?"

"Oh, right." Claire took a seat as Kolya headed over to the bar. "Bernard now has what amounts to a second full-time job fielding questions about the chamber and the highly unorthodox manner in which you decided to release that information on an unsuspecting world."

"I'm not surprised that there are questions."

"Neither are we," she said, struggling to keep the annoyance out of her voice. "We are, however, a bit surprised that we're expected to *handle* those questions on our own when they stem almost entirely from decisions KTI made. Members of our editorial board and a slew of outside sources, including government leaders and the UN, are suspicious that this is a massive hoax. And since they aren't getting responses from you beyond the very basic KTI press release that you sent out that afternoon, all of those questions and accusations are landing on Bernard. That makes him unhappy. And when Bernard is unhappy…well, he's not the kind to keep the misery to himself. Major story or not, I think he's about ready to kick this *junior reporter* to the curb."

Kolya sighed. "That part wasn't intentional. It's just that recent events pushed this whole thing to the back burner. When we were on the *Ares Prime* and I told you that I would be busy for the next two weeks, I was telling the truth. I anticipated that in addition to tending to some very necessary oversight tasks to keep stage six on schedule, some of my time would be spent dealing with the various requests and, almost certainly, *complaints* about my decisions regarding the chamber."

He poured some amber liquid into a glass and held up the bottle. "Krambambula. It was the Belarusian national drink, before we merged with the Eastern European Union. Each region has its own special blend. Languages may die, but liquor lives on. This is the only thing I continue to import from Minsk, because we're still missing a few of the spices here on Mars. Have you tried it before?"

Claire shook her head.

"If you would prefer not to experiment, I can…" He waved a hand at the shelves behind him.

'No. The krabam…the whatever you called it sounds fine."

"Krambambula. Anyway, to get back to the issue at hand, I had my schedule planned out for everything I just mentioned but did *not* anticipate being hit the very next morning with a major labor crisis that could unravel the entire terraforming effort. I've been up for more than…" He glanced at a clock behind the bar. "More than thirty-two hours."

"You do look beat."

"Truth in advertising," he said with a grin. "As I told you before, I'm an open book."

She resisted rolling her eyes and took the glass he offered.

"Have you eaten?" he asked. "I'm going to call down for a pizza. You can order something else if you like, but I need food that doesn't require anything more complicated than lifting my hand to my mouth."

She told him that she hadn't eaten, that pizza was fine with her as long as he avoided mushrooms, and then took a sip of the drink as he called down to the kitchen. It was mildly sweet, considerably stronger than she had expected, and wonderfully spicy, with hints of honey and coffee.

Kolya collapsed onto the sofa next to her and cast a questioning eye toward her glass.

"It's good. Very good, in fact."

That earned her a delighted smile that almost, *almost* made Claire forget that the man was a dirty rotten liar. "You have exquisite taste," he said, holding the glass up to examine the amber liquid in the late afternoon sunlight. "This is the nectar of the gods."

The drink *was* good, but for someone who claimed to now be a citizen of Mars (although technically, he must have at least dual citizenship), Claire found Kolya's absurd pleasure that she liked the national drink of his homeland a little odd. Or maybe he'd simply reached the stage of exhaustion where every emotion was magnified.

"Has it occurred to you that you might need a bigger staff?" she said, pulling them back toward the subject.

Kolya's lip curled slightly at the suggestion but there was a hint of amusement in his eyes. "Sounds like you've been talking to Stasia."

"No," she said, not adding that she had barely spoken to Stasia since the day of the ill-fated debate. "But I *have* spent much of my life observing the behavior of a high profile CEO. My mother travels with an entire pack of assistants, even when it's only a short trip."

"I have over two thousand employees in Daedalus alone. Twice that many on Mars as a whole, and nearly a million employees on Earth. I just prefer to keep a very small *personal* staff. That's partly because I like my privacy and partly because I'm the world's worst delegator, as Stasia frequently points out. But delegating requires you to trust people, and I have learned over the years that trusting too many people can come back to bite you in the ass. I also function better if I can keep the number of people who communicate directly with me to a bare minimum. Stasia is my liaison with KTI's science and engineering arms, and she handles all communications—well, except for communications security. Macek handles all security and he's my lead person on legal issues and corporate negotiations."

Claire wondered if what she'd seen Macek doing outside with Wes counted as *corporate negotiations*. If so, it seemed like a major euphemism.

"So most of the time," he said, "I deal directly with only two people—Macek and Stasia. And, occasionally, Caruso. We added him about three years ago because Stasia was getting overloaded. When we're in Minsk, she can shift more of her responsibilities onto the main KTI staff, but here..." He shrugged. "Caruso is off handling something for me now, in fact, so everything has been on the three of us. Stasia and I traveled to Elysia on Tuesday, hoping to avoid the need for a full conference. Macek was out there, too. He only got back this morning. I don't think any of us have had more than fifteen hours of sleep *total* since this thing began to heat up Monday afternoon. And we almost, *almost*, had a resolution. I was literally seconds away from striking an agreement with the MFL when all of their phones went off at once with messages about the disaster."

"What exactly is the MFL?"

"Mars Federation of Labor. Or maybe it's Mars Federated Laborers. I can't remember. The group started organizing in Elysia a few months back, and they've picked up steam more quickly than I'd have thought. A chapter started at Cerberus about six weeks ago."

"What are their demands?"

"The right to unionize, to begin with. That's not assured in the other colonies and definitely not in the unincorporated areas. But the key issue is that they want full pay, with the usual bonuses, during the six months of downtime. Just to be clear, Daedalus isn't a nonunion colony. We have four different labor unions here, and apparently, they're all supporting this bullshit last minute stunt. Which is their right… but if housekeeping doesn't show up tomorrow with fresh linens, just remember that you can blame it on the MFL."

"It's not *really* last minute, though, is it? I mean, stage six isn't set to launch for nearly a month."

"Twenty-four days. And when you're talking about a multifaceted planetary wide initiative, anything less than a year counts as last minute."

"There were dozens of people in the executive pavilion," Claire said. "Do you really think the news about the strike hasn't already spread?"

"Maybe. And I'm sure that it will eventually. But the people in that room have every bit as much reason as I do to hold information about a potential strike close to their chests for the time being. Something like this can tank stock prices. Every company involved in these negotiations has a parent corporation back on Earth to answer to. But yeah, some of them may already be short selling with their personal funds, and if we don't get the union reps back into the room by tomorrow morning, that's going to increase…which is why I'm really hoping that explosion at the Cerberus mines was an accident."

EIGHT

"BUT YOU DON'T BELIEVE it *was* an accident, do you?"

Kolya shrugged and poured himself another shot. "Let's just say there have been threats. I was hoping they were idle ones, similar to the saber rattling that the new iteration of Shepherd's Flock has been doing on Earth."

"Are those threats why Stasia edited out every reference to the location where the chamber was found? Twenty-five hundred kilometers or so from Daedalus City is really vague and that lack of precision about the location is one of the most frequent complaints we're hearing about the story."

He nodded. "It's also why I wanted to have *both* chambers excavated and transported back here. As I said before, it wasn't just convenience, but also security."

"That's troubling, then, because I don't think you can count on the location being secret much longer. Two of the people who were in the elevator with us knew the name of the contractor whose workers found it. I heard them talking just before your negotiations with the MFL came to an abrupt end. She didn't mention the crater or even Icarus Camp, but she knew it was a firm called Pada."

"I'm not too worried about Elizabeth. Who was she talking to?"

"The man in the Jodhpuri jacket."

"Thanks for letting me know. I'll have Macek increase security at Icarus, *again*, given the attack on Cerberus. This whole thing is going to piss him off royally. It's hard to add new security personnel quickly and Macek hates being spread so thin.

Most of the threats have been at locations connected in some way to KTI."

"Does that include the Cerberus mines?"

Kolya nodded. "They're in an unincorporated area, operating under one of our contractors, Miller Excavation, usually known as Millex. But they supply about a third of the tridymite for our operations, so yeah, there's a definite connection. They also supply Elysia, which is the colony they're closest to, and apparently, they have a new contract with Lyot." His huff with the last part suggested to Claire that he wasn't exactly happy about the new contract. "But, yeah, we're still their biggest client."

"Tridymite…that's a form of silica, isn't it?"

"Yes. A form that works better than others as an insulator. It's a major component in KTI's tridygel—which is the aerogel that Daedalus and most of the other colonies use to make the domes. We're still at least a few decades away from being able to dispense with the domes entirely—possibly more than a few decades, but I'll deny the hell out of that if you repeat it. And even after we're able to slow down the rate at which we're building domes, there's maintenance to consider. The sheets have to be replaced periodically. And even after *that*, tridymite is a component in another project in the developmental stages…" He stopped and shook his head, glancing down at his drink. "Whoa. I need to watch my rambling tongue. And maybe I should pat you down for hidden recording devices."

Claire raised an eyebrow. "You could *try*. But since you just said that you're too tired to even manage a fork, I think you'll have a difficult time catching me."

"True," he said, laughing softly. "And, to be honest, that seems like an activity that would be much more fun when I'm not exhausted."

It seemed like an activity that he was unlikely to get a chance at either way given what Claire had learned that morning. But he didn't know that yet, so she simply gave him a prim smile. "I'm not recording. In fact, I assumed we were off the record. But I *am* curious—not about your super-secret project but about the explosion. Assuming it wasn't an accident, who do you think might be behind it?"

"Several of the most likely suspects were in the executive pavilion just now. I should have had Macek lock the doors and let you play detective for a bit."

"You mean the smaller mining companies? If they're the ones who stand to lose the most during the mandatory down-time, I guess they *would* be the ones most likely to try and throw a wrench in the...machinery." Claire realized as she spoke the words that they were the same ones Ben Pelzer had used a few days back. "That's the same thing KTI thought about the Icarus chamber at first, isn't it? That it was an attempt at sabotage."

"At first? Yeah. And, you're right that it's *mostly* the smaller companies that want to stop—or at least delay—the terraforming. But now that we're looking at a potential intercolonial strike, the situation is considerably more complicated. Many of the people in that room today are closely connected to the polit-ical leadership in their respective colonies. And some of these colonies are run like private fiefdoms."

"Some? I was under the impression that they all are."

"Okay, yes, but to varying degrees. Rather than looking at the long-term best interest of the planet and investing workers with economic and political rights, some of the colonial leaders want carte blanche to employ what are basically indentured servants. That's not how they phrase it, of course, but no matter how they polish it up, that's what it boils down to in the end. It's been a huge sticking point in the negotiations for a Martian constitution, something that we need to iron out. I knew this conflict was coming, but I'd hoped we'd be able to postpone it until later in the year, once stage six was behind us. Because I really do think we're going to have a surge in investment coming into Mars after that. And that surge would be exponential if we could promise the solid foundation that comes from a stable, cohesive government."

A bell went off then, and Kolya fetched a large pizza from the room service window behind the bar. The smell of pepperoni wafted up from the box, and Claire's stomach rumbled in anticipation.

For the next few minutes, they simply ate without talking. Her mind continued to work, however, thinking back to the dinner discussion with Wyatt when he had mentioned Kolya's ongoing labor issues. And then there were the picketers that she'd seen during her brief stay at Tranquility. To Claire, the labor disputes back home didn't mesh with the image Kolya was trying to cultivate on Mars.

"You seem to be relatively pro-worker here at Daedalus and yet there was a crowd picketing KTI at the lunar base. And I also recall reading something about KTI having similar issues back home."

He gave her an annoyed look. "I'm *pro-worker* on Earth, too. That still doesn't mean that I cave in to every little demand, so yes, we get protests from time to time. Although, if you read beyond the headlines, you'll see that most of the complaints aren't from my actual employees, but rather from employees of smaller companies whose owners bid low on contracts with KTI in order to beat out their competitors. Rather than the owners and shareholders tightening their own belts, they slash worker salaries and blame it on KTI. That happened recently with one of the lunar contractors, which resulted in the protest you saw while we were there."

His story seemed dodgy to Claire, and woefully familiar, since she'd heard her mother making the same excuse on more than one occasion. "But...can't you require subcontractors to follow fair labor practices and give workers a decent wage?"

"Sure. But good luck finding a definition of *fair labor practices*, let alone *decent wage*, that is acceptable not just across nations, but now across planets. And to be honest, we need a higher standard here than we do on Earth. I'm trying to convince people to set down roots, to make Mars their permanent home. To do that, I need to offer extra incentives and some degree of job security. If my workers on Earth don't like the pay and benefits, they can easily go elsewhere. Here, though? That's a much more difficult prospect and it's one reason that people are reluctant to give Mars a go." He stifled a yawn and said, "You probably have five minutes at most before I'm completely useless. What do you need from me to appease your editor?"

"It's not just a matter of appeasing my editor. The issue is more appeasing the multitude of people who are hounding him. They want to know why you decided to release the information the way you did. For example, the press office at the White House wants to know why the *Atlantic Post* was given this information before they were. Pretty much the same question from NASA and…" Claire scanned the notes on her tablet. "And thirty-two other national or regional space agencies and military organizations, several of which are claiming that there are clear national security implications. That's one reason there's still a big fat disclaimer at the top of our coverage although Bernard says the *Post's* lawyers are fairly confident that the story falls under First Amendment protections. So…at a minimum, could you please tell me why you opted to break the news the way you did—specifically, to a single junior science reporter operating under an NDA that prevented advance editorial scrutiny—rather than going through what were apparently the appropriate channels for a story of this magnitude? And before you start, I should let you know that I did a bit of digging earlier today. It seems that my mother isn't the *only* one on Columbia University's Science Advisory Board."

NINE

KOLYA ACTUALLY HAD the nerve to laugh, leaving no doubt in Claire's mind that her guess had been correct.

"I've been on the advisory board for the past twelve or thirteen years," he said. "In fact, if not for the generous discounts KTI offers on transportation and lodging, the university's Mars program probably wouldn't exist. Government grants tend to be pretty meager."

"You *lied* to me. Back at Tranquility Base, you said you assumed my mother was the reason I'd gotten the assignment."

"I did not lie. What I said was that *Dr. Brodnik* assumed your mother had gotten the assignment for you. And she absolutely did assume that."

Kolya might have been right on that point. Claire couldn't remember his exact words, and once again wished she'd been running a recording device that night.

"But you did say you assumed Kai might be placing a spy in your ranks. I remember that."

"No...I very clearly said it would be *reasonable* for me to assume that she might send a spy, given her threats of legal action."

"Fine. Either way, it's semantics. You're playing stupid word games. Maybe you weren't technically *dishonest*, but you were most definitely disingenuous."

"You're hurt. I'm sorry." He actually did look contrite, and for some reason, that pissed her off even more than the earlier laugh.

"Not hurt. *Angry*," she countered, although he wasn't entirely wrong.

"Would it matter if I told you that the decision wasn't... personal? Stasia—or maybe it was Caruso—suggested your name along with four or five other candidates when we were deciding the best way to deal with the publicity. Given your mother's very open disdain for me, they thought people would be less inclined to believe that you would be biased toward KTI."

"Not if they'd bothered to do some basic research. There are very few subjects on which I take the same position as my mother."

Even as Claire spoke the words, she remembered Beck pointing out, correctly, that Kolya was probably the only subject on which she and her mother agreed. A few days earlier, Claire might have said she'd judged the man too hastily, but she and Kai were now squarely in the same camp again.

Kolya ignored her interruption and continued. "Second, we wanted a respected media outlet and a journalist who was relatively inexperienced but had a good reputation—"

"So that you could trash it?"

"*With a good reputation* so that they could weather the inevitable firestorm at the beginning." He yawned again. "I mean, there's no way that the *Atlantic Post* would cover up for KTI if this were some sort of hoax. There were several other things that my tired brain can't dredge up at the moment. But finally...well, to be honest, the final part *was* somewhat personal. Your mother seems bound and determined to sue us over the biobots. I think it's more due to pettiness on her part than to any actual belief that we've engaged in industrial espionage. The woman is still holding a grudge over things that happened more than a decade ago, things that weren't even my fault. Weren't anyone's fault. I get it, but at this point, it's kind of ridiculous."

"You're right," she said, thinking of how angry Kai had been about the Zimmer award. "It wasn't reasonable. But she already had a spot waiting on her shelf."

He frowned, then gave his head a little shake as if trying to fathom that degree of pettiness. Or maybe he was just trying to clear away the fog of exhaustion.

"Anyway," he continued, "she would lose a lawsuit on this. I have absolutely no doubt about that. *None*. But lawsuits suck up time, money, and energy. I try to avoid them when possible. And I thought that if you were the journalist assigned to cover the chamber, you could take back evidence—evidence with a clear chain of custody, as Kimura would put it—and maybe you could convince Kai to back off. Let bygones be bygones. Because as I said before, our work going forward should be on a complementary, not a competitive track."

"I'm certainly willing to take samples back to the lab and to vouch for their origin. Joe will be overjoyed, to say the least. But if you think I can convince my mother of anything, you're sadly mistaken."

"That may be true," he admitted. "But you *can* convince your brother. And I believe he can convince Kai. Anyway, that was the final straw that tipped the balance in your favor. I pulled a few strings with my contacts at Columbia, pointing out that they'd probably earn some brownie points with your mother at the same time for giving you such a big break. In my defense, though, I didn't think I'd find myself interested in you. I'm rarely attracted to women who are so much younger."

Was that true? Claire had no idea. But it really didn't matter, and she definitely didn't want to discuss it at the moment.

"And," Kolya continued, "I certainly didn't think you'd have any interest in me. To be honest, I would have assumed that the situation with your mother would..." He shrugged.

"Let's set that aside for the moment. Since you've now admitted that the release strategy wasn't an accident—that you basically set me up—could you at least explain to me why you went to all this trouble, rather than going through what were apparently the proper channels for this sort of discovery?"

"I'd think that would be obvious. If I'd gone through the so-called proper channels, this information would *still* be in the hands of a very small number of people. And who knows how long it would have remained there? At a minimum, there would have been months and months of top secret negotiations on how to release the news to the public, as they called in a vast array of psychological experts, religious leaders, and who knows what other variety of charlatan, to debate the impact this sort of news—which was purely hypothetical, they'd be quick to note—might have on society and the global economy. *Years* might even have passed before we had any firm decision on when or even whether to release it."

"So, you were afraid it would delay stage six? That the Ares Consortium would demand further analysis?"

"The Ares Consortium—or at least, the committee that I deal with on this project—already cleared us to move ahead once they confirmed that there were no unique lifeforms in the chamber. But yes, I was worried that their decision might be...over-ruled...if too many people were involved, so that *was* a consideration. A major one, if I'm being honest, and I clearly need to do a better job of being honest with you going forward. But it wasn't the *only* consideration, Claire. I wasn't joking about governments colluding and deciding not to release this discovery to the public. It wouldn't be the first time."

"Are you talking about rumors like Area 51? Or that thing they supposedly dredged up near Bermuda?"

"Those would be two examples, I suppose. I'm just saying that there are things the public never learns because it's deemed too disturbing."

Claire wasn't naïve enough to think that governments released everything they knew. On the other hand, she didn't believe that something of this magnitude could be kept under wraps in the long run. She wasn't even sure that they'd bother to try. Too many people would have known already. Even before the story went public, there were probably a dozen people who knew about the chamber at Columbia alone. She had no idea how many knew at KTI. On Mars, there were the miners at Icarus Camp, the CEO of this Pada company, the people that CEO decided to tell, and the people that *they* decided to tell…which she now knew for certain was a non-zero number. And communications might be laggy between Earth and Mars, but the multitude of amateur videos of the chamber that had been posted by Kolya's guests over the previous few days was proof positive that a bit of delay wouldn't stop a good story.

"Personally," he continued. "I think people have a right to know. They have a right to know that there was advanced technological life on this planet in the very distant past. They have a right to know that this ancient civilization managed to wipe themselves out to the point that the only evidence that remains is a couple of metal boxes deeply embedded inside a crater. Maybe it will be a wake-up call, a reminder that we can't pin all of our hopes for survival on a single fragile planet."

Claire flashed back to Tobias Shepherd, standing at the porthole on the *Ares Prime*, telling her how the view perfectly captured the fragility of Earth. And even before that, Kolya at dinner, saying that he and Shepherd had the same end goal—the survival of humanity.

"Where is Dr. Shepherd?"

As soon as the question was out, Claire realized that it was a weird non sequitur for anyone not privy to her internal monologue. But Kolya didn't seem to notice. Maybe he thought it was another one of the questions that her editor wanted answered.

"Shepherd is safe. He's in a remote location and we have a guard assigned to him. I suspect it's overkill, however, given that everyone was checked thoroughly before leaving the *Ares Prime*."

Claire nodded, even though she remembered him saying

everyone would be checked thoroughly before they *boarded* the ship at Tranquility, and the drone had still made it through their sweep. "He had no lasting ill effects from the attack?"

"None. The speed of his recovery surprised Dr. Yadav and the doctors here at Daedalus who checked him out upon our arrival. They all said that the neurotoxin should have killed him well before Yadav was able to administer the antidote. Shepherd was damned lucky. Of course, Macek has a different theory. He says the man is so paranoid that he probably built up an immunity to every toxin he could get his hands on."

"Like iocaine powder."

He frowned. "I don't think I'm familiar with that one."

She laughed. "Just an old movie I watched as a kid. I think it's more likely that Shepherd is extra healthy from all of that clean living on the Flock's farms."

"Pfft," Kolya said. "He looks anemic to me."

Claire thought that was actually kind of true. "Anyway," she said, "getting back to the chamber, I guess I can understand you wanting to be sure that the information actually makes it to the public. But you may have inadvertently guaranteed that most of them will think it's a hoax. Have you been following the coverage back on Earth?"

"No," he admitted. "As I believe I noted, I've been very busy for the past few days. But I'm not surprised that's the view right now. It will change in time, though, especially after they see video of the excavation of that second chamber." He stopped and cocked his head to the side, considering something. "Do you think it would help if you could send your editor footage of the *first* excavation? And the video that Brodnik recorded?"

Claire's eyes widened. "Of course. Absolutely. I didn't even know that there *was* footage of the first excavation. That would probably go a long way toward convincing some of the skeptics."

"I wouldn't count on that," he said. "There are still people who believe the Earth is flat, after all. That we've never been to the moon, let alone Mars. But if you think it will help, send a message to Stasia, and tell her I okayed the release. And you should probably tell Brodnik before sending the video that they took— technically, KTI now owns the rights, but just as a courtesy. As for the security camera footage, we didn't release it because it's nearly two days' worth of video and it's pretty low quality. Poorly lit and jumpy. Your editorial board may not be as pleased as you think when you dump this on them."

"They have interns."

"Ah, yes, the civilized form of indentured servitude," he said teasingly. "And yet you jab at me about KTI's labor practices. Do you have any other questions before I toss you out and get a few hours of sleep?

Claire opened her tablet again. "No…but could you give me a quick quote summing up your reasoning? I don't want anything to get twisted."

He nodded and she pressed record.

"Presenting this discovery to the world as a fait accompli was the safest way to ensure that it was shared with the public. I wanted to make sure that there was no chance for it to be…" He paused, searching for the right phrase. "To be swept under the rug. To be *disappeared*, if you prefer. No laws were broken, no treaty commitments violated. The chamber was found on KTI property. In the end, it was *my* decision to make, and I made it."

"Okay, I'll have to take your word on that last part since I'm not an expert on Martian colonial law. But, assuming that it's true, do you really think a decision that big should be left up to *one* individual?"

Kolya thought for a moment. "I'll answer that one, but only *off* the record."

She sighed and stopped the recording.

"No. I absolutely do not think that sort of decision should be left up to one individual." A slow, somewhat devious smile spread across his face. "Although, if it *has* to be made by a single individual, I'm obviously glad that it's me. I'm simply working with the tools at hand, though, and they are limited. As long as we have no united government, each individual Martian colony—which actually boils down to the major corporations that run those colonies—has its own internal rules and directs its own foreign policy with the various governments on Earth. Frequently, those decisions end up hurting the other four colonies, and often even hurt the colony that made the decision, too, because it keeps all of us at each other's throats. Until this planet has a constitution and a legal code..." He shrugged. "Paul Caruso put it very well. He said Mars is the Wild Freakin' West. In many areas, there is no effective rule of law. And if this experience helps a few more people to understand why that's not a good thing from both a practical and an economic standpoint, I'll consider that a wonderful bonus."

"Fair enough. I'll go and let you get some rest now."

"Hold on a minute. You asked me questions. Now I have a question for *you*. Would you have agreed to travel here to Mars if you'd known I was the one calling in favors to get you on the contract?"

"Yes." At the back of her mind, she heard Wyatt asking if she'd taken the job to irritate her mother. It wasn't entirely true, but Claire had admitted it was icing on the cake. Knowing Kolya was behind it would have piqued her curiosity as to why, but it wouldn't have been a stumbling block, by any means.

"Yes," she repeated. "And it might have made..."

"Might have made what?" he prompted.

"Well, I was going to say that it might have made things easier with Brodnik's team, but that's probably not true. Kimura would have been even more of an ass than he already is." She stashed the tablet into her daypack. "Thank you for dinner. And for introducing me to kram...bambula?"

Kolya nodded. "Close enough. I'm glad you like it. I'll have a bottle sent to your room."

Before she could get up, he leaned toward her and placed a

hand on her arm. "I'm sorry that I wasn't honest with you from the beginning, Claire. Are you still interested in traveling to Ehden with me?"

Claire *was* still interested in the trip, and she definitely still wanted to get those samples for Joe. But she was now far more inclined than before to keep things on a strictly professional level.

"Sure. My audience will be very interested in stage six, especially after these other segments are posted."

Kolya gave her a rueful smile, seeming to pick up on her wording. "I think your editor will be pleased. Always assuming he doesn't—how did you put it? Kick you to the curb?"

"I think I can appease him with the video footage you promised. Do you think we'll still be leaving on Saturday, though, given the current situation with the MFL?"

"Yes. We're leaving Saturday morning. The trip isn't one that I can postpone if we're going to keep to our schedule for the next stage. We'll likely need to stay over at Ehden for one night, so that I can make a quick solo trip over to Cerberus for a few hours and pay my respects to those who were killed and injured."

"But…what if the labor dispute doesn't resolve in your favor? I thought you said that it could entirely derail stage six?"

He gave her a grim look. "It could. Which is how I *know* that the situation will resolve in my favor. It has to. The only question is how much of the burden for that settlement I can push onto the shoulders of other companies who also stand to benefit from everything going ahead as planned and how much of it will fall on KTI."

TEN

ON THE ELEVATOR ride back down to her room, Claire felt the tablet vibrate inside the daypack. It had gone off several times in the executive pavilion and once when she was in Kolya's apartment. She was tempted to simply shut the thing off entirely for the rest of the evening, but she needed to message Stasia about the video. And maybe send Bernard the quote from Kolya so that he could disseminate it to the slobbering wolves at his door.

The two most recent messages were indeed from Bernard. Another one was from the press office of a US senator whose name Claire vaguely recognized. The first one, though, was from Ro, so she had an excuse to delay opening the others.

> Hey! Hope you're doing well and managing to work in a little fun. I've heard Daedalus is pretty wild. 😉 Things have been wild here, too. Jemma's cat had another run-in with that sheepdog next door. The neighbor, of course, blames everything on our poor little kitty. But I suppose the old fossil is right in a way. It's a very bad idea to tangle with the hound from hell…now I just have to be sure kitty steers clear so that things don't blow up. This is already strike two, and I don't want to end up in mediation with the HOA.

Okay, then…not a message from Ro, but rather from Wyatt. That was established by the first two sentences and carved in stone by the emoji. Ro hated the things in general but had a particular loathing for Mr. Winkyface.

The rest of the message was sheer nonsense. One set of neighbors owned a dog, but it was a fluffy little Pomeranian puppy—definitely not a *hound from hell*. Siggy had never even met the neighbors' pup, because she was strictly an indoor cat. She liked to look out the window but seemed to consider the great outdoors as the equivalent of a viewscreen. The one time they had tried to take her into the yard, it freaked her out. She had scrambled back through the door so fast that she left a wicked scratch on Ro's arm. The neighbors were also both male, which meant the pronoun was wrong. Both were in their thirties, too, so *old fossil* definitely didn't fit either one of them. And Claire didn't even have a homeowners' association, thank God.

So, she began breaking the message down. In light of recent events, *blow up* wasn't ambiguous at all. *Hound from hell* was clearly a reference to Cerberus. *Sheepdog* was oddly specific, and Claire thought it was probably intentional phrasing, but she had no idea what Wyatt meant by it. Maybe it was just to reinforce the fact that he was talking about the Cerberus mine, but she would have thought he'd use *guard dog* in that case. No clue about *old fossil*, either—although, again, a fossil was something you dug up, so it could be another reference to the mine. *Strike* and the bit about mediation with the HOA were probably in reference to the MFL negotiation, so Kolya had apparently been wrong about the others keeping that story quiet.

When she opened the *Post*, however, she didn't see anything about the explosion or about the strike. A quick search of other Earth outlets also showed nothing. It was most likely due to the communications lag, although she supposed it was possible that Macek's crew was once again engaging in a bit of censorship with the media sources available to guests at the resort.

The fledgling *Red Planet* news service based in Daedalus City was the only source that had news of the bombing, but it was just a brief developing story blurb. There was no mention at all of an impending strike, which Claire found odd when pretty much every mining executive on the planet was in the city at the moment. You'd think that would at least have raised suspicions among the local journalists. Assuming, of course, that there was more than one. She could easily see the *Red Planet* website being the province of a single person.

And then Claire remembered the source on Mars that Wyatt had mentioned. He'd said that there were rumors about forming a union, and that had been nearly a month ago. She was pretty sure that his contact was in Elysia, though, and she didn't know whether the source was a fellow journalist or someone who worked in the mines.

She sat on the bed for several minutes, trying to come up with a response that would let Wyatt know that she was aware of the explosion and that she wasn't going to Cerberus. Kolya had plainly said his trip to pay respects would be solo and a quick look at the map showed Ehden was about twenty-five hundred kilometers from the mine that was hit. That was basically the distance between DC and Denver, so surely it had to count as steering clear of the *hound from hell*. And it was probably a moot point, anyway. If it was actually a terrorist attack and not an accident, it seemed unlikely that they'd hit the same location a second time.

It was sweet of Wyatt to worry, but also a little amusing that he seemed to think there was more of a lag in communication between various points on Mars than there was between Mars and Earth. Information passed between Daedalus and Elysia in the blink of an eye, and news of the bombing would have reached the Red Dahlia long before it reached DC. Unless, of course, Wyatt was less worried about the speed of communication than he was about the state of the free press on the planet. He almost certainly knew more about censorship on Mars than she did.

But…then she remembered that this had been the *first* message in the list. The first message that she'd ignored. Had it come in when she was at the piano? No, when she was at the bar waiting for her drink.

Claire checked the timestamp and saw that it arrived at *14:58 DMT*. So just before three p.m., Daedalus time, which would be just before eleven a.m. Eastern Time. Add in the communications lag, which was usually just over fifteen minutes, and that meant Wyatt had sent this message from DC around ten forty.

From what Kolya had said in the conference room, the explosion couldn't have happened much before five…or around one p.m. back in DC.

Which meant that Wyatt hadn't been telling her about an attack that had already happened.

He'd been warning her about an attack several hours *before* it happened.

ELEVEN

CLAIRE'S TRAM pulled into Dome Two a little after seven thirty on Saturday morning. The dome, which sat just off to the side of the main launch area where they'd touched down the previous week, was about five times larger than the one that held the Icarus chamber. Much deeper, too, with high cliff faces all around. Three tunnels led into the dome—the one she had come in on, one leading off toward the main launch area, and a third tunnel that simply disappeared into the side of the crater.

In the center, atop a metal platform, a single, two-passenger ship was waiting. The cruiser was a seamless curve, sort of an inverted U, with the ends nearly touching. It was almost blindingly white under the lights on the landing pad, with black trim along the sides and a red KTI logo on the hatch, which now stood open. Kolya was in the cockpit, looking a little annoyed, probably because Claire was late.

"Why are there no wings?" she asked as she climbed the steps up to the cabin. "This thing looks like a folded-up boomerang."

"The wings unfold once we're airborne. I think a paper airplane might be a better analogy than a boomerang, though. Yes, we're going to be flung into the air, but we won't be spinning around. Well, *hopefully* not, at any rate."

He grinned with the last remark and reached up to take her bag, which he stashed behind the passenger seat. It was a tight fit. She had been instructed to pack for Icarus Camp, too, since she would be joining Brodnik's team there on Sunday. Stasia had added a cautionary note that there were no hotels and no stores of any sort in Ehden, and only a small general store at

Icarus, so she should be sure to carry anything she might need for the next few days.

"You're certain you know how to fly this thing?" she asked Kolya. "And *land* it?"

"This baby? No problem at all. You should have seen the contraptions I flew back when there was almost no atmosphere. The first one had more blades than a knife factory, and it was still almost impossible to maintain lift. Those were a lot heavier, too. The *Excelsior* is a feather in comparison." He tapped the wall next to him with his knuckles. "Ultralight carbon nanotube-infused polymer. And thanks to the earlier stages of terraforming, Mars now has enough atmosphere for her to ride on."

Claire stepped down onto the seat and then lowered her legs into the slot, stashing the small daypack she carried under her knees. It was more spacious than it had looked from above, closer to first-class than economy-class legroom, but Claire had no doubt that she would be ready to get out and stretch by the time they reached Ehden.

"What took you so long?" he asked. "I was beginning to think you'd changed your mind."

"Miscommunication. I was on the tram at seven, as instructed, but no one told me I'd be the only passenger. After about ten minutes, one of the security guards came over and informed me that you'd already left for the airport."

What she didn't add was that she'd thought Macek or Stasia, or possibly both, were coming with them, based on what Stasia had said when she mentioned the trip to Dr. Brodnik. At the very least, she'd thought that Stasia would have assigned Meadow or Pax to handle the recording, since that had been the case for everything else she'd filmed so far. She'd most definitely had no idea that they would be making the trip alone in a two-person craft, although she *had* assumed it would be smaller than the shuttle that they'd traveled in from Ares Station given that she was instructed to wear the biosuit.

"Sorry about that," Kolya said. "I like to check everything over personally when I'm the one behind the controls. And that goes double when I have a passenger, so I got Macek to tag along and make sure I didn't overlook anything. Strap in and take a quick look at your stats, okay?"

The helmets displayed a constant oxygen reading in the top right corner of the face shield, but you could pull up vital signs and other details by quickly tipping the helmet toward your right shoulder and back. Claire did so, then asked if Kolya wanted the readings.

"You don't need to call them out unless you've got a red or a yellow."

"Nope. All green."

"Okay, then. Let me get our audio synced and we'll be set."

There was a short pause, and then his voice came through the speaker inside her helmet. "Do you read me?"

"Loud and clear. Can you sync my recorder, too?" she asked, pointing to the camera she'd attached to her helmet after discovering that she'd be filming this on her own. "I think my subscribers would like to see the takeoff."

Once they had all devices talking to each other, he pulled a lever, and they began moving slowly toward the mystery tunnel. Off to the side, Claire noticed Macek getting into a KTI buggy. He gave Kolya a thumbs up. Kolya returned it, and then Macek's buggy took off toward the tunnel that would take him back to Daedalus.

Claire told Kolya she was going to start recording and then asked if he could give her an overview of how the plane operated. It was partly for her work, but she was also curious. And more than a little nervous.

"Happy to oblige," he said, turning slightly to look at the camera. "This is pretty much the same system as the ramp that goes up Arsia Mons...the one that you'll take when you head back to Ares Station next week. You may have noticed when you came in that this crater is about three times as deep as the ones housing the other domes here at Daedalus. But instead of the slow, steady descent that you had on the ride over from Daedalus City or the one in the tunnel on the other side of the crater that brought *Excelsior* in from the launch area, that tunnel you see ahead shoots up at about a thirty-five degree angle. That's not quite as steep of an ascent as the Arsia Mons lift, because we don't want to escape the atmosphere. All we want is to get enough of a boost so that we can ride on it."

The craft paused at that point, adjusted slightly to line up with the tunnel, and then continued.

"So, it looks like this is all automated?"

"For the take-off? Yes. We're on a maglev platform that goes back and forth between the landing pad we just left and the launch pad inside the tunnel. Once we're in place, we'll zip through just like your viewers do when they ride the Loop back on Earth. When we reach the edge of the tunnel, we'll detach. The platform we're on will return back here to Dome Two, but the *Excelsior*..." He jabbed one of his hands out at an angle. "She keeps going. Once we're clear of the launch area, the wings will expand, and the ion thrusters will kick in. They're actually pretty powerful on their own and can generate enough lift for us to make short hops as long as we have a bit of a runway to get started. But if we relied on the thrusters alone without this turbo boost that we're about to get at the beginning, it would take all day to get to Nepenthes. We'd also have to stop at Memnonia to recharge. That's what we had to do up until about six years ago."

"Back in *my* day," Claire said in a querulous old lady's voice, "we had to *walk* to school. It was uphill both ways and it snowed year 'round."

"That's right. You youngsters don't know how easy you have it."

A few seconds later, they entered the tunnel. Runway lights ran along the top and sides, but it was still dim enough that the light on her recorder flicked on. They made a wide curve and then slowed to a halt. Something whooshed into place behind them, and the ship seemed to tremble with anticipation.

"What about the return trip?" Claire asked. "Do they have a similar set up at Ehden and the other places we're stopping?"

"No. There's a launch crater at Nepenthes Station, which is just a quick hop from there. That's where we'll be landing. The other stops are a short ride away from the station by maglev. You'll pick up the ship you're coming back on at Nepenthes, too. It's a little bigger than this one, but Caruso's a good pilot. Maybe even better than I am. Don't tell him I said that, though."

"I'm still recording, you know. You'll just have to hope Paul isn't a *Simple Science* subscriber."

"Not a problem. I'll have Stasia tell them to take it out in post-production."

Claire smiled, but it was yet another reminder that everything she recorded would have to go through their internal review process before she turned it over to Bernard. Kolya had claimed on several occasions that he had nothing to hide. Maybe he actually believed that since Stasia, Paul, and the rest of her team did most of the hiding *for* him.

And what was Paul doing at Ehden? She filed that away to ask later when the camera was off, and chuckled at the thought of what a job listing for Kolya's personal staff must look like. *Looking for a skilled videographer, copywriter, hostage negotiator, xenobiologist, and licensed pilot.*

Although, could you even *get* a pilot's license on Mars? She didn't know, and that now had her wondering how many hours Kolya himself had behind the controls.

Almost as if reading her mind, he turned and gave her a grin that bordered on nightmarish in the dim light. "Are you holding on tight, Claire?"

Holding on was completely pointless. There was no way she was going anywhere in the harness, and if something went wrong, the fact that she was gripping the armrests certainly wasn't going to save her. But grip them she did.

The countdown clock on the flight panel stood at seventeen seconds.

"Ready to place your life in my hands?"

"I guess?"

"Good," he said. "Because it's too late to abort. Any last words?"

Claire thought of several she'd have liked to fling in his general direction, but since she was recording, she just gave him a tight smile and said, "*Carpe diem*."

"Good choice. Let's rock and roll."

Music blasted into her helmet at the same instant that the *Excelsior* shot upward toward the tiny pinpoint of light. She tried to place the opening bars of the song but had no luck. Something from the 2040s psychedelic revival, maybe?

Several seconds later they burst out into the morning sky. Daedalus was a brief blur of color in the periphery of her vision and then it was gone. She felt a mad rush of adrenaline as they ascended for about fifteen seconds.

And then, without the slightest warning, they began to fall.

TWELVE

CLAIRE PULLED in a breath to scream, but before she could get it out, the wings deployed, the motor kicked in, and the ship leveled.

"You…absolute…bastard," she said between clenched teeth, thinking that would be something else for Stasia's team to edit out.

Kolya laughed. "One hell of a rush, isn't it? That little dip, like on a rollercoaster? The design team said they could probably level it out by changing the timing of when the wings deploy. But where's the fun in that, right?"

"Oh, you mean the dip that felt more like a *plummet*? You might have at least warned me …"

"Again, where's the fun in that? The rollercoaster is always a bigger blast the first time, before you know exactly when you'll drop."

"True," she said, trying to keep her voice steady. "But I generally don't *go* on rollercoasters that can crash into the surface of an alien planet and burst into a ball of flames."

"Oh, come on. That's not even possible."

"So you're saying none of these ships have ever crashed?"

"Well, sure. Several of the unmanned ships crashed during development and there have been a couple of accidents, even the occasional fatality, since we started marketing them to the other colonies. There was one last year, in fact. Some guy took a single-seater model off autopilot so that he could swoop down into Eos Chasma. Probably trying to recreate a movie or game he played as a kid and thought he had the skills to pull it off. He hit the side of the canyon at full speed and *wham*. They had to bring in a rescue crew from Noachis, and it took them the better part of a week to find the flight recorder. Wasn't much left of him or the ship. But, to be clear, he did *not* burst into a ball of flames. There's not enough oxygen in the atmosphere yet, so that's not possible. He might have smoldered a little, but no fire. Maybe by the end of stage seven we'll—"

He stopped when she reached up to turn off the recorder.

"Sorry. Forgot you were recording. I was going for a little gallows humor to ease your nerves. It was in questionable taste anyway given what just happened at Cerberus. Not that it's the same thing, but…"

"As you noted before, Stasia's team can edit it out to preserve your image. Did they find any other bodies? At Cerberus, I mean."

"No. It's just the four people who were mentioned in the early reports, as far as I've heard. Another half dozen were injured. One is critical, but the doctors seem to think that he'll pull through."

"Good. I was worried that there might be more. I read the news reports yesterday morning, but I haven't checked since then."

The full truth was that she'd gone out of her way to avoid all news about the attack after her first glance at the headlines on Friday morning. After several days of being on call for Bernard's multitude of questions, she'd given herself a day off and spent most of it wandering around Daedalus City. With no idea how long they'd be at Icarus, she told herself it might be her only chance. She did some souvenir shopping and recorded some touristy things to incorporate in a future segment, but also a few clips for her own use, so she'd have something to send to Ro and Jemma and some vacation pictures to bore everyone with when she got back. At the end of the day, after nearly a week of gourmet meals (mostly room service) from the four restaurants at the Red Dahlia, she had pigged out on wonderfully greasy junk food at a place called Podkayne Fries. Judging from the many framed book covers on the walls, it was named after the main character in a Robert Heinlein book about a teenager from Mars. Claire hadn't read the book and had no clue whether it was good, but the fries were delicious.

The day off did a decent job of keeping her from harping on things she couldn't change. Things that, realistically, she couldn't have changed even before they happened. The odds were slim that she'd have been able to decipher Wyatt's warning correctly without the context she had after the explosion, and even if she *had* put the pieces together that there was going to be an attack on the Cerberus mines, there had been no indication when it would occur. Wyatt may not even have known when it was being planned. Most likely, he'd been warning her on the basis of vague rumors his source had passed along.

With enough time and complete information, Claire *might* have been able to get someone to believe her. But since she'd had neither of those luxuries, there was no logical reason to think she could have stopped the attack. No logical reason for her to feel responsible for those deaths.

But she still did.

Claire and Kolya rode in relative silence for the next half hour or so. She turned the recorder back on for a few minutes from time to time to get footage for her segments, and Kolya occasionally pointed out landmarks including a couple of domed cities, the largest of which was near the mining camp at Mangala Valles.

"That one is about the same size as Icarus Camp," he said. "Maybe a little smaller. You'll probably be sleeping in borrowed barracks while you're there. The workers are organized into seven units and one or two of the groups are usually on leave at any given time."

"Kimura made it sound like we'd be *literally* camping out. I was imagining what it would be like to sleep inside a pressure suit. That didn't sound like fun, even in the biosuits."

He snorted. "Yeah, right. Forty years ago that might have been true. But even when my dad took his earliest trips to the planet, back when the first camps were opening, they had portable habitats for the mining crews."

"Speaking of mining, I didn't see any stories on the *Red Planet* about a strike. Does that mean the dispute was resolved to your satisfaction?"

Kolya tilted his hand from side to side, *comme ci, comme ça.* "There's satisfaction…and then there's *satisfaction*. Let's just say I can live with the outcome without too much distress. Especially since I think that the—" He glanced up at the camera. "That's off, right? And we're off the record?"

"Yes, and yes."

"Okay. Especially since I think that the sacrifice will get us closer to a functional government on Mars. The governors of Arcadia and Lyot still restrict voting to those who've lived in their colonies for at least five years…which means that fewer than twenty percent of the people living there have any say in the government. I'm hoping I can exert some subtle pressure to ensure that Mars is more democratic than most constitutional republics, at least in the long run."

"As long as it's a *unitary* system, though, right? One central government?"

He shrugged. "Issues that are strictly local or regional would still be handled at the lower levels, but yes. One central government for things that affect Mars as a whole. It's really the only solution that makes sense with a population this small."

"But you don't intend for it to *stay* this small, do you?"

"No," he admitted. "We have to stay flexible to allow for new colonies to form and join the union over time. I'm actually trying to help establish a self-sufficient agricultural colony at Ehden right now which wouldn't have ties to any of the corporations. But even if we grow to millions of people and dozens of colonies, a unitary system will be better. You've seen firsthand what can happen in federal systems. There's constant discord and very little incentive to strive for the common good. The *United* States is still…what? Three states short of the fifty-one you started out the century with? I'm not an expert on American politics by any means, but I do know there are still active separatist movements in several of your renegade states a decade after their governments finally woke up to the fact that they weren't economically solvent on their own."

The US had actually started out the century with *fifty* states —DC and Puerto Rican statehood came later, after the first three secessions. But she didn't correct him, because she thought he was basically right. Tribalism can take root more easily in a federal system. On the other hand, it did keep ultimate power from ending up in the hands of a single individual.

"Aren't you putting a lot of faith in this proposed constitution?" Claire asked. "Especially when you don't really have a democratic political culture to build on. What you've got right now, at least in the other colonies, is corporate oligarchy—a corporatocracy. And those corporations are used to calling the shots. People rarely give up power without a fight."

Based on everything she knew and what Wyatt had told her, Claire was being very diplomatic in leaving Daedalus out of the corporatocracy group. Yes, the colony had elected leaders and universal suffrage, but Wyatt had implied that those leaders didn't sneeze without requesting advance permission from KTI —and Kolya *was* KTI. The Daedalian press didn't seem free and unfettered, either, in her limited experience, although she supposed it could simply be that a media outlet for a colony with a little under six thousand permanent residents lacked the staff for real investigative journalism. And that had to be even more true in the colonies where most of the workers were on temporary contracts. Lyot had fewer than a thousand permanent residents, and one of the others wasn't much larger.

"Every single one of those corporations made a commitment to shift to more representative government when the colonies were initially founded," Kolya said. "They'll either abide by those commitments or lose their lease. So far, they've all made some progress in that direction. We need a basic set of guaranteed rights to attract more colonists—I mean, would you want to relocate without that? We also need to speak with a single voice when negotiating with world leaders. It's chaotic enough that Earth has so many divisions. Even after the reforms, the UN is next to useless."

Claire smiled, thinking how close this was to Wyatt's characterization of the UN as a toothless dinosaur—and how much Wyatt would probably hate knowing that he and Kolya were *simpatico* on that point.

Kolya raised his eyebrow. "You disagree?"

"No. I was just thinking of a friend who holds the same opinion. But I don't have any firsthand experience with the organization, so I couldn't really say."

"Lucky you. I avoid them whenever possible."

"But…I thought KTI worked closely with the Ares Consortium on the terraforming project. They're part of the UN, right?"

He laughed. "Technically. But ACon is more of a commercial adjunct. The various member states set it up when they realized the only way that terraforming would ever happen was if they privatized the operation. Governments clearly weren't going to fund it, but they figured it might eventually be feasible if they could find a way for people to make money out here and get them to coordinate their efforts, more or less. I guess you could say ACon is the buffer that allows things to actually get *done* here on Mars without drowning every initiative in an endless sea of bureaucracy."

"Is that…" Claire stopped, trying to think how to word the question in a neutral fashion. "Is that how you were able to keep stage six on track when you switched to the recombinant biobots? And no. My mother isn't behind the question. Neither is my brother. It's just something I…overheard."

"Kimura, no doubt."

It had actually been Wyatt, although as Claire thought about it, the question also tied in a bit with the conversation she'd had with Joe and Beck on her trip to Jonas Labs. Kimura had certainly voiced plenty of skepticism about the cozy relationship between the Ares Consortium and KTI, though, so she decided to neither confirm nor deny Kolya's assumption. "*Someone* merely said that the recombinant variant was a game changer, and if the Ares Consortium had any real integrity, they'd have held up stage six pending a complete review of the science."

"They'd *already* reviewed the science. The experts on the panel agreed—unanimously, I might add—that there was no reason to hold things up given our extensive tests inside the domes. I do agree, however, that this is a game changer. And you're going to see exactly what I mean by that in…" He glanced at the time. "In about three hours when we reach Fenris —that's our third and final stop before Ehden."

"What's at Fenris?"

"We're going to watch a preview of stage six in real time. I've watched it twice before in other domes, and…" He grinned. "As you said. Game changer."

THIRTEEN

CLAIRE FOUND herself looking at the viewscreen map inside the *Excelsior* far more than she looked at the terrain below them. The ship was going too fast and flying too high to properly take in the scenery, anyway. After a while, the novelty wore off and it was like traveling across a massive desert. Any fears she might have had about Kolya's piloting skills were rendered moot by the fact that he really didn't seem to be doing much aside from occasionally glancing at the dash.

When the viewscreen shifted about twenty minutes after they passed Kolya's former pit stop at Memnonia, however, she realized that their flight path would take them a little closer to the site of the accident than she had told Wyatt in her response on Thursday night. It was hard to be sure exactly *how* close, though, given that there were several locations in and around Elysia that began with the name Cerberus. One of them, Cerberus Palus, was almost in their flight path.

"So, where exactly is the Cerberus mine located?" she asked Kolya. "The news account simply said the attack happened at the Millex mine in Cerberus, but it looks like that covers a pretty wide swath of territory."

"I believe the news account is still referring to it as an *accident* rather than an attack," he said, "and I'm really hoping it stays that way. But it's the one up near Tartarus Montes. Cerberus Fossae." He cast a questioning eye in her direction. "Judging from your change of expression, that information seems to have caused an epiphany."

It had. *Fossae* was what Wyatt had been trying to get across with the bit about their fictitious neighbor being an *old fossil*.

"Not an epiphany, exactly," Claire said, hunting for a plausible excuse. "I was just thinking about the ...Greek origins of these names. Isn't Tartarus the deepest pit of hell or something like that? I suppose it stands to reason, then, that Cerberus would be nearby."

The message she'd sent to Wyatt and Ro had said that she agreed the kitty should steer clear of the hellhound, adding that she hoped the old fossil would finally decide to join her daughter in Denver, so that their kitty would be a few thousand kilometers away from the dog. Cerberus Fossae was the location farthest from their flight path, but instead of the distance between DC and Denver, it was more like DC and Boston. Still, that had to qualify as *steering clear*, by any stretch of the imagination.

The largest landmark they passed over was the city of Elysia, which became visible a few minutes before they reached it. Kolya touched the controls for the first time since take off and slowed as they approached. "What do you think?"

To Claire's surprise, there was no dome, just four tall spinning cones. They looked identical to her.

"It might be more impressive if I hadn't already seen Daedalus. Those huge cone-shaped buildings are interesting, but there's not much variation in them. And no plant life. But I guess there really couldn't be much of that without a dome."

It was both the truth and what she suspected Kolya wanted to hear. Elysia definitely wasn't a showplace, and the designers hadn't put forth any effort to make it look like Earth. Claire wasn't sure whether that was good or bad, though. It was a Martian colony, so you could make a valid point that they shouldn't be wasting valuable resources in an effort to recreate their home planet.

"More plants can grow out in the open now than you'd think," Kolya said. "We'll see some good examples at Doba, which is our first stop. And Elysia did have a dome at one point. They took it down in favor of tunnels between the cones, which they call pods, about five years ago. And the whole setup is a little deceptive. The pods aren't just buildings, but complete communities. They look a lot more like earth on the inside, with parks and other recreational facilities scattered about. And they're mostly self-sufficient. One of them is an agricultural pod, which produces the majority of their food. A lot of the residents live and work within the same pod and rarely venture onto the actual surface of the planet. I think they figured why waste a lot of resources beautifying the surface or constantly making repairs to the dome when their people don't spend enough time there to make it worthwhile. Most of them seem to view the outside in the same way that you might think of a major highway on Earth. Or maybe the hyperloop. It's basically a way to get to other colonies, to the mines, or to some of the smaller cities within Elysia. I suspect that the majority of the people in the pods wouldn't even notice stage six was happening, if not for the fact that they're going to be a bit overcrowded for the duration. They usually have one group of the colony's miners out of every three in the pods at any given time—sort of like a shore leave system—but they'll have the full contingent joining them during the quarantine. Well, *almost* a full contingent. One of our concessions in the recent negotiations was that Daedalus will take in twenty percent. An easy concession to make, given that we're not going to have as many tourists during that time."

"As *many* tourists? I'm surprised that you'll have any."

He shrugged. "I originally planned to close Daedalus to visitors, but we had people expressing interest in an extended stay during the quarantine. Mostly researchers, at first, but then KTI's travel unit began listing it as an option and we're a little over half-booked now. The bulk of the tourists will be coming in on the maiden voyage of the *Ares Prime*'s sister ship, *Diamante*, which departs from Tranquility next Friday. You'll pass them on the way back to Earth...although I don't think you'll be in visual range."

"If you're booking tourists, then you're fairly certain that people will be able to leave the domes in six months, right?"

"Yes. And not just *fairly* certain. I'm certain." He said this with the exaggerated patience of a man who has answered the question far too many times. "You can ask the lead biologist on the project when we get to Fenris, and you'll get the same answer. In fact, she thinks we might even be able to give the all-clear earlier."

They arrived at Nepenthes Station a little less than an hour later. At first blush, it appeared to be just another crater, and not an exceptionally large one, at that. The only difference, aside from the dome, was a paved landing strip and a parking lot with several small maglev shuttles just outside of it.

Landing the *Excelsior* apparently did take more skill than flying it, at least to the point of knowing when to hit the various buttons on the dash. Something that Claire assumed was the landing gear whirred and clicked below her feet as they began their descent. The craft circled the tiny dome once and then slowly lowered them onto the nearby runway. She felt a slight jiggle when the wheels hit, but not as much as she had on the Jonas Labs corporate jet she'd traveled on a few times as a kid.

Kolya pushed a button that simultaneously opened the roof and retracted the wings. He grabbed their bags, then lowered a canvas ladder over the pilot's side of the plane.

"Congratulations," he said as Claire followed him down the ladder. "You survived. Here, let me help…there's a bit of a drop at the end."

The drop was less than a meter, and given the lower gravity, Claire wouldn't have felt it at all. Kolya had to have known that as well as she did, but he stepped to one side and lifted her down anyway. His hands lingered on her waist in a way that told Claire the move was less about gallantry than an excuse for physical contact. With both of them still in the biosuits, complete with gloves and helmets, it was almost laughable.

She looked up at him through the face shield. "So, tell me... who grants pilot's licenses on Mars?"

He grinned. "Why? Are you planning to lodge a complaint?"

"Not at all. It was an exceptionally smooth landing. Let's just say I'm the curious type."

"Some questions are best left unanswered, Claire. I wouldn't want to jeopardize your continued peace of mind."

"How very kind of you."

A buggy similar to the one they'd used at Tranquility was now approaching from the airlock tunnel leading out of the dome. Two men occupied the front seats. Both were fully armed, which was startling until Claire saw the KTI logo on the front. Kolya said he'd be right back and walked over to speak with them, taking their suitcases with him. A private conversation, apparently, because he turned off her helmet speaker.

About a minute later, he motioned for her to follow him to the area where the maglev shuttles, also bearing the KTI logo, were parked. The guard stayed behind and unpacked several boxes from the cargo bay at the rear of the *Excelsior*.

Once Claire and Kolya were inside the shuttle, he pressed his thumb to the ignition pad and pushed a button marked *Doba*. The shuttle moved a few meters, then spun around about forty-five degrees and shot off like a bullet across the sand. A viewscreen on the dash lit up with their current speed (*305 kph*), the distance to Doba (*111 km*) and their estimated time of arrival. Just below that was a route map that looked like a slightly misshapen diamond. Lines were drawn between Nepenthes Station and the three domes—Doba, Canillo, and Ehden—and from each dome to the other two, so that it looked like a kite, minus the string and the tail. Several smaller locations were noted along the paths, including Fenris, which Kolya had mentioned earlier.

"So, are all of the facilities here run by KTI? I was under the impression that most of the work you do outside of Daedalus is through subcontractors."

"It depends. If it's something directly connected to the terraforming effort, I like to keep it within KTI. Nepenthes Station and the other areas we're visiting today are leased to us on the same extended, renewable terms as Daedalus. We have about fifty small leases scattered around the planet with over two hundred people who are Daedalian citizens living and working there. And I believe that number is going to more than double in the next year. Elycorp—that's the main employer at Elysia—has at least a dozen outposts. The other colonies have them, too, although some of them reserve citizenship for those who live within their primary borders. That's another reason that we need a unitary government. Much of the planet is unincorporated, and borders are increasingly meaningless."

"But isn't there a basic code of laws that covers the planet as a whole? I mean, for the big stuff like capital crimes. Otherwise, how would you address any crimes that happen at…let's say a mining camp that isn't within any of these pockets of civilization."

Claire didn't add people traveling *between* two pockets of civilization, but she was definitely thinking it.

"We do have a basic legal code. *Thou shalt not kill* and so forth. The Ares Consortium saw to that before they allowed colonization to begin. But a code is only as good as its enforcement, and outside colonial territory, there's no mechanism for that. Even within the colonies, you're talking mostly private security. In the end, if there's a dispute between two people out here, it's usually a matter of frontier justice."

"So if they learn that the explosion at Cerberus wasn't an accident and they find the person responsible, you think frontier justice will decide the fate of the accused?"

"Yes." His jaw was set in a firm line. "And given that it's the only sort of justice that exists out here at the moment, I'd say I'm even counting on it."

FOURTEEN

CLAIRE SPOTTED Doba on the horizon about fifteen minutes later. Not the crater itself, but the bamboo forest just beyond it, with tall trunks and deep green tops that stood out starkly against the midday sky.

"Those look even bigger than the ones I saw inside the dome at Daedalus," she said as she tapped the camera on her helmet to begin recording.

Kolya was looking down at his messages. "Yeah. They're a new variety that's engineered to be hardier, and they can grow higher outside the domes. But you'll get better information on all of that from Dr. Ademola."

Once they were a bit closer, the interior of the dome came into focus. From above the crater, the varying shades of green seemed to be one massive lawn, acres upon acres of grass. Claire couldn't even see a road. The shuttle taxied to a slow crawl, then turned and parked on a landing pad about fifty meters from the entrance to the dome, next to one of the buggies.

"Idi—that's Dr. Ademola—is over at one of the smaller craters," Kolya said. "I just messaged him, and he said he's about fifteen minutes behind us. He's already eaten so we should go ahead and have lunch. We can save the forest part of the tour for last. I don't know about you, but I'll be happy to find a bathroom and get out of this suit for a while."

They took the buggy into an airlock tunnel, emerging a few seconds later onto a straight road so narrow that Claire wasn't sure two vehicles could even pass each other. What had appeared to be grass when viewed at a distance was actually young bamboo plants that stood a meter or so higher than the buggy.

Kolya pulled off his helmet and gloves. Claire followed suit, enjoying the fresh air and the breeze against her skin as they sped through the bamboo fields.

"How do machines get in here to cut these down?" she asked.

"Robotic harvesters. They're about half as wide as the buggy we're in now. Smaller bots go through the fields first to measure and tag the ones that are ready. This is the last of the experimental bamboo crops, though. Unless we have a new frontrunner, that variety you spotted from the shuttle is the winner and they'll all be grown outside the tunnels in the future. And after stage six, Ademola will be shifting to a wider variety of crops, including apples."

Kolya smiled and sang a few bars of a slow, haunting tune. It sounded Russian. Claire couldn't understand the words, but his voice was a pleasant baritone.

"That's pretty, but I have to admit that I didn't follow a word of it."

"An old Soviet cosmonaut tune. The meter is better in the original, but roughly translated it's something like, all the astronauts and all the dreamers say there will be apple blossoms on Mars someday. To be fair, we already have apple trees growing *inside* at Daedalus City and in the pods at Elysia…but that's a cheat in my opinion. The goal here—as with the bamboo—will be to select the varieties that can survive in the open. For the apples, that won't be until after stage six. Even the modified trees will take a few years to bear fruit. Bamboo is easy—we get two fully grown crops during each growing season."

"As big as the ones we saw out there? You're kidding."

"Nope. Not kidding at all."

A few kilometers into the fields, they entered a clearing with a cluster of buildings near the center. Instead of bamboo, there was a garden that looked like it was for personal rather than industrial use, including a small vineyard near the back. Four buildings flanked the road, all of them basic, functional rectangles, which appeared to be made of bamboo. At the end of the row on the left, two much larger and more modern buildings were in the final stages of construction. The primary sections were torus shaped, with a hollow center. These sat atop a circular base and were perched at an angle like the Red Dahlia and the various housing units Claire had seen from a distance in Daedalus City. Propped up against the side were two panels that looked like massive theatrical flats depicting an apartment building. There were holes for doors, but the windows looked painted on.

"What the hell…?"

"Sleeping quarters under construction," Kolya said. "They just need to put the façades on the front. Turns out people really don't like to dwell on the fact that their beds are inside a glorified hamster wheel. Even at Red Dahlia we have to disguise it a bit."

Claire had a ton of questions about that, but she stored them away for later because they had now stopped in front of a building with a handwritten sign reading *Café Doba*. Like the others, it looked fairly new.

It was also completely empty, making her wonder if the sign was a joke. Inside, there was a kitchen with a small cooktop, a refrigerator, a table, a dartboard—and thankfully, a bathroom. It was a relief to get out of the biosuit, which was much too warm now that they were under a dome.

Lunch was in the refrigerator—a grain salad with cucumbers, peppers, and little strips of something that turned out to be bamboo shoots, along with a cheese plate. On the counter, they found a loaf of rustic bread, a jug of wine, and a plate of small, greenish-gold globes.

"Are those scuppernongs?"

Kolya shrugged. "I'm not familiar with that word. They look like oversized grapes to me."

Claire popped one into her mouth, savoring the way it burst when her teeth pierced the thick skin. "*Definitely* scuppernongs. The outside is a bit tart, but the inside…"

And in that odd way that tastes and smells can take you back through time and space, she was no longer in a tiny café on Mars. She was at the picnic table of a beach house on the island of Ocracoke in North Carolina that her parents rented the summer she turned fourteen. Claire had just come in from the water, and she and her father were eating the grapes that he'd bought at a roadside stand while they watched Joe navigate a kayak out beyond the breakers.

"Mars to Claire." Kolya waved a hand in front of her face.

"Oh. Sorry. The…um…outside is a little tough and kind of sour. I like it, though. The inside is very sweet. Just be sure to swallow the seeds without chewing them. They're bitter."

"You're not exactly selling me on the idea, but…." He tried one and grimaced. "Yeah. I believe these may be an acquired taste. Maybe the fermented form is better." After he poured both of them a glass of the wine, he said, "Where did you go a minute ago? You had such a happy smile and then it…faded away."

"I was just thinking about our last family vacation. My dad bought some of these. Kai left early, saying she needed to get back to work, but Dad, Joe and I stayed an extra week. A month after that, we found out about his cancer, so it's one of the last uncomplicated happy memories with him." She picked up another grape. "I don't know if they grow scuppernongs outside the Carolinas, but that was the last time I had them. How odd to find them here."

"Maybe the variety is extra hardy. We'll have to ask Idi."

Kolya dug into his salad at that point, seeming uncomfortable at the shift in their conversation. Perhaps he thought it had made her sad. And it had, for a moment. But it had also given her a more vivid memory of her father than she'd had in several years and Claire was grateful for that.

"So," she began, attempting to change the subject. "I take it there aren't many people living here in Doba? Or does the place liven up when everyone comes in from the fields?"

"Right now, the population of Doba is zero. Idi lives in Ehden, with his wife and daughter. But they'll be relocating here next week, along with about sixty others. This way, they can continue their work on upcoming projects during stage six. Doba has underground tunnel access to the Nepenthes lab, which we keep off the shuttle map for security reasons. The buildings currently under construction are multifamily sleeping units. This was originally designed to be a breakroom for people working here rather than an actual café, but I think they're planning to use it as a communal kitchen of sorts. We'll be adding a park and a few other amenities that Ehden currently lacks."

"So they'll be here with families during the lockdown? What if someone is injured or becomes seriously ill?"

He laughed, shaking his head. "They'll be flown to the closest hospital, of course. That would be Elysia, in this case. We *do* have provisions in place for emergencies. They just require full biohazard suits, level A decontamination, and an extreme degree of caution. Did you think we would just leave people to die?"

"Well, no. To be honest, I actually hadn't thought about it at all until just now. But if you're not completely locked down, then couldn't similar exceptions be made for some of the businesses?"

"The mining camps and other worker outposts don't have the facilities to do anything close to the level of decontamination we can do in the major cities. And we're talking about a handful of exceptions for life-threatening situations. Even those will involve some degree of risk. Now multiply that risk by thousands of people over one hundred and eighty days and…"

"And it becomes unmanageable."

"Exactly."

They had finished eating and were taking their plates to the sink when the door opened, and a man stepped inside. He was carrying several bags, which he deposited on a nearby table.

"Ah," Kolya said. "Our host has arrived."

Ademola was younger than Claire had expected. For some reason, she'd been picturing a weathered sage in a white coat. This guy appeared to be in his mid-thirties.

"Kolya, my friend. It has been too long." He clapped Kolya on the back with a broad, genuine smile.

"Claire, this is Dr. Idi Ademola, the preeminent botanist on Mars. Idi, this is Claire Echols, a journalist with the *Atlantic Post* who is here to cover our recent find and to tell her subscribers back home a bit about what we're doing in stage six."

"A pleasure to meet you," he said. "I have seen your face on the video where you revealed the chamber, but you are even more lovely in person."

"Thank you, Dr. Ademola."

"No, no. You must call me Idi. Kolya throws titles around to impress people. How was your lunch?"

Claire told him it was delicious and asked about the scuppernongs. "Kolya thought perhaps you planted them because they're resistant to the cold."

"Not especially, but they do like sandy soil, which is probably why I've had some success with them here at Doba. One of the only fruits, so far. My wife likes the wine I made from them but says the grapes themselves are nasty."

"Your wife is right," Kolya said. "Claire, however, seems quite partial to them."

"Then I am very glad that I ignored Renata. She tried to talk me into bringing you some fruit grown over in Ehden instead, but I wanted to serve foods produced here. Well, except the cheese. And the bread. Those *are* from Ehden. Maybe one day. But the salad, the grapes, the wine—those are all from our garden. A year ago, we were joking that we'd have to make it through stage six on those nasty packaged meals and bamboo shoots, but I think we'll have quite a nice variety now. Speaking of bamboo, though, leave your plates on the counter and come with me. I want to show you something absolutely *amazing*."

"Have you found a variety you think will work better than the ones growing outside the dome?" Kolya asked.

"No, no. *Dendrocalamus amara* is still the best choice until at least stage seven. But this bamboo is more exciting to watch. Bring your wine."

Claire exchanged a look with Kolya as they followed their host outside. How could bamboo be exciting to *watch*?

"That is *Phyllostachys bambusoides*." Idi nodded toward a small patch of bamboo that was a little less than a meter tall. It was in a row of about a dozen plants. A card with the number 4 was inserted into the soil nearby. Behind this row was an unplanted section where several bots appeared to be mulching the remnants of a previous harvest.

Idi moved a short bench in front of the row of bamboo and motioned for them to sit.

"Technically," he said, "it's a variant of that plant that we haven't named yet, thus the number on the card, but it is quite similar to the one that is native to Earth. It grows faster and taller here—more CO_2, less gravity—and these babies spit a lot of oxygen into the air. Kolya, can you start a timer on your phone for me, please? Ten minutes on my mark."

"Is it okay if I record for my subscribers?" Claire asked.

"Of course, of course."

She ran inside to get the recorder from her helmet. When she got back, Idi was holding a thin white pole. He jabbed it into the ground next to the clump of bamboo, then pulled a pen and a little ruler from his pocket. The first black line he drew was flush with the top of the closest shoot. Then he held the ruler against the pole and made another mark just above it.

"Okay," Idi said, "Start the timer. Ten minutes. That second mark is one centimeter above the first. Maybe a smidge more because this pen draws a thick line. And this shoot will be *above* that mark before the timer goes off. If your viewers watch closely, in fact, they might even be able to see it grow in real time."

Kolya chuckled. "Idi, you've been in Nepenthes for too long if you think anyone back on Earth is patient enough to stare at a clump of bamboo for ten minutes."

"Hey. Don't insult my subscribers," Claire said, keeping her camera pointed at the plants. "But, for those of you who have other things to do, we'll have a button allowing you to view it at 2x, 5x, and 10x."

They watched for a few seconds and then Claire added. "I'm doing the math in my head, Dr. Ademola. Are you saying this grows about a meter and a half a day?"

"I am, indeed. And if speed were the only factor, we'd be going with *Phyllo* here after stage six. But as you can see, the culms—the stalks, that is—on this variety are rather thin. *Dendrocalamus amara*, which I took the liberty of naming for my lovely daughter, is a sturdy plant with culms thicker than my waist."

Idi wandered off at that point to check on the mulching bots. Kolya also got up and walked back toward the café entrance. Idi had no doubt given him this demonstration before, so Claire couldn't really blame him. Watching bamboo grow is pretty much on par with watching paint dry. She remained still and kept the camera focused on the plant but was beginning to wish she'd placed it on a chair.

A minute or so later, she heard Kolya on the phone, probably checking in with Stasia or Macek. Judging from his tone, it didn't sound as if things were going especially well. He came back when the timer went off, and even before she looked away from the bamboo, Claire could tell that he was on edge.

She tapped to pause the recording.

"Are you okay?" she whispered.

He waved a hand, but Claire didn't know if the gesture was

supposed to mean *nothing's wrong* or *ask me later*. She decided to interpret it as the latter, since Idi was heading back their way and she needed to start the camera again.

"It's over the one centimeter line," Idi said after measuring the new growth. "Nearly two millimeters above, in fact. And now, if the two of you want to get back into your suits, I'll take you out to see the big boys."

Idi wasn't joking about them being big boys. As they drew closer to the bamboo forest outside the dome about ten minutes later, Claire could see that most of the culms were wider than she was and looked like the trunks of palm trees. One was so large that even Kolya couldn't wrap his arms around it.

"For about thirteen months out of the Martian year," Idi said, "or from roughly mid-spring to mid-autumn, *Dendrocalamus amara* survives fine outside the domes. It grows at a little over half a meter a day and tops out at maybe forty-five meters."

"So is that how you're able to get two full crops each year?" Claire asked.

"Yes. It sometimes grows even higher near the aquifers. The challenge here at Doba is keeping it fully irrigated. Once they begin switching to this variant it should double, maybe even triple, the current yields of those forests."

"At that rate of growth, Mars is going to be overrun with bamboo before long," Claire said.

Kolya shook his head. "Not likely. Houses, furniture, paper products, clothing...much of what you saw in Daedalus was bamboo although we currently get most of it from the forests around the Pettit aquifer, which is about five hundred klicks north of Memnonia. If I'd thought about it, I'd have flown you past that this morning. I'll get Paul to take you over the bamboo forest at Lake Tombaugh on the way to Icarus. It's smaller, but not by much."

They bid Idi farewell a few minutes later and Kolya directed the shuttle to take them to the second dome on their schedule, Canillo.

"What happened back there?" Claire asked once they were on their way. "Did they find more bodies at Cerberus?"

"More bodies, yes. Not at Cerberus, though. Remember the guy in the elevator? Westmoreland? He left Daedalus to head back to Lyot this morning and his plane crashed. About two hours ago. It was him, the pilot, and one of the other men who was in the elevator. The Indian guy, Navneet Rao. They were landing at Mamers Valles to drop Rao off."

"Did any of them survive?" Claire was pretty sure that she knew the answer from his expression alone, but she had to ask.

He shook his head. "No survivors. It's been…five years, at least, since we had an accident of that magnitude here on Mars. I'll be the first to admit I didn't like Westmoreland. Or trust him. A standing rule at KTI was not to make any agreements with the son of a bitch if you could avoid it. He'd renege on them anyway, so what was the point of negotiating? But…something like this…" He shook his head, letting out a shaky sigh.

"When did they leave Daedalus City?"

"I don't know for certain. Had to be after we did, though. We were first on the launch schedule."

"Do they have any idea why the plane crashed?"

"Not yet. Pilot error, most likely. Maybe a malfunction. It wasn't one of our models, if that's what you're concerned about."

"No. Just…curious. Comes with the job."

And the safety of the KTI planes really *wasn't* what worried her. She was far more concerned about Macek's confrontation with Westmoreland on the patio of the executive pavilion two days prior, with both men looking as if murder was very much at the front of their minds.

She was also concerned about Macek having been in the departure dome earlier that morning and the way he'd given

Kolya a big thumbs up. And the way that Kolya had given him a thumbs up right back.

Kolya's reaction to the news about Westmoreland seemed sincere, but Claire already knew that the man was remarkably skilled at deception. He'd used that skill on her more than once in the past few weeks. The little bit at the end there, where Kolya had trash-talked the dead man proved nothing. She'd already had the sense that Kolya didn't like Westmoreland, so he could very easily have added it to throw her off.

The simple truth was that Claire wouldn't put it past Macek to kill someone who got in the way of KTI's objectives.

Her only question was whether Kolya would authorize that killing.

She wasn't sure. But either way, she needed to be very, very careful what she said and did until she was back home.

Because if they'd kill Westmoreland, it stood to reason that they'd kill again to cover it up.

FIFTEEN

THEY ARRIVED at Canillo a few minutes later. Claire was happy about that, because it gave her an excuse to push all thoughts about the plane crash aside for the time being in order to focus on getting the recording.

There was a buggy next to the airlock tunnel, and Claire expected them to drive inside. To her surprise, however, Kolya steered the buggy onto a track that ran around the perimeter of the crater.

"We're not going in?"

"No. We'll talk to the lead KTI biologist at our next stop. Davy said it would be *safe* for us to go in if we wanted—it's day one hundred and seventy-one, and she's been going in and out since day one sixty, even before that with the higher-level biohazard gear. But we've gone the full hundred and eighty days for the other tests with only *her* going in and out, and I don't want to introduce deviations from the norm if we can avoid it. I'll drive around the perimeter so that you can record. Not all the way around...it's something like forty kilometers across. But we have additional video that Davy can send you."

"Okay. Starting the recording now. So...this is completed stage six? Or rather, almost completed?"

"Yes," Kolya said, glancing briefly away from the path around the dome. "Canillo is the final test crater...well, next to final, technically. Fenris is the last one, but it won't have time to fully cook before we launch." He nodded toward the dome. "Just record for a bit. Zoom in and check it all out. Then you can tell me if you notice anything different from what you've seen so far on Mars."

She watched and recorded for about five minutes. The terrain inside the dome was covered by a mat of much darker green than what they'd seen at Doba, and there were a few splashes of color, as well. It was a little hard to judge the scale at first, but then she zoomed in on what looked like a utility shed near the center and realized that the odd-looking grass was probably about ankle high. A few of the other plants came up to midcalf. Some were flowering. Some looked like slightly different varieties of grass or maybe clover.

"Okay, it's not *entirely* different from what I've seen elsewhere on Mars," she said, "but it's considerably different from the plants that you imported from Earth for the domes. The plants inside Canillo look…the only word I can give you is *alien*. I thought the same thing about some of the varieties that I saw on the drive out to Dome Three the day we opened the Icarus chamber. One of those trees was like nothing I'd ever seen before—its leaves were reflective, almost like dark mirrors. The plants inside here are like that tree. All of the grass seems a bit too dark. More like the color of spinach. And there are flowers that look kind of like dandelions, but again, the color is darker. More bronze than yellow. If I had to guess, I'd say these are varieties you adapted specifically for Mars. Like the bamboo forest that Idi Ademola showed us outside the dome at Doba—dendasomething amara. Except these plants are inside a dome, where I'm guessing the atmosphere is altered with more oxygen."

"There *are* slight differences to the atmosphere in there now, but on day one it was identical to the outside. As for them being species or varieties that we've adapted…well, you're close. Let's go." He turned the buggy around and headed back toward the shuttle.

"I'm *close*? Really? That's all you're going to tell me?"

"We've got one more stop before Ehden. Fenris is *five minutes* away once we reach the shuttle. Five minutes, I swear. And Davy can explain it better than I can."

Claire sighed. "Fenris. That's...like...a Norse werewolf or something, isn't it?"

"Maybe? Doba, Canillo, and Ehden were all named when we got here. I think those labels were assigned back around the turn of the century by some international group. But most of the smaller craters are unnamed, so I let the workers pick, just like Idi named his new bamboo variant after his daughter. Fenris is one of the tiny craters. It's named after Davy's dog, although he's more the entire town's dog at this point. You might see him while we're in Ehden."

"That would make him the first animal I've seen. Although...I did think I spotted a couple of fish in the lake. No birds, even though your ambient sounds on the balconies had faint birdsong."

"The fish were imported. They do okay here. But birds wreak havoc with the domes, so they're not feasible until we're fully outside. And even then...we're a little worried about what we might end up with in the long run."

"How so?"

"Given our gravity, I'm thinking birds the size of a ptero-dactyl would have no problem on Mars. We had a couple of farms in Daedalus that imported chickens, which don't fly on Earth if you keep the wings trimmed, and even if you don't, they can't fly far. At Daedalus, though? They literally flew the coop. Which meant dead chickens and repairs to a couple of the tridygel panels. I heard that they tried importing birds from Earth into the pods at Elysia, but they couldn't adjust to the arti-ficial gravity. A while back, someone told me they were going to try hatching a few species and see if they could survive if they were born at that level of spin. Maybe give them a few genetic tweaks to see if they could engineer something viable that could fly without crashing into everything. Not sure what the outcome was, though..."

Once they reached the shuttle, Kolya pushed the button to resume course toward Ehden. They zipped past two other domed craters, both of which looked like smaller versions of Canillo. Those quickly became greenish blobs in the rear window of the shuttle. Fenris, which was smaller still, was just beyond that, a little less than the five minutes away that Kolya had promised. As with the other domes, there was the usual airlock tunnel on the side, but this one also had a biosafety glovebox just to the left of the airlock, like Claire had seen on the lower floors at Jonas Labs. The strangest part was that the box was only about a meter off the ground, almost as if it were part of a kindergarten lab exercise.

Their shuttle pulled onto the landing pad next to a KTI buggy with two occupants, both in biosuits identical to their own. One of the two was an armed security guard. He stayed put, but the other person grabbed two sample cases from the back of the buggy when they drew up alongside.

Shrewd blue eyes stared out from inside the helmet as the woman approached. She was easily the oldest person Claire had seen on Mars. At the time, Claire would have placed her in her late sixties, but she later learned the woman was nearly eighty.

Kolya, who usually led off any conversation, was unusually deferential. Before he could even introduce them, the woman thrust one of the sample cases toward Claire.

"Anton tells me you'll be collecting some samples for your brother."

Claire was surprised to hear the woman's voice, which carried a faint Scottish burr, coming in through the helmet speaker. Kolya must have patched her in when she wasn't paying attention.

"I'm completely fine with that," the woman said, although her tone suggested she was only moderately okay with it, at best. "I certainly wouldn't want to get in the way of scientific cooperation. But you need to be sure that your brother knows that everything we do here at Nepenthes is fully protected by law in multiple countries. On multiple *planets* for that matter, even though Martian law is a pathetic joke. I'm telling you this as a courtesy and as a warning because my name is on these patents, too, not just KTI's. If I see anything misused or misattributed, I *will* sue even if they don't. Are we clear on that, Ms. Echols?"

"Claire, please. And yes, ma'am. We are crystal clear."

She took the case. The woman gave her a curt nod, followed by a surprisingly warm smile as she extended the hand that was now free.

"Dr. Davina Monroe. I will be overseeing the next two stages of terraforming, assuming I live long enough, which I will if *this one*"—she gave a sideways nod toward Kolya—"keeps us on schedule. You look very much like your mother. Except for your eyes. And your smile. In both cases, I like yours better."

Claire opened her mouth to ask how the woman knew Kai, but Monroe had already turned her back on them and was walking at a rapid clip toward the dome.

"Come on, come on," she said. "We need to *do* this so I can get back to my lab and Gentry can get back to his post. I've had another death threat, Anton, and there was the bomb threat last week. Please tell that braindead lunk of yours that I'd appreciate a few more people to help with security. I've only got three for the entire facility, and I don't think that's nearly enough now that you're playing your silly little games over at Ehden. I still can't fathom what the hell you're thinking with that. We don't *need* those people."

Kolya sighed. "Yes, Davy. We do. I'm looking at the long term here, not just the next few months. As for security, we're spread a little thin for at least a week. We're helping to look into the Cerberus explosion. And one of the aircraft that left Daedalus today crashed, so Macek is going to have his hands full."

Does he have blood on those hands, as well? Claire wondered, thinking it was incredibly convenient that Macek would be the one investigating anything that might have happened to Westmoreland's ship before it departed for home.

"Once we get the second chamber to Daedalus," Kolya continued, "I'll have him assign four more guards…two tasked with the Ehden arrivals and two general purpose guards for the lab. Is that okay?"

"I suppose it will have to be, won't it? Maybe I'll have Gentry or one of the others train a few of the new lab assistants in case the current guard on duty has to step out and go to the damn bathroom."

Several parts of their conversation made little sense to Claire, especially the part about Ehden. But she filed her questions away with all of the others she intended to ask Kolya at some point and followed the two of them to the edge of the crater.

And that's absolutely all that it was. A desolate crater encased in a dome. There wasn't a hint of green or any color other than the tawny red of the Martian regolith identical to the soil on which they were standing.

As if reading her thoughts, Dr. Monroe turned and looked directly at Claire. "This dome is brand new, as of yesterday. It is roughly half—"

"Is it okay if I record?"

"I *assumed* you already were." She gave a little huff of impatience as Claire started the recorder and moved back a few steps so that she could get the woman fully into the picture.

Once Claire was settled, Monroe continued. "All right. As I was saying, the dome is brand new, as of yesterday. It is a little under half a kilometer in diameter and the ground inside is unmitigated aside from the overall increase in oxygen levels that occurred planetwide as a result of the earlier phases of terraforming. That means the regolith is still heavy with perchlorates. No changes have been made to the air inside the dome, although it might be a degree or two warmer in there by now thanks to the insulation provided by KTI's patented tridygel."

Claire had to stifle a laugh at that. The woman's tone was

identical to Kimura's snarky *and now, a word from our sponsor* when they were on Ares Station.

"But I don't expect you to take all of that on faith, so..." Dr. Monroe nodded toward the airlock tunnel. "Go on in, grab a soil sample. Grab a few, if you want. Take one from out here, as well, for comparison. You've got ten empty CL-2 canisters in that case. Just be quick about it."

Kolya tapped Claire's elbow, and they headed over to the airlock tunnel. Before they went inside, Claire opened the case, removed the first of the Containment Level-2 canisters, then bent down to get a control sample. Once she placed the lid back on the canister, the vacuum kicked in to seal it tight, and a green light came on for a few seconds to let her know that everything was secure. The only way it could be opened now was by the safety sensors inside a Level-2 containment unit.

Unlike the other domes that had been wide enough to drive the buggies through, Fenris had a narrow airlock tunnel that had to be entered on foot. Claire followed Kolya inside and they stood on the small platform. There was about a minute of the same suction sensation she'd experienced in the other tunnels, only it felt much more intense given the smaller space.

When the all-clear light went on, they stepped into the dome. Kolya turned off the helmet communication and motioned for Claire to do the same. "As I'm guessing you've noticed, Davy can be a bit much. But she's the best synthetic biologist I've ever known."

"I like her. So many people *claim* to be open books, but Dr. Monroe seems like she might be the real deal."

Judging from his raised eyebrow, Kolya picked up on the shade she was casting his way but decided to let it slide. "She is. I'd say to ask your mother, but since that doesn't seem to be an option for the two of you, I'm sure your brother is familiar with her work, as well."

"What did she mean about bomb threats at Ehden? That

seems like the kind of thing an *open book* might have told me before we left Daedalus."

"Seriously? There are threats everywhere right now. Like I said before, Mars is the Wild West. It would be easier for me to tell you the locations that haven't been on some sort of security alert in the past few months."

"Thank you. That makes me feel *so* much better."

"It should. Because Cerberus is the first time anything has actually *happened*. And we're still not certain that was sabotage."

"But you already said you thought it *was* sabotage. You were just hoping the media didn't pick up on that fact. Did something change your mind? And you've now got an *accident* that kills two mining executives and their pilot a few days later? Doesn't that seem rather suspicious to you?"

The question was out before it even occurred to Claire that it was a stupid one to ask if she thought there was even the slightest chance that Kolya had been involved in setting up that accident. Maybe it was because she couldn't quite make herself *believe* he was involved. She had little doubt that Kolya engaged in questionable business practices, but the more she thought about it, the harder it was to buy him as a cold-blooded killer, even indirectly through Macek.

"Listen…" He sighed and pointed at the dirt below their feet. "Let's just get the sample, okay? Before Davy gets fed up with our dawdling and leaves. We can talk about all of this later."

Claire gathered one interior sample, stashed the container back inside the case, and then took off at a slow jog toward the center of the crater. Running wasn't as easy as she'd thought it would be in the suit, so she didn't make it more than about fifty meters before she decided she'd gone far enough to collect a second random sample. After she had it safely stored away, she headed back to where Kolya—who had apparently decided to conserve his energy—was waiting.

Once they were outside the dome, they rejoined Dr. Monroe next to the thigh-high glove unit.

"Okay, then. You've collected your samples, so let's get started. First, I want to clarify for the sake of your audience that most of the domed craters on the planet are here to protect what's on the inside from the harsher Martian environment, much as our pressure suits protect us. This dome, however, is here to protect the *outside* by containing the spread of what we're about to release, which could be very hazardous to human health during its active phase."

"Hazardous in what way?" Claire asked.

"Let's just say you wouldn't want this particular strain of bacteria to form a biofilm in your lungs or on other mucous membranes during its metabolically active phase given the modifications that we've made. That's why we'll be keeping everyone inside during stage six." She opened the other sample case to reveal three canisters. Two of them were labeled *6A Fenris*. "The *6A* canisters are identical. Put one of them and the canister marked *6B* into the two extra slots in your case."

"So it doesn't matter which of the two—"

"No," she said, with a look that suggested Claire was being obtuse. "That was the *entire point* of my telling you that they were identical. One will be used in our experiment. The other goes back to Earth with you. This way you can be reasonably certain they're actually the same. I'm afraid you'll have to take *6B* on faith, for reasons that I will explain to you in a few moments."

Claire picked the one on the left, then placed it and the *6B* canister next to her two soil samples, and again closed the case.

"Very good. Now take the other *6A* canister over to the glove station. Anton, if you want *her* to do the honors, you're going to need to make yourself useful and hold something instead of just standing there twiddling your thumbs. She's obviously going to need both hands in those gloves to open the canister. Have you ever worked one of these boxes, Claire?"

Claire nodded. "Not with anything even remotely hazardous, of course. But my brother let me play around with one in his lab when I was younger, so I know how it operates."

"Then cop a squat and let's get to work."

She copped a *kneel*, instead, preferring to get the legs of her biosuit a little dusty rather than risk falling on her ass. Then she unlatched the window on the side of the box and placed the canister on the ledge. Once the box was again resealed, Claire stuck her hands inside the gloves, slid open the door on the other side of the dome, and held the canister up to the security panel just to the right of the opening. The light blinked yellow a few times as the security system processed the code. When it flipped to green, she reached forward into the dome, twisted the container open, and poured maybe a quarter liter of white, viscous liquid onto the ground. The regolith darkened as the liquid began to seep in.

Claire pulled the canister back into the box, closed the inner door, and removed her hands from the gloves. "What next?"

But even as the words left her mouth, she noticed a small, vivid dot of green forming inside the pool of liquid. It was stationary for about five seconds, and then it surged outward. Another pause, then it multiplied again. And again.

Claire kept watching and recording. After only one more cycle, a green film had reached the spot from which she'd taken the first of her two samples.

And then it was off, picking up speed exponentially as it moved further into the dome.

SIXTEEN

CLAIRE'S EYES remained fixed on the floor of the crater so that she could record the entire transformation. Behind her, Dr. Monroe was asking Kolya about getting the samples back to Earth.

"Does she know the protocol?"

"Probably not," he said, "but the team she's traveling with does."

"Good. Just be sure that you give her the proper paperwork so NASA or one of the other bureaucracies doesn't confiscate the damn case. It took me nearly six months to get my samples cleared the last time I went through and several of them were completely ruined."

Kolya chuckled. "The last time you went through was over fifteen years ago. There's an actual process now that we have thousands of people a year going back and forth."

They were both silent for a moment, and then Monroe said, "I just hope you know what you're doing, Anton. First, we get the *clusterbùrach* at Ehden, and now this. I'm beginning to think you've lost your damn mind."

Claire didn't know what a *clusterbùrach* was, but she could make a guess. Between Dr. Monroe's colorful language that the *Post* would censor and the many things she was sure KTI would censor because they considered them security breaches, she had to wonder whether there would be any audio left.

Kolya and Dr. Monroe continued arguing in a softer tone, and Claire was again struck by the familiar banter between the two. The conversation seemed less like one between employer and employee than one between family members, with frequent callbacks to conversations and disputes from the past. And as Kolya had noted back at Tranquility Station, there were only a few people who still called him Anton. Dr. Monroe was the only one Claire had heard...

No. Not the *only* one.

Stasia had also called him Anton at least once. Definitely in that message about them being tied up with the mining conference, but Claire had a vague memory of hearing Stasia say the name, too.

It probably meant nothing. As Kolya and Paul had both said, Stasia was his trusted right hand. But thinking back, Stasia had been perfectly friendly on board the *Ares Prime*. Claire had dinner with her several times, and Stasia had been joking with Claire and Paul when they were rehearsing the lighting cues for the debate.

The chill had happened after that night.

After Kolya visited her room. *After* he talked to Stasia about bringing Claire along on this trip.

Was Stasia more than just his right hand? Or did she perhaps *want* to be more? Claire hadn't picked up on any signals from either of them, but...

She'd been so focused on her internal train of thought that she hadn't even noticed that the green slime was no longer spreading out.

It had taken about two minutes to spread roughly a quarter of the way.

Now, in the blink of an eye, the entire ground was carpeted in a bright, dayglo green that reached to the edge of the dome and stopped, forming a perfect circle. Although, on closer inspection, it looked like the greenish film that had formed earlier was more vibrant near the point of origin, so Claire thought perhaps the stuff was working its way *down* into the soil, as well.

When she stood and brushed the dust from her knees, she noticed several blue splotches on the fabric. There were even tiny blue dots on her gloves.

"That's why I told you to *squat*, not kneel," Dr. Monroe said. "The dust and gravel have jagged edges. That blue dye is released from microcapsules along with a self-healing agent and it will disappear in a couple of minutes once the fabric is completely repaired. It's just showing you that you damaged the suit. Not a big deal for tiny punctures like that. It can even heal some degree of damage to the nanofiber shell layer. But the suit has its limits, so you should be more careful. Now…what did you think of our little demonstration?"

"Very impressive," Claire said. "But I'm afraid I need one of you to explain exactly what it was that I just saw. Is this what will happen in stage six?"

"Well, it's *part* of what will happen," Dr. Monroe replied. "The first part, as was suggested by the label on the canister —*6A*. The solution you just released contained a few million modified *Azospira oryzae*. We've obviously edited the bacteria's reproductive genes to vastly increase the speed at which they multiply. Instead of the usual binary fission, it now uses multiple fission, splitting into five daughter cells. And, of course, we added that garish color that appears when they feed —which I will note was Anton's choice. Personally, it reminds me of pictures of this horrid carpet in my great-grandmother's basement. But he wanted something easily visible so there you have it. The green will eventually fade as the perchlorates are consumed—that's the only food source this modified strain can survive on, so they'll die off once it's exhausted. The surface will then return to its original color, and that will be our signal to release *6B*. That will be in about twelve hours for this little dome but will take over a month after it's released planetwide to about five thousand locations. The *Azospira* needs time to digest the perchlorates in the regolith. As it consumes the toxin, it will release oxygen into the air, which gets us a little closer to eventually being able to walk around on the surface without these suits."

"So…what happens when you release the canisters marked *6B*?"

"We move from microscopic to macroscopic life. Macroflora, to be more specific. Things that will turn the planet a more *realistic* shade of green instead of that fluorescent abomination. But when I say realistic, I mean realistic for Mars. As I've told Anton, he should keep the dome around at least part of Daedalus City even after the final stages are complete and rename it something like Earth City or Daedalus Disney, for those who are feeling nostalgic for home. Because most of the plants beneath that dome aren't a good choice for this planet. We're too far away from the sun. But with some modifications, Mars *can* eventually have a lush microbiome. The fauna, too, will be tailored specifically to the Martian environment, although that stage isn't strictly necessary. We need plants to have a viable atmosphere, but we could survive without animals."

Judging from the look Kolya gave the woman, this was a long-standing point of contention. "True. But no one will consider the place completely terraformed without animal life. And as Idi has noted, we could use earthworms to till the soil. They require less effort on our part than introducing biobots or machines to do the job. Ants, beetles, millipedes…they're all useful for agriculture. And yes, so are bees."

"Stage ten is the bug-monsters," Claire said.

Kolya looked at her and frowned. "What?"

"Nothing. Just a little joke my roommate's daughter made," Claire said with an uneasy laugh, although the stage ten part had actually been Wyatt. "She's four, and she saw a movie where there were bug-monsters on Mars. Big nasty ones that gave her nightmares."

Dr. Monroe smiled. "You can tell your young friend that there's nothing to worry about. No bug-monsters—no spiders, wasps, or scorpions. No mosquitoes, either. Given that most fruits have self-pollinating varieties, we wouldn't even need bees if Anton wasn't obsessed with a few types of apple. Although I suspect it's less about the apples and more because he wants honey for his precious krambambula. So, let me amend what I said a moment ago. The fauna will be tailored to the Martian environment *and* the whims of the brilliant Anton Kolya. But to be clear, we *do* have strict parameters for our AE biobots. For example, they can't select anything poisonous or venomous to humans."

"AE biobots?" The term was new to Claire, and she added it to the list of things to talk to Joe about when she got back to Earth. "How do those differ from the run-of-the-mill recombinant variety?"

"AE is for accelerated evolution," Dr. Monroe said. "We could simply seed the Martian landscape with genetically altered selections from Earth's microbiome. But that's not really optimal. Life on our home planet had the advantage of evolution, enabling it to adapt to the existing conditions in each environment or to die off and let something better suited take its place. KTI's *patented* AE biobots are designed to do something very similar...only within a radically compressed timeframe. We have a few dozen basic varieties, each programmed to switch key genes on or off to form the most viable variant of that family or genus for a particular section of the planet."

"How do you plan to distribute them?" Claire asked. "I assume you don't have people positioned around the planet waiting to open canisters like I just did."

"We'll be peppering the surface from Ares Station to accomplish the bulk of stage six," Kolya said. "And any of the quadrangles that we can't target from the station's orbit will be handled by suborbital aircraft drops. Not just the more temperate areas near the equator, which is all that you've seen so far, but also the polar regions. Think of these as biobot cluster bombs...only they will be *seeding* life rather than destroying it."

SEVENTEEN

"YOU'RE UNUSUALLY QUIET," Kolya said about ten minutes after their shuttle left Fenris. "I thought you'd be assaulting me with questions by now."

Claire's mind had actually been pinging back and forth between her suspicions about the fight Macek had with the man who was now dead, the Stasia situation, and everything they'd just witnessed. That sort of mental chaos didn't happen to her often, but when it did, she'd learned to just let the thoughts bubble away and see what rose to the top.

On the former, even if Macek had done something to Westmoreland's plane, she couldn't be certain that Kolya was aware of it. That thumbs up could have been about anything. For all she knew, the two of them might exchange thumbs up before every trip, in a sort of preflight ritual. Maybe Macek had been telling Kolya he'd gotten lucky the night before. Or saying he hoped Kolya would get lucky tonight.

And on the possibility that she'd angered Stasia—or worse, hurt her—by entertaining the idea of a fling with Kolya, Claire had pretty much decided that asking Paul would be a mistake. Asking Kolya himself was problematic, too, since she didn't want to leave him with the impression that Stasia had in any way given her the idea that she was interested in him.

In both cases, she thought the best thing to do at this point was to keep things strictly professional between herself and Kolya and try to put everything else out of her mind. Tomorrow morning, she'd be on her way to Icarus and might not even see the man again before she left for Earth.

"I was just lost in thought," she told him. "And you were

busy scowling at your messages. Are you actually complaining about my silence?"

"Not complaining. Just a bit surprised. I guess it *is* a lot for you to take in all at once."

"Absolutely. I have a major case of information overload." That was true, even if some of that overload was from things that had nothing at all to do with the terraforming project. Claire nodded toward his phone. "Was that more news about Westmoreland's plane?"

He shook his head. "Not yet."

"So…how long have you known Dr. Monroe?"

"And…the silence has ended," he said with a teasing smile. "I believe the phrase is since I was knee-high to a grasshopper. Davy worked for KTI long before I took over, and the woman rarely lets me forget it."

"She appears to be the only person at KTI who calls you Anton," Claire noted, thinking he might correct her and mention Stasia, but he didn't.

"It's a fair trade," he said with a little shrug. "I'm the only one—well, the only *adult*, at any rate—who she lets call her Davy. Those are the names we've used for each other from the beginning. She probably still thinks of my uncle as Kolya and… they had their differences near the end of his tenure at KTI so I'm fine with her keeping us separate in her mind. To be honest, I'm not sure that I'd be in charge of the company today if she hadn't marshalled the tech leaders—and quite a few of the shareholders as well—into my camp. Davy would rather be working in her lab than pulling strings and calling in favors, but when that woman sets her mind to something, she is a force that you challenge at your peril."

"And yet you've clearly challenged her on at least one occasion, since Mars will have apple blossoms…and honey."

He laughed. "And eventually, krambambula. The truth is that Davy is a bit of a softy under the gruff exterior. But I've also known her a very long time and I'm smart enough to pull back if I get the sense that I'm pushing her too close to the edge."

"She really hasn't been back to Earth in fifteen years?"

"Ah, you *were* listening, then. You were staring so hard at the floor of the dome that I wasn't sure."

Claire tapped the front of her helmet. "Because I was recording, remember? The video gets jumpy if I move my head too much."

"Right. To be honest, it may be getting closer to twenty years since she's been back. At some point, she had to make a choice. There were no habitats with artificial gravity when she first started her work here. She exercised, but...let's just say that Davy is the type who will forget to eat if she's working. I think she'd forget to breathe if it wasn't automatic. And you needed to spend a lot of time exercising to stay in Earth-shape back then. You still do, really. By the time the newer sleeping quarters were being built, she'd decided that Mars was home. The small amount of time she spent on Earth was no longer very enjoyable because she was tired and could barely get around. Her work is her home, and her work is here."

"Will you be following her lead in a few years?"

"I don't know. At one point, I would very likely have said yes. But I now see that my work doesn't end here, and much of my value to KTI lies in my ability to convince people of the potential for our projects. Not just convincing them of the *need* for the project but clarifying how they might make money from fulfilling that need. And all of that is better accomplished on Earth, face to face. On the other hand, our next steps aren't quite as expensive, so I might not have to spend as long on Earth sucking up to investors."

"That makes sense," Claire said. "Compared to the early stages, with the orbital mirror and laying the wire for the magnetosphere, seeding the planet with life must seem relatively cheap."

"No...I mean, *yes*, the earlier stages were more labor intensive and costly than what we're doing now, but I'm not talking about Mars. What I said during the debate wasn't just to score points against Shepherd. Becoming a multiplanetary species is the first step to insuring that humankind survives. But we can't let that be the end. If humans are, as I truly believe, alone in the universe, then we have an obligation to ensure that those who come after us have a backup option."

"That sounds like you're planning to build a generational ship. But unless KTI has suddenly developed warp drive or discovered a stargate or some other technology that I'm pretty sure exists only in science fiction, there's no other way to reach habitable planets in a single lifetime…even if the travelers end up living a few extra decades thanks to Rejuvesce. And I can't imagine that a generational ship would be an *inexpensive* step at all, even compared to the early stages of terraforming."

Kolya was quiet for a moment, staring out the window at the blur of sand and sky. Through the front window, Claire could see a green dot that, judging from the dashboard map, had to be Ehden.

"We haven't developed faster-than-light travel," he said finally. "Nor have we managed to corral a wormhole or anything of that sort. I don't think I'm quite at the point where I'm willing to talk specifics beyond that. Not yet, and not even off the record. *But*…if you'll have dinner with me tonight, I promise you'll be the very first reporter I call when I'm ready to make that announcement. How does that sound?"

She rolled her eyes. "It *sounds* like a somewhat ethically questionable quid pro quo…except for the fact that we're traveling together, and I doubt that there are multiple dining options for me to choose from at Ehden. So, with all of that clearly understood, I accept your terms."

"It's a good thing my ego is bulletproof," he said with a chuckle. "Otherwise, I'd be wounded by all those caveats."

Less than a minute later, the shuttle pulled onto the landing pad. They grabbed their bags and transferred them to one of several KTI buggies parked near the entrance to the airlock tunnel. From the outside, it looked like a considerably smaller, non-commercial version of Daedalus, in the sense that the plants beneath its dome weren't odd or alien, but very close to ones you'd find on Earth. A lake was also visible off in the distance, near the center of the dome. But Ehden was simple and utilitarian, without the garish lights and massive buildings she had seen at Daedalus. There was in fact, only a smattering of buildings.

Claire pulled off the helmet and gloves once they were inside the dome. Her hair was sopping wet, as if she'd just stepped out of the shower. After a brief, fruitless search for something to tie it back, she tucked the damp strands behind her ears and put on her visor cam. Travel could be tiring anyway, but it seemed to be amplified by the biosuit. She could only imagine how much worse that was in the puffsuits she'd seen Brodnik and the others wearing in that first video, which was now in the hands of Bernard and the *Atlantic Post's* editorial board.

"Before you turn your visor back on," Kolya said, "I have a confession to make."

"That sounds ominous."

"Yeah…although on second thought, I guess it's *two* confessions. First, there are other dining options at Ehden. But the communal dining hall will likely be rather…rowdy this evening. And certainly more crowded than usual. Ehden residents aren't even eating there this week because a construction crew arrived two days ago to build habitats and some common buildings for a few hundred new colonists that will arrive prior to stage six. The first of those new arrivals is already here, and I need to talk with him for a bit. Paul says he can have him at the dining hall by the time we arrive, if you're okay with us stopping there first. Shouldn't take more than half an hour. An hour at the most. We need to hash out a few legal issues, so I'd prefer to patch Macek in on the meeting, and the dining hall has the most reliable communications system in Ehden."

"That's fine," she said, even though she was more than ready to get out of the suit and the increasingly sweaty clothes underneath. "Are these new colonists what Dr. Monroe meant by saying you're playing games at Ehden?"

"They are. But Davy is overreacting. I made a deal that will benefit Mars as a whole, and Nepenthes, too. She wouldn't be complaining if not for the fact that it's happening in what she thinks of as her backyard. I swear, the woman detests any sort of change to her personal surroundings, which seems odd to me given that her line of work deals with some pretty monumental changes."

"For a man who runs a company full of scientists, you really haven't spent much time with them, have you? That description fits at least half of the truly gifted scientists I know."

"Fair point. Either way, we were already planning to move her crew over to Doba before stage six. And I think I've found the perfect new caretakers for Ehden."

Claire thought the place *did* need quite a bit of caretaking. Acre upon acre of land stretched across the dome, and while it looked fertile, at least compared to the desert beyond, only a small amount of it had been cultivated.

"But we can talk about all of that over dinner," he said. "I need to make my second *mea culpa* before we stop. When I originally talked to Stasia and Paul about setting up this trip, back on the *Ares Prime*, I told them that we'd be staying at my cabin."

"You have a cabin here?"

"Yes. It belonged to my uncle. I sort of inherited it with the company."

Claire stifled a smile at that. If the stories she'd heard were true, it was less that Kolya had inherited the company and more that he'd shoved his uncle off of a corporate cliff and taken it. The cabin was probably just one of many spoils that went to Kolya the Younger as the victor of that battle.

"Ehden was one of the first domed craters and the cabin is original construction," he said, "so it's fairly rustic compared to my place at Daedalus. But I like it. I'm not here often, and I treat Ehden as a vacation from sleeping in artificial gravity. You can actually sleep with the windows open here most of the year. There are three bedrooms, so I wasn't being entirely presumptuous. Just a tad… hopeful?"

He gave her that smile again, the one that made him look ten years younger and a bit vulnerable. The one that she found attractive, even though she still half suspected he practiced it in the mirror. And, Claire reminded herself, the sort of smile that might be worn by a suave sociopath who removed business foes from the picture with the help of his lefthand man.

"Anyway," he said, "I informed Stasia that you were annoyed with me—she said you were a smart girl for keeping me at arm's length, by the way—and I told her that we needed to make other arrangements for our night here in Ehden. But based on the message I received from Paul a few minutes ago, that information never made it to him. Stasia is usually very much on top of things, as you know. I'm guessing this just got lost in the shuffle with the labor crisis and the explosion at Cerberus."

Well, that blew her theory about Stasia and Kolya right out of the water. She might have told him that Claire was a smart girl for keeping things on a strictly business footing merely as cover. But if Stasia was at all interested in the man, wouldn't she have made absolutely certain that Paul got the message to find another place for her to sleep?

"We can figure something else out, though," Kolya said, seeing Claire's expression. "As I told you, Ehden is unusually crowded at the moment, to the point that they even have some of the construction workers sleeping in tents. But Paul *did* offer the sofa in the quarters he's sharing with Ayman as an alternative."

"It's not a problem," she said. "Assuming the bedrooms at this cabin have doors?"

"They do. And the doors even lock. But, of course, as the owner of the cabin, I probably *do* have a key somewhere..."

Claire laughed. "You're making Paul's sofa sound tempting."

"Seriously, though...if you're uncomfortable, we'll work something else out."

"We've just covered several thousand kilometers of perfectly good spots to bury a body," she said. "And, based on what you told me earlier, there's no one out here to enforce the few laws there might be against it. So I suppose that if you were a mad slasher intent on killing me, you'd have done it by now. Plus, there are at least a dozen people who know that we're traveling together. Some of them don't even work for you."

"True." He was quiet for a moment and then said. "In the interest of transparency, I should probably go ahead and admit that I *remain* hopeful. My optimism is legendary. Just ask KTI's investors. But I will absolutely respect your wishes either way."

"And they say chivalry is dead."

"Not dead. Although, while we're on the topic, I should note that out here in the hinterlands, chivalry might be on life support. There's this very old movie called *Mars Needs Women*. Fiction, obviously, but flash forward over a century and...well, it's not wrong. The planet is still about three-quarters male outside of the more urban areas. Many of these guys on construction and mining teams see only a handful of real live women each year."

Kolya didn't elaborate on the *real live women* point, and Claire definitely didn't push. It was common knowledge that of the dozens of varieties of robots on Mars, sexbots were by far the most numerous.

They were now nearing the center of the village, and Ehden appeared to be a good deal larger and far busier than sleepy little Doba. There were five single story buildings, along with a tall structure that Claire assumed was one of the torus-shaped sleeping chambers. A wooden—or more likely, bamboo—façade covered the front. It was almost identical to the one she'd seen propped up at Doba earlier in the day. Two other housing units were under active construction, with several dozen workers and an assortment of helper bots clustered around the site.

"Bring your things," Kolya said as their shuttle stopped on the parking pad in front of one of the generic looking buildings. "And if you want to send any messages back home, you'll have much better luck getting them to go through here than you will at either the cabin or at Icarus Camp."

Claire wedged the sample case into her daypack and struggled with the zipper. The case fit—barely—but there was no hope of getting anything else inside, so she stashed her gloves in the helmet.

A group of men, maybe half a dozen in total, were gathered on the other side of the narrow street, surrounded by a cloud of vapor. The official sign-up age for work in the Martian colonies was twenty-one, but some of these guys looked like they were in their mid-teens. Claire was surprised to see that the youngest looking of the bunch was smoking an actual, honest-to-God cigarette. She hadn't seen one of those in public since she was a small child. People still smoked on their own property, but only if they purchased them on the illegal market or grew and rolled their own.

The kid stubbed the smoke out on his shoe when he saw her watching him. At first, his expression was angry, so maybe the things were illegal on Mars, too. As soon as she stepped out of the buggy, however, he gave her a leisurely head-to-toe appraisal and his scowl morphed into a wolfish grin. "Ooh, babe, ain't you—"

Whatever he was planning as a follow-up to those four words shriveled and died on his tongue as soon as he realized that the man coming around the side of the buggy was, at least indirectly, his boss. The kid flushed a deep red, gave Kolya a nod, then faded back into the group, where his buddies promptly began ragging him.

"You weren't joking," Claire whispered as they headed toward the door. "Can't believe the little twerp was on the verge of catcalling me when I'm in this shapeless suit."

"If you're disappointed, I'd be happy to catcall you later when you're out of it." Kolya grinned when she flipped him off, then he stepped forward to open the door. "Davy said they gave *her* the eye when she came into Ehden last night, and she's well past the age of most of their grandmothers. *Of course* they were looking you over."

Ehden's dining hall consisted of a large enclosed octagonal area at the front and a covered patio at the back. It was mostly empty, although Claire guessed that would change in an hour or so when the sun went down, and the men outside were off the clock. Aside from her and Kolya, there were only a few people at the tables inside—three middle-aged men with mostly empty plates in front of them and two men in KTI security guard uniforms. All of them were watching a football match on the viewscreen.

The two men at the bar were also watching the match. The first was Paul Caruso, which didn't surprise Claire in the slightest.

The second was Tobias Alvin Shepherd.

EIGHTEEN

CLAIRE GRABBED Kolya's arm and yanked him back outside. "Your new colonists are the *Flock*?"

"Not *all* of the Flock."

"Well, *obviously*. This dome wouldn't support more than a tiny fraction of them. When did this happen? And *why*? No wonder Dr. Monroe is pissed. After two decades of harassing scientists on Earth, you can't actually believe members of the Flock are going to be good neighbors with the ones you're moving over to Doba?"

"I do believe that, because Shepherd will make sure of it. Two worker transports will arrive at Ares Station in a little under three weeks with one hundred and twenty of his most loyal followers. If all goes well, we'll bring in another group after stage six is over. KTI's worker transports may not be the Sentinel motherships that Shepherd promised them, but they will find an unspoiled paradise where they can work the land and live uncomplicated lives while they wait for the real deal to arrive and whisk them off to Alpha Centauri or wherever. It's a mutually beneficial arrangement."

"So this was your plan when you invited him to Mars?"

"Well, it wasn't exactly a plan at that point. I mean, it *did* occur to me that Mars needs a few agrarian colonies as…agents of civilization, I guess? The same way the western US needed homesteaders. Miners aren't really a civilizing force, but farmers put down roots."

Claire groaned. "That was really bad, Kolya. And for a guy from Minsk, you seem to know a lot about the Old West."

"My graduate work *was* at Caltech."

"In planetary science, though, not history."

"True. To be honest, most of what I know is secondhand from Caruso. He watches a lot of movies. But leaving my terrible pun aside, what I said is accurate. The Flock has a lot to offer Ehden. I thought I might have to *pay* Shepherd to get him to even consider the move, but with the recent schism, he needed a safe haven and so did his more devout followers. Still, I thought it would at least take a few months to get enough volunteers. I certainly didn't plan to bring them here in time for the stage six isolation. But many of his people have no place to go, no money. They left behind family and friends years ago. Once they found out that Shepherd was here, they were happy to make the move, and the sooner the better."

"What if all of them get here and decide they were happier with the dream than with the reality?"

"Then they'll be sent home. We're not going to hold anyone against their will."

"Except there have been reports for years that Shepherd did just that. At a minimum, the ones who left the Flock did so without the money they handed over when they joined, and with nothing to show for years of labor on the communal farms."

"The Flock provided room and board. Health care, clothing, and other expenses."

"I can't believe you're defending that business model. It's basically voluntary slavery."

Kolya sighed. "I'm not defending it. And I can't guarantee that they'll leave with whatever resources they sank into the Flock if they're not happy here. All I can promise is that they'll be up the price of one Martian vacation, and I'll be down the cost of a round-trip passage. No harm, no foul." He opened the door a second time and waited for her to enter. "Just grab a table anywhere. I'll be back as soon as I can. What do you want to drink?"

"Water will be fine."

Kolya, who was already halfway to the bar, gave a thumbs up to indicate that he'd heard her. A completely innocuous gesture, but it reminded her once again of the exchange between him and Macek that morning at Daedalus.

He said something to Paul and spoke briefly to the two guards. Paul turned and gave Claire a wave, then went to the fridge behind the counter. Shepherd didn't even spare her a glance. He just grabbed his glass from the bar and followed Kolya and one of the guards out to the patio.

Unlike the café in Doba, the dining hall smelled heavily of fried meat, onions, and beer. Not bad smells when they're fresh, but less pleasant as lingering aromas. There was also a strong odor of sweat, some of which Claire realized was quite likely coming from her. So she found a seat near a window that looked out over the lake and raised it a few inches to get a bit of fresh air.

Claire pulled her tablet from the front pocket of the daypack and began scanning through the video clips from her touristy afternoon in Daedalus City. If Kolya was right, this might be her last chance to send anything home until they were back at the Red Dahlia.

When she looked up, Paul was at the table with both the bottle of water she'd requested and a very large glass of white wine. He set them down in front of her and then slid a package of crackers across the table.

"Yes, I know you said just water. But, believe me, you're going to be here a while. Shepherd is convinced that they need to renegotiate something in the charter for Ehden. Or, as he pronounces it, *Eden*."

"As in the *Garden of…*?"

"Precisely. He says to come back in a year and his people will have turned this into a paradise. I told Stasia we ought to assign them one of the domes that hasn't been terraformed. If Shepherd and his handmaidens could turn that into a paradise, I'd be less likely to chalk him up as a pretentious poser."

"He *is* getting a considerable head start, so it does seem a little presumptuous to claim godlike powers."

"Tell me about it. I've spent the past few days with the man and Shepherd's ego is bigger than you-know-who's…and while we're speaking of Kolya, I'm glad to see that you survived his little take-off joke. The man's sense of humor has a definite evil streak. Stasia keeps telling him he's going to give someone a heart attack one of these days. Or piss them off enough that they kill him as soon as he sets the plane down. But Kolya thinks it's freaking hilarious. And even though he couldn't have known it at the time, it's kind of awful to think that Westmoreland and the others on that plane had to experience that same nasty jolt only a few hours before they ended up actually crashing at Mamers. Is that little stunt the reason you're now looking for other housing options?"

"No." She started to give him a full explanation but since Kolya said Paul had been in on the whole scheme to get her this assignment, she decided it might be best to avoid specifics for the time being. "The cabin will be fine, though, now that Kolya understands the boundaries."

"Good. Because the couch in the little apartment we're using is hard as a rock. And Ayman and I both snore, so you probably wouldn't get much sleep anyway. Listen, I need to get in there. We'll catch up on the way to Icarus, okay?" He nodded toward the security guard who was still watching the game. "Jackson over there will stay here to keep an eye on things. The cooks will be in shortly to start prepping to feed the hungry hordes, but we *should* be done before they actually arrive. Hopefully. Oh…and the bathroom is at the rear of the dining hall if you want to get out of that suit."

"Thanks." Claire waved the tablet. "Is there a password? Kolya said it might be my last chance to message Ro and Jemma."

Paul pulled his phone out, pressed his thumb against the screen and then held it to the back of her tablet. "That should do it. There's more wine in the fridge behind the bar if you need a refill."

Claire changed out of the biosuit, wishing that she had thought to pack an extra set of clothing in her daypack. A shower would have been nice, too, but she splashed cool water on her face and patted her clothes down with some paper towels until they were merely damp, rather than dripping wet. She still couldn't find her hair tie but decided it would have to do. Back in the dining hall, she draped the biosuit over the back of the chair currently holding her helmet and gloves and took up her tablet again.

For the next few minutes, she typed out a message to Joe and another to Rowan and Jemma, keeping things vague but letting everyone know she was safe and sound. Then she began going through the videos in chronological order, attaching a few clips from the hotel, including the dizzying view from the so-called balcony when it was at full spin, a photo she'd taken of the red baby grand on the mezzanine of the executive pavilion, and a few shots of the lake outside the Red Dahlia. She had just switched to looking at the videos she'd recorded on the main strip when she heard a raised voice from the patio. Claire was pretty sure it was Shepherd, but she couldn't make out the words.

She slipped her earbuds out of her pocket and opened the amplifier app that Wyatt had given her a few years back. It wasn't legal to use in many US states, at least not without the consent of one or both parties. There was a chance that it might be illegal on Mars, too…but Kolya was always pointing out that this was the Wild, Wild West in terms of law and order, so Claire decided they probably hadn't gotten around to laws about eavesdropping.

That left the ethical quandary. She wrestled with that one for even less time. Kolya had just told her that there were threats everywhere out here, which meant that she had a vested interest in learning *what*ever she could, *how*ever she could. That went double after hearing about Westmoreland's plane crash. Macek and Kolya might both be entirely innocent of any involvement in that, but since she couldn't really ask Kolya about it, she'd have to get information on her own.

For the first few seconds after she turned on the amplifier, all she could hear were construction noises from across the street and the football match the guard and the three men at the back of the dining hall were watching. She filtered those sounds out, along with a few other bits of ambient noise, and then zeroed in on the voices out back.

Macek was talking now, explaining something about the need to keep the charter for Ehden aligned with other colonial charters and the proposed planetwide constitution. "We can't make exceptions. The other four are all on board with Ehden being included as a provisional member, but you'll have to send representatives to parliament. You'll need to hold elections for those, and for offices in the colony."

Shepherd said, "I don't have a problem with holding elections within the colony. We've always done that. But I was told that Eden would be self-governing."

"It *will* be," Kolya said, "for any matters that exclusively affect Ehden. And your people will have a voice in matters that affect the planet as a whole, the same as every other citizen."

"But that's the entire point! We don't *want* to participate. I fully expect the Sentinels to rescue us within the next few years. While we wait, we'll help to rehabilitate this ruined planet. It's certainly better than staying back on Earth and watching those idiots destroy a verdant one. As I have said before, we will welcome other colonists here with open arms. And any of my group that wishes to leave and join another colony will be allowed to do so. But we have no more desire to get embroiled in the petty political squabbles of Mars than we had to get involved in those of Earth. If that means we're not full citizens, then so be it."

It went on in the same vein for the next fifteen minutes.

Round and round, and if they were making any progress toward a compromise, Claire certainly couldn't detect it. Despite the boredom, she was torn between continuing to listen and her need to finish the message to Ro and Jemma. The thought of Jemma was what finally tipped the scales toward turning off the amplifier app and opening another video. All of her messages home lately had been coded notes to Wyatt, and Claire wanted to add two videos she'd recorded just for Jemma on the main drag at Daedalus the day before.

The first was taken at a combination bakery and candy shop, Galactic Goodies, where the clerk informed Claire that they did indeed carry peanut butter cookies but had already sold out for the day. She had mugged a sad face into the camera for Jemma and then told the clerk that she'd check back before the trip home. That one didn't need any editing, so she added it to the message and moved on.

At the toy store a few doors down, however, she'd purchased a Martian plush creature that actually did look a little like a bug-monster—the big-eyed friendly variety that hopefully wouldn't inspire nightmares. That one she *would* need to preview and probably edit before sending. The store had a fabulous display window with lots of animated toys, including a few that interacted with each other. Claire had recorded a couple of minutes there but was pretty sure the bug-monster was somewhere in the mix, and she didn't want to spoil the surprise by Jemma seeing it before she got home.

About ten seconds into the video something in the window caught Claire's eye. At first, she thought the blip of green light was coming from one of the toys, but then she saw it again.

The light wasn't inside the store. It was a reflection in the store window.

She zoomed in. A tiny drone, not much bigger than a fly, was hovering a few feet behind her, blinking a very familiar pattern.

Dot, dot, dash... Dot, dot, dash... Dot, dot, dash...

NINETEEN

THE ODDS that the nanodrone was still tailing her halfway across the planet seemed non-existent, but Claire's skin continued to crawl as if she were being watched.

Over by the counter, the guard still had his eyes glued to the viewscreen. At some point while she was looking through the videos, however, the three men who were watching the game had departed and four new people—a man, two women, and a girl of around twelve—had arrived. They were pulling bowls and trays from the refrigerator, and Claire noticed that the girl *was* sneaking looks at her, possibly because she recognized her face from the video about the chamber. The girl also seemed oddly familiar, and Claire realized that she was probably the daughter that Idi had mentioned.

It felt ridiculous to be nervous given how far she was from Daedalus, but she still couldn't relax until she looked out the window next to her, and out the front windows, as well. There was no sign of the nanodrone, but then she'd already been pretty sure there wouldn't be.

Claire hadn't even touched the wine Paul had given her up to that point, but she picked it up then and downed half of it in a single go. For several minutes, she simply sat there, taking deep breaths, and trying to organize her thoughts. Then, she began scanning through the rest of the videos she'd taken that afternoon.

Most of the clips had been intended as possible background footage for a future *Simple Science* segment, along with the general sort of things that you record on vacation. In five of them, the nanodrone was clearly visible. In three others, Claire could see reflected green light that might or might not have been the drone. The videos weren't taken during a brief period of time, but spread out over the course of the afternoon, with the last one being at the Podkayne Fries place where she had grabbed dinner. That was among the clearest images, with the drone reflected in one of the framed book covers on the walls.

It had been *following* her. And, as best Claire could tell, she was the only one who'd had an insect-o-bot escort that day. She had taken more than a dozen videos and still shots of other tourists walking along the strip and around the grounds at Red Dahlia, and even when she zoomed in at the maximum resolution, there was no sign of any other drones in those pictures.

Claire had no doubt that it was the same model as the one that attacked Shepherd. Even though she was not an expert on nanodrones, as she'd told Macek, he'd left the smashed version that was inside the vial on the table while he questioned her on the *Ares Prime*.

Macek hadn't disagreed with Claire when she told him that, for all she knew, it could have been a common brand of drone. In fact, he'd even tossed that observation back at her when ordering her to keep quiet. But she couldn't shake the sense that he'd recognized the thing and that he'd been surprised that she'd spotted it in DC. Surprised, as well, that she thought it might belong to the Flock.

Would Macek, who was almost certainly much better acquainted with this sort of device than Claire was, have been surprised to hear that a commonplace, off-the-shelf drone was following her? Probably not. But what if it was a very specific model? What if it was the *same* model used by his own organization? Maybe even a model exclusive to KTI?

It didn't make sense that Kolya would want to kill Shepherd, though. Not if he was hoping to convince the man to bring his followers to settle in Ehden. Which left only a few options that Claire could think of offhand. One was that Macek believed someone outside their organization had stolen one of their devices and was trying to frame KTI for Shepherd's murder. Another was that someone inside KTI had gone rogue and had their own reasons for wanting to kill Shepherd. Perhaps they'd even been hired to kill him by this Drexel guy who was taking over the Flock.

Or…maybe the attack on Shepherd had only been designed to *scare* the man? He didn't die, after all, and it played right into Kolya's hands for Shepherd to believe that he was in too much danger to go back to Earth. And Kolya had just told Claire that he'd thought he might have to pay Shepherd to get him to consider the move to Ehden.

Still, would Kolya really think it was worth setting up an assault—and a risky one, at that—just to convince a cult leader and his pack of free laborers to move to Mars?

Despite the fact that Claire now felt like there was a target printed on her back, she had to admit that it was possible that Macek or even Kolya had authorized the drone simply to keep her under surveillance. Given that Claire was still alive and hadn't wound up twitching uncontrollably on the sidewalk from a dose of neurotoxin, she thought that was quite likely. There was even a chance that they'd justified the surveillance as being for her own protection.

Claire wanted to believe that. In fact, she spent several minutes trying to convince herself that it was true. But it felt off. The whole situation felt off, and a ravenous little worm of panic began gnawing at her stomach as she realized there was no one on the entire planet she could talk to about this. No way was she telling anyone at KTI that she'd spotted that drone. And telling Brodnik or anyone on her team was pointless. What could they do? Call the cops? The only police she'd seen were private security like the guy across the room, still watching the football match, whose salary was paid by one of the people she considered a prime suspect. And as Kolya and others kept pointing out, the entire concept of law and order was rather shaky on Mars right now.

Either way, on the off chance that the drone following her *had* been armed to kill but just never found a good spot to take her out, Claire decided that she needed to tell someone back home. And while it was possible that messages going out of Ehden didn't go through Macek's censors, she couldn't afford to risk stating her concerns openly.

Which meant that she and Wyatt were back to speaking in code.

Claire opened the draft of her message to Ro and attached the two videos for Jemma along with a few other clips and photos that showed the drone, including the really clear image from the diner. Then she added a note at the end:

> Ro: Thought you might be interested to see the little ship in the window in the toy store video. Isn't that the same one you bought for your nephew at the Space Museum in DC? The one that he lost on the Metro? How odd that they'd have it here at Daedalus when we couldn't find it anywhere else! Check and see if it's close enough and if so, I'll grab a replacement for him. Hugs!

Given that Ro was an only child with no nieces or nephews, the entire story was obviously bunk. If any of Macek's security team bothered to check, they could probably find her family information without much trouble, but there was also the possibility that Jemma's dad was the source of the nephew, so they'd have to check him, too. Hopefully, they wouldn't bother. And if Ro and Wyatt looked closely enough at that display window, they would see the drone in the reflection behind her.

She held her finger over the send button for a long time, though. This was going to scare the hell out of them. If Wyatt was keeping Joe informed about all of this, as she assumed he was, it would scare him, too. And what good would it do? It wasn't like they could send in the cavalry to rescue her when they were nearly a quarter of a billion kilometers away. She was completely on her own.

Still, if anything *did* happen to her while on Mars, Claire wanted someone back on Earth to know that it probably wasn't an accident, no matter what they were told. They might not be able to *do* anything about it, might not be able to save her, not when she was on a part of the planet where the only sort of justice was apparently the frontier variety.

But at least they would *know*.

TWENTY

ONCE THE MESSAGES WERE SENT, Claire tuned in once more to the Back Porch Accords, where Shepherd was making what seemed, at least on the surface, to be a self-contradictory argument about security. He said they didn't want or need KTI guards on the premises, and then immediately shifted to talking about the explosion at Cerberus.

"And don't try to tell me it was an accident. One of the construction foremen has a brother who works for Millex. Not at Cerberus, but at their other facility over at Orcus Patera. He said there have been threats for several months now, something that I would note you did *not* tell me prior to our agreement. Millex is one of *your* companies. Why would I want to pull my followers out of one violent situation and into another?"

"Millex is a subcontractor, not part of KTI," Macek said. "How about this as a compromise? Ehden handles its own internal security. We'll scan anyone coming to Ehden when they arrive at Nepenthes Station and have them leave whatever weapons they might have in their possession, but you can feel free to scan them again when they get here."

They dickered back and forth for a while, then Shepherd excused himself. The door opened a moment later. He nodded to Claire as he passed and headed toward the hallway with the bathroom.

Through the earbuds, she heard Paul asking if they had any more information about Westmoreland.

"No," Macek said. "But the plane with the MFL delegation was on the schedule just after Kolya's takeoff this morning. And you heard them in the conference."

"He actually didn't," Kolya said. "Paul was here with Shepherd, remember? As soon as they got word about the explosion at Cerberus, Gergen—that's the head of the MFL delegation—accused Wes point-blank, but I don't know if he thinks Wes ordered an attack directly or just blamed him for the situation in general. To be fair, I wouldn't be surprised if Wes *was* involved. To use Davy's term, it's a complete *clusterbùrach*. Which means I may have to stay at Cerberus for a few days, so—"

A hand fell on Claire's shoulder. She jumped and turned to see Tobias Shepherd staring down at her. He was saying something, so she yanked the earbuds out.

"I'm sorry. What did you say?"

"I said I believe this must be yours." He held up a bright pink hair tie. "It was under the sink, and I can't really see it belonging to anyone else in here. I'm sorry if I startled you."

He glanced at her earphones and then at the open window. The tablet was closed. There was no way he could have seen the amplifier app or could have known what she'd been listening to, but she flushed anyway.

"I should really stop listening to scary books," she said with a nervous laugh. "They have me jumping at every little thing."

Shepherd nodded, but Claire had the oddest feeling he knew she was lying. Then he said, "I also wanted to take the opportunity to thank you."

"For what?"

"Paul Caruso, who has been my...chaperone for the week tells me that you were the one who first spotted the drone and told them it might be a neurotoxin. Without your sharp eyes, they might not have gotten the antidote into me in time, and I would likely be dead. So, again, thank you."

"You're welcome." Claire debated for a second and then as he was about to walk away, added, "I actually saw something very similar in DC, just before we left. Otherwise, I'm not sure I'd have noticed it. The thing following me. In fact, I wondered whether it might have belonged to one of the factions of your group, since I'd just interviewed a...well, I suppose you'd call him a whistleblower who came into the *Post*. Is the drone that attacked you similar to any that your group has used in the past?"

Shepherd frowned. "Not that *my* group used. We never employed any drones at all. I can't speak for the Drexel faction, though. And I wouldn't know what the drone looked like anyway. I never saw it. From what I was told, the thing shattered when I knocked it across the stage."

Well, that was interesting. Macek seemed to have dismissed her theory about the Flock without even looking into whether they owned the drone. Which seemed like yet another indication that he already knew the drone's origins.

"That's okay," she said. "Just curious. I understand that you and some of your followers are planning to settle here in Ehden?"

He nodded. "For the time being, yes. My Flock, as I believe your paper calls them, enjoys a challenge. And now I should really get back in there to hash out these last few issues so that the ships can leave Tranquility. Enjoy the rest of your book, Ms. Echols."

Paul returned to the dining area before Claire could even get her earbuds back into place, and she couldn't help but wonder if Shepherd had clued them in that she was listening. Even if he didn't know about the app, he might have assumed she could hear the conversation unaided given the open window.

"All of this is going to take a bit longer," Paul said, "so I convinced Kolya to let me drive you out to the cabin rather than hanging about here until the hungry horde comes pouring in. Give me just a sec, though, so that I can help these folks get the rest of those pans out to their buggy. Oh...and be careful with your bag. Looks like the zipper is busted."

He was right. Claire muttered a curse under her breath, then scooped up the daypack and her other things. The pans Paul had mentioned were being transported outside by the group she'd spotted in the kitchen earlier. Her arms were full, but she held the door open with her back so that they could get through.

Another man, who had apparently just arrived, stood at the counter now, looking impatient. When the girl came around the corner, she had a few bags over her shoulder and a small dog tucked under one arm. Or at least Claire thought it was a dog. It was doglike at any rate, with thick chocolate-colored fur and a long ringed tail. The dark eyes seemed unusually large, though, and it was holding something green in one…paw? It looked like a bamboo leaf.

"That mutt of yours shouldn't be in the kitchen," the new arrival told her.

The girl lifted her chin and now Claire could definitely tell she was Idi's daughter. "I couldn't leave him home or outside. All of your construction noise scares him. He's fully housebroken, and he was only on the floor. I didn't let him on the counters."

"I don't care if the thing is housebroke or not. It's a *code* violation and that's my kitchen, too, for the next ten days. What kind of dog is that, anyway?"

"It's a Bavarian Shih Tzu." Paul leveled the man with a stare as he approached, carrying the last container of what looked like a pasta salad. "And *Anton Kolya* gave it to her."

Once the girl was through the door, Paul turned back to the man, who must have been the chef for the construction team, and added in a lower voice. "I'm sure they've left the kitchen spotless, but there's plenty of disinfectant. Feel free to scrub everything down from top to bottom if you're worried. Oh, and I'll be sure to pass your concerns about the code violation along to the Ehden Department of Health…in a decade or so when they have one."

Claire followed Paul outside to where the others were loading their buggy. The vehicles were identical, so she had no idea how anyone could tell which one they'd been driving. Did people just remember where they parked? Or maybe the buggies were like community bikes and boards in large cities on Earth and you just grabbed one from the landing pad?

The girl was leaning against the front of the buggy that the others were loading. She'd put the bags on the seat but was still holding the little creature.

"This must be Fenris," Claire said. "And you're Amara, right?"

She nodded. "Mr. Kolya didn't actually give him to me. He really belongs to Dr. Monroe, but I help take care of him. How did you know my name?"

"Because your father introduced me to an entire forest of your bamboo namesakes earlier. I'm Claire Echols."

"You were on the news this week."

"I was. Would you mind if I take some videos of you and Fenris for my subscribers on Earth? You'd need to ask your mom, though."

A few moments later, Amara was back with her mother.

"Are you planning to publish this?" the woman asked after Claire introduced herself.

"If KTI clears it, sure, although I mostly wanted my roommate's daughter to see it. But I'd send you a release form and let you review the footage and how we use it, if they decide it's okay to air. And if you decide you don't want Amara in it, we'll edit her out or scrap it entirely."

Amara's own preferences in the matter were clearly evident from her expression, so her mother laughed and said, "Okay, okay."

Claire tapped the record button on her visor.

"Claire Echols, coming to you from Ehden, Mars. I'm speaking now with Amara Ademola, who is going to tell us about her pet, Fenris. So...what kind of dog is Fenris?"

She smiled and shrugged. "We don't know. A brand new kind, I guess. Davy...oh sorry, that's Dr. Davina Monroe. She calls him a *Canis Mars*, which means Mars dog, but she says there are also a lot of similarities to the *Hapalemur* genus, which isn't even in the *Canis* family. I think they're going to need to set up whole new categories for our planet. That's what I want to help do when I'm older. Right now, we just call him a lemur dog. He's very gentle. You can pet him if you like. On his back, though, since he doesn't know you yet."

Claire ran her hand over the soft, thick fur, and moved down a bit to get a better look at what she'd first thought were paws, but which actually looked a lot more like hands.

"Lemur dogs eat bamboo, mostly. My dad hopes there will be whole families of them eventually to help clear away the debris after the bamboo harvests and help fertilize the soil. They'll be wild, though. Fenris got hurt, and I helped Davy nurse him back to health. He was *supposed* to go back to the test dome with the others, but they wouldn't accept him. So we all sort of share him now."

"How old is he?"

"Almost a year. Are you coming to dinner at the meeting house? If so, I can show you the tricks we taught him. He's *super* smart."

"I'm sure he is. And I really do wish I could join you." It was true. Given everything Claire had just overheard, she'd have much preferred taking the girl up on the invitation instead of spending an awkward dinner with Kolya dodging conversational landmines. She glanced over at Paul, who was now waiting in one of the buggies and sighed. "Unfortunately, I have a work engagement. But it was really nice meeting you, Amara. And Fenris, too."

Claire slid onto the bench next to Paul. "Okay, spill. Dr. Monroe told me that they'll be including animal life in future stages, and I guess I was thinking more along the lines of things that hatch out and are self-sufficient from birth. But that's a *mammal*. How—and, for that matter, *why*—did KTI cross a lemur with a dog?"

TWENTY-ONE

JUDGING FROM PAUL'S EXPRESSION, he fully understood that there was a third question underlying Claire's basic *how* and *why* they had decided to cross a canine with a primate—namely, how was this even legal? Back on earth, there were strict guidelines on genetically engineered lifeforms. And even if there were no such laws on Mars, she thought that kind of thing would generally be frowned upon by investors who were even slightly risk averse.

"Hold on just a sec." Paul keyed in some coordinates from his phone—apparently Kolya's cabin wasn't programmed into the buggy's navigation system—and they backed out onto the road. He didn't answer until they were well past the building crew, and Claire had the sense that he was taking a bit of time to formulate his response.

A few moments later, once they had veered off the main road onto a path that curved around the lake, he turned toward her. "First, I can *promise* you that bit of footage won't make it off Mars for at least a decade, so let's just pretend I'm Macek"—he scowled in a decent imitation of the guy—"and you have now been duly warned about your NDA. Which this does cover, beyond any shadow of a doubt. By the time KTI security clears that clip, if they ever even do, Amara won't need parents to sign her release form."

"Okay. Guess I won't be showing the cuddly little lemur dog to Jemma, then. Probably just as well, because she'd want one."

"Second," he said, "*technically speaking*, KTI didn't create Fenris and the other lemur dogs. All that our scientists did was set parameters for the AE biobots—you know what those are, right?"

Claire nodded. "Accelerated evolution. Dr. Monroe gave me a brief overview."

"Good. So, the scientists simply set the parameters for these biobots to meet the needs of a specific environment within one of the test domes—an environment that closely mimics what will exist in some regions of Mars by the time we're at the final stages of terraforming. *Canis Mars,* AKA the cuddly little lemur dog, was one of the creatures that emerged. Dr. Monroe and her colleagues can't say for certain it's a creature that *would* have evolved over time, but they have computer models that say it *could* have evolved because it is one of the optimal lifeforms for that ecosystem."

"But…KTI programmed those AE biobots. They didn't just come with lemur dogs as an option. That means KTI created them, even if they did so indirectly. It's a little like programming a bot to kill someone and then claiming you didn't do it."

"No, because there are laws against that, even here on Mars. But there are no laws against programming the biobots to create optimal lifeforms for an otherwise uninhabited planet. Pretty sure there's a whole legal team back on Earth who researched that prior to stage six. I mean, I'm not a scientist—and by that, I mean I'm really, *really* not a scientist—but isn't that the entire point of recombinant biobots? They combine to create new forms of life."

"Not…always. Not even most of the time. Usually, we're talking about changes at the cellular level. I mean, Rejuvesce is a good example." Now it was Claire's turn to measure her words, making sure that she didn't reveal anything beyond the information that Jonas Labs issued in what Kai referred to as the company's public-facing statements. "The biobots my brother works with combine to create the best possible version of the patient's cells in an earlier form, before they become degraded through the aging process. It's not like creating a new person—or, let's say, a lemur dog—from scratch."

"So, what would you propose? Thanks to billions of years of evolution, there's a base to work from on Earth. There were many, many mistakes along the way, too…and I'm not merely talking about failed humans, although I've certainly encountered my share of those. But all of those lifeforms are optimized for Earth, and they don't always do so well here. We need life that's specially formulated for Mars, and as I understand it, the biobots let us skip past all of the trial and error stages. Fenris and his fellow lemur dogs will be fat and happy in the bamboo forests. They've figured out the optimal lifespan and even engineered a low reproduction rate so that we won't be overrun with the little critters."

"Again, though…they're mammals, right? So, KTI had to do something other than just program the biobots. Otherwise, the first batch would have died."

"Oh, sure. They were incubated in the lab and then nursing stations were placed in the dome with milk until the pups were old enough to start foraging. Fenris was the runt of the group. The others kept pushing him away, even though there was plenty for all of them. Kolya says Dr. Monroe would generally have just let nature take its course. But she had two student helpers that month. You just met one of them…so you can probably guess why she made an exception. And there's now a new rule at the Nepenthes lab: no student helpers at the domes if the creatures are even remotely cute and cuddly."

"So at what point are they going to do the same with humans?"

"What do you mean?" Paul looked puzzled.

"I mean the humans living and working here weren't optimized for Mars."

"Well, you and I aren't. But it's already been established that babies born on Mars do just fine here. While they wouldn't fare so well if they were sent back to Earth, we can create optimal humans the old-fashioned way."

He was right, at least on the surface. The first baby born on Mars was now fifteen years old. That pregnancy had been an accident—a case where one of the workers either didn't realize she was pregnant or else didn't want to admit it to her employer and be sent back to Earth. By the time it was obvious even inside the Stay-Puft suit, the woman was nearly seven months along. As she was in her second year of a two-year contract, there was no question that the pregnancy had originated on the planet. At that point, there was far greater risk in transporting her back to Earth for delivery than remaining on Mars. That pregnancy and successful delivery had provided KTI scientists with a test case. When little Marta was three years old and doing well, they began a small test group for prospective colonists. To date, fourteen babies had been delivered on the planet and all were apparently doing very well. The only catch was that their families wouldn't be able to return to Earth.

But there were several things wrong with Paul's line of argument, including an underlying assumption that humans were the pinnacle not just of evolution on Earth, but also on Mars. To Claire's mind, there was a major difference between humans who *do just fine* on Mars and humans who were *optimized* for Mars. She wasn't sure there was much point in continuing that line of discussion, however. It was becoming more of a philosophical debate, and she wasn't even certain where she stood on the issue. After all, she'd been perfectly okay with the idea of plants that were engineered to the Martian atmosphere. She had even thought that it was kind of silly to try and mimic Earth. So why did the idea of animals that were tailor-made for this environment feel different?

They were now on the other side of the lake, near one of the few sections of trees she'd seen in Ehden that looked to be fairly robust, and Claire could now make out a house through the branches. She had half expected Kolya's place to be gargantuan, something that only one of the world's wealthiest men could think of as a cabin, but it was fairly modest. Not a shack by any means, but still a good bit smaller than the house she shared with Ro and Jemma.

Paul apparently wasn't done with their philosophical discussion, however, because after a moment of silence, he said, "And it's a very good thing that we *can* create optimal humans without scientific intervention, because there *are* laws against that sort of tinkering, for obvious reasons. With the lower life-forms, though, it just falls under selective breeding, and people have been creating hybrids of one sort or another for thousands of years."

"Have they created a lot of other…hybrids…at the Nepenthes lab?"

"Oh, sure. Hundreds. And there are hundreds more to come. Maybe you can take another trip back here and see the full zoo when we get closer to stage…" He frowned. "I *think* that would be stage nine? Pretty sure that's at least ten years down the pike, but if you're interested, I can mention it to Stasia."

Claire pulled a hesitant face. "Maybe not. I don't get the sense that I'm Stasia's favorite person right now. Do you have any idea what I did to upset her? For a while there, I was thinking that she and Kolya might be…well, that she might not like the fact that he was…"

"Stasia and Kolya? *Oh my God no.*" He looked rather horrified at the thought. "I don't think Stasia is entirely asexual but she's *definitely* aromantic. Direct quote: *I don't have time for that nonsense.* The woman says it so often that I told her she should get it inked. She was close friends with Kolya's ex-wife. I think they even knew each other from before. College or something. But that wouldn't be a problem. His split with Jenelle was completely amicable. If it had anything to do with Kolya at all, it's just Stasia being protective of him. Which isn't entirely unreasonable…"

Claire gave him a questioning look, but they were at the

front gate now and he didn't seem to notice. He'd made it sound like Kolya was a defenseless young thing and she was some sort of predator going in for the kill. Then she remembered they probably *did* have trouble fending off women who were only interested in his money. Claire had made it clear that she didn't get along with her mother, and she worked a full-time job. Maybe they had lumped her in with the gold-digging opportunists?

"But," Paul said, "if I had to guess, I'd say it's not you at all. She's just in a really bad mood about this thing with the Flock. Stasia was *firmly* opposed to Shepherd coming on the *Ares Prime* in the first place, and then not long after we get here, Kolya tells her he's decided to bring Shepherd's followers in as colonists. Macek believes it's a good idea, which means she lost this round, even with Davy adamantly on her side. All of this came to a head in the middle of the labor crisis, and I think Stasia's sort of licking her wounds. As I may have mentioned before, Stasia usually comes out on top in any battle with Macek. I think she's a little annoyed at me for not taking her side more firmly, but…I'm ambivalent about the whole thing, to be honest. I mean, they're all adults, right? They know what they're doing."

Claire gave Paul a noncommittal nod, and grabbed her belongings from the back while he typed a code into the keypad on the door. What he'd said was mostly true. Some of Shepherd's followers had brought children when they joined and even more had given birth as members, but they *were* mostly adults. On the other hand, they were adults who had been deluded enough to join the Flock, so she was less convinced of his assertion that they knew what they were doing.

The door opened to reveal a room that was the epitome of midcentury upscale design. Two walls had the era's ubiquitous floor-to-ceiling viewscreens, with bookcases and a stone fireplace taking up another side. A glass door at the back led out to a patio and beyond that, a pond.

"Okay," Paul said, "I'm going to put the final touches on dinner. And I suspect you will want a bath. Even if you don't, you should take one." He pointed her toward one of the bedrooms. "Those biosuits don't breathe...for obvious reasons...and you may end up with a truly unpleasant rash if you're not careful. I'm speaking from painful personal experience here, so off you go."

Claire definitely hadn't been planning to argue. The clothes she had on were the same ones she'd worn under the suit, and to use one of Wilson's pet phrases, she reeked like a wild hog.

Her original plan had been to simply shower, but the guest room was equipped with a bathtub that was too tempting to resist. It was carved out of the same dark red granite as the conference table back at the Red Dahlia and was deep enough for a long, decadent soak.

The shelves nearby held an impressive assortment of toiletries and Claire scanned them for shampoo and soap. Whoever cleaned the place had dusted the front of the shelves but hadn't moved the bottles and jars around, and the layer of dust on top made it clear that they hadn't been used recently.

Claire selected a bottle of jasmine bath salts and spent the next half hour rejuvenating. Afterward, she went in search of a hair dryer and eventually found one in the cabinet next to the sink. It was on top of a picture frame, which was face down, and curiosity got the better of her. She flipped it over to find a photo collage of Kolya and a woman she assumed was Jenelle, the ex-wife that he and Paul had both mentioned. There were five pictures, all taken on a beach with the ocean in the background. One shot showed her laughing as she held down a floppy hat to keep it from blowing away in the wind, which was wreaking havoc with her long auburn curls.

Claire stared at the picture for a long moment, trying to figure out why the woman seemed so familiar. Maybe she'd seen her in some paparazzi shots with Kolya back when they were together? Or maybe the woman was famous in her own right, and she'd seen her in a movie or something?

But it felt more recent than that. Claire could almost hear her laughing and couldn't shake the image from her mind. Once her hair was dry, she went to replace the dryer and picked up the photo again. It was the smile and the hand holding the hat that was familiar, not the hair. If the woman's hair was up, though…

New York.

Outside the building at Columbia where she'd met with Brodnik's team.

They had crashed into each other, and Claire's phone had hit the sidewalk. The wind had nearly blown the woman's hat away and she had laughed as she reached up to grab it.

It was the same woman. Claire had no doubt about that.

What were the odds that Anton Kolya's ex-wife had happened to be on the campus at Columbia University the exact same day that Claire agreed to this trip? That she had *accidentally* bumped into Claire on the sidewalk? And that, instead of continuing on her way as so many people do in the city, she'd actually stopped to help?

Nope. That didn't feel at all like a coincidence. How long had she and Kolya been divorced? Was she still working for him? Paul had said it was an amicable split, and implied that Jenelle had still been in the picture when Stasia was hired, but Claire had no idea how long ago that was aside from being longer than the three years that Kolya said Paul had been with KTI.

Claire put the picture frame and the hair dryer back where she'd found them and got dressed. The only thing aside from jeans was her black dress and the one thing she'd bought for herself during the shopping excursion in Daedalus City—a dusky blue jumpsuit of soft bamboo with buttons made of tiny Martian fire opals. It covered far more skin than her little black dress, so she slipped it on and went back into the main living area. Finding it empty, she followed her nose to join Paul in the kitchen.

She hadn't realized how hungry she was until she caught a whiff of the food. "That smells incredible. Let me guess—in addition to being a pilot and videographer, you're a Michelin star chef."

"Oh, absolutely not. Ayman learned early on that if he wanted anything beyond a grilled cheese, he'd best get himself into the kitchen. I am, however, perfectly capable of following written instructions from the chef at Della Marte for reheating the lobster Newburg—don't worry, no mushrooms— and tossing the salad."

"Kolya brought all of this from Daedalus?"

Even as she asked the question, Claire remembered the guard unloading something from the plane at Nepenthes Station when he took their bags.

"Yes," Paul said. "There was also dessert and wine in the box, both of which I opened and placed in the fridge. They packed candles, too, but I did *not* light them. If Kolya wants to set a romantic mood when you've clearly stated that you're not so inclined, he can light them himself."

"I'm surprised that candles weren't already in the cabinets," she said, trying to nudge the conversation toward something that would answer a few of her many questions. "The bedroom seemed to have a lot of feminine touches, so I'm guessing this is his regular romantic getaway."

"Not to my knowledge. Stasia did say that Kolya and his ex spent a couple of weeks here just before they split up. And Stasia has used that room herself on a few occasions, so she may have left a few things behind. Oh...speaking of things she left behind." He grabbed a white daypack with the KTI logo from one of the chairs. "This was in the closet. I know it's not the height of fashion, but beggars, choosers, and all that."

"Thanks. I was going to ask if there was tape or something

for a temporary fix, but this is much better. I hate to take it if it's Stasia's, though. She might—"

"Oh, no, no. We overordered for a contractor event KTI held a few years back. There are still dozens of those things, maybe even hundreds, in the supply closet back at the Daedalus office. Stasia once said she thought they were multiplying when our backs were turned. I doubt she even remembers she left it here."

"So, how long has Stasia been with KTI?"

"She's coming up on nine years. Aside from Macek, that's the longest anyone has put up with Kolya. Well, except for Dr. Monroe, but she sees him maybe three weeks out of the year."

"Does his ex-wife still work for the company?"

"Jenelle?" Paul frowned. "I don't think she even worked for KTI when they were married. Where did you get that idea?"

Claire shrugged. "Most couples meet at work."

"Do they really? Personally, I found Ayman the same way my grandparents met—on a dating app. Would you mind listening for that timer on the bread? I just got word that Kolya is heading here now, so you won't have to wait long. And if I don't get back to Ehden soon, all of that lovely pasta that Renata made will be gone."

"Or you could just stay here for dinner. That looks like way too much food for two. Maybe you could call Ayman and we'll make it a foursome."

It was a joke, but Paul must have detected a tiny hint of hope in her voice.

"Sorry. I'm still on duty until Shepherd is tucked safely inside his sleeping quarters. But...bring me your tablet before I go."

Claire frowned, unsure what he wanted with her tablet. But she went back to the bedroom to fetch it, double-checking to be sure the amplification app she'd used back at the dining hall was closed. She held it out to Paul, but he shook his head.

"No, no. Just activate it."

She did, and he tapped his phone against the back.

"You now have my private number, which I rarely give to anyone. Personally, I have never witnessed Kolya being anything less than a gentleman. But...there are always rumors with any man as wealthy as he is. At any rate, send a message if you need me and Ayman and I will head straight over."

Claire smiled and told him that she was sure everything would be fine. Because she really wasn't worried that Kolya wouldn't take no for an answer. She was far more nervous about having to spend several hours talking to the man without letting it spill that she was now aware of at least some of the secrets that he and Macek had been keeping.

TWENTY-TWO

DINNER WAS SURPRISINGLY PLEASANT, in part because the food was good and in part because Kolya seemed determined to stick to neutral topics while they were actually eating. It wasn't until they finished the chocolate mousse that he apparently decided the time for polite dinner conversation was over.

He poured two shots of krambambula and sat one in front of Claire. "Shepherd says you told him that the drone was following you in DC."

"I did. But only after he told me that no one had even shown him the thing. I guess Macek had already discarded it by the time he recovered. You may be bringing *some* of his followers here, but he still has thousands of others who are loyal to him back on Earth. If there is any chance that Drexel's faction is weaponizing those drones against them, they should be warned, don't you think?"

He nodded, and then asked how much of the conversation with Shepherd she'd overheard.

She decided to admit a tiny portion of the truth and see if they could move back to neutral subjects. "I'm sorry. I didn't open the window with the intention of eavesdropping. The dining hall smelled bad, and I was overheating from the pressure suit, so I cracked the window. Not long after I did, Shepherd started yelling about not wanting Ehden to participate in parliamentary elections. A few minutes later, he raised his voice about something else. Security, I think. I put in my earbuds and finished my messages back home, as you'd suggested. Played my piano app for a while, then listened to a book. And yes, I know that what little I did hear is covered by the NDA I signed."

This elicited another nod. Claire got the sense that he didn't entirely believe her, which was fair enough. After nearly a minute of increasingly awkward silence, she asked if they'd been able to make any headway with Shepherd.

"Yes. I'm happy to report that the worker transports will be leaving Tranquility in a few hours."

"Will Ehden be sending a representative to parliament?"

"We actually tabled that. For the time being, Ehden will be a…a protectorate, I guess?…of Daedalus, rather than applying for colonial status. I think Shepherd likes that idea better anyway since he views this as a temporary waystation while they wait for these Sentinels."

"But if Ehden is part of Daedalus, won't they have to abide by the various employment regulations?"

"Not an issue. He won't have any employees." He laughed at her expression. "Don't start holding back now, Claire. Why is that such a problem?"

"It just seems hypocritical. You were talking about the other colonies treating workers as indentured servants, and yet you're about to hand Ehden over to someone who'll be doing the exact same thing. It's even worse than the other colonies, because he doesn't pay them anything aside from room and board."

"It's not worse or better. It's an entirely different sort of agreement. The others are paying wages. Their contracts are manipulative and dishonest, and they're duping people whose entire reason for taking the job is financial gain. Shepherd's people are happy to work for next to nothing because they believe he also offers some sort of salvation."

"Do *you* think that there's some mothership coming to save his people?"

"Of course not. But their contract—if you can even call it that, given that it's verbal and nonbinding—isn't with *me*. It's with Shepherd. He *does* believe in these Sentinels. And so do they."

"I guess it just doesn't make sense to me that you'd go to all this trouble. Your friend Davy was right, you don't *need* these people. Almost all of the labor in a place like Ehden could be handled as easily by farming bots like the ones we saw at Doba as by Toby's...sheep."

Toby's sheep.

Toby's sheep...are mostly ewes.

"Is something wrong?"

"No," she said. "I'm just mentally kicking myself for being so slow on the uptake. Just like the Wild Freakin' West, right? You're bringing in mail-order brides as...how did you put it? Agents of civilization? People who put down roots?"

"As I told you before, it's a mutually beneficial arrangement. Mars attracts a lot of young, single men. And, for some reason I can't entirely fathom, Shepherd's ideology attracts a lot of young, single women."

"I'm guessing women of childbearing age were given priority on the manifest?"

He shrugged. "Age is a consideration for all colonists."

"And the women were *informed* that they are being imported as breeding stock?"

That question broke through Kolya's nonchalant demeanor and Claire thought she heard an actual touch of anger in his voice. "Why must you put the most negative spin on everything? *No one* will be forced to enter a relationship. Nor would they be forced to bear children. There will be generous incentives for those who *do* make that choice, however. As to whether they were informed beforehand, you'd have to ask Shepherd. I told him how many people we could fit on the ships now and how many we could bring in the second wave, after stage six is complete. He took the entire process over from there."

"But Shepherd understands that you're more interested in female colonists than male."

"I think so. He was not, as you say, slow on the uptake."

"Touché. So you've subcontracted out to someone in order to keep your hands clean. At least I know why you and Kai can't stand each other. You're too damned much alike not to be at each other's throat."

"Is that what she told you? Because the truth is that Kai and I rarely fought. Well, not until right at the end, at least, but as you know, there was a lot going on by the time…"

He trailed off, probably in reaction to Claire's dumbstruck expression.

"What exactly do you mean by *at the end?*" She was almost certain that she *knew* what he meant, but she needed to hear him confirm it.

"You're telling me you didn't know. Seriously?"

For a long moment they just stared at each other. Her mother's unreasonably petty anger at Kolya suddenly made a lot more sense. So did Kolya's confused expression when she'd told him that Kai had cleared off a shelf for the stupid award.

"I thought that was the whole point," he said. "Okay, maybe not the *whole* point. I believed you were at least somewhat attracted to me, but from what you said, it seemed pretty clear that pissing off your mother was at least a factor. Maybe a competitive sort of…"

He thought she *knew*. And not only that she didn't care, but that she believed it added a little extra spice.

"You truly thought I was petty enough to have a fling with someone that my mom…that she…" Claire shook her head, unable to even go there. "When? *When?* And for how long?"

"About five years after I took over KTI. It actually started back when it was still just KI, when we were still dabbling in pharmaceuticals and a few other sidelines. I met her at a conference in London and—"

"Spare me the details. When did it *end?*"

"A few months after your father's diagnosis. Kai said she needed to make a clean break, even though I told her I was willing to...wait." He flinched, apparently realizing how that sounded. "And then, about six months later, I met Jenelle and things moved pretty fast. The last time I saw Kai, she was furious that I'd won some award we were both up for, although I think it was really because I brought Jenelle to a conference that she and I had attended together on several occasions. It had been sort of a regular vacation for us, but in my defense, I didn't know Kai was going to be there."

"Maybe she was looking forward to not having to sneak around anymore."

"Your father *knew*, Claire. Kai was honest with him from the beginning. She *did* love him."

"The hell she did! She knew damn well that my father couldn't hold on until Arvectin was approved for human testing. If she'd *loved* him, she'd have been there with him at the end, holding his hand like I did. Like Joe did. Or better yet, she would have ignored the possible sanctions against her precious company and started him on the drug before it was approved. Instead, she hid inside the lab, day in and day out. She saw him for maybe an hour during those last two days. At least now I understand why. She was too ashamed to face him..."

At that point, a tiny shred of sanity began to return, just enough that Claire held back the rest of that sentence—*because she'd been screwing around with you*. Leaving aside all of her suspicions about Westmoreland, about the drone, about Kolya's ex-wife following her in New York, Claire still had to deal with KTI until she was back home, and Kolya could make things difficult for her if he wanted.

Looking at him right that minute, though, she didn't get the sense that it was going to be a problem. Claire thought there was a touch of embarrassment in his expression, which was surprising because shame wasn't something of which she'd thought the man capable. More than anything else, though, he seemed sad. And she wasn't vain enough to think it was because she'd dashed his last bit of optimism about a potential sexual encounter. He seemed to genuinely regret that she'd been hurt.

"I'm sorry," Claire told him. "I shouldn't have lost my temper. It's obviously none of my business and the outburst was unprofessional. You just caught me by surprise."

"Swear to God, Claire, I thought you knew."

"Well, I know now. It answers a lot of questions and again... beyond that, it's really and truly none of my business. I'm just... I'm going to try to get some sleep, okay? It's been a long and..." She gave a rueful laugh and tossed back the last of her drink. "I really do not have words for this day. And I don't mean that in a totally—or even a *mostly*—negative way. Let's just say it's been eye-opening. I'm looking forward to sharing what you're creating here with my subscribers."

"Would you like to take the krambambula with you? I can open another bottle."

Claire shook her head but then remembered she'd be facing the first night in a strange place hurdle on top of this utter fiasco and poured herself another hefty shot. "This will be more than ample. I have another long day of travel tomorrow. Facing it with a hangover seems ill-advised."

"An excellent point. I'll most likely be gone by the time you wake up. I, too, have a long day ahead and want to get an early start. Paul will pick you up at seven with breakfast, so that you can head straight to Nepenthes Station. He should have you in Icarus by noon, which is just after Brodnik's crew is scheduled to arrive. I wouldn't be surprised if the excavation goes fairly quickly. The second chamber is smaller than the first one and the crew has already done this once. But it will probably still be sometime on Monday at the earliest. I had asked Dr. Brodnik to wait for me, but...."

There was an odd questioning note to his voice, almost as if he were asking Claire's permission. Which was ridiculous. Finding out about him and Kai was a shock, but it wasn't as if it had shaken Claire's perception of her mother. If the two of them had been close, it might have been different. She mostly just felt like an idiot for not having picked up on it earlier.

"Of course," she told him. "You should be there when they open it. Have a safe trip and I'll see you at Icarus."

The next time Claire saw him, however, wouldn't be at Icarus Camp. It would be in what passed for the ICU at the tiny hospital in Daedalus City.

TWENTY-THREE

WHEN CLAIRE OPENED the door at five minutes after seven the next morning, Paul shoved a mug of coffee and some sort of breakfast sandwich into her hands and grabbed her suitcase.

"First," he said as he piled the bag into the back of the buggy, "I am so very sorry. Second, you look like you slept much better than Kolya did, if that's any comfort at all. He seemed a bit...mortified. As well he should. I don't think he'd have told me at all if not for the fact that he knew we were flying together. Just to be completely clear, any assumptions that Stasia or I might have made about all of this were based on *his* assumption that you knew all about him and your mother."

"That was pretty much what I thought. And now can we never, ever speak about any of this again?"

"With pleasure."

Claire had actually slept surprisingly well. It had seemed unlikely at the beginning, given the usual issue of the first night in a strange place and the bizarre events of the day. But she took another long hot bath during which she went over every single thing she'd said to anyone, and to Kolya in particular, concerning her mother since she'd arrived at Tranquility Base. At some point during her soak, she reached the conclusion that the entire misunderstanding was Kolya's fault. She had barely mentioned Kai to anyone else. In most cases, Kolya had mentioned her first. And the more Claire thought about it, the more it seemed like Kolya might have been trying to get back at Kai by pursuing her daughter.

All in all, it seemed like a fairly straightforward case of

projection on Kolya's part. And once she had concluded that bit of amateur psychoanalysis, Claire crawled into bed and slept straight through until her alarm went off.

It was a short drive to the housing unit where Ayman and Paul were staying in Ehden. Once Ayman was on board, Paul said, "We're not talking about you know what. But if you want to say Kolya is an egotistical ass, that's perfectly acceptable."

"Kolya is an egotistical ass," Ayman said. "Who pays you an obscenely high salary to do a job you mostly love for work toward a cause you believe in. For the record, that's number four hundred and sixty-seven."

"Thank you." Paul turned to Claire. "Ayman is tasked with giving me a silver lining reminder each time I bitch about Kolya requiring me to do something I hate. Or Macek. Or Stasia."

She smiled. "You've been with them for three years, right?"

"Nearly four."

"So…that comes out to a few times a week. That's really not bad. I probably gripe about my boss more often than that."

"Oh *no*," Ayman said. "I reset the count each month. And the way this month is going, I may need to switch to a weekly tally."

The *Peregrine* was waiting for them on the platform when they arrived at Nepenthes Station. It looked exactly like the *Excelsior* from the outside, but this model traded a bit of cargo space to make room for an additional passenger. Or two, if they were very close friends.

To Claire's relief, their takeoff from the hyperlift was gloriously uneventful, with no heart-stopping plummets. Once they were airborne, Paul asked how badly she actually wanted to see the bamboo forest at Lake Tombaugh. Claire had to think for a minute, and then vaguely recalled Kolya saying he'd get Paul to fly her over it on the way to Icarus.

"Because we can definitely *do* a flyover," he said, "but it's about forty minutes out of our way. I was just thinking that after yesterday, you've probably already seen scads of bamboo and if you'd rather get to Icarus a bit earlier, Ayman can show you a lovely video that KTI recorded just last year."

"That works for me."

"Perfect. But if Kolya asks…"

"It was my idea to get to Icarus faster. In fact, I begged you."

After she watched the video of what was admittedly a massive tract of bamboo surrounding the aquifer, Ayman put on a movie—something Kolya hadn't even mentioned as an option on the trip to Nepenthes. That might have been because it was her first long-distance trip on Mars and he thought she'd want to focus on the scenery, but she thought it equally likely that he'd simply wanted to ensure an attentive audience for his legendary brilliance.

The trip passed quickly, and shortly after noon, the little dot for Icarus Fossae appeared on the dashboard map. Before they reached it, however, Paul nodded toward a huge crater off in the distance.

"That's Clark. If you look over to the far left, that second dark spot in the wall is the cave where they're currently excavating the second chamber. It's wider than the others, because they had to get the first chamber through the opening. If you turn on the zoom inside your helmet, you can probably see them working on the second one. And the dome over to the right of that spot at the bottom of the crater is the current location of Icarus Camp."

Claire zoomed in, but all she could see were slightly darker shadows moving around inside the tunnel. Ben Pelzer had described the face of Clark Crater as Swiss cheese, and she thought that was pretty much dead on. Holes of varying sizes had been bored into the crater wall. Paul explained that the smaller holes around fifty meters down from the top were carved out to get samples because that level was the most likely to contain veins of opal. If the initial sample showed significant traces of the gem, then they widened the hole into a full tunnel and sent in a crew to extract them by hand, since that yielded larger, more lucrative stones.

"You said that's the *current* location of Icarus Camp. Is it mobile?"

"Yeah. Pada—the company name means *dig* in Korean—is working in Clark right now, but they have mining rights for a total of five craters in this area. The buildings are modular, so they pack up camp and move every few months, either within or between craters. Hussey Station, where we're landing, serves as a hub between the various locations, sort of like Nepenthes does for Ehden, Doba, and the others. It will take a half hour or so to get back here on the shuttle, but Hussey has a hyperlift to give us a boost when it's time to head back to Daedalus. That cuts the trip home almost by half, so it's worth it."

A few minutes later, the *Peregrine* touched down on the landing strip next to a spartan dome that was maybe five kilometers in diameter. Two large buildings stood just inside the airlock tunnel, with three more off in the distance. Otherwise, it seemed to be a motor pool, with thirty or forty trucks, trams, and shuttles of various sizes. One small plane was currently on the tarmac, but the only people Claire saw were a couple of armed security guards. It looked as if most of the traffic in and out was via maglev.

After Paul cleared them with the security detail, they transferred their bags over to a shuttle. This time, instead of the KTI logo, there was a graphic of a shovel with foreign characters on the blade and the letters *PADA* on the handle.

During the drive, Claire learned that she would be rooming with Chelsea and Dr. Brodnik in the female quarters at the camp. "Pada is one of only three companies that even *has* a female barracks," Paul said. "In fact, two of the seven miners on the team that found the chamber were female. Kolya has been incentivizing his contractors to work toward a better gender balance, and Pada is putting forth more effort than most."

"Well, if Kolya's Ehden experiment goes according to plan,"

Claire said, "he'll have a dome of mostly women. Mostly *young* women. I guess he can tell at least a few of his subcontractors they can relax."

Paul laughed. "Most workers don't have access to a plane to carry them halfway across the planet. When these guys go on leave, they visit Memnonia, or Daedalus if they've saved up enough credits."

"Even if they had access to a plane," Ayman said, "a four-hour flight one way isn't exactly feasible for a date."

"Just to be clear," Paul said, "Kolya isn't planning for Ehden to serve as some sort of agrarian brothel. If that were the case, I'd have taken Stasia's side against it. What he's *hoping* is that some of the people here on temporary contracts will decide to stay on at Ehden or someplace like it, rather than returning to Earth when their two years are up. The fact that there will be a surplus of young women there will be a draw…at least for *some* of them." He gave Ayman a smile. "More of the miners are happy with their lives in the barracks than Kolya assumes. And from what I've heard, not all that many of the Flock he's transporting in are going to be looking for husbands. For someone who likes to think of himself as cosmopolitan, Kolya's thinking can be extremely traditional on many issues."

Claire was very close to making a quip about Kolya not putting much value on the sanctity of marriage, but she held her tongue. "You said two of the miners who discovered the chamber were female. Do you think it would be possible for me to interview them? The men, too. I'm pretty sure Kolya would be okay with it, because he was complaining that the miners deserved more credit than the academic team, given that they were the ones who actually found the thing."

Paul shrugged. "I don't think it will be a problem. But we should probably ask Stasia. Last I heard, she's supposed to leave Daedalus in the next few hours."

TWENTY-FOUR

A FEW MINUTES LATER, they arrived at Clark, where they encountered another security check. Three guards were currently manning the station, with two of them monitoring screens showing about twenty different views from around the perimeter, probably from security bots. Despite the fact that the crater was more than a hundred kilometers wide, it seemed to Claire that it should be fairly easy to secure because there were only two maglev ports. Someone could, of course, land a shuttle at another location, but they'd have to contend with a steep drop of well over a kilometer from every point around the crater. Alternatively, they could try to land a plane *inside* the crater, but that seemed incredibly dangerous given that there was no landing strip, and the surface was pitted and pocked with deep channels and subcraters.

Since the vast majority of the crater wasn't domed, there was no need for an entry tunnel. They simply boarded a lift—a cage made of wire mesh, which Claire found rather terrifying—that carried them down to the bottom where several buggies were waiting.

They were still over thirty kilometers away from the site and the buggies weren't nearly as fast as the shuttle, so it took almost as long for them to get from the lift to Icarus Camp as it had taken to travel the much longer distance from Hussey Station to the rim of the crater. Along the way, they traveled past the ghosts of former campsites, which were now just utility sheds surrounded by massive slag heaps, some with debris that was ground almost to dust and others with larger chunks that Paul said would be sent to the processing center in Hussey.

There, they would be washed and spun repeatedly in something similar to the barrel of a concrete mixer until the debris was cleared away and only the gems remained.

The air, which had been dusty from the beginning, was now clouded to the point that you couldn't see more than a few meters ahead. Claire was glad the buggy was on autopilot and doubly glad that they were in suits with heavy-duty filters.

Their buggy automatically slowed as they approached the mining site. Beneath the Swiss cheese cliff face, the crater floor was a bustling hive of activity. Huge lifts similar to the one they'd taken from the top of the crater were positioned outside five of the tunnels, only these appeared to be even more open. To Claire, they looked like giant versions of the window-washer platforms she'd seen in old movies, in the years before cleaning skyscraper windows was automated. Miners, a hundred or maybe more of them, mostly clad in the bulky puffsuits with hardhats attached to the regular helmet, moved in silent efficiency around machines equipped with shovels and drills for boring the tunnels.

It was hard to imagine how those massive yellow behemoths could operate so quietly.

And then, in the space of a second, Claire's ears were assaulted by a hellish cacophony. Drills, grinders, conveyor belts, people yelling. It was almost as if the buggy had pierced an invisible membrane that had been shielding them from the sound.

"It kind of sneaks up on you, doesn't it?" Ayman's voice came from inside her helmet, but it was still nearly drowned out by the din of the equipment. "The thinner atmosphere plays tricks on your ears. Paul has gotten used to it, but it took me by surprise when we stopped here on the way to Nepenthes. Give it a couple of seconds, though, and…ah, there. We're back in the quiet zone again."

Claire glanced back over her shoulder, almost expecting the mining site to have vanished like a mirage. Everything was still running at full speed, but the tableau once again seemed to have fallen silent.

"It's a good thing," Paul said. "Otherwise, they'd have to worry about noise pollution inside the dome. The drills that pull rock samples are automated to run twenty-four seven. If the sound carried like it does on Earth, no one would get any sleep."

Like the dome at Fenris, Icarus Camp was equipped with a narrow pedestrian airlock, as opposed to the drive-through variety. Aside from the standard solar panels and a few utility shacks, the camp itself was just four buildings grouped around a center quad, where there were several dozen tables arranged in rows. Off to the side was a recreation area, with a container about knee high filled with what looked like arrows and something that resembled a cornhole board.

Three of the main buildings were around the same size. The fourth, which Paul said was the men's barracks, was larger than the other three combined. No rotating sleeping quarters here, but then Claire supposed they'd be hard to set up in a temporary camp. And maybe the workers got enough exercise in their daily jobs that they could get by with an hour or so of exercise a day and still stay reasonably Earth-fit.

They stopped by the dining hall, which was empty aside from a maintenance bot, and grabbed sandwiches and water from a refrigerated case. Paul said he wanted to check in with Stasia and rest for a bit before they headed over to the dig site for Claire to plan out the shots for the next day, so she left him and Ayman outside their building and took her lunch across the quad to her room.

Claire didn't expect anyone to be there, but Chelsea was sprawled out on one of the three bunks looking at something on her tablet. She glanced up and gave a nod when Claire said hello.

"I thought you'd be at the site."

"Brodnik and Pelzer are watching over things. There's really not much Kim and I can do until they get the chamber open, and apparently that's not going to happen now until they transport it to Daedalus. Kim says he's going to ride on the transport carrying it, just to make sure they don't try anything underhanded." She was quiet for a minute, then added. "Did you enjoy your trip?"

It was an innocent enough question, aside from the tone, which Claire chose to ignore.

"Yes. I got some excellent footage. Now the challenge is to see how much gets past KTI security. Speaking of security, when we were on the shuttle—"

"Oh, I'll bet you can get Kolya to approve anything you want to use if you ask nicely."

And that was the final straw.

"Would you just *drop it*? I signed the same NDA that all of you did. Every message, every video, every picture that I take will be scrutinized before it leaves the planet. And I'm *not* sleeping with Anton Kolya. I'm here to do my job, just like you are, and your snark is getting really old. Just because you work with Kimura doesn't mean you have to join him in acting like a juvenile."

Chelsea ignored her outburst, so Claire opened the sandwich. The label read *Icarus MC: Egg* with foreign characters beneath. It was surprisingly good, especially for something grabbed out of a case—sort of like egg foo young with spicy pink mayo between slices of toast.

When she was about halfway through, Claire realized that Chelsea had put her tablet aside and was now watching her.

"You said you were wondering about something that happened when we were on the shuttle?"

This was as close to an apology as she was likely to get from Chelsea, so Claire finished the bite and said, "The others seemed to be ribbing you about Shepherd when we were on the shuttle into Daedalus last week. Did you see something at the debate?"

Chelsea snorted. "Yeah. The same thing you did. I watched you dive onto the floor when you thought it was coming your way."

"I *did* think I saw something, but the lights were in my eyes, so I wasn't sure. That's why what you said stuck with me. What did you see?"

"Pretty sure it was a drone. There was a flashing light. Green or maybe blue. That walking refrigerator Kolya has for a security chief grilled me for about half an hour the next day, after someone in the audience told him they heard me say I didn't think it was just a seizure."

"And this drone…exactly what do you think it did?"

Chelsea shrugged. "All I know is that the thing zoomed toward Shepherd and then he went down. Not that I'm all that worried about the guy's wellbeing. He and a bunch of his weirdos camped out near Rabi Hall for about a week last year. We couldn't even get out of the building for lunch that first day. Campus police finally ran them off, but it was hard to get much accomplished with all the chanting going on."

"Then you may be happy to know that Shepherd is staying on Mars. And, apparently, a few hundred of the Flock are joining him over at Ehden as colonists."

Was that bit of information covered by the NDA? Claire wasn't sure, but at this point, she really didn't care.

"Is that the story Kolya carted you over there to cover?" Chelsea asked.

"No. I was recording some advance materials for stage six. But I can't talk about that part or print anything about it until his press conference following the launch."

"I'm kind of surprised that Shepherd and his flock want to set up residence in the middle of the weird science they're practicing at Nepenthes. Did you get a look inside their test domes?"

"A few of them, yeah."

"So did we. On our last trip, which was mostly over at

Hyblaeus, we flew out of Nepenthes Station. Our plane passed over a couple of small domes as we were about to land, and I took some video. It was from a distance, so it made it past the censors…but if you zoom in really close, there are some freaky animals in a couple of them. Animals none of us could identify. Kim calls Nepenthes the Island of Doctor Monroe, which I thought was him mispronouncing the H. G. Wells book, but KTI has this doctor—"

"Davina Monroe, yes. I met her briefly. She's…interesting."

"That's one way to put it. I'm glad she found her niche on Mars because cooking up the things I saw inside that dome would get her banned from working in pretty much every country on Earth."

TWENTY-FIVE

PAUL MESSAGED CLAIRE a little after three. She slipped on the biosuit and met him outside in the courtyard area, where he was trying—and failing—to pitch the arrows into the vase.

"It's called *tuho*," he said. "Or pitch-pot. And I truly suck at it. You want to try?"

"If I do, we'll never make it to the site. I would probably suck at it, too, but I have a bit of a competitive streak and wouldn't be happy until I got them all into the pot. Is Ayman joining us?"

"No. He said he's seen enough sand and rock for one day, by which I'm pretty sure he meant for one lifetime but he's not willing to admit it. Hopefully, he'll find Mars less depressing once there's a bit more greenery." Paul made one more try at the pitch-pot, missed, and then they headed toward the airlock tunnel. "I just heard back from Meadow. They've got transportation problems. Should be here by early tomorrow. Still nothing from Stasia, but I got an automated message saying she was in transit to Cerberus. I guess she decided to join Kolya. So…I made an executive decision and messaged Byeon—he's the head of Pada—to ask if we can go ahead and record a brief chat with the mining team that found the chamber while we're over at the site today."

"Are you sure?"

He shrugged. "Stasia can always kill it—or me—if I've overstepped. Alternatively, we can wait until tomorrow when Meadow and Pax arrive if you want professional equipment. Or if you need time to come up with questions."

"Oh, no, I can wing it. I just want to get some basic reactions.

What they thought when they hit metal and realized it wasn't a natural formation. Stuff like that. Brodnik came back to the room about an hour ago—"

"Really? I'm surprised. Kolya said she wanted to be there to oversee every move they made."

"I think she and Pelzer got evicted until tomorrow morning. The excavation crew isn't actually chipping away at the chamber right now, but simply digging a wider trench so the workers will have easier access for the rest of the job. Anyway, she told me they're fairly certain they'll have the chamber out and ready to transport to Daedalus sometime tomorrow. And Pax and Meadow will be busy filming all of that, so it's probably best for me to get this interview out of the way. I can just use the visor. Or you can use it, if you don't mind handling the recording."

"Don't mind at all. Making sure you get what you need to properly cover this story is the entire reason I'm here."

Claire was happy with this. The simple truth was that either one of them would likely get a better end result than what she'd seen from the apprentices so far, even using the lower quality visor cam. She didn't say that to Paul, but she was definitely thinking it. And given that Paul had suggested jumping the gun on the interview, she thought that he might have been thinking it, too.

They took one of the buggies over to the site, even though it was less than half a klick away. Personally, Claire would have welcomed the opportunity to walk for a bit. As they drew closer, Paul reminded her to turn on the noise filtering feature in her helmet. It dulled the sound to a faint roar when they crossed into the audible range, but it wasn't nearly as stark as the change she'd noticed earlier. She wondered what the effect would be like if you approached on foot and decided to test it later. It would make a good short clip to tack on as part of a *Simple Science* episode.

The crew that found the first chamber was working further

inside that same tunnel on a vein of opal. Paul flashed his KTI badge at someone who must have been a manager and had him call for the excavation team to take a break. Several minutes later, the square platform outside the tunnel began its descent to the crater floor, running along the maglev track. As soon as it reached the bottom, one of the men shoved open the gate in the center and the other four followed.

Pada's manager issued them special hardhats that fit over the biosuit helmet. The extra layer stretched the strap of the visor cam to its limit, but they finally managed to mount it on Paul's head.

The lift was even more massive close up. Fifteen people could have stood fingertip to fingertip without any fear of someone being jostled over the edge. Two metal bars wrapped around all four sides, one at about Claire's hip and another at shoulder-height, and there was a solid barrier from about the knees down. You would have to actively work at falling from the lift.

None of that did much to settle Claire's nerves, however. The thing was about to take them straight up for more than a kilometer. Once they were on the platform, she went as far as possible from the gate, remembering how effortlessly it had popped open when the excavation team unloaded. When the platform began moving upward, she clutched the bar with a two-handed death grip.

"Are you acrophobic, Claire?"

"No. That would imply an *irrational* fear of heights. Being nervous about this thing is perfectly rational. I didn't have a problem coming down in the cage earlier, remember?" That wasn't entirely true. She'd had a problem. It just wasn't a *major* problem. "This thing, on the other hand, has to violate several dozen safety regulations."

"Safety regulations? Oh, you sweet summer child, this is *Mars*. Seriously, though, sit down if you need to. I've been on these lifts many times now, so I've gotten used to it, but it can definitely be a little unnerving at first."

Claire just grunted. *Unnerving* didn't begin to cover it.

"If it helps," Paul added, "remember that this elevator is designed to handle tons of weight. This is what lifted that chamber you saw at Daedalus to the top of the crater. That thing had to weigh at least a hundred times as much as the two of us."

"Yeah, well...I'm going to keep my eyes closed and pretend we're in an elevator."

"We *are* in an elevator. Technically. Just an open-air elevator going really, really—"

"Shush," Claire said. He was clearly enjoying the situation way too much.

"Yes, ma'am. May I record you?"

"Not if you want to live. Record anything else you'd like but keep that camera away from me until we're inside the tunnel."

According to Paul, the ride lasted less than a minute. It felt considerably longer to Claire. The platform quivered as they came to a stop, or maybe it was her knees shaking. Either way, she would have strongly preferred to cling to the bars and work her way around to the tunnel entrance. But the miners down there might well have zoom features similar to the one in her helmet, and the thought of them viewing her terror close up stiffened Claire's spine enough to let go. She pulled in a deep breath, opened her eyes, and crossed over to join Paul...who, judging from the light on the visor, was filming her.

"Don't kill me," he said. "I'm doing you a favor. No one else has to see it, and you might find it amusing as a memento later."

"Remember back at Ehden when you said Kolya's sense of humor had a streak of evil? Well, you might want to curb the amount of time you're spending with the man because it's definitely rubbing off on you."

Claire had intended it as a joke. And Paul did smile, but

there was another look behind it, almost as if she'd confirmed something that he already feared.

"Sorry. Do you want me to delete it?"

"No. I can do it later. Let's just get off this thing."

From the bottom, the tunnel had appeared fairly small. Now that they were closer, however, Claire could see that the space was wider than most of the buildings at Icarus Camp. The chamber, which she'd assumed was farther inside the tunnel, was barely ten meters from the edge. That seemed rather suspicious to her at first, but any lingering questions as to whether it might indeed have been planted were dispelled when she saw how thoroughly the thing was embedded in the rock, even after nearly a full day of work by the excavation team.

It was maybe three-quarters the size of the chamber already at Daedalus. They'd had a bit of a head start with this one since the top was mostly uncovered in the process of removing its larger counterpart. The center of the exposed top held the only marking Claire had seen on the exterior of either chamber—a large circle, slightly left of center. According to Brodnik, it was probably an entryway. They hadn't seen a similar portal on the bottom of the first chamber, but it might have been located under that pedestal in the center, something that Brodnik wanted to check when they returned to Daedalus. She was hoping the hatch would make this one easier to open, but in order to keep within the bounds of her recently revised contract with KTI, they wouldn't be testing that until the box was out of the tunnel and stored with its big brother inside Dome Three at Daedalus.

So far, the excavation team had managed to chip away about a meter of stone, resulting in a rectangular block of metal protruding from the bottom of what looked like a moat that they'd dug on the right side of the tunnel floor. Several digger bots were frozen in place until the team returned to start them up again. Tools and personal items were scattered around the chamber, including one of the KTI packs that Paul had given Claire to replace her busted daypack.

"So, the excavation team is employed by KTI, not Pada?"

Paul shook his head. "Not KTI, not Pada. It's another group we contract with on occasion. They mostly work out of Noachis, where a lot of the dwellings are underground. Why?"

"Nothing. I just spotted one of the KTI bags."

"The lead guy was probably at the conference. Like I said, Stasia won't miss the bag I gave you. She hands them out like business cards."

Farther inside the tunnel, Claire heard people talking. It was in another language, presumably Korean. An electric hand-tool buzzed and hummed steadily in the background. When one of the women looked up and saw them approaching, she called something out to the others and the noise subsided.

The inner section of the tunnel was brighter than the exterior, thanks to four large portable lights that were aimed at the walls. It was wider, as well, and farther back inside Claire could see two tunnels that sloped slightly downward forking off in opposite directions. This area seemed more like a natural cave, with bumps and grooves in the floor and ceiling instead of the more regular and obviously artificial curve of the tunnel where they'd entered, which was covered in a thin layer of sediment.

Beams from the lamps illuminated a strip of brightly colored translucent stone embedded in the wall. It was as wide as Claire's forearm in some places, swirling in and out of the reddish-gray rocks. It didn't yet look much like the sparkling, polished Martian opals that she'd seen in jewelry stores both on Earth and at Daedalus City, or even the seed pearl sized versions on the jumpsuit she'd bought, but given the price usually charged for the larger gems Claire thought this section of the tunnel was going to make Pada a very nice profit.

None of the miners were eager to talk at first, so Claire broke the ice by getting a few of them to explain the tools they were using. Another showed her how the UV lamp on the helmets helped her spot sections where opal might be lurking just below the surface. All but one of the team spoke at least a bit of English, which was a good thing since Claire had forgotten to bring her earbuds and the helmet didn't include a translation app among its features. One of the men in the group spoke fluently, with a British accent every bit as posh as a grad school classmate of Claire's who had attended Eton College. He was able to translate for the others on the occasions when they hit a conversational roadblock. She suspected there was an intriguing story behind how a guy with that accent had ended up in an opal mine on Mars, but she couldn't think of how to get at it without sounding condescending.

Paul recorded one of the women for about ten minutes as she carved out a chunk of opal nearly the size of her fist. Then Claire gradually worked back around to questions about the chamber. The guy with the Eton accent told her that the second woman on the team, the one whose English skills were almost nonexistent, had been the first to discover it.

"There was only that one corner jutting out, and Nari thought perhaps it was black opal. Then the chisel broke." He nodded toward the hand tool that the other woman had just used to extract the opal. "We cleared away enough rock to see that it was perfectly smooth, breaking a second chisel bit in the process. That's when we called the foreman to come up and see what he thought it was."

Claire turned to the woman who had found it and asked, "Were you surprised to learn that it was something left behind by an ancient civilization?"

Once the question was translated to her, the woman shrugged and shook her head, although Claire couldn't really tell if it signified a negative answer or just ambivalence. She spoke briefly in Korean. The guy who was translating listened, then gave her a brisk, almost angry shake of his head and turned back to Claire. "She says she was very surprised. None of us have ever seen anything like that here."

Claire had the strong sense that this wasn't at *all* what the woman had said, but she moved on, asking whether they were eager to get back to Earth when their contracts expired. Five of them said yes, but one of the men and the woman who had demonstrated extracting the chunk of opal said that they planned to apply for permanent residence.

At the end, she asked each of them to give their names and where they were from originally. "You deserve a share of the limelight for finding something this important, so I want to make sure that we have all of your information correct for the history books."

One of the men said something in Korean, and then all seven of them burst into laughter.

"Can you translate?" Claire asked.

The Eton guy grinned. "He says he's just happy that Kolya is giving us five percent of the revenue that tourists will pay to see the big black boxes."

"Really?" Claire said. "I didn't know he was doing that."

That triggered a second round of laughter, louder than the first.

Paul whispered, "I'm pretty sure that was a joke, Claire."

Claire smiled, even though she could feel a flush of embarrassment rising to her cheeks. They finished collecting the miners' names. Then Claire thanked them for talking to her and said they'd go and let them get back to their work.

"It *shouldn't* be a joke," she said to Paul on the way out. "Someone should tell Kolya they deserve a finders' fee at the very least. Otherwise, all of his talk about how they did the *real* work here rings very hollow."

Paul nodded, but she could tell there was no way he'd be passing her comment along to the boss.

The ride down was a bit less terror inducing. Claire even screwed up the courage to peek out once during their descent before deciding not to press her luck. Once they were back on Martis firma, she asked for the visor cam so that she could get some closer shots of the massive machines nearby. Paul handed it over, but Claire thought she detected a hint of hesitation. Had he also noticed that the woman's mannerisms didn't sync up with the translation the man provided? If so, he'd have had plenty of time to wipe the entire video while she was standing petrified on that platform with her eyes squeezed shut.

Claire did a quick walkaround, grabbed maybe twenty seconds of video, and then headed back to the buggy. She was now much more interested in getting to her room back at Icarus Camp so she could check the status of that clip than she was in recording a bunch of very big rigs.

TWENTY-SIX

BRODNIK AND CHELSEA were both in the room when she arrived. Claire gave them a perfunctory greeting, then slipped out of her biosuit, located her earbuds, and started syncing the visor cam with her tablet so that she could check the recording. It was still listed, although she supposed it was possible that Paul had simply erased that section of it. He could always claim that he'd accidentally turned off the camera.

Claire had built her suspicions up to the point that she was actually surprised to find the entire interview intact. She rewound to the part where she'd spoken with the woman who first spotted the chamber, then switched her earbuds to translate mode. There was a short delay after she played the woman's words, and then the translation came through.

Not really. We've seen tool fragments in some of the caves. Nothing this big, though.

Tool fragments?

When Claire looked up, Dr. Brodnik was staring at her expectantly.

"Sorry. Did you say something?"

Brodnik laughed. "Yes. I asked if you wanted to go down to dinner with us. As soon as the shift ends, the dining area is likely to be packed. Are you okay?"

Claire trusted Brodnik enough to play the clip and ask if she'd heard any rumors about tools being found inside subterranean—or would it be submartian?—caves. But she was less sure about Chelsea. They might have broken the ice a tiny bit earlier that afternoon, but Claire was quite certain that Chelsea would repeat anything she said to Kimura, and Claire definitely didn't trust Kim.

"I'm fine," Claire told them as she slipped on her shoes. "Just double-checking to make sure we got all of the shots I wanted."

They headed down to the courtyard to find Kim and Pelzer already at one of the long bench tables with their plates in front of them. A few minutes after the women joined them, Pelzer laughed and nodded over Claire's shoulder in the direction of the mining site. "Looks like we have a stampede."

She turned to see a cloud of dust moving toward the dome, so thick that you could barely make out the figures inside it. Some of the particles were being churned up by the lone buggy in the group, but most of the dust cloud was coming from the twenty to thirty workers bringing up the rear on foot. They weren't exactly running, but they were all moving forward at a pretty rapid clip.

At first, Claire wondered if it was simply a rush to be first in the chow line, but then she realized they had a second motivation—there was only one airlock tunnel. It could handle no more than two people at a time, and it usually took a good ninety seconds for the system to give you the green light indicating that it had cleared all of the hazardous particulates from the pressure suits and from the air around you. The managers seemed to be releasing the miners in shifts, since she'd seen at least a hundred people at the site, but anyone who arrived at the tail end of their assigned cohort was still looking at about a twenty minute wait.

After they finished their meal, Chelsea suggested a game of cornhole. Brodnik cried off, saying that she was tired, and Claire did the same.

As soon as they were back in the room, Brodnik plopped down on her bunk and said, "Okay, what were you wanting to ask me that you weren't willing to say in front of Chelsea?"

"Was I that obvious?"

"To me, yes. But I don't think *she* noticed, if that's what you're worried about."

Claire rolled the video back to her conversation with the miner and let Brodnik listen to the translated answer.

"Interesting," Brodnik said. And she *did* look interested, but much like the Korean woman in the mine, she didn't look surprised.

"So, you were aware of this?"

"There have been rumors. I wouldn't say that I believed them, but given the discovery of the chambers, it would be kind of odd if they were the only signs of previous advanced life on the planet."

"True, but...shouldn't something like that have been mentioned in the terraforming plan? Not necessarily to cancel it, but to at least allow scientists a bit more time to investigate the finds."

"One of my professors was part of several early expeditions. He said that they found something he thought might be a rudimentary knife in a cave near Valles Marineris. But it was stone, and they eventually decided it was natural and the shape was just an odd fluke. I never had the sense that he fully accepted that explanation, despite the fact that he would have no doubt gotten a lot of pressure to do so in order to avoid losing funding. Most of the rumors are more recent, though, coming from miners who return to Earth at the end of their contracts. Mining crews are much more likely to find unexplored caves, after all, given that these companies are punching massive holes in the rock. Chelsea and Pelzer did hike back into one of the natural tunnels on the other side of that cave the last time we were here, mostly out of curiosity. They didn't have time to explore both of them, but Chelsea said they didn't see anything unusual in the one they checked out. Not too surprising they came up empty handed, really. If you believe the rumors, the first thing these mining companies do when their machine-made tunnels connect with one of the natural caves is to send a ground crew in to scoop up any odd articles that might be…problematic."

"I would think that you and other astropaleontologists might have complained about that."

Brodnik shrugged. "Any fossil records in those caves aren't going to be harmed by the terraforming effort. Biological life is an entirely different story, although I think it quite likely that any unique lifeforms that might have remained have already been wiped out."

"You mean by the early stages of terraforming?"

"Yes. That's one reason Kimura and Chelsea tend to be a bit…prickly…about KTI. But as Kimura learned the hard way after his presentation at the Ares Consortium conference, questioning the powers that be is an excellent way to end your career. That can be true even for scientists who study entirely on Earth, but it's doubly the case for those of us who require funding for off-planet travel in order to do our jobs. Kimura is smart. And I think he's right that something is off with those samples. Unfortunately, he's politically inept. A lot of people, including yours truly, had to stick their necks out in order to get him this second chance. So…I'd appreciate it if you didn't mention any of this to Kim. And I'm glad you didn't say anything about it in front of Chelsea. They may bicker back and forth, but she tells him everything and it's hard enough to keep Kim from mouthing off without adding extra fuel to the fire."

TWENTY-SEVEN

CLAIRE WAS AWAKE WELL before dawn the next day, but she couldn't blame Chelsea this time. Both of her room-mates were sleeping soundly and quietly, so maybe the crazy snoring at Tranquility Base had been a fluke. It wasn't even that the bunk was all that bad. It certainly wasn't the most comfortable bed she'd ever slept in, but it wasn't the worst, either. She was just awake, with well over an hour to go before dawn.

Her first instinct was to get a shower, but the two communal stalls were occupied. Claire was apparently not the only early riser, and the fact that there was a third woman waiting reminded her that the other occupants in these barracks almost certainly had to be at work at a specific time. So instead of joining the line, Claire pulled her biosuit back on, attached the visor cam, and jotted a quick note to tell Dr. Brodnik where she was going. Then she headed outside the dome to record the short piece on how sound carries in the Martian atmosphere. While she could have waited to record it later, it would be more dramatic in the predawn silence against a twilit sky. She just hoped that Paul was right about the sampling drills operating around the clock. Otherwise, there wasn't going to be much to compare and contrast.

There were a few shadows moving around in the dining hall and someone jogging around the inner edge of the dome, but unless there were people already at the mining site, Claire seemed to be the first person of the day to venture outside the dome. The sun would probably be coming up by the time she came back, and it would be nice to get some footage of that, too.

While she'd seen several Martian sunsets during the trip, this was the first time she had been up before sunrise.

About halfway to the mining site, Claire turned on the visor cam and began recording.

"Good morning from Clark Crater on Mars. I'm outside the dome this morning to demonstrate an odd quirk about the Martian atmosphere. There's this tagline from an old horror movie that I watched as a kid—*In space, no one can hear you scream.* While that's not entirely true here on Mars, it's definitely in the ballpark. Someone *might* hear you if you screamed, but only if you were very loud and they were very close."

Claire walked for a bit in silence, and then continued. "Sound creeps up on you here. Not conversations, of course. Those usually come through the speaker in my helmet, and our voices sound pretty much the same as always. And you can hear people talking when they're nearby. In fact, if you listen now, you can hear my footsteps against the soil, because they're so close. But ambient noises off at a distance? Instead of growing gradually louder, as they do on Earth, those sounds spring at you out of nowhere, due to the carbon dioxide and the thinner atmosphere. The pressure has been increased planetwide during the first stages of terraforming, but it's still less than ten percent as dense as the average on Earth. As a result, the air here acts like a muffler, deadening even loud noises until you're right on top of them."

Her destination was within clear visual range now, marked by a ring of vehicles out front and bright orange flags around the perimeter of the dig site. The guard shack was occupied, so apparently, they kept someone on duty full time. Scanning up the face of the crater, Claire found what she was looking for near the top. One of the large drills was steadily boring into the rock and sending a slow trickle of debris down an attached chute that ended about twenty meters above the ground. She thought it was a very good thing they did that at night, when there were no workers around to get hit by stray fragments.

Claire zoomed in slightly. "On Earth, you would gradually begin to hear the whine of that drill we see off in the distance and it would grow steadily louder as we drew closer. Here, however, the sound is lower in pitch and when it arrives, it comes almost without warning. One second, it's eerily silent and the next, the sound assaults your ears. It's almost as if the machinery was taking an unscheduled break and flipped on the power when it saw someone approaching with a camera. We're getting pretty close now, so I'm going to be quiet and let you listen for it."

She continued walking for about thirty seconds and just as she passed the orange flags, the noise began. It wasn't blaring the way it had been the day before, when the drills were combined with a host of other noises, but the *thwup thwup thwup thwup* was still loud enough and sudden enough that Claire startled, even though she'd been expecting it.

After a couple of seconds, she walked backwards about five steps, and everything fell quiet. Five steps forward and the noise started again, joined this time by someone yelling in Korean. She turned to see the man from the guard shack running toward her.

He didn't appear to be armed, but he sounded angry. And it was hard to read facial expressions inside the helmets even in full light, let alone when the sun was barely up.

She stopped and raised both hands at shoulder level. "Claire Echols. I'm here to make a video for KTI."

Technically, that was true, even if it wasn't the reason she was outside the dome at the moment.

The guy relaxed visibly. "Oh, okay," he said in heavily accented English. "No big. I didn't know you had another member coming."

"Another member?"

"Your film crew is already setting up cameras. So they get the best shots. You want me bring the lift down so you can go up?"

Ah, she thought. Either Pax and Meadow had arrived the night before or they'd gotten a really early start from Daedalus.

Claire knew that she probably *should* join them. Who knew where they were positioning the cameras? It would have been nice if they had talked to her first. But she rationalized that they could just as easily go over the game plan once the other two were back on the ground. Whatever they were doing could be changed…it's not like the cameras were welded in place. And no way was she going to take an extra trip on that hellish lift if she could avoid it.

"That's okay," she told the guard. "I'm just getting some exterior footage." She thanked him for his help and then headed back to the camp.

Claire had just passed back through the sound barrier when she spotted a tiny dot in the sky. There was far more dust in the air here than there had been at Daedalus, and aside from that one bright spot, no stars were currently visible.

Was it Earth? At first, she wasn't certain and then a massive wave of homesickness hit her as she zoomed in and the little blue orb came into sharper focus. Claire hadn't looked back at Earth since that last view in her room on the *Ares Prime*, and the sight drove home how very far she was from everyone she loved. She had checked her messages throughout the day to see if anything had come back from her note to Ro about the drone, but there was nothing. Of course, it was entirely possible that Ro—and by extension, Wyatt—had never even gotten it.

Kolya had been sending and receiving messages all the way from Daedalus to Ehden, but he was probably on a more reliable network than the one that Claire had been connected to after checking in at the Red Dahlia. She hadn't even gotten a response to the proposed script she'd sent to Stasia. She was beginning to think Icarus was a dead zone.

That should have had her looking forward to getting back to the Red Dahlia and all of the benefits of civilization, but she was dreading it. Walking alone in a dark crater was nowhere near as scary as the thought of that stupid drone tailing her through the city. So while Brodnik and the others were clearly hoping the chamber would be on its way to Daedalus by late afternoon, Claire would have been happy with a few more days of relative isolation at Icarus.

Claire had come close to confiding in Paul about the drone on several occasions. Once when they were at Kolya's cabin, and once on the drive over to the mining site. She had even made up her mind to tell him at dinner the night before, but he and Ayman must have already eaten by the time she went down with Brodnik and Chelsea because she never saw him.

She trusted Paul.

Okay, she *wanted* to trust Paul.

But her mind kept circling back to two things. The first one probably wasn't fair, since he'd apologized, but he *had* joined in on Macek's little stunt after her interrogation. The second thing she couldn't quite shake was Ayman's ongoing count of silver linings. Claire suspected the actual number he'd quoted was a joke, but it was still clear that Paul had done a lot of things he really didn't *want* to do in order to keep this job. Would reporting back to Macek that she knew about the drone be another thing that he groused about to Ayman? Would it be tallied up as the four hundred and sixty-eighth thing that he'd hated doing but had done anyway in order to keep the job that Ayman had said he mostly loved in service of a cause—presumably the terraforming project—that he believed in?

Claire stood still for a few minutes, watching the tiny blue Earth fade away as the sky grew lighter. Then she looked a quarter turn to her right to see a white dot—more like the moon than the sun she was used to seeing on Earth—hovering on the horizon, in stark contrast against a sky the color of summer storm clouds.

That's when it occurred to Claire that she was going about this all wrong. Paul had implied more than once that Stasia and Macek were competitive. He'd also said that Stasia was angry at

Macek over the Flock immigrating to Ehden. Claire didn't like that situation either, and while her opinion hadn't been solicited and wouldn't matter one whit to anybody at KTI, maybe she could use the situation to sound Stasia out in general. Because if she was already angry at Macek, she might be very interested to learn that he'd nearly come to blows with a man who turned up dead two days later. And while she was at it, maybe Stasia could figure out whether Macek was the one having her followed…and why.

TWENTY-EIGHT

PAX AND MEADOW were in the courtyard area when Claire went down to grab breakfast a little after seven. She slid onto the bench across from them and engaged in a bit of polite chitchat about their trip from Daedalus and hers from Ehden before shifting over to planning for the upcoming shoot.

"So," she said, "I was thinking we should at least capture the last ten minutes or so of the excavation with KTI's equipment. I'll have my visor cam running, too, and if the quality difference isn't too major, we may be able to use some of it. My suggestion would be to set up a little farther inside the tunnel, close to where it broadens out into the cave. Or did you see another spot you think would work better when you were up there this morning?"

"Oh, no," Meadow said, after a quick glance at Pax. "That should work fine if you think it's close enough."

The fact that Meadow was playing with her long green braid, along with the little look the two of them had exchanged before she began speaking, suggested to Claire that they had indeed been planning to do something different. She really hoped they hadn't set up somewhere that would get in the way of the excavation.

"If there's room for us to come in closer, then we definitely will. But the tunnel is going to be pretty crowded. And keep in mind that Stasia may veto me on all of this. I haven't even heard back from her on the script I sent. Is she still expected to arrive this morning?"

"I think she's coming in with Mr. Kolya," Pax said, "but it will probably be early afternoon. And she told us the script was

entirely in your hands. She said we'd just edit things out if…
you know, there were issues."

"Sure," Claire said, thinking that it would have been nice if
Stasia had sent her that information directly. "Are the two of
you okay with heading over around ten? That's what Brodnik's
crew is planning. The excavation team told her they'd have the
last of the trench created by then and could start back on the
chamber."

Meadow glanced at Pax again. "We actually have something
we need to film this morning with Caruso. Something for the
terraforming project. He said we'd be done by noon, so maybe
we could just all go over to the site then? Dr. Brodnik's team
might want to wait, too. Based on what we saw this morning,
the excavators still have a *lot* of digging to do. Caruso said he
spoke to the lead guy, and he says there's no way they'll have
the chamber out before late afternoon. It might even be as late
as tomorrow."

She was right, but Claire knew Brodnik and Pelzer, at the
very least, would be spending the entire day over there. And
she'd planned to go over early as well, since she had a little
digging of her own to do. This time, she'd have her earbuds in
place and the tablet in her daypack so that she could translate
on the spot. Hopefully, she would be able to get the miner who
mentioned the existence of artifacts alone for a couple of
minutes. The woman probably wouldn't talk to her after the
scowl she'd gotten from the guy with the Eton accent, but Claire
really wanted to find out if she'd seen anything odd herself and,
if so, where she'd seen it.

When they reached the site shortly after ten, however, Claire
discovered that group of miners wasn't there. Maybe they had
been assigned to work another tunnel for the day. It made
sense, given that this one was going to be crowded with Brodnik's crew hanging about in addition to the five-person excavation team.

As Claire stared into that now-empty section of the cave, she debated going in farther, maybe even into one of the two tunnels that forked off from the main section. It would be interesting footage for *Simple Science* and there were enough empty CL-2 canisters in the sample case that Davina Monroe had given her at Fenris that she could spare one or two if she found something that warranted collection. She needed to tell Brodnik what she was planning, though, and maybe see if Pelzer and Chelsea wanted to tag along. Poking around inside a cave seemed like an activity designed for the buddy system.

Maybe that's where the bug-monsters are hiding, Claire.

She smiled at that thought and then turned back to join the others. When she found the team, however, they were huddled near the chamber with the head of the excavation crew, whose name tag read *Valentine*. He was pointing to something at the back, and whatever it was, none of them looked happy.

"*Probably* not," Valentine said. "Or at least, not yet. It's only a hairline crack and I don't believe it goes all the way through. But when I noticed it yesterday, it was little more than a scratch. It's definitely wider now, and there's a chance that it could get even worse as we continue with the excavation."

"What do you think we should do?" Brodnik asked.

He shrugged and spread his hands, clearly uneasy about giving recommendations. "We're still going to try to get it out of there in one piece. But if you think there's anything inside that might be damaged by exposure to air, I'd suggest collecting your samples before we go any further."

Brodnik looked torn. "We were supposed to wait until Kolya arrives. I could call him, I suppose…"

Kimura grabbed Brodnik's arm and pulled her off to the side. Claire and the other members of the team followed. Kim gave her a brief glare, as if wishing she'd go the hell away, but began speaking anyway when he realized she wasn't budging.

"We need to go in *now*. If you call and Kolya says no, we're screwed."

"He's right," Pelzer said. "And *technically*, all the contract says is that we'll wait to pull the thing out when Kolya arrives, unless he gives us the go-ahead to proceed without him. It doesn't say we can't crack it open and go inside."

"Yes!" Kim said. "That's exactly how I interpreted it."

Claire didn't believe there was even the slightest chance that Kim had read the contract. Based on her little eye roll, neither did Brodnik, but she thought for a moment and seemed to come to a decision.

"You're right. This is clearly one of those cases where it's better to beg forgiveness than ask permission."

Brodnik walked back over to Valentine and asked him if it would be safe to use the laser while the chamber was still in the tunnel.

"Should be," he said, "but I'll bring up the technician to test the air and make sure we don't have any volatile gases leaking into this section."

"How long do you think it will take?"

"Half hour? Maybe a little longer since we'll have to do the last centimeter or so without the laser to avoid damaging anything that might be on the inside."

"And it's stable enough to enter?" Brodnik asked.

"Yes…" He stopped and decided to step it back a notch. "That is, I *think* so. But I can't guarantee it. That's the only crack that we've located, but it doesn't mean it's the only one that exists. I'd send one person down at a time. Two at the most."

"According to our contract, it *has* to be two." Brodnik turned back to the others. "Claire and Kim, you go first."

"What?" The two of them said the word in perfect unison.

Brodnik motioned for the team to follow her and again lowered her voice. "I still think there's a chance that Kolya will view our going in before this thing is at Daedalus as a violation. At a minimum, we're depriving him of his chance to sell tickets to the tourists. But the contract clearly says that entry into these chambers must be recorded by *the neutral third party*, and that means Claire."

"Neutral?" Kim said. "That's ridiculous. She's in bed with Kolya. Literally."

Brodnik took one threatening step toward Kim. While he wasn't a large man, he still had several inches and probably fifty pounds on her. Nevertheless, he flinched at the fury in her face. "One more crack like that and you're on the bench, Kimura. Chelsea might be a better choice to go in there, anyway, given the weight differential."

"No. I'm…" He floundered for a minute and then turned to Claire. "I'm sorry. That was uncalled for."

"Uncalled for and untrue," she said.

"Yeah, okay. Sure. Again, I'm sorry."

Claire nodded her acceptance, even though it was clear that the apology had left a bad taste in Kim's mouth.

"Okay," Brodnik said. "Claire will go first. Keep your camera on Kim as much as possible. Don't give me that look, Kim…it's for your own protection. If you do find something out of the ordinary, we don't want anyone claiming that you planted it. Make it quick and once you have your samples, get out. I'll join Claire after that, assuming you find anything in there for me to examine. Ben can follow after I'm done. Chelsea…"

"Yeah, yeah," she said. "I know. I'm superfluous. Kim can get whatever we need."

"No point in me going in, either," Ben said. "Nothing that I need to examine is going to be damaged by exposure. And that ceiling looks even lower than the other one, so I'll be happier waiting here with Chelsea. There will be plenty of time for me to check the thing out once we get it under the dome."

While they waited, Claire messaged her errant video crew and explained the situation. Surely, whatever Paul had them doing could be delayed for a couple of hours? He'd said, after all, that the only reason they were even at Clark was to make sure they got the footage they needed of the excavation. Shortly after she hit send, Claire got the little blinking light that indicated a response was in process, but five minutes later the light went out and there was still no answer. Frustrated, she tried the private number that Paul had given her back at Ehden. She supposed there was a *slight* chance that he'd try to veto opening the chamber, but she didn't think it was likely. They were, after all, doing this on the advice of the excavation team that Kolya had hired.

"No luck with the video team?" Brodnik asked.

Claire shook her head. "I thought I had a message coming in, but then it vanished. Maybe we're on the edge of a communications dead zone. Earlier this morning the guard said that Pax and Meadow were setting up cameras, but I don't see any equipment here. Either he misunderstood and they were just planning the shots…or maybe they came back and got them. They probably needed the equipment for whatever it is Paul has them doing right now. But yeah, it would have been nice to have something other than my visor cam recording this."

"There's also the security camera," Brodnik said. "It's not the best quality but…"

"That's true." Claire had scanned through the security footage of that first excavation before she sent it off to Bernard. It definitely wasn't high quality—far worse, in fact, than what Pax and Meadow produced. But it would have to do.

As soon as the air was tested and deemed clear of anything that might not play well with the laser, the technician headed back down to the crater floor. Three members of the excavation team went with her. Either it was breaktime or they simply had no desire to be in here when the mystery box was cracked open. Claire hadn't been all that nervous about going in prior to that, but now she was wondering if maybe they were onto something.

The fact that the lift was no longer at the mouth of the tunnel made Claire nervous, too, which was ridiculous given how she felt about the thing. Still, it was their only way out of the tunnel, and she felt better a few minutes later when it returned to its usual spot.

About forty minutes after they began working on the hatch, the team leader positioned a magnetic arm over the section they'd been lasering. Then the second guy began cutting away at the last sections of the circle with their usual hand tools.

As Claire stepped into one of the two harnesses, she noticed that the lift was descending again. Perhaps her missing camera crew had decided to just come straight to the site if their messages weren't getting through?

There wasn't much time to think about it, though. The lid popped off with a metallic clink as it hit the magnet, and they began lowering one of the floodlights into the chamber. Claire grabbed the sample case from her pack. Her tablet was still inside, so she leaned the pack against one of the digger bots to keep it from getting trampled. Then, Claire hurried over to the head of the excavation team, who was waiting to hook her harness up to the hoist and drop her inside a chamber that, according to Pelzer, no one had entered in more than three million years.

TWENTY-NINE

CLAIRE STUMBLED and very nearly fell when her feet hit the bottom of the chamber. The top surface had appeared level enough, but the thing was actually sitting at an angle. A slight angle, to be sure, but still enough that the floodlight the excavation crew lowered down had slid toward one of the back corners and tipped on its side, casting her elongated shadow against the walls.

As soon as Claire caught her balance, she moved out of the light and turned in a slow circle to record the full view. There wasn't nearly as much to see in this one. Unlike the first chamber, there was no dais in the center. If there had been a body in here, as Brodnik seemed to hope, it hadn't been placed on a pedestal, or at least not on a pedestal that survived for millions of years.

The symbols looked like the ones Claire had seen in the larger chamber, but here they were etched into only one wall and there weren't nearly as many of them. A large single character that reminded her of the head on Jemma's teddy bear, Cordy, was sandwiched between two short clusters of symbols at the top and a third cluster at the bottom.

Below *that* was the source of their current crisis—a large crack running from the bottom line of symbols all the way to the floor. Judging from the way that light reflected along the edges of that crack compared to the rest of the wall, moisture was also seeping through.

As they began lowering Kim into the chamber, Claire pulled one of the empty CL-2 containers and a collection tool from her case and began collecting a sample of the liquid. On closer inspection, it didn't look like water, which was what she'd assumed at first. It seemed more like an emulsion of some sort.

Kim stumbled backward, exactly as she had, when he landed. Claire thought she should probably have warned him, but on the other hand, did she really owe him any favors?

"Where did you get that canister? And what exactly do you think you're doing?"

Claire dropped the tube into the container and sealed it. "Collecting samples to take back to my brother."

"The hell you are."

As soon as the green light on the CL-2 flashed, Claire placed it in the case and pulled out another canister to sample the liquid on the opposite edge of the crack. "I also took samples at Nepenthes. Kolya approved it. In fact, he *requested* it."

This was only sort of true. Kolya had requested that she take back samples of the biobots they were using. He'd only said to feel free to take any other samples she liked. But she was tired of Kim's attitude.

"Are you saying he *gave* you samples from Dr. Monroe's menagerie?"

"Yes. In fact, I have another entire case full." The bit about the second case was, of course, a complete lie, but Claire wouldn't put it past the man to try to overpower her and take the samples she was holding. It was probably for the best if he thought she had backups. "Maybe Kolya wants an insurance policy against any future claims of tampering."

"Yeah, well, we'll see about that. Whatever you did at Nepenthes is outside of my purview. But you collecting biological samples here violates our contract." Kimura took out one of his own canisters and collected the same sample that Claire had. Then he reached down to turn off the light next to his feet.

Claire clutched the case to her chest, expecting Kimura to lunge for it. Instead, a blue glow shot out from his hand. At first, she thought it was a weapon, but he pointed it toward the wall instead of her.

"What are you doing?"

"My job."

"Yeah, well, I'm doing mine, too, and the lack of light is a complicating factor."

"Too bad, so sad." He moved the light slowly across one section of the wall and then moved to the next.

Claire didn't argue the point further. Now that she saw what Kim was doing, it was clear that he needed the gadget, and she could still record with the light on the visor cam and the faint glow coming from the hatch above them. He might at least have given her a heads up, but maybe that was karma getting back at her for not warning him to watch his footing.

Kim stepped closer to the left wall to examine something glowing faintly along the lower half. After staring at the splotch revealed by the device, he collected a sample and placed the canister in his own case.

Claire also collected a sample from that spot, even though she had to guesstimate because Kim had already moved on to the other wall. It was more to prove that she had the *right* to collect it than anything else. She didn't intend to follow behind, grabbing everything he did. Kim was being territorial, but he probably thought the entire world was out to steal his research agenda. He was an academic, after all—trying to survive in a realm where the fights are so brutal because the stakes are so small.

After another minute or so, Kim switched to a green light. His sweep across the room was much more rudimentary this time, so maybe he hadn't expected to find anything under that frequency. But just before he switched the light to purple, Claire noticed a luminescent patch out of the corner of her eye. Given his surly attitude she was tempted to just grab the sample herself but decided not to stoop to his level of pettiness.

"Something lit up over there when you had the green light on. Right under the teddy bear's left ear."

"It's not a teddy bear," he said with a snort. "It's Mickey Mouse."

"What?"

"*Water*, obviously. It looks like the symbol for H_2O. The Mickey Mouse molecule? Isn't that what they call it in remedial courses? You know, the ones that teach *simple science*?"

Claire ignored the jab. She'd never actually heard the phrase, but then she'd never taken *remedial* science, either.

For the most part, she kept the camera on Kim as he switched the device to several other colors of light. In all, he took ten samples. Then he positioned himself under the hatch.

"Hey, Val. Pull me up."

Kim hadn't bothered to turn the light back on, of course. And before he was even all the way out of the chamber, she could hear him complaining to Brodnik.

Using the light from her visor, Claire worked her way over to the floodlight and flipped it back on so that Brodnik wouldn't be disoriented. A few seconds later, the woman's feet appeared just inside the hatch.

"Watch your footing," Claire said. "The floor tilts a bit."

"Thank you." Brodnik cast a cursory glance at the case in Claire's hands, then began taking photographs of the wall that contained the etching as she spoke. "Kimura is...unhappy."

"I gathered as much. But Kolya did ask me to take back some samples to Jonas Labs. He seems to be attempting a... détente or something with my mother. I'll gladly sign something promising there will be no academic publications based on the material. And there certainly won't be any Jonas Labs products based on them. I've already been threatened with a lawsuit by Dr. Monroe if her patents are violated in any way."

Brodnik continued taking still shots of the tiny room. "I'm not sure signing anything would help, to be honest. I should have left Kim on Earth. He's too insecure to function as part of a team, especially after the Ares Consortium fiasco. And we have twice as many hoops to jump through because he's here. The man is probably out there bitching to Kolya right now."

Someone *was* speaking loudly and rather excitedly outside the chamber. The voices were distorted, though, and Claire couldn't tell if it was Kim or one of the others.

"If it's any consolation, I doubt he'll get the phones to work, either."

"Oh, no. Kolya's here. Macek, too."

"Good. Maybe they brought Stasia and my camera crew with them."

"No. They weren't on the lift. The others were getting off just as Valentine started lowering me down. Kolya looked... agitated, so I don't think he's happy we cracked this thing open without him."

"Well, he didn't yell for you to stop, so I guess that's a good thing."

"True. But based on the noise out there, I think that could change at any second...which is why I'm snapping so many pictures. If he pops us on the next worker transport back to Earth this is the only look I'll get. I don't think that's likely, but..."

Claire glanced toward the wall Brodnik was currently photographing. "Do you see anything different from what we observed in the top chamber?"

The professor moved in and traced one of the symbols with the finger of her glove. To Claire, it looked like a leaf, or maybe a fish standing on its tail. The one next to it was an almost perfect lollipop, and another resembled a staircase with three steps. That one had been on the wall they removed from the upper chamber, next to the backward number two.

"I don't see any new symbols," Brodnik said, "except for that large one in the center. It looks like this cartoon koala from a game I played as a kid. What was that character's name?" She shook her head. "Can't remember."

"Yeah, I thought it looked like a teddy bear. Kim, on the

other hand, thinks it's Mickey Mouse. Or a water molecule, which probably makes more sense."

"True. But that substance on the wall doesn't look like water." Brodnik nodded toward the crack, then stepped all the way back to get a full picture. "I take it Kim got a sample of whatever that is?"

Claire was about to say yes, but then she heard someone outside the chamber yelling, "Get them out of there. Right now!"

Kolya.

Brodnik made a sound that was something between a sigh and a chuckle. "Yep. Kolya's—"

Whatever else she was going to say was lost to the sound of the explosion.

THIRTY

CLAIRE AWOKE to a faint beeping noise and opened her eyes a few moments later to almost total darkness. No floodlight, and the faint glow that had filtered through the hatch was gone, too. The only reason she could see at all was because the tiny red light on her visor cam was undamaged.

The pain in Claire's side and lower leg, however, suggested that she hadn't been as lucky as the visor.

Her camera explained the beeping, too. The power conservation feature issued a warning tone after ten minutes without motion and stopped recording thirty seconds later if you failed to tap the button. Which meant she'd been out at least ten minutes.

Moving gingerly, Claire reached up to tap the button on the visor. A beam of white light filled the chamber and she somewhat reluctantly looked down at one of her two major sources of pain. There was a faint blue line running from a few inches below her left knee to her boot, which was wedged under a long jagged chunk of sandstone. The biosuit was doing a passable job of mending itself, but the stone that had cut the suit had also cut her leg and the fabric was stained with blood. Worse, she could feel blood pooling at the bottom of her boot. It seemed very likely that she had broken bones in her foot or her ankle or both.

Claire couldn't see her other injury to tell whether the suit had begun to mend, but she could definitely feel it. The cut was on the left side of her back, a few inches out from the spine. Nothing felt broken back there, at least not that she could tell so far. Oxygen was at sixty-nine percent. Low, given that they'd replaced their air packs before leaving camp, so there was a leak somewhere.

Thinking about replacing the air packs reminded Claire that she hadn't been alone when the accident happened.

"Dr. Brodnik?"

No response.

"Dr. Brodnik? Are you okay?"

She was almost certain the answer was no. Brodnik had been almost directly under the hatch, and most of what Claire could see inside the chamber were the chunks of rock and silt that had poured in through the opening.

Gritting her teeth against the pain that she knew was coming, Claire tried to push herself into a sitting position so that she could remove the rock from her foot. As soon as she moved, however, she felt something that could only be described as a fist punching the wound in her side.

She screamed and tried to scuttle away from whatever was attacking her, and in the process kicked the rock off of her boot more roughly than she had intended. A second massive jolt of pain shot through her lower leg, but at least nothing punched her in the back again.

Had she fallen on top of Brodnik? Maybe the punch had been the woman trying to push her away.

Propping herself onto one hand, Claire looked around and found nothing—and no one—behind her. That's when it occurred to her that what she'd felt had probably been the biosuit repressurizing. Dr. Monroe had told her that the inner shell could also do a limited amount of self-repair. She just hoped the suit hadn't caused further injury to its occupant in the attempt to heal itself.

Claire tried calling for Brodnik again and this time she thought she heard a faint noise. It might merely have been the chamber shifting position, but it gave her a tiny bit of hope.

The electronics in the helmet were still functional, so she turned up the internal volume as high as it would go. At first, all she could hear was her own respiration and heartbeat. She held her breath and after a few seconds, picked up the sound of someone else's shallow breathing. It had to be coming from the other side of the chamber, beyond the pile of rubble that had poured in through the hatch before it tipped into…

Into… *what*? Into a hole left by an explosion?

She needed to try and reach Brodnik, but there was no way to stand given the angle of the chamber, even if she could have walked on her injured foot. And she was going to have to move very, very carefully. Leaving aside the fact that it hurt to even breathe, she couldn't afford to keep damaging her suit on the rock fragments. One option would be to take the hardhat attachment off her helmet and use it to clear some of the rocks away, but that seemed like a spectacularly bad idea under the circumstances.

No. She could use the sample case. But where was it?

Claire pivoted the light from the visor around in a circle and finally detected a glint of silver beneath a spray of gravel. As she shook the rock fragments off the metal case, she heard Brodnik again…not just her breathing this time, but a faint whimper.

"I'm coming, " Claire said, although she had absolutely no idea what she was going to do when she reached the woman.

She began to clear a path around her, brushing aside what she could with the sturdy case and then clearing away smaller bits with her hands. The gloves had extra layers of the protective self-healing polymer, but she kept remembering Dr. Monroe's caution that the suits had their limits.

"CLAIRE?"

A man's voice boomed painfully inside Claire's helmet, which was still at maximum volume. She jumped, sending waves of pain through her leg and side, and quickly turned the speaker down.

"I'm here!" she said. "Brodnik is alive, too…but I can't see her. I can barely even hear her. She was near the hatch. I'm trying to get over there to check on her."

"Are you injured? We heard a scream."

The man was Macek. Claire thought there was a certain measure of irony in how very glad she was to hear his voice. Yes, he was the person she trusted least on the entire planet. But as Paul had put it back in Ehden...*beggars, choosers, and all that.*

"Yes. I have a broken foot and a couple of deep cuts. I was bleeding inside the suit but it repressurized, so I don't know how bad it is."

"The fact that it repressurized should help stanch the bleeding. It's going to get really loud in there as we try to pry this thing out far enough to reach you. Just hang tight."

So many questions were flooding through her mind. First and foremost, was everyone else okay? Claire couldn't form the words to ask him, though, partly because she was terrified of the answer. She and Brodnik were inside a big metal box, and they'd been injured just from the impact and the rock fragments that fell through the hatch during the blast.

The explosion had happened *out there*, so she didn't see how the answer to her question could possibly be anything other than no.

Those thoughts weren't going to help her right now, though. She adjusted the audio balance in the helmet to damper external noise but keep the internal connection steady. Then, she began inching her way toward Brodnik.

In retrospect, it was probably a good thing that she had to stop and clear away the debris to get to the other side. Even staying still hurt like crazy, and she needed a few moments to recover from the extra bolt of pain that hit each time she dragged her body forward.

The third time Claire moved, she was yanked backward by the harness that she'd forgotten she was wearing. She moved the rock that was weighing the tether down and pulled on the end to see if it might still be connected to something. Any hope she had of it being used to lift her out, however, was dashed when the frayed, blackened end of the tether slithered through the dust toward her like a flattened snake.

Macek checked in once more to tell her that they were about to start the equipment. That time, she couldn't stop herself from asking.

"Is everyone else all right?"

Stupid question, Claire. Stupid, stupid question.

"Um… No. We managed to get *most* everyone onto the lift before it went off, but we do have…casualties. For now, let's just focus on not increasing that number, okay? Get yourself and Dr. Brodnik to the edge of the chamber and clear any heavy materials away from you if you can so that they don't hit the two of you when we right this thing. There may be some additional rubble coming through the hatch, too, when we try to flip it."

"Okay. Just let me know before you do it, okay? There's a lot of rock in here, and I'm not moving very quickly."

"Understood."

Macek's answer had given Claire several things to ponder as she cleared debris away and pulled herself along. He said they'd gotten *most* of them onto the lift before the thing went off. That meant they'd known something was about to happen. It also put an entirely different spin on Kolya yelling *get them out of there.* She hoped that he and Paul had made it onto the lift in time. Maybe that was why they hadn't brought Pax and Meadow…

Claire had a sudden flash of Meadow playing with her braid. Telling her that there was no reason to go into the tunnel until late afternoon.

In retrospect, that seemed like a warning.

Your film crew is already setting up cameras. So they get the best shots.

But there had been no cameras in the tunnel. What if they'd had something else in their bags?

Would the Pada night watchman have checked? She

doubted it, given that the guards around the perimeter, who seemed to take their jobs considerably more seriously, hadn't bothered to search their bags once they verified that Paul was with KTI.

Even with the external noise reduced, Claire heard the equipment when it started. Worse, she felt the vibrations shaking the surface beneath her. On the plus side, the mini quakes were clearing some of the rock away for her, but she was worried that it was sending more pieces sliding down to where Brodnik was.

Claire was also worried because she could no longer hear Brodnik. It was probably just that the ambient noise was blocking the sounds of her breathing, but she didn't like it.

As she got closer to Brodnik's position, Claire was surprised to see that the professor's tether had survived. It had been obscured by one of the larger rocks, so she was only just now able to see it. There was a very real possibility that the other end connected to nothing, but from this side, the belt curved upward and disappeared into the hatch.

Claire glanced down at her gloves and the knees of her pressure suit. They now looked like speckled robin's eggs—sky blue with splashes of cobalt here and there. That was probably not the most serious of her threats, though. As Stasia's avatar had noted when they were at Ares Station, most of the planet was now well above the Armstrong limit. So if the suit failed, at least the blood pooling inside wouldn't begin to boil. A far more pressing issue was that she was beginning to feel lightheaded.

When she finally managed to clear the last of the bigger rocks away, Claire got her first clear look at Dr. Brodnik. The good news was that she was already right at the edge of the chamber, which was a very good thing since Claire doubted that she could have moved her. The bad news was that Brodnik's helmet was pinned between a large chunk of sandstone and the metal wall, and there were multiple tears in her suit.

"Dr. Brodnik? It's Claire Echols. I don't know if your speaker is working, but they're trying to get us out of here. I'm going to move this rock and clear some of the stones away from us so that we don't get hurt again when they right the chamber, okay? Just hold still."

It was one of the heavier blocks she'd had to move, and Claire very nearly screamed again as she pushed it aside. But she could now get to Brodnik.

While the woman's helmet appeared intact, there was a spatter of blood on the screen. The fabric around the seal between the helmet and Brodnik's suit was also blue and there still appeared to be some gaps. That was true for another, triangular flap that had been carved out of the suit's right arm. Unlike the rip along Claire's leg, both of those pieces appeared too far apart to fully seal on their own.

The gap in the helmet seal worried Claire the most. She couldn't tell if the air recycling system was intact. If it was damaged, and the suit was leaking oxygen or not scrubbing out carbon dioxide, that might be the reason Brodnik was unconscious. The only thing she could do was try to patch the seal. She pushed the edges of the fabric against Brodnik's helmet as best she could without touching the rip. Claire's knowledge of how the polymer worked was minimal but she thought there was a very real chance that her gloves might adhere to the cut if she touched it. Getting them out of the chamber one at a time was going to be a big enough challenge without her fusing their suits together.

At first, Claire couldn't get it to work, but then she realized that the problem could be that the biosuit had already released all of the sealing agent stored along the torn section of the fabric. Hoping she wasn't about to make the situation worse, she grabbed a rough section of rock from nearby and scrubbed the jagged edge against the two torn sides. Then she tried again. This time, the seal took, and the blue color began to fade, although there were still darker blue areas here and there.

She did the same thing for the triangular tear, and as she

was pressing the edges together, Macek came over the helmet speaker again.

"Claire? Are you in position?"

"Yes."

"Okay, good. They're saying five more minutes, maybe ten, and then we're going to try and flip you. One question…we've got one of the harnesses still attached over here. Is it attached on your end, too?"

"It appears to be. Mine broke, but Brodnik's tether runs up to the hatch. I tugged on the end connected to her harness and it seems secure, but I can't move her to check. Tell them to hurry. Her helmet seal was loose. I've done everything I can, but she's barely breathing."

"Understood," he said. "Hang in there."

Then he was gone again. The triangular patch was mostly healed, so Claire went back to physically holding together the seal at Brodnik's neck.

"Did you hear what he said, Dr. Brodnik? Five minutes. Maybe ten."

Brodnik said something in response, but her voice was so quiet that Claire couldn't make it out. "What did you say?"

"Laura, damn it. Call me… Laura."

Claire laughed and then winced at the stabbing pain from the wound in her side. "Okay, *Laura*. Macek said to hang in there."

"I wouldn't… have cast him… as our knight… in shining… armor."

"Well, he has the build for it, I guess."

She gave a barely audible laugh. "Claire?"

"Yes, Laura?"

"Can't move. Think it's… spinal. Tried fingers, toes. Nothing. Last thing… I remember… is rock… hitting helmet."

Claire felt a rush of panic as she activated the comm. "Macek? We have another problem."

"What's up?"

"Brodnik is conscious, but she can't move. She thinks it could be a spinal injury."

A long stream of curses came from the other end, every one of which Claire wholeheartedly seconded. "Can you keep the chamber level as you lift it out?"

There was a long pause with mumbled voices in the background. Then, Macek was back. "Eventually. He says it will take longer, though, and there's no way it's ever going to be a perfectly clean lift. You could be in there a while." Then, in a quieter voice, to someone outside the chamber, "Can you run a check on their vitals? Both of them. No, damn it. Give it to me."

Claire could have given him a basic overview of her own vitals. She didn't even have to tilt her head to check them now, because anything tagged as red caused the display to stay on. Right now, her heart rate was at 182, in the low red zone, but maybe that was to be expected given that she'd just overexerted while injured. There was a yellow reading, too. Her blood pressure always ran a bit low, but 84/57 was unusual. Oxygen was now at fifty percent, which meant she had a leak, but it wasn't yet critical.

Almost as if reading her mind, Brodnik said, "They... have to... risk it... soon. Otherwise... I'll run... out of air. Already... at seventeen."

"What is she saying?" Macek asked.

"Her oxygen is running out. Seventeen percent. I patched the leak, though. Unless there's another one I can't see." As Claire spoke, she placed the sample case between Laura's helmet and the wall to brace her neck. She looked around for the rock she'd just cast away, wishing she'd left it in place to help keep the woman stationary when they moved the chamber. It was too far. She'd just have to do the best she could with her body and the case.

Macek said, "Okay, I'm tracking vitals on both of you now. We're getting you out of there ASAP." A click on the other end told her he was gone.

"There's… another leak," Brodnik said. "Sixteen… now. And Kooky. That's it. The symbol. Kooky…Koala."

"Shh. Don't talk. Save your breath, okay?"

Brodnik ignored her. "Get our… story out. Whatever… that is." Her eyes moved to the symbols on the wall. "Those symbols… are important. Make sure… the world… sees them."

"Yes, I will. And you will, too. You're going to be the first person I interview about this when we get back to Earth. Understand?"

Brodnik's eyes closed then. Claire couldn't detect any sign that she was still breathing but kept talking to her anyway. "I'm going to try to squeeze in here so that I can keep you stationary when they pull us out." She began inching between Laura and the wall. Even that small amount of movement seemed harder than dragging herself across the chamber had been.

Still no response from Laura. After a few seconds, Claire opened a channel to Macek. "Brodnik's unconscious again. I'm… in place now so I can wedge her… against the wall when you flip the chamber. Just *hurry*."

"Claire." Macek spoke so gently that it didn't even sound like him. "I can see Brodnik's readings from here. She's gone, okay? And you need to lie still."

"It's only been a minute. Not too late. My arms are *fine*. I can brace her."

But her heart rate reading was now flashing red inside the helmet. Claire's mind began to feel…floaty.

Her internal voice spoke up then, the voice that sounded so much like Kai, ready to rebuke her. To say *I told you so*. To remind her that she should have stayed home.

And it *was* a rebuke, just not the one she expected.

Don't you dare quit, Claire Jonas-Echols. When you quit, you lose every time.

Now it was her father's voice, there next to her, softer.

Your mother is right, you know. Keep trying. You'll get it.

Then, Claire felt piano keys beneath her fingers and heard

the first hesitant notes of the evil second half of *Für Elise*. The song that nearly made her quit piano.

Music continued, now mixed with the sound of Jemma laughing…*where the bug-monsters…*

…Don't you dare quit.

Then the voices faded, and it was just sights and sensations rushing past.

Jemma on Christmas morning when Ro brought out her new tricycle.

Wyatt on his side, watching her as she slept …*uncharacteristically sentimental…*

Joe swinging her around and around and around in the backyard when she was seven or eight, as she laughed.

Go higher, Joe.

Higher.

Higher.

THIRTY-ONE

CLAIRE once again awoke to a faint beeping noise, but this time it was accompanied by sunlight filtering through her partially open eyes and the unmistakable smell of a hospital. She had spent so much time with that odor when her father was sick, and right now, she wished for nothing more than to sink back into oblivion.

Wish granted.

She surfaced again to the same. More beeping. The reek of the hospital. Only this time, she heard Kolya talking to someone. That brought back a vague memory of the cabin. Kolya and Kai. Kolya yelling *get them out of there!*

No...she was not ready for this. Darkness was better. Easier.

The third time Claire awoke, memories of the explosion and its aftermath came roaring back. Dr. Brodnik...

Laura, damn it.

and Macek had said there were others...

we do have casualties.

The hospital stench was still there—antiseptic, flowers, and something far less pleasant that Claire could never quite pin down. Maybe it was the smell of pain. Or fear. She had quite a bit of both at the moment.

Again, she reached for oblivion.

But it was no use. The throbbing in her back and the questions in her mind weren't willing to be silenced this time. Her lower left leg was trapped in some sort of gel case. She was thirsty, too. So very thirsty. There were tubes in her arms, but her mouth felt drier than the Martian regolith.

She opened her eyes and immediately spotted the flowers

she had smelled before, the only pleasant element of the hospital odor. A large bouquet sat on the window sill. Deep green leaves and burgundy blooms. They looked native to Claire, like a plant from one of the Nepenthes domes. Next to the bouquet was a familiar silver case, also from Nepenthes. Maybe Joe would get his samples after all.

Outside the window, the Red Dahlia was in full spin. The hospital was spinning, too, no doubt. Which meant that Claire had to be looking at a viewscreen, not a real window. Did every room in the hospital have the same view? It was a clever bit of marketing for the resort, although most of the workers probably couldn't afford that hotel and any tourists who wound up hospitalized here might not be too keen on a second vacation in Daedalus City.

A noise drew Claire's attention to the other side of the room where Paul Caruso was reading something on his tablet. The right side of his forehead was plastered with a large bandage and the skin under his left eye was a deep, mottled shade of purple.

"Paul?" Claire's voice was almost unrecognizable to her own ears. "Water?"

"Sure. Hold on." He pressed a cup against the dispenser on the wall and brought it to her. "They said you should take it easy, though. Your stomach hasn't seen any action in the past few days."

"Days?"

He nodded. "Three days, to be precise. It's around ten a.m. on Thursday. We very nearly lost you on the flight back. The good news about your suit repressurizing is that you'd likely have died in the chamber otherwise, but the bad news is that it repressurized *around* the sharp chunk of rock that you fell on. The suit helped stop the external bleeding, but the rock nicked your kidney, either before or after the suit sealed, so there was a lot of internal bleeding. Plus, you now have a pin in your ankle and two broken toes, so I hope you weren't planning to run a marathon anytime soon."

"No." She glanced at his face. "So, you were there when the bomb went off?"

"This? Oh, no. I got my little makeover the night *before* the explosion. Pax packs more of a wallop than I would have assumed based on his build."

She took another tiny sip of the water. "He and Meadow set the bomb, didn't they? They were up there before dawn."

"Yes. That's what the security footage from the tunnel showed. Carried it in a KTI bag. See...I told you they were everywhere."

"They said they were...working with you until afternoon."

Paul gave a bitter laugh. "Ayman and I spent the morning—and most of the night before it—in a utility shack. We flew to Daedalus to pick them up shortly after you and I finished the interview with the mining team. I should have messaged you, but it's just a few hours round trip. They were supposed to travel to Icarus with Stasia because they haven't been with the company long enough to take a vehicle out unaccompanied. And Stasia...well, we have absolutely no idea where she is."

"You said she was going to Nepenthes."

"That's what her automated message said. But Kolya hasn't seen or heard from her since before the two of you left for Ehden on Saturday morning."

"Oh my God. You don't think they..."

"No, I think Stasia's fine. In fact, she's almost certainly the reason I have this"—he gestured toward his injured face—"but I'm still alive."

Claire was too stunned to speak. And maybe it was just as well, because it hurt to talk. That meant she was left to Paul's rather circuitous method of delivering information. But he generally made it to the key point eventually, so she just nodded and waited for him to go on.

"As I said a minute ago, we spent Sunday night in one of the utility shacks inside the crater," Paul said. "Meadow told us it was for our own good, that they wished us no harm. When Kolya and Macek arrived at the checkpoint late the next morning, they found two very upset guards who had no idea why they'd fallen asleep on watch—but one of them was certain some sort of insect bit him just before he passed out. They woke to find the plane gone, which means not only that one of our two apprentices knew how to fly it but also that they had a security code that allowed them to launch from the hyperlift."

"Stasia?"

"That's the working assumption. Either they asked me to come and pick them up because they didn't think the drone trick would work on the larger number of guards at Daedalus Station, or Stasia thought it was the best option to keep me out of harm's way. And I'm grateful for that, but…damn." He shook his head. "Macek thinks she was the one who brought the drone on board the *Ares Prime*, too. And the one who had it following you that day in Daedalus."

Claire's eyes widened. "How did you know about that?"

"I'm going to skip over giving you grief about not trusting me since you're in that hospital bed. But luckily for you, Macek's people scan every message leaving the planet— including the ones from the outposts like Nepenthes. And they've obviously been on alert for any sign of the drones…one of which they spotted in the attachments you sent to your roommate."

"They're KTI drones, right?"

"I can neither confirm nor deny the owner of the drones. Let's just say the digital security team got a message to Macek. Something must have pointed toward Stasia. He and Kolya left Cerberus a few hours early, hoping that she would be at Icarus Camp with us and that she could explain. But she never showed, of course."

"Why would Stasia…?"

"I don't know. Money, apparently, but the question is who

paid it and why. Macek thinks it's someone who wants to stop stage six. He had some suspicions that Westmoreland was trying to do that by stirring up labor unrest, but then…" He shrugged. "Anyway, Macek thinks the goal was to scare Kolya enough that he'd call it off. Fortunately, that narrows the list of suspects considerably because it would have to be someone who has never actually *met* Anton Kolya."

Claire laughed and paid for it with a sharp pain from the wound on her back.

"Should I call the nurse? Before he left, Kolya said you were due for pain medication in about an hour, so…" Paul glanced at the time. "That means about twenty minutes."

She shook her head. "So Kolya's okay? I heard him in the tunnel…"

"Yes. He only left a little while ago. Now that you mention it, I have to send a group message to let them know you've decided to join us. Kolya and I have been taking turns, along with Ayman and the remaining members of Brodnik's team, so that someone you knew would be here when you woke up."

Hearing Brodnik's name brought tears to Claire's eyes. She squeezed them shut for several seconds as Paul finished tapping out his message. Then her head cleared, and she picked up on the operative word in what he had just said—*remaining*. "Who else? Macek said there were other casualties."

Paul sighed. "Are you sure you want to do this right now? Maybe you should rest for a bit. You look like death warmed over and you sound like a frog with a bad case of laryngitis."

She took another sip of the water. "You said *remaining members of Brodnik's team*. Who else?"

Paul took the water away and brought her a cup of chipped ice. "Okay. Just let these melt in your mouth. Don't talk. I'll tell you what I know."

He sat back down and took a deep breath. "The foreman of the excavation crew, Valentine. He didn't make it. The other guy is a few rooms down. He'll need some prosthetics, but he'll survive. Probably more of the team would have been lost since they were about to head back up from break when we arrived, but Ayman and I went over to tell them to stay on the ground, while Kolya and Macek took the lift up."

"Why didn't they just message the foreman to evacuate?"

"Couldn't get through. The guy said they'd had trouble all day. Macek thinks there was a jammer of some sort in the same bag with the bomb because when it went off, comms started working again. And…he didn't *know* there was a bomb. The explosion at Cerberus wasn't inside a tunnel, but outside next to some of the heavy equipment—they're thinking Stasia may have hired someone to do that when she was there with Kolya last week. Anyway, Macek thought drones were more likely at Icarus since that's what Pax and Meadow used on the security guards. Given the video of the drone that you took in Daedalus, he and Kolya assumed you were the target. Even if they'd *known* there was a bomb, they wouldn't have known it was about to go off. Macek wanted to clear everyone else out, and…"

He was stalling. Claire stared at him, then he took a deep breath and went on.

"Okay, okay. Kimura was holding the bag with the bomb when it went off."

Claire was hit by an odd mix of emotions. Of the three people on the team that it could have been, she had obviously liked Kim the least. She hadn't wanted him dead, by any means, but she'd have been far more upset to hear it was Ben or Chelsea. So yeah, sadness, relief, and a dollop of guilt in the mix, too.

"Why was—"

"Shh. Just eat your ice. I'll tell you. Kolya said Kim came out fuming. Something about you collecting samples, which are over there on the window sill, by the way. We had to pry the box out of your hands. Which reminds me…before I forget, we agreed to share your samples with the team from Columbia.

Kimura's were…well, unusable…and anything still in the chamber would probably be tainted. I hope that's okay?"

"Absolutely."

"Everything was handled in the KTI lab, and we handed them over to his assistant—the blond woman. I keep blanking on her name."

"Chelsea Friesen."

"Yes. And so you wouldn't feel like you didn't get anything out of the deal, she agreed to share two samples she collected from the surface on their last trip. You'd have to ask her the name of the bacteria, but it's the one that caused such an uproar. They're in your last two canisters."

"That really wasn't necessary, but okay." She was actually glad, though, since that was the sample Joe had said he'd like to have. This way, he'd have the full set, even though she suspected he'd be far more intrigued by the stage six samples.

"*Anyway*," Paul said, "where was I? Oh, yes. Kim must have thought the bag holding the bomb was yours. Kolya saw him head around to the other side of the chamber about thirty seconds before it went off. He was about to go after him, but… well, let's just say Macek vetoed it. I don't know if Kim was carrying the bag, or if he spotted it there. But if he hadn't been crouched down behind that chamber, I'm not sure Macek would have made it." He stopped, taking in her expression. "Are you okay?"

Claire shook her head. "I told him…" She stopped, trying to get her emotions under control. "I thought Kim was going to take the sample case from me when we were in the chamber. So I told him I had more. Another entire case of samples from Nepenthes. Which is probably what he was looking for."

"Stop it, Claire. It's not your fault. I mean, I'm not saying the man deserved it, but he was trying to steal something. He *might* even be the reason that the bomb went off when it did. Macek's expert said there was a timer, but they think there may have been a motion trigger, too. And it could have been so much worse. Pelzer and Chelsea were both off exploring in one of those tunnels just beyond where we filmed the interview with the mining team. They're damn lucky that it connected to another cave and another sampling tunnel. Otherwise, Pada would probably still be trying to dig them out. It gave them a nasty scare though. They thought they were trapped until we were able to reach them on the comm system."

"I tried to reach you, too. On the phone, but—"

"Oh, that wasn't because of the jammer. Meadow took our phones when they locked us into the utility shed. Didn't turn them off, though, and left them outside...which is how Macek located us. Meadow and Pax both kept saying over and over that we'd be fine. That they were trying to minimize casualties."

"I think they tried to warn me, too...although they didn't go to quite the same extremes. Said there wasn't much point in any of us going to the tunnel before early afternoon."

A nurse came in at that point to take Claire's vitals. He said the doctor was on his way and ushered Paul out.

Claire's first question to the doctor was when she could travel, but he wouldn't give her a firm answer. He just checked her over, pressed his thumbprint to the device to dispense more pain medicine, and told the nurse to bring her a small cup of apple juice. After taking the few sips she was granted, Claire closed her eyes.

THIRTY-TWO

WHEN CLAIRE OPENED her eyes again, it was dark outside and Kolya was in the chair that Paul had vacated. There was a bruise on his jaw, but otherwise, he seemed unharmed.

He gave her a tired smile as she groped for the apple juice.

"Glad you decided to stick around. It was touch and go there for a while. I take it Caruso filled you in on what happened?"

"Mostly. Do you know anything more about..." Claire was going to say *about Stasia*. But she had the sense that Kolya was bracing for that question because it hurt. She remembered what he'd said when they were in his penthouse at the Red Dahlia about the dangers of trusting people. Stasia was one of the few people that Kolya had trusted completely and trusting her had indeed bitten him in the ass.

"Macek is still trying to figure everything out. Someone clearly doesn't want us going ahead with stage six."

"And are you?"

"Of course. Yielding to terrorists is never a good idea. It just encourages the next group. At least now we know how they were getting past our security. My own right hand turned against me, and my left hand didn't know what the other one was up to. Of course, my left hand quite possibly saved my life by punching me and tossing my ass on the lift when I was heading off to confront Kimura." He rubbed his jaw. "You may be interested to know that he's been vindicated. Kimura, that is, not Macek. We agreed to let his assistant use one of KTI's labs when they were dividing up the samples you collected. Kimura was right that the bacteria sample shows evidence of tampering. In fact, it's even more evident in the new sample because it was spared several million years of exposure on the surface. Fortunately for me, it's a bit hard to paint KTI as the culprit, given that the vault was sealed tight. Although I'm sure someone will try."

Claire gave him a sympathetic smile. She suspected he was looking for more…perhaps her assurance that Joe wouldn't be one of those trying to pin the tampering on KTI. But the truth was, she couldn't even agree that the lower chamber had been sealed, given the ooze that was seeping out of the crack in the wall below the markings.

"So," Kolya said, "why didn't you tell me about the drone following you at Daedalus?"

"I didn't figure it out until we were at the dining hall in Ehden when I was looking back at the videos. And…to be honest, I thought Macek was behind it. It was pretty clear that he recognized the drone when he was interrogating me, so I thought it most likely belonged to KTI."

"Well, you were right about that."

"I thought maybe KTI staged the attack on Shepherd—not to kill him, but to scare him into staying on Mars. And then there was the whole thing with Macek and Westmore…land." Claire trailed off, thinking she should probably have left that bit out. And that she should probably have avoided Kolya entirely until she wasn't on painkillers.

"What *thing* with Westmoreland?" There was a slight edge to his voice now.

"Just…a disagreement I saw. But you're saying you probably wouldn't be here if Macek hadn't tossed you onto the lift. And he was driving the charge to get me out of that chamber. So, I owe him an apology as well as a thank you."

Claire would definitely give Macek both of those things when she saw him. She just hoped he wouldn't realize that while her thanks were heartfelt, the apology really wasn't. The man had rescued her, and he apparently hadn't been behind the drone. Still, if Claire were forced to bet, she'd say Macek had been behind the crash that killed Westmoreland. She wouldn't guarantee it, but she thought it more likely than not.

Did Kolya know what Macek had done? Claire didn't like to think he would have authorized it, but she also wasn't willing to rule it out.

"Well, you'll have to send him a note," Kolya said, "since he's currently not in Daedalus and you'll be gone by the time he returns. We were originally thinking that you would have to travel back to Earth with us in a few weeks. We'll be going on the *Diamante* after we observe the launch of stage six from Ares Station. But I've convinced the doctor to let you return on the *Ares Prime* as scheduled. He said you were quite adamant about getting home, and…" He laughed. "Given how the last part of your trip has gone, I can't say that I blame you."

"Thank you. You're not staying behind for the lockdown?"

"No, I'm not. I know I'll take some political heat for it, but I need to be back on Earth for the next few months. The conditions of your early release are that you'll spend the first week in the med bay and you'll need to check in with Dr. Yadav regularly during the trip."

"I can definitely do that."

There was a brief, awkward silence, and then Kolya said, "I'm glad you woke up in time for me to say goodbye. I'll be leaving in the morning to handle some things Stasia was going to take care of, but as I am now one-handed…"

Claire started to say that he had a very capable replacement in Paul but decided it would be best to steer clear. Given that Stasia seemed to have gone out of her way to protect Paul, it might take a while before Kolya would be fully convinced that he wasn't in on the plan.

None of it made sense to Claire. Yes, Stasia had made jokes about looking for another job and, obviously, there were people who could never have enough money. But Kolya was far and away the wealthiest man on Mars. He was in the top ten on

Earth. If she needed money, she could most likely have doubled her salary simply by saying she had another job offer. And as Paul had said earlier, only someone who didn't know Kolya would think that a few attacks on facilities connected to KTI would stop him from going forward with the terraforming. Stasia had to have known that this wouldn't work.

And if she was really aiming to stop the next stage of terraforming, Stasia would have known that there was another spot she could hit on Mars that would be far more likely to put a halt to the project than Icarus.

"Has Macek upped the security at Nepenthes?"

Kolya nodded. "Yes. That's where he is now. He had already requested several teams from Tranquility and a couple of our suborbital resorts when the first threats started a few weeks ago. Those teams should be here within the week. Until then, we're halting work on the new shelters at Ehden, and we've moved Davy's people—and Shepherd—into temporary underground shelters at the lab. Tight quarters for a bit, but now that we know for certain that KTI-related facilities were being specifically targeted we can't take any risks."

"Good. What about the tourists coming in on the *Diamante* who were supposed to be at Daedalus for the lockdown?"

"If they hadn't already left Tranquility, I would cancel, but it's too late. We'll probably turn them around at Ares Station. And this *may* mean that we have to delay stage six for a week or so. Everything is still a bit crazy. On that note, I need to get back to work. I just wanted to stop in and let you know that I'm very sorry for…all of this."

She gave him a wry smile. "Well, I can't say it wasn't an adventure."

"Very nearly your last one, though." He nodded toward the window sill. "If you check behind the sample case, you'll find a bakery box. Macek said that your video included a stop for peanut butter cookies. They will undoubtedly be stale by the time you reach Earth, so feel free to indulge once you're able to eat. I've sent an order ahead for a fresh batch from Della Luna to be waiting for you when the *Ares Prime* docks at Tranquility Base a few weeks from now. If you put those cookies in that box, your young housemate will be none the wiser."

"Thank you. That was kind of you."

"The least I could do." When he reached the door, he opened it slightly and then turned back. "One other thing, though, before I leave. I know it's absolutely none of my business, and it's going to piss you off—"

Claire had a premonition where this was headed. "Then perhaps you shouldn't go there."

He chuckled softly. "Oh, I go lots of places that perhaps I shouldn't. You're free to ignore my advice, of course, but you're a captive audience right now so I'm afraid you're going to have to listen. I was very close to your mother at one time. People change, but back then, I knew Kai better than anyone aside from your father. And if you think the reason she wasn't in that hospital room when he died was because she felt guilty about us or because she didn't love him—well, you're wrong."

"Really? Why don't you explain it to me then?" Claire's voice was bitter and petulant, even to her own ears. He was right—not about Kai, but that it was none of his business and he was pissing her off.

He smiled. "Nope. Sorry, Claire. That's a conversation you'll need to have with your mother."

PART III: TERRA FIRMA

FROM THE JOURNAL
OF EBERIN DAS

18.13.508

THIS WILL BE my last entry. My fellow "soldiers" know that I am
here. They really do still view themselves as such, despite
decades in their new lives. Some even have families. And yet I
know that they will do their sworn duty.

They will find me. I will not be able to reason with even the
most reasonable among them. While some of them may find it
harder to kill one of their own, I fear that others will find it even
easier, because I have made their jobs more difficult, and they
are angry. They will feel relief rather than remorse, because once
you are proclaimed a traitor, you cease to be one of the fold. You
become instead a *threat* to the fold, one that can be put down
with no shame or regret.

The label of traitor still stings a bit. I love my people. I
cherish the culture we built over the [*ages? iterations?*] and I do
not, as they have claimed, seek its destruction.

But in the deepest sense, *these* are my people, too. They are
my heart-kin. Not just because I have lived and worked among
them for so very many years, but because I see in them so many
shared attributes. Their tenacity, for one thing, to grow and
thrive even on a planet so inhospitable. What they have over-
come, how they have advanced in such a short time is too

admirable for me to continue to see them as lesser than, and in the mind of my blood-kin, that alone makes me a traitor.

They also claim that I lack kindness. That my actions were cruel when there is no hope for a reprieve. On this charge, they may be right. Perhaps it would have been kinder to simply let my heart-kin go on, never knowing the fate that awaits them. To be fair, most of them still have that comfort, as the denials and refutations planted by my fellow soldiers have convinced the vast majority of those who once followed and believed me that I am insane.

In truth, convincing the people of this world was never my goal. From the beginning, I have known that my only hope was to convince those who will now end my life. Through moral suasion and combined effort, we *might* have started a revolution, not just here, but throughout the sector.

It goes without saying that I have failed. My blood-kin will continue to ignore the rank hypocrisy of holding others so rigidly to rules that we were allowed to break with impunity.

And so, I come now to a test of will that I suppose is a fitting companion to my test of conscience all those years ago. He died by my hand. So shall I. Neither death will have been in vain, however, if these words live on as a warning for those who reach out to explore.

Because, future explorer…they *are* watching you. Watching and waiting. To my mind, fairness dictates that you be informed of the rules of the game in which your people, your blood-kin are, like it or not, a player.

You will not be allowed to opt out. You will have no warnings, no second chances.

But if you find this, if you learn the rules, then maybe you can also learn to live without breaking them.

(Confidence interval: 86.3%)

ONE

CLAIRE HAD PLANNED to hire a car when she landed at Dulles, but two very familiar faces were waiting for her when she came out of customs. Jemma took off running, and Claire was afraid she would expect to be scooped up into a hug the way she always did. But Jemma halted about ten steps away and approached with exaggerated caution, as if Claire might break if she didn't tiptoe.

"Mommy said you're hurt, so no piggybacks or swing-arounds. Can I touch your boot though?"

"Absolutely. And then we're going to sit down over there so that I can get my hugs. I have missed you so much. Both of you," she added, looking over at Ro.

"Oh, no. Don't even bother. I know where I stand. As soon as you spit out a cute kid, no one ever says hello to you first again." She pulled Claire into a tight hug. "You scared us big time. Which means you're grounded. No leaving the planet for an entire year."

"Only a year? Could you make it permanent?"

Claire cautiously lowered herself into one of the chairs and pulled Jemma onto her lap. The wound on her back was just a small scar now, still red, but no longer a source of pain. The fracture boot—which looked oddly like the biosuit boot she'd been wearing when the ankle was injured—would be with her for at least another few weeks, and she'd have to continue the physical therapy that Dr. Yadav started on the *Ares Prime*. It was getting better, but the only time it had felt normal was on her brief visit to the Zero-G play area during their layover at Tranquility Base.

"Can you hand me my daypack, Ro?"

Paul had presented Claire with the new daypack when he and Ayman visited the morning that she left Daedalus. It contained the tablet and other items she'd been carrying in the KTI bag at Icarus, along with an unopened bottle of krambambula that Kolya had apparently sent. The new pack was bigger than the one Claire had taken to Mars, so there was no fear of the sample case splitting the zipper, and this one was totally unbranded. Claire was pretty sure that if Paul had anything to do with it, all of the remaining bags with the KTI logos would be incinerated.

She unzipped the pack and reached inside. "I found the place where the bug-monsters were hiding, and you know what? They're actually kind of cute."

Jemma's slightly worried look morphed into a grin when Claire pulled out the plushie.

"Does he have a name yet?" she asked. "Because he should have a name, you know."

Despite their best efforts, Jemma had not yet been willing to name a single one of her toys. She would usually gender them without hesitation but insisted that they must have had a name before she got them, which meant that Claire or Ro had to come up with something. Jemma's belief in intrinsic names had, unfortunately, been reinforced when Wyatt had delivered Siggy to them already named, not that the cat ever responded to it.

But realizing that things could have changed in the past few months, Claire decided to hedge a bit. "He does have a name… but he'd be happy for you to give him a new one."

Jemma shook her head resolutely. "No. What's his name?"

"His name is Fenris."

"Fen…wis?"

Claire nodded. *Fenris*. But he says you can call him Fenny. He doesn't have a stinger, or a biter, and he's not allowed to hurt people. All he can eat is bamboo."

"What kind of bug is he?"

"A Martian lemur bug. See the big eyes? And if you peek into my bag, you can see your other present, but we can't open it until we're in the car and on our way home."

There was a hitch in Claire's voice with that last word. The viewscreen in the med bay on the *Ares Prime* had been set to default back to her vital signs and helpful tips for healthy living, but once she was cleared to return to her own stateroom, she had spent hours staring at Earth, willing the ship to move faster so that she could be *home*. She'd occasionally flipped to the ship's version of the rearview mirror, as well, and watched as Mars receded, but the emotions that sight raised were far more complex.

Would she actually be willing to never return as she'd just joked to Rowan?

Probably not. As the terraforming moved to the next stages, Claire was pretty sure that her curiosity would eventually win out.

On the ride from Dulles to Columbia, they ate peanut butter cookies from the box marked Galactic Goodies, but actually from Della Luna. Claire gave them an abbreviated, kid-friendly version of what she'd done on Mars and how she'd broken her ankle. Then Jemma filled Claire in on the new kid at preschool who she claimed was kind of a meanie and told her what she'd been doing in the afternoons with Ethan.

"We did the museum a few times. And swim lessons. We mostly had to stay home watching WonderKitties, though, cause Mommy said there were nasty bugs at the park. Not like Fenny, but the bitey kind."

Ro gave Claire a slightly sheepish look. "Yeah, yeah. You were right. Better safe than sorry. I even let Siggy's dad bring in one of his buddies to make sure the house was safe and bug-free."

Claire would have liked to tell her that she could relax a bit now, but she wanted to hold off until she talked to Wyatt. They had continued to maintain radio silence on her trip back, communicating through Ro. While Claire didn't really believe that Kolya or Macek would ding her for violating the NDA after everything that had happened, she had the feature about stage six coming up and didn't want to risk it. Ro's last message had asked whether Claire thought she'd feel up to Siggy and her father having dinner with them on Friday, which was still two days off.

"So, I gather that Wyatt is out of town until Friday?"

"Yes," Ro said. "Covering some political conference in Texas. But I wouldn't be surprised if he comes back early."

"Really? Why?"

"*Why?*" Ro gave her a look like she was incredibly dim. "Jeez. He's been a total wreck, Claire. I don't think he really understood why you didn't tell him about the..." She glanced at Jemma. "About the bitey bugs. I told him that I probably hadn't helped matters, since I didn't really take you as seriously as I should have."

It was kind of true, but Claire shook her head. "Not your fault. As for Wyatt, we just didn't...talk much when he first arrived."

Ro snorted. "I bet you didn't."

"*And* by the time the sun came up, I was even thinking maybe I'd overreacted. Not enough to cancel the extra security—"

"Because better safe than sorry."

"Exactly."

They ordered Thai food from Claire's favorite takeout place and picked it up on the way home. It was the one cuisine that was pretty much ignored by Red Dahlia's restaurants, which she suspected meant that Kolya wasn't a fan. As Dr. Monroe had noted, Kolya's whims were part of the equation for the planet's flora and fauna. He had probably tailored the menus to suit his tastes, as well.

The only two Thai foods Jemma would eat were the crunchy tips of the crab rangoons and the chicken satay, as long as they took it off the pointy stick and let her stab each piece one by one with a chopstick. As Claire watched Ro sliding the chicken onto a plate, she flashed back to Kimura pulling the chunks of meat off his skewer at Ares Station.

"Did I tell you he had a kid?" she asked Ro. "Kimura, I mean?"

Ro shook her head.

"A little boy. Eight years old. He lives on the West Coast, so Kim mostly saw him in the summer. Chelsea mentioned him on the one occasion I met her and Ben Pelzer, the geologist, for dinner on the trip home. Just in passing," she added, when Ro frowned. "I don't think either of them were trying to make me feel guilty or anything—"

"Because there's no reason for you *to* feel guilty."

"I know." And she did know. But the kid's college account would be fully funded. If KTI didn't do it, she'd handle it herself.

Ro gave Jemma her plate and shooed Siggy away. She'd be right back, though. The cat might be picky, but she loved chicken and there was likely to be at least one fat chunk on the floor before the meal was over.

"What about the head of the team?" Ro asked. "Brodnik? Did she have kids?"

Claire shook her head. "An older brother. And her mom's still alive. But Chelsea said she was pretty much married to her job. They're going to turn the images she took over to a philologist at Columbia, but—"

"A *what*?"

"Philologist—that's a linguist for ancient languages. I hope they can decipher it, because that was kind of Brodnik's last wish. She asked to get the story out, which I'll be doing in the literal sense. But she meant more than just the existence of the chambers. She was talking about the message on the walls. And she even said herself that it's going to be really hard for anyone to decipher those engravings without some sort of Rosetta stone."

After dinner, there were work messages to answer, but Claire ignored them. She'd caught up as much as possible during the last few days on the *Ares Prime*. Bernard now had the edited, KTI-cleared footage for stage six that she'd shot at Nepenthes so that he could show it to the *Post's* editorial board and have it ready to air as soon as Kolya's press conference ended on Monday. In her last message, she'd informed him that she had no intention of going into the office for at least a week. Bernard had told her to take all the time she needed. That was, no doubt, partly in deference to her injury, but she suspected he was also happy for any excuse to delay the inevitable office fireworks.

Claire had messaged back and forth with Joe on the trip, but she called around the time he usually quit work. It was mostly just to hear his voice, but also to ask whether Monday would be a good time for her to come up to Boston to deliver the souvenirs she had brought back for him and Beck. Joe undoubtedly thought that meant a kitschy mug—the gift they always bought each other when they traveled, since you can never have too many. Claire didn't let on that she'd brought back a bit more than that. She wanted the sample case to be a surprise.

Joe had immediately said yes, even offered to come down to DC if she didn't feel up to making the trip to Boston. That would have been a first and Claire might have taken him up on it, just to get him out of the lab for a day or two. But the customs form authorizing travel with the sample case was in her name and she had no idea what the protocol was for transferring it.

Once Jemma was bathed, bedtime stories read, and sound asleep, Claire gave Rowan the full, uncensored version of her trip. As she expected, the part that Ro zoomed in on was the relationship between Kolya and Kai, probably because it was the one piece of entirely new information.

"Okay," she said. "That's...creeper territory. In *my* opinion, at any rate. If some guy I dated were to start sniffing around Jemma, even years later, I'd go nuclear."

"Yeah. But I really do believe he thought I knew. And that I was...I don't know, into it or something."

"Still ick. Probably a big boost to his ego, though...although I doubt the man needs it."

Claire nodded. "I'd already decided it wasn't going to happen but finding that out was like someone dumped a giant vat of ice over me."

And that was true, even though she still had a hard time disliking the man. He was driven and determined, yes, but there was an odd, almost childlike desire to please. Jemma's cookies, for example. Admittedly, it was easy to perform that sort of gesture when you could snap your fingers and get an employee to take care of the details, but she actually couldn't imagine Kai even thinking to do it.

Claire didn't get the sense that this sort of consideration had been reserved strictly for her, either. Despite their teasing, most of Kolya's employees seemed to genuinely like the man. She would have sworn that was even true of Stasia, if not for the fact that she had completely betrayed his trust. But then again, she would never have thought Stasia capable of arranging the murders of at least half a dozen people.

"There is a bright side, though," Ro said with a devious little smile that reminded Claire very much of Jemma. "Next time Kai starts giving you crap, you can just stare her down. Because even if you never say a single word about the affair, she's going to wonder if you know. I mean, I doubt the two of you are ever going to do mommy-daughter spa dates, but wouldn't it be nice if she at least started treating you with some respect?"

TWO

A LITTLE AFTER TEN, Claire went off to unpack and get ready for bed. Just as she was stashing her empty suitcase in the closet, she heard a tap at the bedroom door.

"It's open, Ro."

"Not Ro. But she *was* good enough to distract the furball."

Wyatt slipped through the door, dropped his backpack to the carpet, and pulled her into his arms. A long, hungry kiss later, he stepped back and just looked at her for several seconds before speaking. "You scared the holy hell out of me, Claire. We were already worried, and then Ro gets the message from that Paul guy saying you're in the hospital. In the ICU, no less."

"I'm sorry you were worried. But…welcome to my world. Do you have any idea how many times I've sat at the computer worrying about you making it back from some assignment? And it's not like I could have predicted the chamber would be blown up."

"I know, I know. Although, I did *try* to warn you about things blowing up."

"At *Cerberus*. And I didn't *go* to Cerberus." She reached up to kiss him again. "Not complaining, by any means, but I thought you weren't going to be back until Friday."

"I'm going back in the morning. If anything major happens in the early session, there will be plenty of videos online. I wanted to see you…and we need to talk. Did Ro tell you I brought my friend Kes in to do a full sweep for listening devices?"

Claire nodded.

"Well, what she doesn't know is that they found one. If you

want to tell her at some point, that's fine with me, but Kes disabled it, and I didn't want her to freak out."

"Where was it?"

"In your closet. Attached to the side of your shoulder bag. The black one. Kind of square shaped?"

"My messenger bag?" Claire hobbled over to her closet and removed the bag from its hook. "This?"

"Yeah." Wyatt sat on the bed and slid over to make room for her. "Would you get off that boot? You're making me nervous. Anyway, Kes sent me a picture, then disarmed the bug and left the bag. Can you remember when you used it last before you left?"

"Definitely. I took it on my trip to New York and…" She sucked in a sharp breath. "And Boston. The guard at Jonas Labs thought she picked something up at first but said it was an error."

"Kes nearly missed it, too. He said the device was fairly high-end. It alternated frequencies and sent out a jamming signal when it picked up his detection equipment. But he saw a little blip, made some adjustments, and finally tracked it down."

Claire cursed softly. "It must have been Macek. I don't remember him touching my bag, but he was in the meeting with me at Columbia. And it sounds like something KTI would do to make sure I didn't violate their stupid NDA. They couldn't use it in court, but…I'm not sure they handle everything through the judicial system, to be honest. Maybe they've gotten too accustomed to frontier justice on Mars. There was an incident—"

A fevered round of scratching at the door was quickly followed by a loud meow. Wyatt sighed. "Well, that didn't last long. Stay put. I'll let her in."

The cat gave Claire a disdainful glance and began kneading Wyatt's chest, which was by far her favorite perch. Once Siggy was settled and purring contentedly, he said, "Okay. You go first. Tell me about this frontier justice incident. And everything else. Then I'll fill you in on what's been happening here."

When she wrapped up about a half hour later, he said, "So, what aren't you telling me?" He reached over and tugged on her ear. "You've done the little hair tucking motion four times now, even though that bit of hair hasn't budged."

She stuck her tongue out at him. "A girl has to have some secrets, Wyatt. Seriously though…there *are* a few things I still have to hold back concerning stage six. But we should be able to talk about all of it in a few days once they put the first part into motion."

"Okay. After the launch, then. I am impressed that you managed to keep the purpose of the trip a secret from me before you left. Although I should have known you were hiding something when you wore your hair up that night."

"Hey, I had an NDA to protect."

The stage six information wasn't actually the *only* secret Claire was keeping. She also hadn't told him the Kolya and Kai bit, mostly because it meant telling him the Kolya and Claire bit. She *should* tell him. He didn't exactly keep his other women secret.

But right now didn't feel like the time, partly because she wasn't willing to admit how big of a role Wyatt's quip about breaking a few hearts had played in her interactions with Kolya. If not for that comment, she thought it entirely possible that the trip would have gone very differently. She wouldn't have been actively thinking about a fling, that was for sure. There was a decent chance that Kolya would never have invited her to Ehden, and she'd still be blissfully ignorant about his relationship with her mother. Would Stasia still have had the drone following her? Probably. And, either way, Claire would almost certainly have still been inside the chamber at Icarus. There might have been an even higher death toll if those videos hadn't given Macek reason to be suspicious. Claire was pretty sure she would tell Wyatt eventually, but at this point, she needed a bit more time to sort all of it out in her own head.

"I do wish you had at least mentioned the drone," he said. "Especially since it worried you. That wasn't part of the NDA."

"True. But by the time you got here, I was half convinced that I was jumping at shadows. I'd been on edge about the interview with Devin, the guy from—"

"Oh, no. Devin and I have now met. He's a very useful source for someone actually willing to listen. I got him hooked up with a camera and he's been transmitting photos and occasional video from the East Coast compound down in Culpeper. Bryce Avery should have been taking the man a lot more seriously. You didn't actually think that Devin—"

"Not really. It was more that it might have belonged to someone keeping tabs on him. Although, the guy was kind of intense when I spoke to him."

"Yep. That's Devin."

"And that was just a few days after Wilson's warning about the bomb threats, I just assumed the drone was probably the Flock."

"You weren't wrong."

Claire frowned. "No. The drone belonged to KTI. Kolya and Paul as much as confirmed it."

"Maybe initially. But I think you're going to be interested in a couple of photos that came in last week..." Wyatt glanced over at his bag and then down at Siggy.

"I can get it," Claire said. "She'll be all grouchy if you move. The boot may be clunky, but I'm not an invalid."

After she handed Wyatt the bag, he removed his tablet and played a short video of a car pulling up in front of a large white farmhouse. As the farmhouse door opened, three people—a tall woman, a short woman, and a man of medium height—got out of the car. Another woman stepped out of the farmhouse and onto the porch to greet the trio.

"Do you recognize any of these people?"

Claire took the tablet and paused the video, then zoomed in on the ones getting out of the car. While she had never known the tall woman to wear jeans—she was more the linen suit type—Claire definitely recognized her.

"That's Stasia Ljubic, Kolya's former CCO," she said, tapping the screen to zoom in some more. "And I'm not sure I would have recognized the man on his own, but see that bit of green on the other woman?"

"Yeah. Looks like a scarf, maybe?"

"Nope. A braid. That's Meadow. Which means the guy is almost certainly Pax. No clue as to their last names, but I can probably find out."

"No need. Whatever last name they were going by at KTI, I'm almost certain their legal name is Shepherd. Despite the schism in the Flock, most of the members haven't changed their names back. This video was taken by Devin two days ago. He said the tall woman left Culpeper on a private plane the next morning. Probably going to the main EWA headquarters in Ohio, but he wasn't sure."

"And the other two are still there?"

"Probably."

"They're the two who set the bomb that killed Dr. Brodnik and the others. The police need to know—although I'm not sure what the jurisdictional issues might be given that their crimes were on Mars. Kolya needs to know, too."

"Oh, I think he's going to know soon enough. I'm guessing you don't recognize the woman on the porch?"

Claire hadn't even looked at the other woman yet, but she zoomed in as Wyatt was speaking. "I recognize her, too." She had only seen the woman once in person, but she'd stared at her photograph for a very long time in the bathroom at Kolya's cabin, trying to place the face. "Her name is Jenelle. She was married to Kolya about a decade back."

"That's also what our facial recognition software came up with. Jenelle Tuller, married to Kolya for about four years. She's going by a different name these days. According to Devin, that's the EWA's new leader."

"But I thought the new leader was a guy. Drexel…something."

"I made that mistake, too, at first. But Devin says *that* woman, who we're pretty sure is Kolya's ex, is Corbin Drexel."

"And I'm pretty sure we can also put her down as the person who planted that bug in my messenger bag. Which, unfortunately, means I carried it into Joe's lab."

THREE

CLAIRE ARRIVED at Jonas Labs nearly an hour late on Monday. There were three guards at the security desk this time. That was possibly because it was the middle of the workday, but Claire thought there was a general air of higher alert about the place now. Which was a good thing, since their scanners hadn't picked up the bug the last time she visited.

She had called Joe the morning after Wyatt's visit to let him know about the listening device. Wyatt had already contacted him when he found out Claire's house had been bugged, but neither of them had known when she'd been tagged or whether she'd brought that bag when she visited.

Claire had played the conversation between the three of them over and over in her head and couldn't think of anything they'd said that would have been too revealing. Joe said he didn't think it was a problem, either, but said he'd give their head of security the specs on the device so that they could make sure it didn't get through their scans again. She still felt bad about it, though, and had a feeling that Kai would be far less forgiving if she found out.

The lab's security detail didn't, however, bat an eye at the thing in her bag that made her miss the first train. Unlike the security team at the Loop station in Baltimore, these guards were accustomed to dealing with biological sample cases and the various customs forms that accompanied them.

Wilson was again on duty when the elevator opened at the sixth floor. "What, no dumplings?"

"Nope. Joe gets to feed *me* this time. But I do have something..." She reached into her bag and pulled out the gift she'd picked up during her souvenir shopping at Daedalus. "I thought this would look good on you."

He opened the black jewelry box and pulled out a tie clip. "You didn't need to do that, Miss Claire. But it sure is pretty."

"The stone is Martian opal. I can't say I mined it myself, but I *did* get to learn a bit about the process. If you're interested, it will be on *Simple Science* in a few weeks."

And it would be...minus the bit with the woman who had mentioned the possibility of Martian artifacts in the caves. That had been neatly excised from the version cleared by KTI.

"I'll keep an eye out for it. And thank you again." He glanced down at her boot, shaking his head. "Girl, you have been on quite the adventure. Your face was on more screens than your mama's for a few days there. And since you can't exactly run with that fancy foot gear, I'll just tell you that she is expected back in a few hours, so you might want to stay away from the other side of Olympus. Joe says that Queen Hera is not happy that you stole her thunder."

"I think Zeus is the one with the thunder."

He laughed. "Okay then, Queen *Zeus* isn't happy you stole her thunder. I already told Joe you were on your way up. He's waiting for you in the lab."

A familiar *thwock...thwock...thwock* reached her ears before she was even halfway down the hall.

"So, who's winning?" she asked when she opened the door.

"I assume that's a rhetorical question?" Beck said as the ping-pong ball bounced once at the very edge of Joe's court and then off the table.

"This is just mental relaxation for me," Joe said. "I'm not playing to win."

"*Sure,*" Claire said. "Keep telling yourself that."

Joe scooped up the ball as he came over and swept her into a hug, much longer than the one he'd given her on the last visit. Then he sat her gently back onto the floor. "You do know that ankle is going to take longer to mend than the doctor thinks, right?"

"We'll see about that. Virtual Claire didn't have the advantage of a reduced gravity environment that allowed her to start physical therapy a week early." She suspected Joe was right, though, since she was still on the migraine preventative. And Dr. Yadav had told her that bones usually healed more slowly in low-gravity environments.

"You're late," Beck said. "We thought we were going to have to start the show without you. And rumor has it they're actually going to have visuals aside from the usual soft-focus shots of KTI's mighty leader. Did you see much of him?"

"Quite a bit, actually. He gave me a guided tour of some of the stage six sites, which you'll be able to see on the *Post* about an hour after this is over."

Neither of them asked how she'd ended up with these exclusives. Claire wasn't sure if that was because they thought she was actually a big enough deal to have warranted the assignment—which definitely suggested they knew far more about science than science reporting—or if they thought she'd find the question insulting. Either way, she was glad to steer clear of the topic and anything else that skated too close to Kolya's relationship with their mother. Claire would prefer not to outright *lie* to Joe about anything, but he had to work with Kai every day. Keeping that secret seemed like a small price to pay to avoid totally screwing up her brother's life.

Claire tuned the viewscreen to the *Post's* newsfeed, which was playing an interview that Bryce Avery had conducted with the head of the Ares Consortium. After that, they would play the video from Kolya as it came in, with a little over a thirteen minute lag between Mars and Earth. Journalists would then send questions, which Kolya would answer in the order they arrived. All in all, given the communications lag, it would probably be a two-hour gig, and Bernard had pulled some strings to get Avery front and center for the entirety of the *Post's* coverage, at the desk with the daily news anchors. Avery would also be the one introducing the footage she'd recorded at Nepenthes, with Claire in the role of the field reporter. Hopefully, it would dull some of the man's jealousy.

She still had no desire to hear Avery's voice, so she muted the screen, and for the next half hour, she chatted with Joe and Beck about the trip and what she'd learned about the Flock's connection to the attacks on Mars.

Joe shook his head. "It's weird that they're not claiming credit. I mean, I know that they're under new leadership, but that's usually their thing. Cause trouble, claim credit, and then give a sermon about how science is destroying the planet."

Claire thought back to Shepherd's comments before the debate. *Progress, onward and upward, in the service of the great god Science with no concern for what other slumbering gods we may awaken.*

Beck nodded. "And why Mars? It doesn't make sense. I think this new leader might be even more unhinged than Shepherd. Which isn't good news. Kai is going to need to ramp up security even more, and that isn't going to make her happy."

"Wilson told me she's on the warpath," Claire said. "More than usual, I mean."

Joe exchanged a look with Beck and then shrugged. "She was already pissed because she had to find out about your trip from someone else on the science board at Columbia. Then, the news about the chamber hit about a week after we launched Rejuvesce—"

"Thanks for that, by the way," Beck said with a grin.

"I already thanked her. Twice. Anyway, that revved her up again. But...she *was* worried when I told her about your accident, Claire. Maybe..." He stopped and gave a frustrated laugh when he saw Claire's expression. "Okay, okay. I won't go there. I think your new buddy is about to start talking now anyway."

She turned and saw that the video of Kolya had been recorded in the main concourse at Ares Station. She tried to figure out what looked unusual, and then realized they weren't using filters on him. Apparently, those had been Stasia's thing more than Kolya's. He was standing on the same platform where she'd seen the Stasia-like hologram just before they departed for Daedalus, but facing the opposite direction so that the massive, curved window showing Mars formed his backdrop.

Claire unmuted the screen and listened as Kolya gave a brief overview of the terraforming project. There was no direct mention of the recent attacks, just a vague reference to a brief delay as KTI increased security in advance of the lockdowns. There was also a mention, almost in passing, of the discovery of the buried chambers. Aside from that slight deviation near the end, the speech was almost identical to the one she'd watched Stasia's avatar deliver. That made sense—no need to reinvent the wheel, especially when KTI was shorthanded—but it gave Claire an odd sense of déjà vu.

"We have made great strides in increasing the atmosphere of Mars and are well on our way to having breathable air, but one of the primary barriers is the presence of perchlorates in the Martian soil," Kolya said. "We have already remediated this in the sections that are domed, but it must be accomplished planetwide in order to eventually allow plants and animals—including humans—to walk openly on the surface without biosuits and the like. On the screen behind me, is a section of Mars near the equator, known as Terra Sabaea. Earlier this week, KTI released modified *Azospira oryzae* in select areas of the planet, including this one. Normally, this bacteria reproduces through binary fission, but it has been genetically altered to utilize multiple fission, splitting into five daughter cells. And what, you may ask, does *Azospira oryzae* require to fuel its reproduction? Perchlorates…the very thing we need to remove. And the byproduct is oxygen…something we need to increase."

Joe squinted at the landscape over Kolya's shoulder. "What the hell is that?"

FOUR

"SCREEN ONE," Joe said. "Increase magnification to four hundred percent. Focus: upper left quadrant." The neon green splotch was now clearly visible, taking up maybe a tenth of the section they were viewing. As they watched, it mushroomed to cover nearly half of that quadrant.

When they returned to normal resolution, Kolya was pointing to direct attention to what Joe had already noticed. "Given the exponential rate of reproduction, the entire surface of the planet will be covered in that blanket of green by night-fall, from the deepest trenches of the Valles Marineris to the top of Olympus Mons. I've been assured that if you view Mars through a standard telescope from Earth, you will find that the Red Planet will not live up to its name for the next few weeks."

The entire backdrop behind him was now painted with an overlay of dayglow green.

Beck shook his head. "It's like watching a fast-growing cancer spread over the surface of the planet."

Kolya spoke again on the screen, almost as if he'd heard Beck's comment. "But rest assured that the color you see here is only temporary. It will fade over time, and when the soil is again red, scientists will know that all of the perchlorates have been removed. That is when we will set about turning the planet a far more realistic shade of green, closer to what it may have been in the era when the creatures who buried the recently excavated chambers walked its surface."

Kolya talked for several minutes about the AE biobots. Claire wanted to ask Joe or Beck if they were familiar with the term, but both of them were staring so intently at the screen that she decided to wait.

"What this will look like," Kolya continued, "will be different in each part of the planet. Some species grow better on certain parts of Earth, and the same will be true for Mars. We knew that people would be curious about this, however, and decided to give a very limited sneak preview. Luckily, we had Claire Echols of the *Atlantic Post* with us for several weeks and she was able to record one of our test domes. I believe that will be released later today. And beginning next week, there will be live coverage from cameras positioned in various areas of the planet that you can view in real time—well, as close as we can get, given the time differential. And with that, I will take a break and return in approximately one hour so that reporters can submit their questions."

"Screen two," Beck said. "Display live view of the planet Mars."

There was a short delay and then the planet, now covered with several bright green patches, filled the second screen.

Joe laughed, shaking his head. "Now *that* is how you do a launch. I think the main reason Mom hates the guy is because his science is the sort that lends itself to this sort of flashy demonstration. Cure a disease, or even extend lifespans, and all you have are live people walking around. Arguably far more important, but not something you can display like turning Mars into a giant tennis ball."

"Yeah," Beck said. "Adding the color was a stroke of genius. Especially given the rate of reproduction and how he timed the conference for when it would reach its peak in that area. You knew about this, Claire?"

She nodded and picked up her daypack. "I watched as it expanded from just a tiny bit of liquid when I poured it onto the soil to covering the inside of one of the smaller domes—about half a kilometer wide. At the very end, I basically blinked and the whole thing was carpeted in green. And on that note...you may be interested to know that I brought you samples of the liquid. With Kolya's blessing. Happy belated birthday, Joe."

"You're kidding?" Joe said. "Why would he do that?"

"Kolya says KTI hasn't stolen anything from Jonas Labs… and he wants you to convince Mom of that. He doesn't want a lawsuit and says that our work should, and I quote, be complementary, not competitive."

Beck laughed. "I knew the man was an idealist, but I wouldn't have imagined he was that far removed from reality. Has he never met your mother?"

Claire wasn't touching that comment, so she shrugged and handed Joe the sample case. "Kolya only asked that you *try*. There are samples inside here of both 6A, which is what you saw just now, and 6B, which is what they'll release once the perchlorates are clear. Also a couple of control samples. I do have to caution you, however, that those two canisters are copyrighted. And Kolya's lead biologist, Davina Monroe, told me that if KTI didn't sue, she would."

"Not going to be an issue," Joe said. "I was totally joking when I said to bring me back some samples, but…wow. Davina Monroe is something of an icon in synthetic biology."

"Well, that's one way of putting it," Beck said. "Another way would be pariah. No judgment from me, though, as long as she's painting on a relatively blank canvas."

Joe nodded. "And there are rumors she's creating on a pretty major scale. Not just plant life. But no one has actually seen her in…decades. You actually got to *meet* her?"

Claire smiled. They made it sound like she'd met a major movie star or maybe even a demigod. "Yeah. She's…a character. I liked her. And there are plenty of people who've seen her at Nepenthes, but I would imagine they're all under an NDA."

She would have loved to tell them about Fenris the lemur dog, but decided she should hold off in deference to her own NDA. And she had something else she wanted to show them anyway. "I know you guys are going to want to start playing with your new toys, but…I brought back some other samples that I collected, and I was wondering if you could take a look at them for me. They're from the chamber where…" She swallowed and glanced down at the fracture boot. "Where Dr. Brodnik was killed. Chelsea Friesen, the other biologist on the team, examined the samples and claims that they basically confirm what Kimura claimed at the conference…the samples were tampered with. Kolya says he couldn't have done it, because the chamber was sealed, but it *wasn't* completely sealed."

Claire pulled out her tablet and sent the video taken inside the chamber to the large screen, blocking the image of Mars, which was now mostly green, at least on the visible side.

The video was now silent. KTI had removed the audio of Kim's snarky comments and she was actually grateful for that. Watching him moving around the chamber, knowing that he would be dead within a matter of minutes, was hard enough.

At the point where the camera was facing the wall with symbols, she paused and zoomed in.

"H_2O," Joe said. "The big one looks like a water molecule. And is that water on the edge of the crack?"

"No. At least I don't think so. It was thicker. Viscous. I got a sample of it. Two actually. A few other things, as well, but Kimura was getting territorial, so I stopped."

Joe mumbled something under his breath that she suspected didn't adhere to the social norm of not speaking ill of the dead. She started to tell him that they really didn't know whether Kimura triggered the bomb or was simply very much in the wrong place at the wrong time, but did it even matter at this point?

Beck was still staring at the screen. "Are those the same symbols you found in the other chamber?"

"Yes. Dr. Brodnik said the only one that was different was the water molecule, assuming that's what it is."

"Oh, that's almost certainly what it is," Joe said. "I mean, it makes sense. These others, they're probably a language, right? And it's going to be damned hard to translate without some sort of reference. But that water molecule…that's something that I'd think someone from any civilization advanced enough to build those chambers would recognize."

"Any chemist or biologist, at least," Claire said, deciding not to mention that both she and Brodnik had seen something different on this particular Rorschach test.

Beck walked over to the screen. "So…if that's not water, I wonder what these words above and below it are. I'd bet the lower group of four symbols there at the bottom is a label and that's their word for water. See how there's a much smaller gap between it and the bottom of the symbol than between the symbol and the words on top? But these…" He ran one finger over the symbol on the screen that looked like a little staircase.

Claire had a strong, painful flashback to Brodnik doing the same thing to the leaf symbol inside the chamber.

"Are you okay?" Joe asked.

"Yeah. Just…wondering what the other two words might be."

"They're short," Beck said. "That often means more common words. So we'd have *something, something water*."

"Could it be…*this isn't water*?" Joe said. "That would be the obvious translation if it's *not* water, right? So maybe we should head back to the biolab and test it."

The biolab was just off the cavernous main lab, used only occasionally since most of their work was with *in silico* models. A glovebox similar to the one that she'd operated at Fenris was on one side of the room. Joe put the canister inside and unlocked the containment seal. Then, he added a drop from the tube into the testing unit and returned the tube to the canister.

Within a matter of seconds, the computer screen identified the substance and displayed two isolated images. The first was a polymer, a far more complex molecule than simple H_2O. The second was *Deinococcus aganippe.*

"That's the bacteria that Kimura was talking about in his presentation at ACon," Claire said. "The one Chelsea analyzed. I've got a few other samples of it, as well, that they collected from the surface on their last trip."

Joe nodded. "The entire *Deinococcus* genus is extremely hardy. Even the earth species are very resistant to radiation. There's one that they nicknamed Conan the Bacterium after the comic book character because it was so hard to kill. I'm still guessing this sample will be the best of the bunch, though, since it was shielded from the elements." He clicked on the image of the bacteria. "Also, the polymer would be a stabilizer."

"True," Beck said. "But it might be worth noting that it's also a *water-soluble* polymer."

Claire followed his gaze through the window into the main lab, where the symbols were still showing on viewscreen one. "Ah. So, maybe those two words up top are…*just add*. As in *just add water*?"

Joe shrugged. "Easy enough to find out." He added a drop of water to the disk and ran the analysis again.

A few seconds later, the computer zoomed in on something bluish purple growing on the disk. Joe exchanged a look with Beck and then tapped a couple of keys. The computer increased the magnification to five hundred million and separated out two groups.

"The one on the right is the coding DNA," Joe said. "Usually, it's more interesting than the non-coding DNA, but not this time."

He was right. The coding DNA wasn't changing. The non-coding section, however, was expanding rapidly and morphing into the tiny violet-colored particles that were changing the color of the sample as a whole.

"That's not part of the bacteria," Beck said. "Something was inserted into the centromeres of the non-coding DNA. That's why they looked wrong."

Claire told Joe that they reminded her of his critters.

"Yeah, maybe a little," Joe said. "If they were shrunken down a few hundred times."

Beck went over to the second console and pulled up the data on his screen. Claire thought he was going to zoom in even closer than Joe, but he zoomed out, instead, to two hundred million.

The tiny purple dots were moving, just as Joe's critters had been the first time Claire saw them. But those had looked like billiard balls pinging off of each other. These dots were more organized. They were like members of a marching band, falling into line, one by one.

"It's almost like they're..." Beck trailed off as the door opened and the only person who would dare enter without knocking breezed into the lab.

FIVE

CLAIRE TURNED and gave her mother a perfunctory smile, slightly amused at the look of shock on the older woman's face. She'd been dreading running into Kai, but as Ro had said, maybe this was a good thing. Maybe Kai would back off if she realized Claire had the goods on her.

"Oh. Claire. No one told me you were coming to town." She glanced down at the boot. "I'm glad to see that you're back on your feet, more or less. I understand you had a bit of an adventure."

The words were almost identical to what Wilson had said, but the tone was worlds apart. Still, they were pretty much what Claire had expected. What surprised her was the tiny hint of fear in her mother's eyes.

"Yes. I'm doing much better, thank you."

Kai stood silently for a moment, almost as if she'd forgotten why she came. Then she looked down at the tablet in her hand. "Eliza said that you haven't signed the revised distribution plan yet, Joe. Could you get to that today, please? And…what on earth are you looking at?"

"Just an odd sample Claire brought back from Mars," Joe said, without looking away from the screen. "What I think you'll find really interesting are the *other* samples she brought back from KTI…with Kolya's blessing. Sounds like he wants to end the war."

"Really? I'd say it's far more likely that they contain another listening device." Kai hesitated, then gave Claire an awkward smile. "Not that I blame you for that, of course. And at least security knows what to look out for now."

"So glad that I could help."

Claire held her mother's gaze for a moment, packing absolutely every bit of contempt that she could into the stare. She wanted Kai to be fully aware that she knew everything.

Joe looked back and forth between them, clearly confused. Which was reasonable. The first part of their mother's comment had been classic Kai. The last bit, though? Kai Jonas wasn't one to shy away from assigning blame.

"I'm…going back to my office now," she said. "Have a safe trip home, Claire. And Joe, send the contract over to Eliza as soon as it's signed, okay? You should cc Lister, too."

"Will do."

When Kai was gone, he grinned at Claire. "*See*. I told you she was worried about you."

Claire forced a little smile in return. "Not *entirely* heartless, I guess."

That much was true. Claire could have sworn she'd heard the woman's heart pounding from across the room. Kai was absolutely terrified that she was going to tell Joe. Which was further evidence that her mother didn't understand her at all.

Beck was still staring at the screen, but he would have ignored the family drama even without the sample to distract him. There was nothing the man could do that would cause Kai to fire him, because that would mean losing Joe, too. But she could make life unpleasant for any employee, so Beck did his best to blend into the machinery in these circumstances.

And Beck had very good reason to stare. The dots were no longer moving but had organized themselves into clusters of symbols. Not just a few, but row after row after row. These rows were grouped into sections of about fifty. Each of those groups were lined up into ten rows of eight, although the last one was a few short.

He looked up at Joe and Claire. "They're all the same, as best I can tell. I don't mean the symbols within the molecule. I mean, each molecule of non-coding DNA has this same arrangement. I obviously haven't compared them line by line, but they start and end the same."

"So this is why Kimura thought it looked irregular," Joe said. "Someone basically hacked into the DNA and inserted a book. You said you had this same sample from the surface?"

She nodded. "Yes. Chelsea said both showed signs of tampering. They're the last two canisters in the case. Both of them are marked, including the date and place collected."

"Got it." He inserted one of the containers into the box and stuck his hands in the gloves to begin prepping a sample. "They say Arsia Sulci MC and...Hyblaeus Dorsa MC. What does MC mean?"

"Probably...mining camp? It was on my sandwich label at Icarus."

He chuckled. "Okay, then. Any idea how far apart those are?"

"Well, Arsia Camp is near Daedalus and Ben Pelzer said they used Nepenthes Station when they were at Hyblaeus. So... at least five thousand kilometers apart. Probably closer to six."

"And Icarus Camp is a few thousand kilometers from both of them?"

"Yeah. Why?"

Joe shook his head. "Maybe nothing. Just want to check..."

"Take a look at this while he's setting that up," Beck said. "A few of the symbols that were on the chamber wall are here in the first line. Not in the same order, though."

Claire leaned in closer. "Yes. But I've seen that second cluster verbatim. It was etched into the wall they removed from the upper chamber. Dr. Brodnik said it was probably the name of the person who was buried there."

A few minutes later, the two samples from the surface were finished. Both of them turned purple. After zooming down to the same resolution as the first sample, they saw the same tiny particles lining up. Only this time, there were gaps, significant enough in places that the symbols were unreadable.

"Okay," Joe said. "Arsia is the sample Kimura claimed had been altered. And it had...only it was almost certainly done millions of years ago. And samples on two geographically distant sections of the planet were also tampered with. So the remaining question is...were they tampered with in the same way? In other words, is this the same document? I mean, maybe this was just a standard way of transmitting messages for this civilization."

"Good point," Beck said. "We should compare a few random sections. Let's see...four pages over, two rows down, line four."

They enlarged that line in all three samples. There were some minor differences, but it was only due to the gaps in the samples that had been exposed to conditions on the planet's surface.

After four more random tests, Joe leaned back in his chair. "It's the same text. Buried in a chamber capable of surviving millions of years, but also dispersed at several geographical locations across the planet."

"Maybe a religious text," Beck said. "Like the Gideon bibles you used to find in hotels."

Joe gave him a confused look. "What?"

"Olden times. Before everything was online. You said you recognized some of it from the upper chamber, Claire?"

"Just one—word, I guess? The two characters clustered together at the end of line one. Dr. Brodnik said it was probably the name of someone who was buried there. Probably a leader. Or someone very wealthy, since they haven't found any other burial sites. Here..." She pulled her tablet out of the pack and located an image of the wall that was removed from the first chamber. "Yeah. It's the same two words. I remembered because it was just the backward number two followed by the little stair-case. And there was that same leaf at the end of the first cluster."

Again, she pictured Brodnik tracing the leaf with her finger, just moments before the explosion. *Those symbols are important. Make sure the world sees them.*

Claire had taken her words in the academic sense. The chamber and those symbols were clearly important archeological finds.

But what if it went beyond that?

If some ancient resident of Mars had been buried in the chamber where Brodnik died, where Claire herself had very nearly died, they had left no physical trace. All that remained of their knowledge, of the collective knowledge of their culture, was this collection of symbols...these words, lines, and pages. Everything else had been lost to the catastrophe that rendered their planet uninhabitable.

Someone from a civilization now dead for millions of years believed this document to be so vitally important that they had encoded it into the DNA of the hardiest bacteria on the planet.

It could, as Beck had suggested, be a religious text. It could be the history of the great leader whose remains had once occupied the chamber. It could be a cookbook, a romance, the fevered writings of a madman...

It could be any of those things.

But what if it was a warning?

NEXT: FIRST WATCH OF NIGHT
ICARUS CODE BOOK II

MORE FROM RYSA WALKER

IMPROBABLE

Improbable

Slipstream

Split Infinities

The Icarus Code

The Cold Light of Stars

First Watch of Night

Dark Little Worlds (Coming 9/2024)

The CHRONOS Files

Timebound

Time's Edge

Time's Divide

CHRONOS Origins

Now, Then, and Everywhen

Red, White, and the Blues

Bell, Book, and Key

The Delphi Trilogy

The Delphi Effect

The Delphi Resistance

The Delphi Revolution

Enter Haddonwood (with Caleb Amsel)

As the Crow Flies

When the Cat's Away

Where Wolves Fear to Prey

Novellas

Time's Echo (A CHRONOS Novella)

Time's Mirror (A CHRONOS Novella)

Simon Says (A CHRONOS Novella)

The Abandoned (A Delphi Novella)

Graphic Novels

Time Trial (The CHRONOS Files)

Short Stories

"The Gambit" in *The Time Travel Chronicles*

"Whack Job" in *Alt. History 102*

"2092" in *Dark Beyond the Stars*

"Splinter" in *CLONES: The Anthology*

"The Circle That Whines" in *Tails of Dystopia*

"Full Circle" in *OCEANS: The Anthology*

Time's Vault: A CHRONOS Anthology

AS C. RYSA WALKER

Thistlewood Star Mysteries

Baskerville for the Bear (novella)

A Murder in Helvetica Bold

Palatino for the Painter

A Seance in Franklin Gothic

Courier to the Stars

Comic Sans for the Ex

Coastal Playhouse Mysteries

The Phantom of the Opal (novella)

Curtains for Romeo

Arsenic and Olé

Offed Off-Broadway

Exes! Stage Right

———

AUTHOR'S NOTE

Thank you for reading *The Cold Light of Stars*.

This book had its genesis several years back in an extended conversation with my husband that, if I remember correctly, began after watching an episode of *Star Trek: Deep Space Nine*. I'm pretty sure there was some bourbon involved, as well. I was in the middle of several other projects at the time, but I kept coming back to the idea, fleshing out the concepts and so forth. I even started a very different version as a Kindle Vella serial, but quickly realized that there was far too much detail and research involved in doing it right for me to keep up with weekly installments.

Those who have read my author's notes in the past probably know that I am not, by nature, a plotter. I rarely know exactly where my stories will end up. Sometimes I plan to kill off a character in an early chapter and they're still around at the end of the book...or in one memorable case, at the end of the entire trilogy. This project was different in that I've known the endgame from the beginning. That's usually a problem for me, because it takes some of the mystery out of writing. I soon found out, however, that there were still plenty of surprises. Characters continued to head off in directions I never expected. I hope it was half as much fun for you to read as it was for me to write. And I hope you'll stick around for the rest of the story. Book Two, First Watch of Night, is coming soon.

Readers of my previous series are also aware that my academic background is history and political science...not hard science. I pulled in several readers with a strong background in science for the early stages as I mapped out the project and I've endeavored to get the details as close to feasible for the 2090s as possible. That said, this isn't "hard" scifi. My interests have always leaned far more in what science fiction tells us about humanity than in the technical aspects. Where necessary to develop the story and characters, I've employed the most versatile and indispensable element in any science fiction writer's toolkit—*handwavium*.

Thanks go out to my CHRONOS Repo Agents group on Facebook, my beta readers, and assorted friends and family for their feedback and support. Not every name on this list was involved in the current project, but they've all helped along the way: Teri Suzuki, Oleg Lysyj, Cale Madewell, Chris Fried, Karen Stansbury, Steve Buck, Ian Walniuk, Mary Freeman, Meg A. Watt, Alexa Huggins, Alexis Young, Allie B. Holycross, Amelia Elisa Diaz, Angela Careful, Angela Fossett, Ann Davis, Antigone Trowbridge, Becca Levite, Bianca Najjar, Billy Thomas, Brandi Reyna, Chantelle Michelle Kieser, Chaz Martin, Chelsea Hawk, Cheyenne Chambers, Chris Fried, Chris Schraff Morton, Christina Kmetz, Claudia Gonzaga-Jauregui, Cody Jones, Dan Wilson, Dawn Lovelly, Devi Reynolds, Donna Harrison Green, Dori Gray, Emiliy Marino, Erin Flynn, Fred Douglis, Hailey Mulconrey Theile, Heather Jones, Hope Bates, Jen Gonzales, Jen Wesner, Jennifer Kile, Jenny Griffin, Jenny Lawrence, Jenny MacRunnel, Jessica Wolfsohn, John Scafidi, Karen Benson, Katie Lynn Stripling, Kristin Ashenfelter, Kristin Rydstedt, Kyla Michelle Lacey Waits, Laura-Dawn Francesca MacGregor-Portlock, Lindsay Nichole Leckner, Margarida Azevedo Veloz, Mark Chappell, Meg Griffin, Meredith Winters Patten, Mikka McClain, Nguyen Quynh Trang, Nooce Miller, Pham Hai Yen, Roseann Calabritto, Sarada Spivey, Sarah Ann Diaz, Sarah Kate Fisher, Shari Hearn, Shell Bryce, Sigrun Murr, Stefanie Diegel, Stephanie Kmetz, Stephanie Johns-Bragg, Summer Nettleman, Susan Helliesen, Tina Kennedy, Tracy Denison Johnson, Trisha

Davis Perry, Valerie Arlene Alcaraz, and the person (or, much more likely, persons) I've forgotten.

Big thanks to my family—immediate, extended, and chosen. You have my unending gratitude.

And extra special thanks to Pete for being my sounding board and keeping me on track. As the dedication notes, this book wouldn't exist without him.

ABOUT THE AUTHOR

 RYSA WALKER is the author of the best-selling CHRONOS Files series, CHRONOS Origins, and the Delphi Trilogy. Timebound, the first book in the CHRONOS Files, was the Grand Prize winner in the 2013 Amazon Breakthrough Novel Awards. The CHRONOS Files has sold more than half a million copies since 2013 and has been translated into fourteen languages.

Rysa currently resides in North Carolina with her husband, two youngest sons, and a hyperactive golden retriever. When not working on the next installment in her CHRONOS Files universe, she watches shows where travelers boldly go to galaxies far away, or reads about magical creatures and superheroes from alternate timelines.

Check out rysa.com for the latest news or to order signed copies.

Made in United States
Troutdale, OR
04/13/2025

30548800R00270